THE 2ND LIEUTENANT SPY

Peter Roman

Copyright 2017 Peter Roman
All rights reserved.

ISBN: 1981252002
ISBN 13: 9781981252008
Library of Congress Control Number: 2017918720
CreateSpace Independent Publishing Platform
North Charleston, South Carolina

For Sally

WASHINGTON IN THE 1960S

In 1968 Washington, D.C., was mostly a government town. Rank and social position were largely decided by the government pay scale: the General Schedule (GS). Pay grades went from GS-1 to GS-15. The rough rule of thumb was that a GS-15 was a full colonel, a GS-14 was a lieutenant colonel, a GS-13 was a major, and a GS-12 was a captain. Lieutenants were variously GS-9s or -11s. The other grades were for civil servants who were not quite enlisted men, but not quite officers either.

On top of them were the so-called supergrades. These were the GS-16s, -17s, and -18s, of whom there were not all that many. These were lordly creatures who had offices with carpeting and secretaries and special assistants, and who spoke if possible only to executive-level (i.e. political-appointee) officers, who in turn reported to heads of agencies and Cabinet departments.

The military was in D.C., but not terribly visible. When coming to Washington after having been elected president, General Dwight D. Eisenhower was reported to have looked out his car window and said, "Why all the uniforms? Is this city under martial law?" The uniforms disappeared. Instead, the Pentagon instituted "uniform day" once a month.

In 1968 it was still very fashionable to follow President Kennedy's call to arms to come to Washington and help the government save the world. The pay was low but the prestige was high. As a result, the graduating classes of the better colleges headed straight for Washington after they did their military service, which also had a certain cachet, unless you had gotten drafted.

In the Central Intelligence Agency, the Clandestine Service — just renamed the lower-key Directorate for Plans (the DDP) — were the spies. They were only vaguely aware of the people in the rest of the Agency. The absolute top spy was the Director of Central Intelligence, called the DCI or the Director. Just under him was the Deputy Director for Plans — called the DDP, the Deputy Director, or the Deputy — who was the number two head spy. Under him came the Division Chiefs, one for each continent, and the staffs (Counterintelligence, Covert Action, and Special Operations). Overseas there were a hundred-odd Chiefs of station or Chiefs of Base around the world. DDP employees were called case officers, not agents. Agents were the people they recruited to do the actual work of espionage.

James Jesus Angleton really was the head of Counterintelligence staff, and his hunt for suspected moles within the CIA really had pretty much shut the Clandestine Service down in 1968.

THE 2ND LIEUTENANT SPY

"Well, I'll be damned. There actually is a tooth fairy," Harvey said. The three members of his surveillance team were sitting at the street-side café table facing him. They looked a little startled. It was a little hard to hear him because he had ducked his head and put his hand up to cover his face. Harvey Masters was a Foreign Service officer assigned to the U.S. Consulate, but was actually the CIA's man in Frankfurt. Harvey had been sitting in the approved spy position, with his back to the wall of the café. This place was nothing like the famous, or, better, infamous Odeon Café where Harvey, who had a morbid sense of humor, once met a would-be agent. The Odeon, after all, had been a meeting place for spies and conspirators for over a hundred years. Lenin and Trotsky had spent their German exile sitting at those same tables. Mata Hari had danced, naked some said, in the dining room upstairs a few years before World War I. Or during, depending on whom you were talking to.

Harvey explained. "That's my pal T. J. Timoshenko who just went by. And I'm sitting here with a surveillance team in hand.

Hence my belief in the tooth fairy. Sam, Alicia, follow that guy who looks like an ex-football player. The one with the expensive suit that doesn't fit right. He's just coming up to the crosswalk at the intersection. Got him?"

"Got him," said two voices, almost together. The rather plain young woman and the military-looking young man rose and slipped away. "Very discreetly please," Harvey said. "And he's KGB. Watch out for countersurveillance," he called softly after them.

The third member of the surveillance team looked at him, an eyebrow raised. Politely, of course. "Maybe not, Anne," Harvey said. "You'd best stay here. You've already been propositioned once this morning." She had been, too. It wasn't her fault she was good-looking. Today's exercise had been a training session, and the team had been picking people at random in the railroad station and following them. She had been pushing the two-seat stroller up the Zeil a half-hour ago, angling though the crowds of Germans, tourists and off-duty GIs. You could hardly see the WW II bomb damage in most places. The Germans mostly went into or came out of the rows of banks and insurance companies that lined Frankfurt's main business street. The tourists were looking in the shop windows of Louis Vuitton and Worth and Prada and the dozens of watch and camera shops. They were also wandering the half-mile from the railroad station to the Zeil, the main pedestrian shopping street, or down to the river Main. It was all quite pleasant and peaceful.

Anne had been in the standard A position, the surveillant closest to the "rabbit." The Agency always called the person being followed the rabbit. B was across the street and roughly parallel to A; C followed along behind A, hanging back or closing up as the pace of the rabbit and the thickness of the crowds required. On a crowded boulevard like the tree-lined Zeil, surveillance was a piece of cake.

The rabbit, a verging-on-plump businessman, had stopped again, rather suddenly this time. This was odd: the business types invariably marched straight to where they were going. Anne glanced down at the twins, stuffed with chocolate and dozing. The Germans, who were ambivalent about foreigners, loved children. At practically every street corner the starchy Germans got all unstarchy and pressed squares of chocolate into the twins' eager hands. Anne worried about the potential for diabetes if the Germans didn't lay off. It kept the kiddies quiet though.

She looked across the street at B. B was her husband, Sam. Sam Carpenter was playing his part right. He was slouching up the street in the best tourist fashion, vacant gaze and all. Two years out of the Marine Corps, he had had a hard time dropping the automatic straight-backed, 120-steps-a-minute march by which Marines and ex-Marines moved from place to place. She gave him the slight head signal to switch places; his return nod acknowledged it.

But it was too late. The businessman had stopped abruptly, spun around and marched right up to her. Stopping a foot from the stroller, he launched into a barrage of Swabish, the local German dialect. Two paragraphs into it, the businessman realized it wasn't working. He started all over again in French. Now Anne got it: he thought the dark-haired young woman pushing the two towheaded kids in the stroller was the au pair. He was trying to make a date after she got off work today.

Stifling an urge to giggle, Anne instead smiled shyly and nudged a twin with one knee. The twin, startled awake, grumped. Mommy immediately dropped to the other knee and began consoling him. When she looked up the man was already gone, marching up the Bahnhofstrasse even faster than Sam usually did. Behind her she thought she heard C snicker. C was Alicia, Harvey's secretary. No, it couldn't be: Alicia took this all very seriously. Anne stood up and prepared to follow the rabbit. Then she saw Harvey, who had been wandering along behind them, watching. He caught her eye, smiled, and made the very unclandestine gesture of cutting his throat with his index finger. It was time to break off and meet at the café.

Anne sighed and said, "Shit," very softly.

Not softly enough. "Shit, shit, shit," little Sam chirped.

"Mommy said 'shit,'" Johnny announced to the passers-by, who already knew.

Sam and Alicia separated and became strangers before they reached the corner. T. J. Timoshenko was already bulling across the intersection and the pedestrian light was flashing that it was going to turn red. They waited anyway and looked around carefully. Sam spotted him first. Jeez, he thought, the KGB is as ham-handed as we are. Timoshenko's countersurveillance looked like a member of Brezhnev's security detail: burly, cheap gray suit worn buttoned and too tight. Sam looked at Alicia. She had seen him too. They waited at the light and, when it turned, followed the tail.

Timoshenko marched on, looking neither right, left, nor behind him. Clearly security was his backup's problem. But the security guy was hustling too, trying to keep his boss in sight. He didn't have the time, or hadn't been trained, to check behind him. So Sam and Alicia were free to slide through the crowds in close pursuit.

Sam was in high spirits. Finally! Finally some actual operational work. He was beginning to wonder if he was going to spend his entire life in the on-deck circle, kicking the grass and waiting for his first at-bat. He'd joined the Marines straight out of college. First it was Officer Candidate School and then three years in the infantry. There was, he decided, nothing more boring than being in the infantry in peacetime. In his third and last year the Vietnam War heated up. The Ninth Marines went in at Da Nang and it looked like the war might get bigger. Headquarters Marine Corps told Sam and another thousand or two Reserve lieutenants that if they signed up for regular commissions, which added a year to their service, they *might* get sent to Vietnam too. By then Sam and most of his friends had gotten engaged or married, or had lined up civilian jobs. In March 1966 Headquarters got nervous and promoted his whole year group to captain, including him, not that it did Headquarters any good.

But he still thought of himself as a lieutenant. Sam had barely noticed the promotion. He was now madly in love with the luscious Anne. She had murmured that she wasn't terribly interested in being a twenty-two-year-old widow. So forget Vietnam.

Pay attention, Lieutenant. You're working for a change. Timoshenko had been caught at a traffic light and the guard was catching up. Alicia nodded slightly and he winked an acknowledgment. They traded places at the next intersection. The security guy had closed up with Timoshenko and was closely inspecting the crowd between him and his boss for interlopers. He never thought to look back. Sam concentrated on shuffling and walking with his mouth partly open. He had checked it in the mirror last week. Sure enough, it made him look like a spacey tourist. Timoshenko was caught again at the next intersection. Sam looked into the window of the nearest watch store, looking at the glass at an angle so he could see Timoshenko and the security man.

After the Marines he had signed up with the CIA to be a spy. Well, the CIA called them operations officers or more often case officers. Anyway, he would be the guy who recruited and ran spies. So he was a second lieutenant again, only this time a second lieutenant spy. There had been two years of training. It was really good training too. Besides a year of intelligence gathering and analysis, there had been Jump School, Jungle Warfare School in Panama, weapons training, and Explosive Ordnance School. That was at an abandoned seaplane base somewhere in the boonies. He had gotten to blow an old government-surplus Chevy sedan all to hell and gone. All you needed was a soap dish full of C-3, a small magnet, and a blasting cap with a ninety-second fuse. You clamped the soap dish to the gas tank with the magnet, snapped the fuse and got the hell out of there.

He switched with Alicia again. He lit a cigarette, giving him a chance to stop and look at the security guy. The Russian was still focused on Timoshenko and oblivious to his own tail. Well, Sam thought, we're rookies, so why shouldn't the KGB guy be too? Alicia was good, though — damn good, a natural. Alicia was Harvey's secretary. She was maybe twenty, kind of homely, very intense, and a fabulously fast typist. She had been so happy to be recruited for this surveillance training she had practically done handsprings. She tried not to show it but failed. While her face stayed impassive her eyes had lit up like a wolf spotting a particularly yummy lamb. Now she reached for a cigarette, giving her a chance to look at the Russians through the window reflections.

Sam had been in Luxembourg for four months now. Somebody had screwed up his assignment as Harvey's number two guy in Frankfurt. The State Department had canceled his slot, so his cover as a Foreign Service officer disappeared. The support people in the CIA's European Division had just shrugged and gone back to doing the *New York Times* crossword puzzle. Sam had already been to visa school, packed out of his apartment and sworn in to his cover job. He was living in his in-laws' basement. Judging from the lack of action from the front office he might be there until his retirement party. His day job on the German Desk at Headquarters had long since become painfully routine.

Heads up! Timoshenko had veered into Kastenallee and his security guy had caught up with him. Timoshenko turned into number 234A, a standard late-nineteenth-century office building which had somehow escaped the WW II bombing. Timoshenko's guard was now practically walking on his heels. Was the security guy lapsing back into the bodyguard business and forgetting all about his countersurveillance duties? Apparently Timoshenko thought so. He turned around and said something and the guard stopped like he'd walked into a wall. Then he turned around and faced the street. He assumed a position close to parade rest and clearly intended to guard the door while the boss was inside.

Sam and Alicia had already exchanged a quick hand signal. Alicia slid into the office building on the left of 234A. Sam wandered, open-mouthed, past the guard and popped into the building on the right. The buildings were old and narrow, each seven or eight stories tall. Somehow they had survived the war undamaged. All three had small lobbies, even smaller open-cage elevators, and reasonably broad marble steps. Sam sprinted across the lobby to the rear door, down the stairs and out the back door. He turned left in the alley in time to see Alicia pop out of the other building.

Sam opened the back door of 234A and bowed to Alicia as she sprinted in. She frowned. This was Spy Business. Be serious. The building seemed deserted. Harvey had said this was not unusual. German office buildings were all offices. There was no retail, no doctor's offices. In fact, most of the "offices" in Frankfurt consisted of a long list of companies who needed only a European address. The company names were posted on the door and there was at most a secretary or a clerk inside. The clerk or the secretary re-sent official mail to wherever the company was actually located and fended off strangers' questions. No wonder there was seldom anybody around.

They slipped up the stairs and into the lobby. Sure enough, the guard was inside now, facing out the door, still at parade rest. Without pausing they went as softly as they could up the marble steps to the European first floor. Above them the elevator was still creaking and clanking away. They took their shoes off and ran up the stairs. The elevator was so slow that they were catching up.

Finally, with a rumble and two loud clanks, the elevator stopped on eight, the top floor. The door creaked open. Alicia, now on the fifth floor, moved towards the sound but Sam caught her arm and pulled her behind a metal panel that covered the elevator shaft from floor to ceiling, but only on one side of the shaft, and only on every other floor. I wonder what that's for, Sam thought as they listened for footsteps.

There was a pause while everybody counted to a hundred. Well, at least Sam did. Then Timoshenko started moving. They heard his feet on the steps. Sam looked around the corner of the panel and counted. A normal flight of stairs has 13 steps. This building's had eighteen, which probably meant ten- or eleven-foot ceilings. As soon as Timoshenko stopped walking, Sam tugged Alicia's hand and they started moving up. Timoshenko had paused on seven.

Alicia was on to the game now. She gestured for Sam to go ahead. She would stay behind. If Timoshenko was going to come down another flight just as Sam walked up there was a high probability they would run into each other. If so Sam was going to bluff it out. Just before Timoshenko saw him Sam was going to grab a door handle. He would open it quietly and close it vigorously and look like somebody who had just walked out of the office. Then, ignoring Timoshenko, he would go clattering down the stairs and leave the building. Alicia would then have a shot at remaining the hidden observer.

But if Sam had guessed right, Timoshenko had just done the standard trick of going past his destination by one floor and then walking back down a flight. If so, Sam could stop on the stairs just short of the seventh floor, look through the open elevator shaft, and see which door Timoshenko went into. He charged the stairs.

Stopping just before his head became level with the top step, he waited. Pressed against the far wall, he could see though the wire mesh of the elevator shaft. There was a burly figure opening the third door from the end of the hall. He waited. The door closed. He felt a gentle breath on his neck: Alicia had caught up. They looked at each other. Who looked least like a CIA agent? Easy: Alicia. She moved past him, shoes in hand, and went down the hall. She stopped at the third door, put her shoes back on, hauled a steno notebook out of her huge purse and started writing down the names on the door. What was she going to say or do if

Timoshenko suddenly opened the door? He'd have to wait to ask her.

In a little more than a minute she was back on the stairwell beside Sam. She was smiling; he was putting his shoes back on. Alicia was enjoying her morning. Now what? Sam pointed at the stairs. Time to tiptoe up to the top floor and wait. Get above Timoshenko and follow him when he left. What if somebody came along? Well, what of it? They were a young couple who would be excused and instantly forgotten if they just looked dewy-eyed at each other. There was an upholstered bench opposite the elevator door. They sat on it and acted like they were waiting for someone. Well, they were, after all.

Out on the Bahnhofstrasse it was another pleasant September day. 1968 had enjoyed good weather so far. It was mild again, as it usually was in central Germany. In the winter it got a little cold; in the summer a little warm. The newspaper kiosks, of which there was one on every second or third street corner, offered papers from all over Europe. The *International Herald Tribune* reported that American and South Vietnamese forces had launched Operation Sea Lord in the Mekong Delta. *Le Monde* said there was a rumor that President Lyndon Johnson was going to halt all bombing of North Vietnam because of satisfactory progress at the Paris peace talks. England's *Daily Mail* dished about Jackie Kennedy's upcoming wedding to Aristotle Onassis, the Greek shipping billionaire.

In the café, Anne — who did look remarkably like a young Jackie Kennedy — glanced at her watch. Sam and Alicia had been gone for about ten minutes. Then she looked up and smiled at Harvey. Harvey smiled back. Behind him the twins were running up and down the sidewalk beside the outdoor café, chasing pigeons. The not-quite-identical twins were three. They had come as quite a surprise to Sam and Anne. Anne had had to give up her job at the Bureau of the Budget, where she was already a GS-12.

While a GS-12 was only the equivalent of an Army captain, this was unprecedented for a twenty-three-year-old just two years out of college. Anne was very smart. But she hadn't thought twice about leaving her job. It wasn't, after all, as if she'd had a choice.

She looked at Sam's new boss. Harvey had a string of registered aliases, the usual dispatch pseudonym, and, back in his OSS days, was referred to as GRUMPY WOLF. Some Agency folk thought the code name was a joke; others weren't so sure. Harvey's had been the third jeep to roll into the Mauthausen concentration camp in the spring of 1945, which had colored his opinion of the human race. "Grumpy" was thus a fairly accurate description of Harvey's public persona.

"Thanks for helping out today," Harvey said. "How are you settling in?"

"Fine, thank you. It does take some adjusting. I tried calling my grandmother last week. Did you ever try to spell Poughkeepsie phonetically to a French-speaking overseas operator?"

Harvey laughed. "I assume Sam told you the contract agent who was supposed to be here couldn't come?"

Anne was instantly on guard. The rules were Sam couldn't tell her anything. Sam said some of his classmates carried it so far that they insisted on telling their wives they worked for the Department of Agriculture. Most of the rest told their wives everything even though the security drones, hopelessly anal, insisted they shouldn't.

"Contract agent?" she said, smiling brightly.

Harvey burst out laughing. "This is the field, Anne. Out here everybody has a need to know practically everything. Here's how it is. The German Station is stuck with a contract agent who's not all that swift. He misses things like meeting instructions, like he did today. The Chief of Station in Bonn and I would really like to be able to do some modest surveillance work here. Frankfurt is full of Soviets and Poles and Czechs doing trade deals with Middle Eastern and African countries. These countries are sometimes on our side, sometimes on the Russians'. We'd like to keep track of the companies and banks and traders they're dealing with. We might be able to develop some operations from it."

Behind him the twins, victorious over the pigeons, had walked over to the waiter. Johnny, the slightly smaller of the twins, pulled at the waiter's pant leg and asked, "May we have some water please?" Johnny wasn't much for doing what Mommy told him but he had noticed that saying "please" and giving the victim his best smile worked wonders with grownups. Sure enough, the waiter smiled back, took their hands and started leading them to a table. Anne and Harvey came over and said they thought they'd all like to eat inside. Still smiling, the waiter whisked them in. Anne knew her mother would kill her if she found out, but she let the boys eat their favorite German food: *rösti* and *würstli*. Fried potatoes and hot dogs. Ugh. But they loved it.

Harvey looked worried. "I hope Sam and Alicia don't spook Timoshenko. I'd hate to have them made by the Soviets on their first outing." Then he shrugged. Sam and Alicia would succeed or they wouldn't.

Sam and Alicia hadn't been sitting on the upholstered bench by the eighth-floor elevator for only three minutes before all hell broke loose. All hell breaking loose in West Germany was, of course, a relatively muted affair. But by German standards it was shocking. The third door, the one Timoshenko had entered, was opened and banged against the wall behind it. There were two loud voices, one male, one female. They were shouting. In what? Not German. Probably Russian. Whatever it was brought Sam and Alicia rushing up to the elevator cage, where they could just see what was happening.

A solid young woman, reasonably attractive, was rushing down the hall, tugging at her skirt and trying to button her blouse and run at the same time. Timoshenko appeared in the doorway. He was shouting and buttoning his fly. He walked to the elevator shaft and bellowed down the stairs as Sam and Alicia slunk back. After the third or fourth bellow a voice yelled back in what sounded like the same language. Presumably that was the backup guy. It was hard to hear over the *clack clack clack* of the woman's high heels on the marble stairs.

What to do? CIA training at the Farm hadn't included quarrels between Pyramus and Thisbe. Timoshenko decided for them by going back into the office and slamming the door. Follow the woman. This was her office. She didn't have her purse. She likely wasn't going to go far. Besides, from outside they could wait for Timoshenko to appear again.

Sam and Alicia could run a lot faster than a solid lady in high heels, and they were only one landing behind her when she reached the front door. The security guy at the door spread his arms wide and prepared to grab her. She ran right up to him and stopped, gasping for breath. She said something and he smiled a rather ugly smile and backhanded her.

The lady in high heels staggered, and then proceeded to kick the security guy in the balls. Sam winced when he heard the impact. Alicia nodded her head approvingly. The security guy clutched at himself and started sinking to his knees. The woman stepped around him and went for the front door. Sam and Alicia drew back again, judging the distance to the back door and wondering whether they could make it there without being noticed.

As they turned to head for the back door, the security guy managed to get to his feet and stumble to the front door. There were five marble steps down to the street. He lurched to the edge of the top step and just managed to catch her arm.

Sam stood there, frozen. Was that jackass actually going to drag her back upstairs to Timoshenko? It appeared that he was. What to do? Fight or flee? He had no business getting involved in an intra-Soviet shoving match. Harvey would not be grateful. On the other hand, this miserable bastard was clearly going to give this young woman back to Timoshenko. At last sighting, Timoshenko had something unpleasant in mind for her.

That simply would not do. Sam's training kicked in. He had learned the trick somewhere. It was either in "Sneaking up on a Sentry" in the Marines or the brief course in unarmed combat with the Agency. Or maybe it was on the playground in the fifth grade. You came up behind an unsuspecting person and kicked him in the back of the knee. In all cases the surprised person immediately fell down. In ninety percent of cases the victim didn't even know another person was involved.

Sam slid up behind the guy and kicked him behind the knee. As advertised, the guy gave a surprised grunt and let go of the woman's arm. He immediately fell down, and heavily. Even better, or even worse, he hit his head hard on the top step and just lay there. The woman had her head down and was concentrating on running in high heels. She hadn't noticed what was going on behind her.

Sam spun on his heel and dashed back inside. "C'mon," he muttered to Alicia and ran for the door to the back stairs. Behind them they heard nothing. Then somebody outside the building shouted something in Swabish.

Eight minutes later Alicia's head poked cautiously out of the door of the office building next door to 234 A. They had heard the hee-haw of a siren three minutes before. Alicia saw a crowd, an ambulance, and a tiny police car. She stepped back inside and nodded to Sam. Arm and arm they sailed out the door, smiling at each other and seemingly oblivious to the business next door.

CHAPTER TWO

As lunch went on Anne made a decision. She decided she could trust Harvey. He seemed to be what a real CIA man was supposed to be like, unlike those shifty stuffed shirts at Headquarters. Well, not all of them, but too many of them. He told her his real pseudonym was GRAY WOLF, because he had been older than the rest of his Office of Strategic Services colleagues. The GRUMPY was added after his visit to Mauthausen. So she gave him a straight answer to his next question.

"Yes, Harvey, Luxembourg is a lovely little city. But Sam feels like he's in exile. I know he shouldn't have lost his temper when they didn't do anything after his assignment to be your number two got cancelled by State. And he shouldn't have told his boss to give him an airplane ticket and he'd find his own goddamn cover."

"But they gave him the ticket, of course," Harvey said. " Only it was to Luxembourg. It's almost impossible for a foreigner to get a *permis de sejour* as a student to live in Luxembourg. They figured he'd fall flat on his face."

"But he didn't," Anne said. "He talked his way into a slot as a graduate student at the University of Luxembourg. So that got them really mad at him. So they said it was going to be a tour to learn languages and he couldn't have any operational duties."

"We know," Harvey said. "We got the dispatch. But I need help and Luxembourg is only two hours by train from here. So Chief of Station and I decided we'd kind of forget we saw it and use Sam when we could. And you too." The last was an afterthought. "We're desperately short on people and information here. I'm alone. The Station has hundreds of people, but because of restrictions and protocols and inertia we can't move them from Bonn and Berlin."

They jumped when they realized Alicia had returned and was sitting beside them. She had been gone forty-two minutes.

"How do you do that?" Harvey asked. "How did it go? Where's Sam?"

Sam, it turned out, was sitting in a café across the street from 234A Kastenallee. She told them what had happened in brisk, short sentences. Except for the KGB countersurveillance guy falling down suddenly. Alicia was great on the street but was not a skilled liar. Harvey could see she was being evasive about something.

"Alicia, it's me, Harvey. This is business. How did the KGB guy fall down?"

Alicia looked at her shoes.

"I assume Sam was involved. You're not ratting him out, Alicia. Tell me."

So she told him. To her great relief Harvey burst out laughing.

"Christ. Sir Galahad breaks cover and saves the lady from a fate worse than death. Well, I doubt the Russian saw his face, so we'll probably get away with it."

They sat for another five minutes while Alicia wrote in shorthand a list of the businesses on the door of the office Timoshenko had gone into and the lady with high heels had gone out of. Then Harvey issued orders.

"Alicia, please go back and join Sam. Stake out that office building, but discreetly. If the woman comes back, by all means one of you follow her. When Timoshenko comes out follow him. Watch out for Timoshenko bringing up reinforcements. If you suspect even the least little bit that they're on to you, break contact and get out of there. I'm going up to Bonn but will be back by seven. Meet me at my house tonight. If you're not through tonight make it tomorrow. Tell Sam to check for a stakeout when he comes to my house. You can use the front door, of course. Voice code protocols if it comes to telephone calls. OK?" Alicia smiled happily and disappeared.

Harvey turned to Anne. "I'm going to go up to Bonn and talk to the Chief of Station. There may be some opportunities here." He sighed. "Besides, I hate waiting. I'd rather be there. But I'm declared to the Germans and the KGB also knows who I am, so I'm not going to be doing any surveillance work in Frankfurt. It's days like this make me wish we had a secure phone line to the embassy. Anyway, I think Sam's going to be tied up so you might as well head home to Luxembourg. I'll accompany you as far as Koblenz if you don't mind."

Anne smiled. "I'll be glad for the company." She turned to the twins. They had been busy showing the bemused waiter how far they could hop. "C'mon, chums. Time go home."

Harvey paid the bill and led the boys off to the toilet. Anne was relieved. She wasn't sure what the niceties of shipping housebroken but still quite small children off to European toilets were. Sam was always around to take care of that.

Harvey and the boys came back. He overtipped the waiter and wrangled a cab from somewhere. "I've had enough stomping up and down the Zeil and Bahnhofstrasse today," he said. "Besides, I don't want the boys waving to Daddy while he's on a stakeout."

German trains were something out of a travel agent's fondest dream. They were fast, punctual, fairly inexpensive — at least for Americans — and plush. The exchange rate was 4 German marks to the American dollar, so everything in West Germany was inexpensive for Americans. Like the restaurant, the train was uncrowded. It was, after, all, an early afternoon in September. The tourists had gone home by the end of August and the businessmen would be doing business until six.

For Harvey and the German Station, and now for Sam, the trains were ideal. The main rail lines connected Bonn, Frankfurt and, through the connection at Koblenz, Luxembourg City. It was only an hour and forty minutes from Bonn to Frankfurt, and only 18 minutes from Bonn to Koblenz. The trains ran hourly. By 1:45 the twins were sound asleep and Anne and Harvey could talk quietly in one corner of a half-empty smoking section of a first-class coach.

"So Sam's having trouble learning German?" Harvey said.

"He doesn't know why. He's always been the smartest kid in the class, or pretty close. He can read German, of course, but when it comes to understanding what somebody is saying to him he's lost. French is even worse. We're talking about resigning and going home and trying something else. It's not like the people in Headquarters would mind."

"I wouldn't quit just yet. Personnel actually did a study and found that being a successful operations officer wasn't particularly related to language ability. It helps, of course, but there are 118 major languages in the world and CIA people get transferred around a lot, so you can't often operate in the local language anyway. Besides, the people we're after — the KGB and those they associate with — generally speak English."

Harvey found her a sympathetic listener and even unbent enough to grump about having to run a surveillance team with his secretary, a trainee who wasn't supposed to be doing this, and the trainee's wife. Who, after all, didn't even work for the Agency. Then he stopped himself. Why you old fool, he thought. Prattling on to a good-looking woman with big, blue eyes. The eyes do go rather well with the black hair though. He changed the topic.

In answer to his questions, he learned that Sam had become a runner and that he and Anne had access through a friend to a small tennis club on the edge of town that also had a shooting range and weight room. The friend was an American businessman who ran the ITT operation in Luxembourg. Sam of course had friends at the university, a German about-to-be journalist in particular.

Anne laughed softly when she mentioned her best friend — a policeman's wife who lived next door. "It's just Sam's luck, he says. He gets Grant Natz for a Branch Chief and a lieutenant in the counterintelligence office of the *Surete* for a next-door neighbor."

That got them on to Headquarters. Officers in the field always wanted to know what the people at Headquarters were up to, and Anne was glad to oblige. "Sam says Grant Natz, the head of the German Branch, is a really nasty piece of work. He really went after Sam, and Ross Callahan, who is the German Desk Deputy Chief, for no reason. Sam was doing great until Grant showed up. And everybody else thought Ross is the very image of what a street guy is supposed to be."

Harvey nodded. He knew all that. "Grant Natz is the poster child of the classic nasty man. Unfortunately, he's a protégé of Clay van Claire, a very big wheel." Harvey pondered a moment. "Van Claire's no prize either."

"And Sam says the European Division front office is weird. It's like they're not there. He's never seen the Division Chief, of course." Harvey nodded. Division Chiefs did not appear among the peasants. "The top Support people are literally out to lunch all day. Or playing squash or something. Two of the top Operations guys are somebody named E. Howard Hunt, a real weirdo, and some college professor the Division Chief brought in. The college professor keeps saying he wants big, bold operations, not the penny-ante stuff we're doing now."

Harvey nodded again. He had heard the college professor, the new European Division assistant Chief of Operations, wanted to engage in the kind of big dramatic operations that had the side effect of getting people killed. Not him, of course.

"Mostly, though," Anne continued, "Sam said it was like somebody threw a blanket over the whole Clandestine Service. Everybody was keeping their heads down and doing as little as possible to avoid attracting attention. Sam and the other trainees could never figure out why."

But the Chief of Station and I can, Harvey thought. James Jesus Angleton, our beloved Director of Counterintelligence staff, is off on another witch hunt to find the Soviet mole he's sure is buried in the Clandestine Service. He's bringing the whole place to a halt while everybody hides under his desk. If there is a mole — and Harvey didn't think there was — he doubted he was doing as much damage as Angleton was. But the Director and the Deputy Director had been in the OSS with Angleton, and the old loyalties endured. They just wouldn't tell Angleton to sit down and shut up.

As Anne started getting the boys ready to get off at Koblenz, Anne was having second thoughts about being so candid with her husband's boss. It must have shown in her face, or Harvey was just good at reading people.

"Relax, Anne. We're all friends and colleagues here. And tell Sam to take his pack off and be patient. Something will work out." The train slowed and pulled into Koblenz. As Anne stood up Harvey smiled goodbye. At least he hoped something would work out.

Harvey was back home in Frankfurt by 6:45 that evening. As expected, the Chief of Station had been most interested at the prospect of learning more about Soviet commercial operations in Frankfurt, and of the Soviets, which mostly meant the KGB men who ran them. Timoshenko, long a suspect KGB type, was showing some ragged edges in his dealings with the unknown woman. There was a chance to get some leverage on him. And who was the woman? What did she know? The presence of the KGB goon as countersurveillance gave them comfort. So the opposition had budget and control problems too? Instead of bringing in all those soft-footed specialists who could easily disappear in a crowd, the KGB in Frankfurt had to make do with their security people. Those tended to run towards the goonish.

Alicia was already there. She was in the kitchen with his wife, Charlotte, who over the last twenty-two years had become blasé at the prospect of having her husband run operations out of their house. A few minutes after dark there was a tap at the back door and Charlotte let Sam in. Sam had politely introduced himself when she opened the door.

"You have good manners for a spy," Charlotte said. "Usually it's just somebody muttering, 'is Harvey here?'"

"He's not a spy, dear," Harvey said. "He's the new trainee Headquarters exiled to Luxembourg."

"That explains it then. Am I feeding everybody?"

"Yes, please," Harvey said. "Sorry not to give you notice."

"You rarely do, dear. Dinner in fifteen minutes."

Sam explained that he had checked for tails and checked the neighborhood for surveillance. He had noted an Opel with two men in it parked on the next street over.

"Oh, yes, good catch. I forgot. That's the Israeli consul's house. He needs security. The Arabs love to try stuff in neutral countries."

After dinner Charlotte went off to read a book. She favored mysteries by female authors. Harvey, Sam and Alicia sat around the dining room table in a haze of cigarette smoke and got on with it.

"What happened this afternoon? Did you rescue any more damsels in distress?"

Sam looked embarrassed. "Sorry. It was kind of instinctive, you know?"

Harvey smiled. "An action both commendable and regrettable. Let's not mention it to Headquarters. Grant Natz would surely not approve. Now, what happened?"

They told him. The cops and ambulance and the wounded goon were gone within twenty minutes. Then an hour later Timoshenko came out, a lot less blustery than before, and made off down Bahnhofstrasse in the direction he had come from originally. Sam had followed him back to the apartment building next to the Soviet Trade Mission building, which in turn was right next door to the Soviet Consulate.

Alicia had taken Sam's place at the café. Two Dubonnets later she saw the lady with the high heels, now in sneakers, edge cautiously up the street, looking constantly left and right, presumably for Timoshenko. The lady went into 234A Kastenallee. Alicia kept sitting. Four minutes later the lady tiptoed out again, this time carrying her purse. We were right, Alicia thought. She had to come back for her purse.

The further she got from 234A Kastenallee, the less paranoid the lady got. By the time she took a 17A trolley she was no longer looking around and Alicia had no trouble getting on the trolley with her. It had been harder at the trolley stop itself. In Frankfurt you bought your ticket from a machine that time- and date-stamped it. There was no conductor on the trolley. The Germans, though, are not that trusting, so there were on occasion inspectors who climbed on and started checking. If you didn't have a proper time and date stamp, or no ticket, you got a loud chewing-out in Swabish and a large fine payable on the spot. But the woman was looking the other way when Alicia slipped up to the ticket machine, and after that she just stood in the shadow of a large man until the trolley came.

The woman got out right in the middle of town. Alicia got off at the next stop, not a problem since the stops in midtown were only about a hundred yards apart. She followed her to a large apartment building, then looked though the glass door after the woman stopped, thank you very much, to check her mail. Hers was the third mailbox in the fourth row.

Alicia waited ten minutes, then arranged to be fumbling for a key when the next person showed up. Alicia even held the door for the woman and gave her a smile of thanks as she followed her into the lobby. The name on the third mailbox on the fourth row was S. Karpova. She left and headed for Harvey's house.

By eleven they had the requests for name traces, a proposed operations plan, and two cables and a supporting dispatch ready to be typed up and sent to Headquarters. Harvey had started to organize it, then caught himself and pointed at Sam. Sam not only knew what to do but could dictate it to Alicia. Alicia had said she could do 120 words a minute and she proved it. Harvey shook his head. Sam might not know German but he sure knew English.

At 11:30 Sam slipped out the back door and Alicia marched out the front door. Nowhere in the cables or dispatches were Sam or Alicia or, heaven forbid, Anne mentioned. Charlotte had already gone to bed. Harvey actually poured himself a scotch, a rare event for him, and sat sipping it in the big chair in the living room. It would be very nice to know more about T.J. Timoshenko's social life, and the whys and wherefores of all those companies listed on the door of 234A Kastenallee. He wondered if Headquarters would have enough sense to go along with the plan.

CHAPTER THREE

The next day Ross Callahan, the German deputy desk chief, sat at his desk and looked with considerable interest at the small pile of paper generated by Harvey Masters's cables from last night. Two related dispatches had made the last diplomatic pouch from Bonn and would be there this afternoon or tomorrow morning.

Around him, Headquarters was its usual sterile self. The huge, white building off the George Washington Parkway in McLean, Virginia, had opened seven years ago to mixed reviews. Top management, who remembered that the OSS had been abolished right after World War II and not reconstituted as the CIA until two years later, saw it as a symbol of permanence. Other Clandestine Service folk had been outraged. "What in hell is clandestine about a giant building out in the Virginia boondocks with a sign out front saying 'CIA'?" they yelled.

The sign quickly came down, to be replaced by one that said "Bureau of Public Roads." Sadly, that did not fool anyone. In the summer of 1967 Cuban Intelligence had openly hired members of Students for a Democratic Society, a new leftish group, to sit out on the parkway grass by the cloverleaf entrance to the new building and write down the license plate numbers of the cars going in.

CIA security jumped on them, but, embarrassingly, not until after a few hours had passed. The cops marched out and told the hippies to move on. The hippies were told they were endangering national security and were subject to arrest. The hippies pointed out that they were minding their own business in a public park and politely suggested the cops might go fuck themselves. It ended in some violence, two dramatic court appearances, a lawsuit and gleeful coverage in the *Washington Post* and *Evening Star*.

Every day when Ross Callahan drove around the cloverleaf and into Headquarters he looked to see if the hippies had come back. He was disappointed when they didn't. As a GS-13 deputy desk chief he rated a reserved parking spot close in. European Division support people had made sure he didn't get one, just to remind him of his status. So he marched in from West Parking, which, some said, was closer to West Virginia than Headquarters. He shrugged. This was all alien corn to him.

Ross Callahan was a street man. He was Boston Irish, with a long face, black hair and a resigned look about him. He was tall but slightly stooped and dressed in the GS-13's almost-a-uniform of a down-market gray suit and an ugly tie. He had been picked up by the CIA from the Army in Germany twelve years before, when Ross had run an operation against the East German Stasi which was better than what the Agency was doing. Since then he had been the German Station's go-to guy. If you needed a clean car with German plates, a cop to look the other way, somebody at the airport to do something they weren't supposed to, or a safe house in Poland, you called Ross.

He and the Agency had been very happy with each other until eight months ago. Then he had been called in to babysit a Headquarters big shot, one Clay van Claire, who was arriving in Frankfurt to meet a supposed Czech defector. Van Claire had been approached by the alleged Czech directly, and he held the operation close to his bespoke-suited chest. Ross, who was driving, broke it off when he saw a Stasi agent near the meeting site. The East German Stasi and the Czechs did not do joint operations. Among other things, they literally did not speak the same language. Sensing a trap, Ross just drove away with van Claire screaming at him from the back seat. Van Claire, who claimed he hadn't seen anything, said Ross was an idiot and demanded he be fired. Chief of Station Germany refused and the fight was on. Ross sat in his apartment for four months doing nothing until the two truculent executives reached a truce.

The truce got Ross shipped to Headquarters. He was put on the German Desk, where van Claire's acolyte Grant Natz could keep an eye on him with a view towards firing him as soon as he screwed up. Ross assumed that time would be soon. He had never been a career trainee, had never worked in an office. Sam, bless him, had saved him a thousand times when he was here. Sam had done the name traces and written the cables and dispatches and coordinated the correspondence and done the work that Headquarters did. Without Sam, he assumed it was just a matter of time before they got him. He wasn't sure he cared one way or the other.

But this morning he looked at Harvey's cables with some enthusiasm. Now this proposal was worth getting out of bed for. T. J. Timoshenko had been on the "assumed KGB" list for a long time, based on his overseas assignments. He was a *biznesmen* apparently, always attached to the trade missions in the countries he had been assigned to. But what was his *biznes*? Who was S. Karpova? She was, presumably, an employee of one of the five firms listed on the door of the office on the seventh floor of 234A Kastenallee, but which one? Alicia had copied them all down: "Baerversicherunggesellschaft . . ." He wished Sam was here to do the traces. Well, he wasn't. But Maria is, he thought, and she's right down the hall.

María was María de Angelo. She was one of the two intelligence assistants on the German Desk. Ross had originally only known of her existence through her dispatch pseudonym. She had done a lot of name traces for him for years before they ever met. Curious, he had looked her up when he came to Headquarters. He was startled to find a thirty-eight-year-old divorcee with brown hair and brown eyes. She was his age and was quite nice-looking. He had expected her to be like the other assistant, an embittered older Austrian woman who checked with Personnel every week to see whether she had enough time in to qualify for early retirement.

Divorced himself, he started having coffee with Maria, and then lunch. The idea of sex crossed their minds. But they were cautious. The pain of the recent divorces was still there. The divorces themselves had been civil enough. Ross's wife had had enough of his twelve-hour days and Germany. Truth be told, she didn't like Germans either. She went home to California. Maria's was caused by husband Bert having a roving eye. She dumped him the first time she caught him.

Maria tolerated her job as an assistant. The assistants had a lot to be bitter about. When the CIA was first set up, it modeled itself on Britain's MI6. MI6 had introduced the OSS to the world of espionage during World War II. It was customary for MI6 officers to have an assistant. The assistant was generally very smart but from the low or middle classes and a graduate of universities inferior to Oxford and Cambridge. The assistant did the name traces, the administrative stuff, and the surveillance work when it was raining.

Being an assistant went over like a lead balloon with the ambitious ex-OSS agents, the Middle European refugees and the corn-fed Midwesterners who staffed the new CIA. These men looked at MI6 as a P. G. Wodehouse clown show. They had no intention of playing Jeeves to the Eastern Establishment's Bertie Wooster case officers. So the assistant concept lapsed into using women who would do most of the work around the office for low wages.

The Clandestine Service was no more misogynous than the rest of the male population, but they damn well weren't going to have any female bosses either. So the CIA had secretaries and assistants. To try to look modern, Personnel had added a sprinkling of women as career trainees, but not in the Clandestine Service. Gone were the female OSS radio operators from World War II, some of whom were caught by the Gestapo and . . . well, best not to think about it. The surviving radio operators and other female OSS officers were now Washington hostesses or wives of Somebody, or even that tall woman from the Burma Desk, Julia Child, who had a cooking show on some Boston TV station.

"Babe, I need help." Ross had sat down in Maria's visitor's chair next to her desk and dropped the cables in front of her. She looked at him. He did look a little woebegone. But that long Irish face often did. Humph. He was a GS-13 and she was a terminal GS-10. He could do his own damn name traces. Besides, was there a glint his eye?

"Are you trying to con me into doing your work again?"

"Am I?"

"Probably."

"I offer bribes. Dinner at a white-tablecloth restaurant. Flowers. Romance. Sex."

"The nearest white-tablecloth restaurant is in D.C. And I'm holding out: in another six weeks it will have been so long the Pope is going to declare me a virgin again."

"I can save His Holiness some paperwork. Ben and Dottie's at seven thirty?"

She looked around. Her Austrian colleague was calculating her pension again. She reached out and patted his hand. "OK. Why're these traces such a big deal?"

So he told her. When he finished she smiled. "So the German Station is trying to wiggle out from under Headquarters' dead hand and actually do some field operations. Good luck with that."

She looked down at the papers. "T. J. Timoshenko rings a faint bell. I think I'll break out the Green Berets on this one." She pushed the red-line button and dialed an extension. "Sweetlips, it's me. C'mon on up and I'll give you something juicy."

She hung up and looked at Ross. "That's Ernie in Records. He's a sweetie. Poor kid thinks if he works hard enough they'll give him a slot in a career trainee class. Fat chance."

She didn't have to explain more. The Records Integration staff consisted of hordes of smart young people who went through the Abwehr files, all the telephone books in the world, thousands of newspapers, and millions of other documents, doing name traces on people and companies the case officers were interested in. Eventually it dawned on them they were going to be down in the file room as GS-7s and GS-9s forever. So they quit, to be replaced by new platoons of smart, naive young people. Personnel thought they were too kind and gentle to be operations officers.

Ernie came up five minutes later. Ross took one look at him and decided that, if he were still in Germany, he would hire this kid on the spot for the Munich surveillance team. Ernie was absolutely nondescript. Up close he had a mild, intelligent look. Otherwise his was an unmemorable face on a completely unnoteworthy body.

Ernie listened and took notes as Maria talked. He muttered "Timoshenko" once, smiled shyly, and disappeared. Maria nodded approvingly after him. "That kid can do inside the building what you can do on the street. He can find anything and get people to do what they had absolutely no intention of doing." She looked at Ross again. How can this man, a real legend on the German Desk, be so utterly incapable of writing a coherent English sentence? He reacted to paperwork as if it were covered with typhus germs. Oh well, she did rather like him.

"Lunch?" he asked.

"Cafeteria or the Albanian Shithole?"

"Shithole."

"Deal." The Albanian Shithole was the one and only bar/restaurant in McLean. Actually, no one ever dared eat there, or even knew if it served any food beyond the Slim Jims in wrappers on the dirty counter. Old-timers urged newcomers to drink nothing but bottled beer, and then only after wiping the neck off with their handkerchief. The Shithole was informally reserved for nonsupervisory Clandestine Service people ranked GS-12 and below. Ross, being a field guy, was an honorary member.

Ross and Maria walked out the far door of the German Desk. Turning right, they headed for the elevators. All around them, the atmosphere in the huge building was subdued. That befitted its determinedly bleak surroundings. One of the senior wives who had been given a tour before the building opened had been horrified. She had looked at the long, barren corridors, with its dark-gray tile floors, light-gray walls and endless gray doors and off-white ceilings. She got her husband to tell Support to paint the doors in pastel colors. Support somewhere found five very pale, very drab pastel colors and painted the doors. The result, one wag said, made it look like a Montessori school for the criminally insane.

His mood improved by a lunch of two beers and, daringly, a Slim Jim, Ross sat at his government-gray desk and looked at the material the ubiquitous Ernie had already provided. Well, well, Timoshenko certainly got around. He seemed to specialize in shady arms deals to countries in sub-Saharan Africa. These countries were mostly busy throwing off the shackles of colonial rule and taking on the shackles of militant Marxism-Leninism.

Three of the companies listed on the door of 234A Kastenallee were, Ernie found, linked to other companies in other European cities. Ernie and Maria were just starting to unravel the rat's nest of intertwined connections. Maria, it seemed, specialized in tracing companies around the world. Ross leaned back and looked at the far wall, somewhat obscured by the cloud of cigarette smoke.

Usually when the field requested an operation, Headquarters would hop to, assemble an operations file and prepare the documents to go to Counterintelligence staff to ask for a Provisional Operational Approval, or POA for short. This was the hard part of getting an operation started.

Counterintelligence staff (CI) was a real pain in the ass about giving approvals. Was it possible that this might be a Soviet dangle? Might it interfere with some other operation? Might CIA sources and methods be revealed during the operation? Why did they have to recruit foreigners for these operations? Were no Americans overseas available? Ross shook his head. The classic example was the time Vienna Station wanted to approach a left-wing Austrian journalist with a money problem who was often seen in the company of a Soviet consular officer who might by KGB. Might the journalist be willing to trade information for money? Vienna wanted to ask him; CI staff was horrified. The man was practically a communist! They proposed instead a young Mormon missionary in Salzburg whose German was impeccable. Nobody was more true-blue American than a Mormon missionary or more deserving of CI's operational approval. When Vienna Station pointed out that the young Mormon didn't know or have access to any Russians, CI got huffy and refused permission to proceed.

But this time it wasn't working that way. Grant Natz had marched into Ross's office just minutes ago complaining that Ross wasn't there when he had summoned him and waving an angry hand at the cigarette smoke. Grant was a militant nonsmoker. Instead of going to CI staff, Ross was to prepare a briefing for the European Division front office. They wanted to comment on the operation before anything went forward. Ross was to prepare the briefing and be ready to present it tomorrow morning at eleven.

When Ross started to protest that the name traces weren't complete and the dispatches from Bonn hadn't even arrived, Natz cut him off. "Kindly spare me your expertise on how to staff an operational plan," he snapped. "Eleven tomorrow in Henry Cabot's office."

Well, God knows he had done enough operational briefings over the years. Usually they were done on the fly. Documents, if there were any, were generally laid on the fender of a car with somebody holding an umbrella over them if it was raining. He assumed it would be easier in an office. But he'd have to do the Tiny Steps for Little Feet approach. These guys wouldn't know the ins and outs of following people around to get names and using them to assemble a diagram of who was talking to whom.

He worked on it till four, then went over and talked to Maria, who sent for Ernie. The dispatches had come in at six, and they worked until almost nine putting together what they had. So much for a white-tablecloth dinner at Ben and Dottie's. The CIA cafeteria had closed after lunch and they were hungry. There was nothing in McLean except the Shithole, so they gave up and walked out to West Parking together and went their separate ways. Both Ross and Maria lived in the anonymous buildings referred to as Condo Canyon. These were rows of apartment buildings spread along the old Shirley Highway, just renamed Interstate 95. The twenty-story buildings started sprouting up about two miles south of Washington and kept going towards Quantico, the rent falling as you went south. Ernie was living in Hyattsville, north of the city, in even cheaper digs. Ross was profuse in his thanks.

The next morning Ross arrived early, put his briefing papers together, and waited. Usually Grant Natz could be relied upon to go over everything Ross did, word for word, bitching and criticizing. But his Branch Chief was nowhere to be seen. At two minutes to eleven he put the briefing folder under his arm and headed across the hall to the European Division's executive offices. He told the secretary who he was. She nodded. Uninvited, he picked a chair and sat down. She frowned at the *lese mageste*. He settled down to wait. Street guys are good at waiting. This would be an excellent op if they could get it up and running, he thought. All those banks and trade missions and East Bloc spies. Frankfurt was something else. It rose from the rubble of the WW II bombings to become West Germany's financial center. Since Frankfurt was now where the money was, it drew crowds of people who had plans for hiding it or spending it or stealing it. The Soviets had even established a branch of the Narodny Bank. The Narodny Bank had financed the Second and Third Internationales, Russia's part of the Spanish Civil War, the Rote Kapelle and Rote Drei in World War II, and God knows what today.

After fifteen minutes, Grant Natz walked in the door and smiled at the secretary. She picked up her phone and dialed. "They'll see you now, Mr. Natz," she said. Ross made sure his face was still. The old trick: make the bureaucrat nervous by keeping him waiting. Trouble is, Natz, I'm not a bureaucrat. He followed Natz into the Chief of Operations' office. I'll just stand here politely with a faint smile and wait to see how they play this, he decided. Behind the huge wooden desk an older man sat. Behind him, against the wall, were three or four more chairs. The two closest to the older man were occupied.

Natz greeted the man in the middle effusively. The man looked like a body double for Leverett Saltonstall, the venerable Massachusetts senator. He must be Cabot, the Director of Operations. Maybe the Cabots and the Saltonstalls had had adjoining cabins on the *Mayflower*. The man on Cabot's right was wiry, tense, bursting to talk. The third man was the one somebody said was E. Howard Hunt, a refugee from operation WAVE, the failed Cuban invasion. Natz greeted the other two, notching the gushing down just a trifle, and then walked around and took a chair next to the tense man. Ah, Ross thought, them on that side and me on this side. He continued to stand there. It was just getting embarrassing when Natz snapped. "Well, get started."

Ross put his briefing papers on the edge of the senator's desk, which earned a frown from Natz.

"Good morning, gentlemen. I'm Ross Callahan, the German Deputy Desk Chief. It's a pleasure to meet you. This morning's briefing concerns an operation proposed by Chief of Base Frankfurt and Chief of Station Germany. As a result of information which has come their way the Chiefs see an opportunity to penetrate the web of Soviet Bloc finance and trade operations which . . ."

"How did they learn that?" Natz interrupted.

"I have no idea, Mr. Natz. The Soviet Narodny Bank branch in Frankfurt," Ross continued, "has always been active in sub-Saharan and Middle East weapons deals. The Chiefs of Frankfurt and Bonn think the Agency has a unique opportunity here to . . ."

"You haven't answered my question," Natz snapped.

"That is because I cannot, Mr. Natz. I do not know," Ross said in a polite, even tone. ". . . with a very modest and discreet effort on the street and augmented assistance from Headquarters research, Frankfurt and Bonn feel they will be able to use the unique opportunity presented by Timoshenko's weaknesses to . . ."

"They damn well better not plan on using Carpenter for that 'modest effort on the street.' Is that their plan, Callahan? Is it? Is it?" Natz's voice was rising.

Cabot held up an admonitory hand. Natz's face was red. Ross snuck a glance at him. *Jesus, he looks like he's having an orgasm. What a weird way to get your jollies.* Natz caught Cabot's signal and sat back.

Ross went on, laying out the German Station's plan. Natz interrupted from time to time. It was, Ross said, a modest cost in money and manpower in return for the chance of considerable gain. This was particularly true if they could get into the details of Timoshenko's activities, find out more about Miss Karpova, and start putting together a mosaic of the web of companies and banks Timoshenko and his colleagues were dealing with. His entire briefing, including Natz's interruptions, took eighteen minutes.

When he had finished, Ross just shut up and stood there. The first to speak was the tense man. "No disrespect, Mr. Callahan, but the operation you have just proposed is exactly the reason John brought me in here." The three men behind the desk nodded. This was the first time Hunt had indicated he was there. "John" was the Chief of the European Division, whom nobody but this tense man and possibly John's wife dared call by his first name. "This is just the kind of timid operation that eats up manpower and material with only the hope of modest gain. Well, we in the European Division are going change all that. We are going after big, bold operations. We are going to target the Soviet *Rezident*, not some drunken flunky. We are going to start at the top and stay at the top. We are going to know what Brezhnev is going to do before Brezhnev himself does."

He turned to Cabot. "I'm sorry, Lance, but this operation is a no-go. Let's wait for something big."

"Concur. Concur," said Natz.

Cabot, the man who looked like a senator, sighed. His prep school teachers had described him as "not sharp." Other educators had been even less kind. He rather liked Callahan; he thought Natz a bit, well, vulgar. But the tense professor had the Director of Europe's ear, and Natz was close to Clay van Claire in the Deputy Director's office. Best to defer to them. He turned to Ross. "Thank you for your excellent briefing, but I fear the answer is no."

Upstairs on the sixth floor, where the big animals roamed the bureaucratic jungle, Clay van Claire was having an excellent morning. He had gained possession of the DDP's conference room after implying to the DDP's other secretary that her boss had approved letting him use it. She hadn't spotted the absence of a direct "Yes, he had." This was a little surprising for a secretary at that level. Perhaps she wasn't sharp enough. Splendid tits, though. Perhaps that was the reason she was there.

Ten days ago he had gotten an anonymous letter delivered to his house. The writer claimed to be a senior KGB officer who knew

Clay was CIA. As bona fides he offered the name of one Hans Georg Kirst. Kirst was a senior advisor to West German Foreign Minister Willy Brandt. He was also a Stasi agent, the letter said, and had been an agent of the East German service for more than four years. The writer offered to provide much more if van Claire cared to meet him in Koblenz, West Germany, in three days. He gave a time and date for the proposed meeting. And that was it.

Van Claire grabbed at it. Here was a change to overcome the shadow of that Czech mess in Frankfurt last year and, if this guy was genuine, the opportunity for fast promotion. It had been a long time since the CIA had enjoyed a KGB walk-in. He got the necessary permissions except from CI staff, whom he carefully avoided, then took two retired policemen now working for the Office of Security, and headed for Koblenz. Now, flushed with excitement, he was home. He strode into the conference room off the DDP's office on the sixth floor of Headquarters. The bigot list for this operation, still called CITADEL, was in effect and the only people there were three supergrades, one each from Europe, Soviet Bloc, and Counterintelligence. He had given each of them a copy of his contact report covering his meeting with CITADEL and given them five minutes to read it. The Counterintelligence guy was looking angry, as was to be expected. Clay turned toward him and started spreading oil.

"Craig, you shouldn't be aggravated about this. There simply wasn't anything to tell you before I met with CITADEL. There was no risk to the Agency: Everybody knows I'm Agency. And God knows there can't be a safer place to meet than a park bench in West Germany. And CITADEL showed me his hand. In return I told him nothing." That wasn't true, but van Claire had no intention of pursuing the topic. He had, in fact, traded a small thing in return for a big one. It was hardly a quid pro quo, since it was much to the Agency's advantage. But admitting that Grant Natz had given him the name of a minor agent — a German working for Dynamit Nobel, the West German armaments maker — for him to pass on to CITADEL might be embarrassing.

"Willy Brandt is likely going to be the Chancellor of Germany next year, which makes this an extremely valuable piece of information. You have a copy of my contact report," he went on. "Tell me, what should we do about the Willy Brandt staffer and what is your estimate of the situation otherwise?" He leaned forward, eagerly he hoped, and looked at the CI man. He waited.

Craig Withers, the Counterintelligence (CI) guy, wasn't much for chatting. He spent most meetings fiddling with his pipe, looking dour, and limiting his conversation to things like "perhaps," and "let's not jump the gun," and "that remains to be seen." Counterintelligence Staff had been designed from the outset to act as a brake on the cowboys in Operations, and to be eternally wary of the Soviets' ability to penetrate the Agency, the State Department, the Defense Department and even the White House staff. My God, even CI's boss, James Jesus Angleton himself, had been suckered by Kim Philby. Philby had been Angleton's mentor back in the days after World War II, when the Agency was setting itself up and modeling itself after Britain's MI6. They had spent months together, sitting in Angleton's office comparing notes, or enjoying long, boozy lunches at Billy Martin's Carriage House in Georgetown, the mess hall for the Clandestine Service's upper echelons.

The embarrassment had been hideous when the Philby case broke. Philby a KGB agent! It had nearly destroyed MI6. From that day on the Agency had held the Brits at arm's length. Even trainees like Sam had been told to stay away from the British Commonwealth Branch, down the hall from the German Branch on the fifth floor, if they ever hoped to go out under cover. Fortunately, the Agency managed to avoid being spattered by what had hit the fan. The rest of the government and the Washington press corps had never cottoned onto the fact that Philby had milked the CIA, and Angleton in particular, like a cow.

Somehow Angleton, a mandarin in the tightly knit group that included Allen Dulles and Richard Helms and William Colby and the other big names from OSS days, had managed to survive. But his innate paranoia had grown, and even now the whole Clandestine Service was clamped down, being investigated case by case and officer by officer. Angleton was looking for the Soviet penetration that he truly believed was even now operating within their ranks. As a result Craig Withers and everybody else on Angleton's staff was busy saying "no" to nearly everything the operations guys proposed. The whole service was getting bored, restless and sullen. Some of the sharper people around town were asking just what the Clandestine Service did besides spend vast amounts of money and tiptoe around town, drinking heavily and otherwise doing nothing.

Craig Withers sucked his pipe. Finally, he spoke: "Who said beware of Greeks bearing gifts?"

"Oh, for Christ's sake," van Claire snapped. "CITADEL has to be a senior man in the First Chief Directorate. What the fuck else do you want? Brezhnev standing out in West Parking handing out KGB files? This is going to be the biggest intelligence coup in the last ten years and the Muffled Fart Brigade is going to poo-poo it? Like hell you are."

Van Claire was on his feet now, standing over Withers. His face was flushed. "What the fuck is wrong with you people?" He slammed his briefing file on the conference table with a loud smack. "I ought to take your goddam pipe and shove it up your ass. You idiots are wrecking the Clandestine Service."

There was silence for a moment. Van Claire's tantrums were frequent, and only some were feigned. This one seemed real to them. They were shocked, not by the outburst, but by van Claire's saying "fuck." It was not a word gentlemen used. Well, the Marines did, but they were officers and gentlemen by Act of Congress, not real gentlemen.

Withers spoke first, leaning back slightly and holding his pipe out of van Claire's reach.

"Virgil."

"What? What?" Van Claire screamed at him.

"Virgil wrote the phrase 'Beware of Greeks bearing gifts.'"

"But Laocoon was the one who actually said it." This from the Soviet Bloc supergrade.

"Is this the Mad Hatter's tea party?" van Claire screamed. "I'm reporting to you that I just met with a senior KGB official who's interested in defecting in place. To prove it he's given us the name of a top-level penetration of the senior staff of Germany's rising chancellor. And you're showing off that you majored in classics at Yale?" Van Claire's family name was Vonderklagen, a good old Dutch name. They had changed it to van Claire about the time great-grandfather had made a bundle brewing beer in Philadelphia. Fourth-generation rich, he was still a little uncomfortable around the WASP aristocracy who talked in the faux British accent perfected by William F. Buckley.

"Why is a senior KGB-nik suddenly America's best friend?" Withers asked politely.

"How does a senior KGB Headquarters guy get permission to leave Moscow and go to West Germany?" This was the first time EUR had spoken.

"Why did he pick you to talk to?" The WASP from Soviet Bloc. Jeez, van Claire thought, these guys are so effete you wonder how they reproduce. Do they have genitals? He had doubts.

"I wish you'd read your briefing papers more closely," van Claire snapped. They had, actually. Van Claire had been artfully vague about the answers to those questions. "With respect to your first question, he says his boss has been a little cool lately. He's not sure whether it's his imagination or his instinct. Plus he has a new Chief, a real peasant named Komsomol, who might actually be a psychopath. His instinct tells him the time is right to look for an exit." That sounded plausible to them. And an actual psychopath for a boss? Ah, but was it true?

"As regards meeting in Koblenz, CITADEL is kind of the KGB's Mikhail Suslov. He travels around the world inspecting *Rezidenturas* and making sure everybody's dead keen on the principles of Marxist-Leninism." Again, there was silence as the other three men pondered this. Mikhail Suslov was famous as the only man in the Soviet Union who actually believed in Communism. He was its acknowledged high priest. But a lesser Suslov in the KGB? There were dozens of commissars in the KGB and every *Rezidentura*. This explanation sounded a tad facile. But to challenge van Claire? I mean, after all, who knows?

"With respect to why he approached me" — here van Claire figuratively dug his toe in the carpeting and tried to look self-effacing — "Well, he said he's heard of me." The three looked at him. Oh, bullshit, Clay. Your name is a legend in the halls of the Lubyanka? Give us a break.

"Tell us about CITADEL." This from Soviet Bloc. This was safe ground.

"CITADEL says he isn't a Russian, but he got in tight with Stalin's Georgians and survived after Stalin died. He says he's been behind the screen at a lot of high-level meetings. He has four languages and says they tell him he has a way of making the boss look smart. Has travelled in the west under alias a lot and has never been stationed abroad. He's a Headquarters man."

"What was he doing in his travels?"

"Wouldn't say."

"Handling agents maybe?" Withers again.

"I told you: I don't know yet. We'll have to handle him on the basis of what he gives us."

"How does he know about Willy Brandt's guy?"

Van Claire slammed his briefing file on the table again. "Look, you can keep asking questions I don't have the answers for yet, and it will never get us anywhere. Why don't you write down all these questions" — he refrained from saying "idiotic questions" — "and we'll agree on what we'll ask CITADEL. He's the guy who knows."

"And we'll assume he's telling used truth," said Withers sourly. "I'd like to FLUTTER him damn soon." FLUTTER was the code word for polygraph.

"Oh, what a swell idea," said van Claire. "Let's establish rapport with a high-level defector by treating him like a street cleaner. We better get the DCI to sign off on that one." That shut them up. Nobody was going to go to Richard Helms with their complaints.

"So we take him on trust?" asked the EUR guy, the man who looked perpetually worried.

"That's what the analysts are for. They'll assess what he tells us and run it against what we already know, see what matches up."

"Oh, we're going to expand the bigot list?" Won't that damn Withers ever shut up? "No, not yet. Look, let's not try and do steps one through twenty-two at the first debrief meeting. Let's analyze what we have and plan what I'm going to do and say to CITADEL at the next meeting." This, he thought, will also spread some responsibility if things go wrong.

Van Claire held up his hands like the Pope raising his arms in benediction over the prayerful in St. Peter's Square. "Look, we have a really big operation with a huge potential right in our hands. Let's not get ahead of ourselves. We sit on the Willy Brandt business; we rest on our oars and just think. How about three days of prayerful concentration and we meet again on — what would that be? Monday, right? Eleven a.m., all right? May I have the briefing papers back please?" They looked like they wanted to keep them. "Sorry, rules."

There were reluctant nods and surrenders of documents. "Fine, until then." Van Claire nodded briskly and grabbed the briefing papers and headed towards the door. Go slowly, slowly, he told himself. Don't look anxious. Once outside, he walked with deliberate steps down the hall to his office. He walked over to his window and looked out into the inner courtyard. He'd gotten them to back off and not demand answers to the obvious questions. Plus they hadn't, thank God, asked him if he'd given CITADEL anything in return. The obvious had never occurred to them: CITADEL had to have a reason for meeting with him in case it had been noticed, so he needed to have been told a little something to show his bosses if necessary. Let us hope and pray that CITADEL was undetected and would never have to use his little present.

CHAPTER FOUR

Three days later Harvey Masters looked at the dispatch and swore, which he rarely did. The Timoshenko operation had been shot down by Headquarters. He read parts of the dispatch again. "We are going to start at the top and stay at the top. We're going to know what Brezhnev is going to do before he does." And how do these twits propose doing that? They didn't say.

The document bore the dispatch pseudonym for Ross Callahan, who undoubtedly felt like he was chewing ground glass when he was forced to write it. Interesting, that. Since Cabot, the European Division's Chief of Operations, was most probably the man who had done the shooting down, you would think he would write this himself. Unless, unless . . . unless Cabot was giving in to somebody else and didn't want his name on this. It was probably some flunky in the European Division front office with connections to somebody powerful. And, of course, that turd Natz. Natz never wanted his name on anything.

Why? He contemplated the awful thought that some idiot was actually serious. The fool was sitting at his desk coming up with scenarios in which the Soviet *Rezident* in Bonn was going to be recruited at an embassy cocktail party. Some golden-tongued warrior sent out from Headquarters was going to run through the script Headquarters had prepared. In response the *Rezident* was going to fall into his arms, weeping with remorse for his past misdeeds and babbling secrets Brezhnev himself had told him only yesterday. Christ on a crutch.

Harvey looked at the dispatch again. On second reading, there was a note of irony in the retelling of the front office's pontifications. By all reports Ross Callahan wasn't much for writing. Did he have a ghostwriter? Harvey sighed. He had already had a guarded open-line phone conversation with the Chief of Station on this. The Chief said, in effect, that one had to pick one's battles and this wasn't worth the effort it would require. If Headquarters was too dumb to green-light a good solid meat-and-potatoes operation, then to hell with it. There's so much potential here in Frankfurt, Harvey thought. There's a lot of potential in Sam too. But Timoshenko was all the work I had for him. I hope he doesn't go nuts sitting over there in Luxembourg.

Ross really liked how Maria had tweaked his dispatch. He supposed it was amusing that they had selected him to be the messenger and give the bad news to the German Station and Frankfurt. If they were so sure of their bluster about recruiting the *Rezident*, you'd think they'd tell Harvey and the Chief themselves. He looked around him and shook his head.

The day last year he had reported to Headquarters they had sent Sam down to the front desk to help him get checked in and get him a badge. The badge was just an oversized credit card with his name and picture on it. Around the edges were letters of the alphabet, and if some of these letters were in red, it meant you had more access. He looked at Sam. He looked intelligent, but career trainees were supposed to be. Usually your new boss came down to welcome you to Headquarters. The fact that they had sent Sam was a message."

Ross had stood in the lobby and looked at the massive building. "How many thousand spies we got in this place?"

"Practically none, boss. They tell us we're operations officers. They say the field offices hire spies." He pointed. "The right side of the building is the Intelligence Directorate; the Directorate of Science and Technology, whatever that is; and then there's Support and Personnel and Security and Central Cover and whatnot. We don't have access to that side of the building."

"You mean I can't go to the German Desk Chief in the Intelligence Division and ask him what he wants to know?"

"I don't even know whether they have a German Desk."

"That must help this place function smoothly. Where are we located?"

"Fifth floor, this side of the building. Soviet Bloc Division is on four, Counterintelligence staff down on two, and the rest are scattered around. There's Western Hemisphere, Near East and Cord Meyer's Covert Action staff. China Operations are on five. Special Operations Division, the Boom and Bang Boys . . ."

"Special Ops?"

"They're new. Special Ops is mostly retired sergeants and majors who haven't enjoyed successful careers in the military. But they talk a good game. Their critics, which include all the old-line case officers, say they're self-confessed heroes, who, rumor has it, spend their time hanging from the air conditioning pipes in the basement eating bananas and waiting for instructions from on high to go out and kill the wrong people."

"Wonderful. What do we do?"

"Support Bonn and the bases at Berlin and Frankfurt. Try and get operational approval from Counterintelligence Staff for new operations, do name and company traces, coordinate the correspondence with everybody else. Do whatever Mr. Natz tells us to."

"How do you and Mr. Natz get along?"

Sam looked at him for a bit, clearly making a decision. Then, "We don't."

Ross smiled. "Never mind. I heard. You were doing great until Natz came in. I believe the charge against you is 'insufficient servility towards the management.'"

Sam laughed. "Guilty, I guess."

"Well, me too. Welcome to the club."

Now, eight months later, Ross sat back and put his feet up on the desk. He blew cloud of cigarette smoke at the ceiling. Natz hated feet on furniture and cigarette smoke, so it was a double win. He wondered how Sam was doing, sitting out in the boondocks.

Sam and Anne's apartment was on the sixth floor of a big building on a hill just on the edge of the Old City. The small balcony looked down on the ancient city walls, one of the Duke's lesser palaces, the Cathedral and the tile roofs that distinguished seventeenth-century Luxembourg. It was around then that the city fathers had ruled that no further changes could be made to the exteriors of any building. Thus, the inner city looked not all that different from when Louis XIV, Napoleon and various Prussian and German armies had come through. The American 4th Infantry Division had added a few bullet holes when they liberated the city in 1944, but otherwise the old city looked much the same.

In daylight they could see cows in the pastures just over the near hills. Beyond them were the steeper hills of the beginnings of the Ardennes. It was a very beautiful view. Even better, at 7 p.m. every night the Cathedral bells rang. Anne told the twins those were "the beddy house bells." The twins, impressed that the whole city wanted them to go to bed, went quietly. Sam kept meaning to find out why the bells rang at seven. Six was Angelus, but seven? Who knew?

"What's on for you tomorrow?" Sam asked. "I'm shooting with Charlie in the morning and lunch at one at the Gambrinus with Dieter."

"Not much. I'm shopping with Madame Baeriswyl in the afternoon. May I have the car, then?" Madame Baeriswyl was Angelica, their next-door neighbor on the two-door landing. Her husband, Kurt, was a lieutenant in the Luxembourg *Verkehrsbrigade*, the traffic police, which was all right, Sam guessed. But Kurt had told him he was stuck in the counterintelligence section, which had Sam cursing his fate. Why me? Why next door?

"Of course." Charlie was Charlie Berringer, the vice president in charge of ITT's Luxembourg subsidiary. About six months a year Charlie was frantically busy renegotiating key contracts. The rest of the time lay as heavy on his hands as it did on Sam's. The two had taken to playing tennis, swimming in the summer and target shooting at the local tennis club. To kill time Charlie had even started taking long hikes in the nearby hills. Sam, who had had a bellyful of hiking in the Marines, had nevertheless joined in. What else was there to do except go to class at the university, where the lectures were delivered in mixtures of French and German which soon lapsed into Luxembourgerisch. Sam had pretty much given up trying.

Sam had also taken to running. Two years before Kenneth Cooper was enthralling millions with his Air Force studies, which were inaccurately translated by the public as meaning that if you ran a mile in eight minutes or less every day you'd never have a heart attack and would probably live forever. Sam had measured 1.6-kilometer courses all over Luxembourg and tried a different one every day. As always, he quit smoking once a week to help him run faster.

Anne decided Sam wasn't exactly driving her nuts with his restless energy, but he was getting close. She knew he had a tremendous need to have an actual, useful job instead of being, as he put it, the perpetual bridesmaid, sitting around waiting for something to happen. Sometimes she considered going over to CO-OP, a local department store, and buying a cast-iron frying pan so she could hit him over the head with it. Oh well, she sighed, he was kind of cute when he wasn't being a pain in the ass.

She patted him on the behind and said, "Cheer up, sweetie. I'll buy you your own KGB agent for Christmas." He turned and grabbed her in a bear hug. "I've got a great idea. Let's play newlywed."

"Good heavens. I thought you'd never ask." They went hand in hand towards the bedroom.

The next morning was typically middle Europe: gray and mild. The pistol range was in the basement of an old farmhouse the tennis club had converted to a small country club: a swimming pool, two tennis courts, a skeet range and the pistol range. It was minimalist — bare-bones and very functional.

"Shit." Charlie had pulled the targets in and was examining them. Sam had won again. Anne had decided not to come because she usually beat Charlie too. She found the hypercompetitive Charlie's attempts to portray the gracious loser hard to bear. You could practically hear Charlie's teeth grinding. Charlie *hated* to lose. Well, it wasn't her fault she was a good shot. Her father had taught her. She was supposed to have been a boy, after all.

"Nice tight group, Sam."

"Hmm. I had plenty of time to practice in the Marines. We had a week of dry firing every year — 'snapping in,' they called it — before you spent a week at the rifle range actually shooting. Talk about boring."

"Are you sure you don't want a job? I've got a problem at the office. I think somebody's embezzling money. Didn't you say you were an investigator awhile back?"

"Yes, but the Duchy won't allow it. "Still," Sam continued, "I've done some white-collar fraud cases. Back on Okinawa they detailed me to the Armed Services Police. The senior guys got the murders and rapes. They didn't like looking at bank transfers and suspicious invoices. So I got a mandatory learning experience. Anyway, bring the check registers for the last six months over tonight. I'll take a look for free. You don't want me sitting around your office making prospective perps nervous. Come after seven, unless you want the twins to help you crack the case."

    Charlie complied that evening. After he left Sam started going slowly through the check registers. By eleven he had a headache and the first feelings of defeat. The long German words swam before his eyes. Just after midnight the penny dropped. What was this *Eidgenoessische Krankenversicherung*? Charlie was already paying the City of Luxembourg for health insurance. And this agency of the Duchy had a poste restante address? General delivery for a government agency? That doesn't pass the smell test, Sam decided.

    Next day he and his German-English dictionary presented themselves to an official in the City government. He was a student, he said, and could the *Herr Inspektor* help him? Armed with bad German and a good memory, he asked his questions. The *Herr Inspektor* was dismissive of Sam's scholarly abilities: there was no such thing as the "*Eidgenoessische Krankenversicherung.*" Gotcha, Sam thought.

    Thursday was the day the checks went out, so Thursday was the day Sam was seated in the café opposite the main post office. He was partially behind a concrete statue but had a good view of the front door. Frau Neimueller from Charlie's office came by at 9:30. She plumped in the front door and was out again in minutes with a bundle of mail. Normal, Sam decided.

    He tried again at lunch. Lunch in Luxembourg was twelve thirty to two. Half the workers went home; the rest headed for restaurants and cafes. Sam was squeezed in a corner, but he could see. At 12:40 Herr Ürli, the pinch-faced Luxembourger who was Charlie's number three man at the office, slid into the post office.

He popped out moments later. You're my man, Sam thought. Now I need a cop. If I have to have a cop as a next-door neighbor I might as well see if I can enlist Kurt to help us out.

That night Sam and Charlie and Kurt sat at Sam's dining room table, smoking up a storm and drinking the very good local beer while Charlie, who could speak German decently enough to make himself understood, laid the story out. When Charlie finished, they looked at Kurt.

Kurt, blank-faced, looked back at them. Then he unexpectedly switched to English, "Well, so we have two foreigners making accusations against a Luxembourger and I'm supposed to *vefhaften* him? Do I have this right?" His expression changed to, well, menacing. "I should run you two in for perjury and making false charges."

Charlie looked like he was going to swallow his tongue. Sam felt his heart skip a beat. Had he misread Kurt so badly?

There was a long pause. Then Kurt smiled. "So, a little local joke." He looked at Charlie. "Do not shit in trousers, Charlie. Luxembourger jokes are not always . . . *scharfsinnig* . . ." He looked at Sam.

"Subtle," Sam said.

"*Ja*, subtle. No, I think you have a crook on your hands. I think I visit him next time he comes to post office."

Kurt kept his word. Ten days later the blustering ITT employee was arrested just after he took the dummy company's check from a postal clerk's hand. An examination of his bank records showed he had been stupid enough to deposit the checks into his own account for the last two years. It added up to a lot of money: some $72,000 altogether. Charlie got brownie points with the ITT front office for his successful investigation; Kurt got the same from his watch commander. Sam, staying CIA-ish in the background, settled for a beer at the Gambrinus and too much praise from Charlie. He did, however, in his role as an Agency spotter, send full biographies of Charlie and Kurt to Frankfurt Base. He had seen that ITT had a lot of contracts with Middle East companies and did a lot of business with the big European and Middle Eastern banks. Charlie was the kind of guy the Agency might want to debrief from time to time. And it was always nice to be friendly with a cop.

Sam and Charlie had talked about that night off and on since it happened. Charlie still shivered with horror at the memory of Kurt pulling his leg and talking about arresting him. When they finished shooting, Sam cleared his weapon, checking the chamber for empty. Then he partially field-stripped the pistol. He didn't want the twins playing cops and robbers.

The Luxembourgers were funny about guns. You'd be locked up forever if you carried one, but everyone had a gun or two around the house, and that in addition to the automatic rifle that all the army reservists also kept at home. And you were allowed to transport it as long as it was partially disassembled.

His pistol was the M1911A1, developed for the Marine Corps after the .32s Marine officers were using to try to subdue the Moro rebels in the Philippines at the turn of the century turned out not to pack enough power to stop an enraged Muslim with a nose full of drugs. Typically, it wasn't issued until well after the Philippine insurrection had been put down. It would have worked though. If you so much as nicked somebody, the slow-moving, huge .45-caliber slug would knock the guy into the next county. It was Charlie's, but Charlie had an arsenal so he told Sam to hang on to it, since Sam came to the range so often.

The Gambrinus was a cross between a German beer hall and a French restaurant. There was a mix of square and round wooden tables, and a hundred heavy wooden chairs. Coats of arms of the 12 Luxembourg cantons hung on the walls and were hard to see in the dimly lit interior. The round tables, seating eight, were towards the front. The locals called them *Stammtisches* — favorite tables — and they were informally reserved for the city's men's clubs and university fraternities, which used them daily. Sometimes only one member would appear, but the whole table would still be his. The waiters never tried to seat larger parties there or move the solitary drinkers. The place had been like that for 150 years and no one thought to suggest changing it. The restaurant stood in the square just down the street from the main university campus, the campus being an unfortunate mix of Bauhaus and Danish Unmodern. In the other direction from the University was Luxembourg's main shopping district, mostly medium-sized shops and the city's few department stores. The far end of the square in front of the Gambrinus led to the very charming Rue de Bec, all seventeenth-century townhouses and tiny shops. It ran sharply downhill to the Hotel de Ville and the Cathedral. The river did a U-turn just beyond the Cathedral, leaving the Old City standing high above the steep walls that the river had cut over the centuries.

Dieter Volkmann was sitting at the far back of the Gambrinus at his usual table when Sam came in. Dieter gave him a smile and a lazy wave. Dieter was a Bavarian and looked like the music hall caricature of one. He was large, overweight, and red-faced. He had a beer mug in front of him. He seemed to always have a beer mug in front of him. But talk to him and the caricature did not hold. He was smart, sensitive, and had an acerbic sense of humor. His mood varied between jolly and fatalist, sometimes switching back and forth twice in the same conversation.

"Ah, the lazy American. Cutting class again. Hi, Willi," he yelled at an overworked waiter. The waiter glanced in his direction and Dieter held up two fingers and pointed at the chalkboard on the wall by the bar which listed the plat du jour. Willi gave him the barest nod and kept going. The unemployment rate was zero and every business was short of help. But the Luxembourgers didn't want any more foreign workers than were already there, so that was the way it was.

"Out shooting little birds again?" Dieter asked.

"Clay discs, Dieter. Not real birds. And no, we were target shooting."

Dieter sniffed. He disapproved of shooting anything. Five years older than Sam, he was ten years old when World War II ended. It was old enough to remember some things about the war he seldom talked about. Dieter and Sam had met eight months ago, when Sam, nervously arriving in Luxembourg in his search for a way to get a residence permit, showed up at the Journalism Institute. Dieter was manning the reception desk, one of the several jobs he held while he finished getting ready to take his final examination for a *Doktorat*. He liked the younger American on sight for no particular reason. He interrupted Sam's carefully rehearsed questions in spectacularly bad German and said, in English, "So you have an unquenchable thirst for knowledge and that is why you are here. And I have a Brooklyn Bridge I want to sell you. That is how you say it, yes? Come, my shift is over. I will buy you a beer and tell you how to become the Student Prince."

The Gambrinus was two blocks away, and by the time they got there Sam had already been schooled as to how to approach the academic bureaucracy. "Everybody is addressed as *Herr Doktor Professor* this and *Herr Doktor Professor* that, and you go into your spiel about your thirst for knowledge" — Dieter particularly liked that phrase — "and pause dramatically, obviously searching for a word. This permits the *Herr Doktor Professor* to break in and try to show off his English. His English will be even shittier than your German, but you nod admiringly and stick to English so you know what is being said.

"Luxembourg is poorer than West Germany and Luxembourg's university is small, even poorer, and unknown to the outside world.. The only foreign students we have are me and a bunch of German draft-dodgers who hide here until they reach age 26 when they become too old to be drafted into the *Wehrmacht*. Pardon me, the *Bundeswehr*. The authorities want the university spaces for Luxembourgoise, not German draft dodgers, so the *permis de sejour* is hard to come by. But they would love to have an American, and will intercede in your behalf with the authorities." He smiled slyly. "I, by the way, have a reverberated eardrum so I won't get drafted."

"Um, it's perforated, not reverberated, Dieter," Sam said.

"Thank you. In return for my advice you will perfect my English until I can get my *Doktorat* and get out of here."

And it worked. Sam gained entrance to academic offices, burst into his memorized speeches in German, paused in the right places, and let the *Herr Doktor Professors* carry it from there. He was back at the Luxembourg airport with a letter of admission and a *permis de sejour* from the Canton of Luxembourg in two days. Bless Dieter. And almost the best part of it had been the angry expression on Grant Natz's face when he went back to Headquarters. He had done what the CIA bureaucracy couldn't do. Sam was careful not to gloat but it hardly mattered. He had embarrassed them and they were going to get him for it.

The plat du jour was typically German: fresh ingredients carefully prepared and tasting of nothing in particular. Their chat during lunch was mostly about Dieter's upcoming doctoral examinations, and his hopes for a job in journalism or business as immediately afterwards as Dieter could arrange. "This vow of poverty, chastity and obedience is fine for monks but not for me," Dieter said. "As soon as I solve the poverty problem, chastity will follow close behind. I will no longer be a poor, fat German. I will be a rich, fat German and Miss September from Playboy will lust for me. And screw obedience. I was never very good at that anyway."

Sam hoped for the best for his friend but wasn't sure about the chastity business. Dieter was surprisingly prim in many ways, and went back and forth between being too shy and too forward with women. Oh well, he'll work it out. Dieter's a smart cookie.

They split and Sam trotted back to the apartment. It was faster to turn right coming out of the Gambrinus and go down an alley and up the stairs to walk alongside the parapet of the Old City wall, which ended at the Rue du St Esprit. It would have taken a lot longer to drive, assuming he could have found a parking space. Medieval cities were not designed with automobiles in mind.

Life in Luxembourg for Sam was an extended vacation when he didn't want a vacation. But taking trips with Anne and the boys was nice. The boys liked riding in the little VW Beetle, chattering, arguing and dozing and looking out the windows at the pretty landscapes and old buildings.

There was an American exchange program for high school students in Luxembourg and thus an ample supply of babysitters. The Luxembourgers were working too many jobs to sit with someone else's children. Sam and Anne could even manage an overnight trip once in a while. They went to Bonn one weekend, which, they decided, was more than enough. Bonn might be the capital of a major country, but it was by far the most boring of all the cities in West Germany. It was expensive too.

But to be fair, Bonn has its moments. Three months before some Arab diplomats had celebrated the end of Ramadan by slaughtering a goat in the bathtub of their hotel suite on the sixteenth floor of the Intercontinental. Then they started to barbecue it on the balcony, setting off every smoke alarm in the area. Even the concierge, who ordinarily wouldn't have blinked if a paying guest had dragged a dead camel across the lobby, was upset. The newspapers, of course, had a field day.

Standing at the French windows of their Juliet balcony on the second floor of their much lesser hotel, Sam and Anne, arms wrapped around each other, stood one morning admiring the view when Anne suddenly started to giggle.

"My God, look Sam. There's A and B."

Sure enough, two men in cheap suits who could only be German policemen were walking carefully down the Josefstrasse, one fifty feet behind the other. Both walked with the careful tread of a hunter in the forest, taking care not to step on a twig or otherwise startle the deer.

"Right out of the wrong textbook. Do you see C?"

They squinted. Then Sam said, "Yeah, right where he's supposed to be. He's stopped by the bus shelter."

"Got him," said Anne. "And — oh, look, Sam," she said, laughing happily. Look at the rabbit."

And there was the rabbit in all his splendor. Another policeman, another cheap suit, but this time the rabbit was wearing a Tyrolean hat with a little feather, gloriously out of place in buttoned-down Bonn.

"Well, the trainees aren't going to have any trouble following him." Now Sam was laughing. What a town. The place was alive with spies, as was, of course, Frankfurt. Frankfurt had replaced Berlin as the espionage capital of Europe. All those banks, all that money going for arms and bribes to third-world countries who were staunch allies of America one morning and Marxist-Leninist to the core the next afternoon. And there Sam was in sweet, peaceful, beautiful, boring Luxembourg. Shit.

Anne sensed his change of mood. "Why don't you go to class more, sweetie? Maybe that will turn your pilot light down a little."

"Going to class is kind of futile. The way they do it, you sign up for your classes every semester. You take your little red *Tabella Scholarum* to the professor, and he signs it. Then nothing: you go or you don't go to classes, keep signing up for more classes every semester, and when you think you're ready, you present yourself to the examining board to try for a *Doktorat*. That could be twenty years later for all they care. In the meantime, there are no midterms, no papers, no grades, no nothing. If they did that in the U.S. I don't like to think what would happen. And all the damn lectures are in Luxembourgerisch. They start lecturing in the German version of Berlitz German in September and by Thanksgiving they're back to muttering and mumbling. I give up."

Going home, they stopped off in Koblenz for lunch. There was a train every hour, so stopping off for lunch or dinner at the pretty towns and cities along the Rhine and Main rivers was a common practice. They were walking along the waterfront when Sam stopped suddenly. He drew Anne back to a newspaper kiosk they had been passing. The kiosk sported the usual racks of newspapers, lots of magazines, and plentiful offerings of cigarettes and candy.

"Anne, fiddle with a newspaper and look at those two guys sitting on the bench by that big chestnut tree. I'm going to stand on the other side here so they won't see me if they look up."

Anne looked. "All I see is two middle-aged guys, both wearing really good suits. They must be bankers. One's going gray, bald on top, overweight. The other one looks like that guy on TV who wants to clean your oriental rugs. You know, Levantine, maybe Armenian."

Sam risked a peek. "Yeah, funny, I swear I know the bulky guy with the bald spot. I've seen him somewhere before. Well, no sense getting a knot in my shorts over it. C'mon, let's go home." So they left, talking about how they were coming to recognize *Luxembourgoise* in other cities. There seemed to be three giant families. All had somewhat similar features and the same wary, pinched-faced look that stood out from the blockier faces in Germany.

They walked hand in hand back towards the railroad station. "A view like this, it makes you feel romantic."

Anne squeezed his hand. "That's what I like about you. You always feel romantic."

CHAPTER FIVE

"Hooray! Huzzah! Oorah! Yippee!" Dieter danced around Sam and Anne's living room. He was holding one twin, who was squealing happily, up in the air while the other one skittered around the dancing Bavarian, laughing and waiting his turn. Anne looked a little apprehensive as Dieter thundered around. Sam caught the look.

"It's OK, honey. The building's concrete. The floor probably won't collapse. Watch it!" He grabbed Anne and held her close as Dieter blundered by.

"It's not that. I'm afraid he'll trample a twin."

Dieter had burst into the apartment five minutes ago. There could hear him coming, singing, in the tiny elevator. Ugh. The neighbors would be pursing their lips. The grumpies upstairs were probably already on the phone to the management office. In one of his manic moods, Dieter was noisily ebullient. When, as the Irish say, drink had been taken, he was a real handful.

"May I introduce myself?" he had bellowed as he popped out of the tiny elevator onto their even tinier landing. "I am, as of an hour ago, *Herr Doktor* Dieter Volkmann, a doctor of economics at the University of Luxembourg." The other door on the landing opened and Angelica peeked out.

"Angelica, join us" Anne cried. "Our friend just got his doctorate." Angelica smiled, shook her head and closed the door. "Oh God, her kids are napping. Dieter, come inside before the neighbors call the police." Not Angelica, but the others would. Anne had gotten a written reprimand from the Duchy, delivered by a uniformed official yet, for doing her washing on Sunday. That was courtesy of the old farts upstairs. Rules were rules, and by God they were going to enforce them.

"Bah. I shall rout the police by waving my wallet at them. For I," and here Dieter drew himself up triumphantly, "am no longer a poor fat German. I am a rich fat German. Starting in a week I am the East Europe and Soviet Union economic correspondent for a whole bunch of newspapers." He paused for breath. "The *Frankfurter Allgemeine*, then Düsseldorf, two Munich papers, and, here I want the drums to roll, *Die Welt*. The pay is adequate, the expenses are excellent, and the future is unlimited. Miss September, pack your spare G-string and call me. We are off to see the world." It was then that he had begun his victory dance with the twins.

Dieter now gave the other twin a whirl, and then collapsed in their easy chair. "Enough. Give me a beer. Always beer after exercise. It is *gesund*."

"That's great, and *Die Welt* to boot," Sam said. Anne kissed him and beamed at him. "How did you do it?"

"I've been a stringer for the *Frankfurter Allgemeine* for years, and I wrote lots of papers for economic journals, and I sucked up to the great and good at every conference I could get into."

"Was the Journalism Institute here any help?" Anne asked.

Dieter snorted. "The *Herr Doktor Professors* here couldn't get themselves a job writing obituaries for the *Luxembourger Wort*. "

"Where are you going to live?" Sam asked.

"To be decided. I have a sub-Saharan development conference in Moscow in two weeks. There's another conference in Frankfurt the week after. I hope to use the conferences to find out where the trade deals are going to be, and then worm my way into capitalist and communist hearts and find some interesting things to report."

As Dieter chatted at Anne, delighted in her interest, Sam tried not to wince. Dieter in Moscow? My poor, best buddy. Christ, the KGB would be all over him like a cheap suit. A naive, horny newcomer with something of a drinking problem and a penchant for snooping on capitalist and communist trade deals. They'd sic a sweet young thing in an Intourist uniform on him in the airport. He'd be compromised by the time he got to the hotel. I need to talk to Frankfurt about this. As far as I know we've got practically zilch going for us in Moscow these days. Harvey could recruit him and drill him in basic agent survival skills before he went.

"This calls for a celebration. Dieter. If you can still stand up by 7:30, how about we take you to dinner at the Duc Berthold? It's time you learned how to eat French food."

Two days later, in his basement office in Frankfurt, Harvey nodded at Sam and Alicia. "Your German friend looks good. Let's get it to Headquarters. Sam, sit down and draft me a full workup, ops plan, the whole thing. And also a request for a POA. We're going to send the whole thing by cable. I'm sorry, Alicia," Harvey said to his secretary, "but this is important and I want it slugged PRIORITY too. I know it's a lot of coding." Harvey and Alicia had driven up an hour ago. Sam had arrived later and cased the area to make sure nobody was staking out the house, and then slipped in the kitchen door.

"That's OK, Chief. No problem." Alicia practically vibrated with enthusiasm. Harvey wished she would stop saying "Chief" though. There was that TV comedy spy series called "Get Smart," which was very popular, and the bumble-headed Director of the agency was always referred to as "Chief." Oh, well. I'm sure she's not aware of that. I hope.

"Shall I leave how you know about Dieter out of this, Harvey?" Sam asked, aware as always how Grant Natz would react to any mention of Sam's existence.

"No. it's time for him to shut up and play the game. Draft a separate POA request for your pal Charlie while we're at it."

"It was just a happy accident, Harvey," Sam said.

"This business is all either happy accidents or bad luck."

Ross got the cables the next morning and quickly began preparing documents and routing sheets. Hot damn. At last some action, and good on you, Sam. Let's see: He needed a code name for Dieter. How about INGRESS? It didn't mean anything. The days of calling something TOTAL VICTORY and then having it blow up disastrously and show up on the front page of the *Daily News* were over. Even intelligence agencies sometimes learn from their mistakes. And for the other guy, the businessman, Charlie, how about CHECKBOOK? Now for coordination, that would be the German Desk and the Austrians and Soviet Bloc Division and Counterintelligence, and that ought to do it.

He was sitting there, typing and smoking, when Grant Natz strode in. Grant waved the smoke away. "Take no action on the Frankfurt cable regarding the German correspondent. It's being considered for use at a higher level. You may continue with the ITT person. And don't smoke when I am in the room." He about-faced and left.

Ross just shook his head. What the hell was that all about? Is he selling cases up on the Deputy Director's floor to curry favor? Probably. The ass-kissing putz. Oh well, at least the German Station gets the ITT guy. Ross took the draft cables and put them in a folder. He locked them in his safe and went off to find Maria. Coffee time.

Grant Natz moved fast. The INGRESS cable, the ops file, a POA request and an obsequious note from Natz were already in Clay van Claire's inbox when Clay returned from the sixth-floor men's room that morning. The nine a.m. visit there was something of a tradition among the most senior DDP staff. A junior officer unwise enough to enter their domain would see a row of closed stall doors. Below the doors he would see five or six or seven pairs of very expensive suit pants lowered over even more expensive English shoes. They in turn would be covered with sections of the *New York Times*, the *Wall Street Journal*, the *Times* of London, *Die Presse*, *Le Monde* and others. Above the doors there would be clouds of cigarette and cigar smoke. Loud, confident voices would be discussing world affairs, Agency operations, and gossip from last night's cocktail parties. All of them ate heavily and well, so the smell had often been described as unbearable.

Van Claire, smiling a well-satisfied smile, sat down and glanced at his inbox. He read the contents rapidly and then came back again to the material from Natz. This he read again. This German guy, INGRESS, might be just what he needed. Running two major cases was real star stuff. He dialed Grant Natz on the red line.

"Grant, is that you? Van Claire here. What a good idea you sent me. Could you come up right away? Oh, good, thank you so much."

After that things moved with lightning speed. By the close of business in Washington the INGRESS file been removed from the German Desk. Ross had been told the matter had been classified PURPLE and was therefore no longer any of his business. The Provisional Operational Approval was rushed through Counterintelligence on what was supposed to have been the say-so of Angleton, which was not true. A month's worth of paperwork and permissions had been done in an afternoon.

By cable, OPERATIONAL IMMEDIATE again, an angry and now mystified COS Bonn had been told to butt out of the INGRESS case. He could have the ITT guy, CHECKBOOK, as a consolation prize. Harvey Masters in Frankfurt was told by separate cable to arrange a congenial setting by which Augustus G. Hetherington (the dispatch pseudonym for van Claire), alias name Henry Navarre, could be put in contact with INGRESS (identity to be provided under separate cover). He was also told to get a poste restante box for use as a dead drop.

The separate cover cable said, "Identity is Dieter Volkmann." "Under separate cover" was standard practice to ensure that if a document fell into enemy hands, the identity of the agent and his code name would never appear together in the same document.

Harvey, of course, could arrange most anything. He was going up to Bonn the next morning anyway. There he had a chat with one of the economic attaches in the embassy, and an invitation went out by mail that afternoon to Dr. Dieter Volkmann to attend a meeting of businessmen and journalists interested in East-West trade. The invitation implied that it was being extended at the behest of one of Dieter's newspapers.

That done, Harvey and the Chief of Station retired to a restaurant with a view of the Old City of Bonn and tried, quite against orders, to unravel what in hell Headquarters was up to this time. Harvey unlawfully told the COS about the invitation and the mail drop. The lunch featured a particularly good *filet de beouf avec sauce béarnaise*. But the two were still unhappy when they parted.

"Ours it not to reason why, I suppose," said Harvey.

"True. Why should the Chief of Station know what's going on in his country?"

Dieter returned from the East-West economic conference in Bonn even more ebullient than when he had left. Sitting at his *Stammtisch* in the Gambrinus, he told Sam all about his new world. His extravagant arm-waving nearly unbalanced a passing waiter who was holding a giant tray stacked with plates of *Würstli*.

"Sam, I met the economics correspondent for the *Suddeutsche Zeitung*. He gave me lots of tips on how to get interviews. What a nice man. And then, a less nice man, a guy from *Neues Deutschland*, the East German communist paper. He quizzed me about my background like I was under investigation or something. Those communists are a hard-nosed lot."

"What did you tell him?" Sam felt like a mother hen watching her babies cross the road for the first time.

"Ach, I did my jolly fat man imitation, which isn't hard for me, and asked him if it was true, the rumor about Walter Ulbricht having a chancre on his penis. He got all huffy and moved on."

Hmm. Maybe my boy isn't so naive after all, Sam thought.

Dieter wasn't. He didn't mention meeting the heavy man with the silver hair and very expensive suit who said he represented an American economic trade group based in New York. The man was very complimentary to Dieter and was most impressed that he was going to Moscow soon. He asked Dieter to have dinner with him that night.

The man, who said his name was Henry Navarre, fed Dieter an enormously expensive dinner and then made Dieter a proposition. The trade group needed eyes and ears in Europe, and particularly in the Soviet Bloc, where their contacts were understandably constrained. Would Dieter serve as an intermittent correspondent for them at a salary to start at, say, $1,000 a month? Dieter managed not to spill his champagne as he leaned forward to shake hands on the deal.

The next morning, still optimistic through the champagne and schnapps hangover, Dieter thought a little more deeply about his windfall. A new Volkswagen Beetle cost $1,800, so he could buy himself a new car with two months' pay. Nice. Very nice. But why would an American group appear out of the blue to recruit an unknown rookie who hadn't even started yet? This is the first time he had been out of Luxembourg in two years, except to visit his mother in Bavaria. Could the beefy man with the bald spot be CIA? No, that's ridiculous.

Could somebody in Luxembourg be involved? Certainly not those poor souls at the Institute, who flushed with pride if a postman nodded to them. Oh dear, could it be Sam? What the hell was an American with no visible interest in higher education doing at the University of Luxembourg?

In the end Dieter decided the answer was no. Even a government as rich and profligate as the Americans' would not go to the expense of placing an agent in a backwater like Luxembourg. Besides, he had read Eric Ambler's *Judgment for Deltchev*. Spies were little gray middle-aged men who melted into shadows, not crew-cut young men with toothsome wives. The meeting with the American must have been just fortunate circumstance. No, what was the word Sam had taught him? Fortuitous circumstance: That was it.

His thoughts turned to other things. His few possessions were ready to go. He had received an advance and instructions from the economics editor at the *Frankfurter Allgemeine*. His Soviet visa application had been approved with remarkable speed. He had bought his ticket to Moscow, an event that made him doubly nervous. The Russians were reported to be pretty scary, and he had never been in an airplane before. He'd have to ask Sam what it was like, flying in an airplane.

And then by God, he was off. He, Dieter Volkmann, foreign correspondent. He hoped he was going to like Moscow.

CHAPTER SIX

Dieter hated Moscow. Jesus, talk about gloomy. And the poor people. They looked to him alternately sad, sour, resigned, truculent, defensive, and, sometimes, warmly friendly. What an inexplicable mix they were. The one constant was the sour-faced officials. There were endless uniformed myriads of them. The grumpy female attendants on each floor of the Intourist hotel, the brusque officials in every office, the armed militiamen on the street, and the scary-looking cops certainly blended in well with the gray concrete buildings and glowering skies of Moscow's gathering winter. It was only early November and already it was cold and there had been wisps of snow in the mornings. Get me through this conference and let me out of here, Dieter thought.

The only three good things about this trip were flying, the conference itself and Natalia. Flying was fun, after the first scary takeoff. The conference had the usual boring lectures featuring endless recitations of the coming conversion of the world to the precepts of Marxism-Leninism. But underlying that were the loan and construction programs in sub-Saharan Africa. The Congo, universally called Congo-Brazzaville, was becoming more socialist and more closely entwined with the Soviet Union every day. This gave the Belgians next door fits, since they still controlled their colony's vast supplies of cobalt. The same situation applied in Guinea, where the government flirted between China, Russia and France and sent its bauxite to each of them alternately.

It was a situation ripe for exploitation. Loans for dam- and road-building projects were proposed and manipulated and competed. The competition was the American, French, Belgian and Portuguese proposals. Spies and bureaucrats, white Russians, black Africans and, well, the Chinese weren't actually yellow, all wrestled for power and influence and were using money and the occasional muscle to do it.

Dieter met dozens of interesting people, so many he filled most of a notebook with tiny shorthand précis of conversations with them and his pockets with business cards. For communists, these Russians and Czechs and Bulgarians and Poles were pretty businesslike. They all had big plans, and they were all fiercely competitive.

The conference was scheduled for three days, and by the second day Dieter saw patterns begin to emerge. The real heavy hitters were a group of seven men who generally sat in the northeast corner of the main conference room. They didn't hop around the room glad-handing and passing out business cards like so many of the other two hundred attendees. People came to them. The African grandees, all of whom either chose to or were encouraged to wear African-looking clothes, were brought forward to meet the seven by tough-looking Russians who looked more like bodyguards than businessmen. They probably were. The Africans held their chins high and tried to look imperious and grand, as befitted men who had risen to high rank by slaughtering quite a few of their countrymen. They must have been cold in their colorful but thin robes. Besides, the concrete set to their hosts' faces would have unsettled anybody.

The seven men who nodded gravely to the Africans being presented to them were, to Dieter, almost comical. They looked like the finalists in a Leonid Brezhnev lookalike contest, all scowling and jowly and stone-faced. The Africans must have wished they had brought their machetes with them. But progress was being made: folders were appearing, and were being opened, and papers pointed to and discussed. Heads bent over the documents, and grimaces that were supposed to have been smiles flashed on and off. And they must have reached a milestone: Dieter blanched when he saw the trays of glasses and the vodka bottles appearing. Vodka at ten in the morning? Even Dieter, a too-experienced drinker, flinched at the prospect.

Almost unnoticed, or at least until Dieter noticed him, a little man had been circulating around behind the Leonid Brezhnevs. He was pointing to a figure here, turning pages and pointing again for the obviously confused, whispering in an ear and otherwise moving things along. Aha, thought Dieter, the *Dienstmädchen für alles*, the jack-of-all-trades, the indispensable staffer. He was the man behind the curtain who wrote all the briefing papers, made up the spreadsheets, got the right documents in the right order and otherwise did all the work while the Leonid Brezhnevs got all the credit. He was the most woebegone little man Dieter had ever seen. He was small, slightly stoop-shouldered, well into middle age, with a slight grayish tinge to his complexion — appropriate for Moscow, Dieter thought — and had a terribly sad expression on his face. My God, Dieter thought, he looks like Eric Ambler's Deltchev. I wonder if his name is Deltchev.

At a break, the little man headed towards the toilet, and Dieter, still curious and full of coffee anyway, followed along. The men's room was Soviet modern — newish fixtures that looked and smelled like they hadn't been cleaned since they were installed. He chose a nearby urinal and, as they were zipping up, remarked in German, "It looks like you do all the work around here."

The little man flinched, startled. Then he looked a Dieter's smiling friendly face and changed his mind. "So it seems. Thank you for noticing." Also in German! They washed their hands in the filthy sink. A useless gesture, Dieter thought. As they stepped out of the men's room and headed back down the badly lit hall, Dieter said, "You look rather unhappy. I hope everything is all right."

To his astonishment, the little man burst out in tears, turning and leaning his head against the dirty wall, his body shaking. Dieter, flummoxed, shifted his weight back and forth awkwardly and then, deciding it was somehow all his fault, stepped forward and started patting the man on the shoulder, saying, "I'm so sorry. What is wrong?"

When he could finally talk, the man said, "My wife. My wife died Tuesday. They said I had to get the conference ready — no time to grieve. They said maybe I can go to the funeral tomorrow if there's time. I'm sorry; I should not tell you this. But nobody has spoken to me; nobody said a word. It was unexpected, the kindness, you know?" He pulled away. "I'm sorry, I'm sorry. Excuse me. I must go back to the conference."

But Dieter held on. He cursed himself for being so coldblooded, but the thought had suddenly occurred to him that this guy could make one hell of a spy. The little gray man in the center of everything, and abused by his bosses. "I'll go the funeral if you can't," he said, a wild promise that he knew he couldn't keep. Or could he? "What is your name?"

His name was Ivan Goshkorow, not Deltchev. Then he pulled away and headed back towards the conference room, saying something in Russian that sounded like a blessing. At least, Dieter heard something that sounded like "*gospady*" so he assumed so.

Dieter watched him go. Then he went back to the conference room and switched to thinking about Natalia. Ahh, Natalia. She was the Intourist guide assigned to him when he arrived. All foreigners were assigned Intourist guides who were, tourists and visitors were told, there to help them. And, it went without saying, to keep a close watch over them. Most thought spying would also be an appropriate description. But Natalia was no sloe-eyed siren like Dieter had seen in the James Bond movies. Natalia was a Russian Audrey Hepburn — demure, with a small, perfect face and huge, trusting eyes. Rather than come on like a femme fatale, she had been hesitant, shy, and beguilingly awkward. Unhesitatingly polite, she had also seemed uncomfortable in her job. Dieter had fallen hopelessly in love on their first introduction. If she was going to ply him for information, he was prepared to blurt out everything he had seen and heard. That would not, of course, include his connection to the American who called himself Henry Navarre. Dieter prided himself on not being completely stupid.

But he came close. God knows what she did during the day, but she only appeared when he was going to leave the hotel or the conference. As long as he stayed inside the hotel or at the conference center — a grim building on Teatralnyy Promenade just off, gulp, Lubyanka Square, the headquarters of the KGB — she left him alone. Undoubtedly there were others doing the watching inside. Outside the conference he tried desperately to say or do what might please her and succeeded only in looking like a dancing bear, opening doors for her and looking a little desperate.

Rather than ply him for information, Natalia was politely businesslike. She pointed out the sights for him, became a tiny tyrant when needed to bully the slouching restaurant staffs to stop glaring off into space and get off their backsides and at least serve the restaurant's lukewarm, nearly inedible food.

"What is this stuff?" Dieter asked one night.

Natalia glanced down at her plate, glanced up, and said with a slight smile, "Don't ask."

His heart leapt. Finally, a flash of the real Natalia. "Some more wine?" It was all he could think of to say.

"No thank you," she said demurely. "It gives me gas."

Dieter froze in midpour. What? Audrey Hepburn passing wind? He burst out in gales of laughter. She joined him uncertainly. Dieter was swept with a new wave of adoration. What a woman. How droll. He finished pouring the rest of the wine into his glass.

The next day Goshkorow was not there. Thank God, thought Dieter, I don't have to go to the funeral. It was evident that Goshkorow's absence was being felt. A tall man, mean-looking in a way Russians seem to specialize in, was racing around the Leonid Brezhnevs today. He was opening and closing files and was clearly no surer of what he was doing than the Leonids were. The little man's boss, I bet, thought Dieter, and not up to it.

Eventually they seemed to get things together and the Africans were brought in again, and a cameraman appeared and there were pictures. And, oh God, here comes the vodka. I think I'll join in, Dieter decided. I deserve it. I have enough material for a dozen articles and to keep Henry Navarre making that $1,000 a month keep coming.

That November week was otherwise quiet. In the United States, Richard Nixon beat Vice President Hubert Humphrey and was elected president. In England, the Beatles announced that their new album would be released later in the month. At CIA Headquarters in Langley, Virginia, only five people were supposed to know about CITADEL, although twelve actually did. So far the twelve had held their tongues and the story had spread no further. In West Germany, nothing happened at all.

CHAPTER SEVEN

Dieter arrived in Frankfurt a happy man. His dispatches from Moscow had been printed in all his correspondent newspapers, and they had all asked for more. His principal at the *Frankfurter Allgemeine* had even praised him. That had made him happy. Not being in Moscow anymore had also made him happy. The parting with Natalia had not made him happy. She had been her usual polite, careful self, reluctantly surrendering a phone number — "My office, Herr Volkmann; I don't have a phone in my apartment" — and otherwise regretful but not heartbroken to see him go. Plus it was "Herr Volkmann," not "Dieter," as he'd asked her to call him. Well, next time. What was that expression Sam had used when Dieter had asked him how he'd talked Anne into marrying him? Oh yes, "Brother, faint heart never won fair lady."

As previously agreed, he was to meet Henry Navarre on Friday at a small park along the river walk at eight a.m. Fine with him, but had Henry Navarre consulted a weather forecast? It was getting rather chilly, and the forecast was for rain towards the end of the week. Well, Navarre looked old enough to have been in the business for a good twenty years, so he must know what he's about. Dieter went back to his hotel, a nice enough place two blocks behind the *Vier Jahrenseit*. Perhaps someday he could afford the *Vier Jahrenseit*, but certainly not now. He headed for the hotel bar, sat down in a corner and began reviewing his notes.

On Tuesday morning the conference began with the usual turgid remarks about the wonders of Marxism-Leninism. It was dutifully attended by sleepy delegates. The hall in the conference center was a bit too large for the size of the delegations, so people clustered in bits and clumps, with rows of empty seats separating them. Guinea, or more precisely who was going to get its bauxite exports this year, was the topic.

The Africans were less prominent now, and less gaudily dressed. Most of them wore Western suits. Except for the tribal scars on some and the sashes some wore, which looked like German fraternity sashes — and, of course, the very black faces — they tried to look more or less like the normal run of visitors to Frankfurt. This meant that they failed spectacularly, as the Frankfurters, not used to purple-black faces with tribal scars, stared at them with great curiosity.

Dieter looked around the room for familiar faces. There was the guy from the *Financial Times*, who of course did not deign to return his friendly nod, and *Die Presse* and *Le Monde*, and the rest of the financial press pack. Someone had said the *Wall Street Journal* was there too, but Dieter didn't know what its reporter looked like. Some of the thugs looked familiar, or at least the bulges in their lumpy suits did. He nodded a hello to some of them but they had just looked back with blank faces, so he quit trying. Did these guys really carry guns in Frankfurt too? The German would have a fit if they knew. Or, since these guys were protecting the moneyed class, maybe the Germans were turning a blind eye.

Squinting, Dieter looked in the far corner. Ahh, there they were. Three, four — no, five of the Leonid Brezhnevs, and there was poor little Ivan Goshkorow, bustling about handing out briefing papers. I wonder if he really did manage to get to his wife's funeral. The more he thought about it the more Dieter determined to spend some more time with Goshkorow. Who better to get financial information from than the man who prepared the spreadsheets? He'd have to be crafty about it though, since the last thing his bosses would want was to have one of their minions chatting it up with a Western reporter. On the other hand, poor Goshkorow was more or less invisible to them, so he could go where he wanted if and when he had any free time. Dieter was the conspicuous one. And what shall I do about that, Dieter wondered. Lose twenty kilos overnight?

What to do? Even Soviet functionaries were permitted to eat occasionally, go to the toilet, and sleep sometimes. I'll catch him when he heads for the toilet, Dieter decided, and talk him into eating with me somewhere that the Leonids and their goons didn't frequent. He stopped in mid-thought. What was the watchword? Hide in plain sight — that was it. I'll take the man to the *Vier Jahrenseit*. The Soviets never went to such a palace of capitalist excess, Goshkorow would probably faint with happiness to get a really good meal, and I get to write the whole thing off on my expenses! I'll need to be damn careful about the timing though. The Soviets were hysterical homophobes, and lurking about the toilets would be an extremely bad idea. He waited in his seat for an opportunity.

The opportunity came Thursday noon, as the group session began to break up just before lunch. The main business had been done, and the closing lectures would be after lunch. Most delegates would plead the need to make a train or plane to avoid listening to the dialectic, and, since they represented money, would get away with it. Those not representing money would damn well sit still and listen until the very end. Goshkorow had collected the morning's briefing papers and left them in the care of one of the goons. He was headed towards the door with the look of a man with a bursting bladder.

Dieter managed, rather neatly for a man of his bulk, to appear casually at the next urinal to Goshkorow. The room was a little old, but as squeakily clean as only a German could make it. "Herr Goshkorow, how nice to see you again."

The little man looked at him sideways, recognizing the voice. "Good morning." Carefully, just "Good morning." As they walked out, Dieter said, "I'm so sorry for your loss."

Goshkorow looked at him and said, "I wish I were dead."

"No, no," Dieter said. "You must not think like that. She would want you to go on. You never told me her name, you know."

Her name was Anna, and suddenly the little man was full of talk. Dieter laid a cautionary hand on his arm. "Your bosses would not like to see you talking to me. Can you get free for dinner tonight? We can talk about her."

As it turned out, Goshkorow could. The Leonid Brezhnevs had already left for a party congress in Moscow and didn't need him. He was to stay behind and leave tomorrow or the next day. Yes, it would be so nice to have someone to talk to, and particularly Dieter, who was so, so, *sympatisch*.

As he expected, the little man almost fainted with happiness when presented with the *Vier Jahrenseit's* menu. Dieter solemnly told him to revenge himself on the capitalists by ordering anything he wanted. Goshkorow did.

"What is Dover sole?"

"A fish that went to Eton. Try it."

Dieter, being a nice man, genuinely did want to hear about Anna. It was a good thing too, since that was all he heard for the first half-hour. Goshkorow thought the world of his wife. They had huddled together for thirty-five years as the cynical Soviet storm raged around them, drawing their solace from each other's existence. Sadly, there had been no children.

As the topic of conversation changed and moved on, Dieter gave an edited version of his life and, almost accidentally, picked up enough information for a half-dozen articles his newspapers would find most interesting. After dessert, which was something Dieter couldn't pronounce flambéed in something expensive, the two men sat back and looked at each other.

"You are a nice man," Goshkorow said, "but you have connections. All Western journalists do." He said this with the dead certainly of a man who since childhood had been told that all Westerners are CIA agents. "I want to leave. I hate these people. My wife is dead; I have no children. I want to go sit in a warm library and read books until I die. Can you do this for me? I will bring all my notes; they will show how these people are cheating these poor *Schwartzas* in Guinea and the Congo and everywhere else. Can you do this for me?"

Dieter sat looking at him, utterly astonished. My God, a month on the job and I have recruited a valuable defector. Visions came to him of Henry Navarre raising his salary to $2,000 a month. Then he angrily rejected this. Dieter, you pig, stop it. This man has just placed himself in great danger. He had put his life in your hands. You must protect him. Think, Dieter, think!

"Ivan," he said, unconsciously leaning forward and lowering his voice. "Perhaps I can help. But we must be careful, very careful. You do not work for nice people and they can cause you great harm."

Ivan Goshkorow looked back at him. "You, a Westerner, are telling someone who has lived 58 years in the Soviet Union what my masters are like?"

"Sorry," Dieter said. "Of course. When are you going back to Moscow?"

"Tomorrow night, maybe the day after."

"That's too soon for anything to be arranged. When will you be in the West again?"

"In ten days. In Frankfurt again. This time it will be about the Central African Republic. Same conference center."

"Then I'll be here and I'll have something arranged." Please God, let me be telling the truth, Dieter thought.

"Good. And I will bring my toothbrush," Goshkorow said, smiling for the first time all night.

Bright and early the next morning, an ungodly 8 a.m. for Dieter, he hustled over to the riverside meeting with Henry Navarre. As predicted, it was raining, and a little colder than usual. Dieter had the heavy jacket he had bought for his Moscow trip, and an umbrella. He found Henry Navarre sheltering under a bare tree, wearing an expensive suit, a light coat, and a newspaper held over his head to keeps the rain off. It struck Dieter that this was kind of conspicuous: a guy standing out in the rain and obviously not happy about it, but what did he know? Henry Navarre was the experienced agent. There was nobody else around except a couple of fishermen thirty yards away, oblivious to the rain. They weren't exactly dressed like fishermen, but they had fishing poles and they were standing there in the rain looking at them, so what else could they be?

"You're late," Henry Navarre snapped. "Let's get out of here." He turned and marched away before Dieter could offer to share the umbrella. Dieter looked down at his wristwatch. Actually he was exactly on time. Navarre marched over to a riverside café and walked in, looked around, and took a table in the far corner. The place was understandably empty, not even a waiter in sight. Henry Navarre took off his light coat, glared at it, tossed it on an empty chair and sat down, fussing and dabbing at his wet shirt and tie with his handkerchief. Dieter sat quietly waiting for him.

Henry seemed to remember that he was there for an agent meeting about the same time an elderly German waiter poked a nose out of the kitchen, saw them, and slowly approached.

"Two coffees!" he said, snapping again. He looked at Dieter. "How do you say 'two'?"

"*Zwei Kaffee, bitte. Und ein Helles, Herr Ober.*" I have a lot to say and I need beer to keep my throat lubricated, Dieter thought. Besides, I hate coffee. He might have asked.

When the coffee and beer came Henry Navarre looked disapproving and said "You shouldn't drink beer in the morning."

Dieter suppressed a flash of irritation. Navarre represented the money. He needed to be nice to the money. He sat quietly. Navarre must have seen his expression because he suddenly remembered he had an agent meeting on his hands, that he was the case officer, and that it was time to follow the formula.

"Sorry. I hate wet clothes." Big smile, look sincere. "How are you? Was the retainer deposited in your account correctly? How was your trip to Moscow? Tell me all about it."

Dieter took a sip of beer and began. Yes, he was well and the money had been deposited. The Moscow conference had gone far better than he had expected. He proceeded to lay out a précis of what he had in the documents in the manila envelope he had slid across the table to his case officer. He laid it all out: the loans, the arms deals, the probable size of the bribes, the intense concern expressed by the seven Leonid Brezhnevs that the Chinese or the French might gain the upper hand on them. He was holding Ivan Goshkorow until the last.

Van Claire alias Navarre kept nodding enthusiastically and saying, "Very good," and "They will be most interested in that." Actually, he was more than a little bored. Africa Division would be interested, of course. Soviet Bloc would want even more details about the Russians involved, and any indications of who might be KGB and who might not. This was all very good, and very useful. But to him it was just a tale of a bunch of niggers getting money from the Russians to run around in the jungle killing each other. Who gave a rat's ass? His interest was the Great Game of spies where gentlemen of the equivalent rank of colonel and general crossed swords in Europe. If this guy can't come up with something better

I'll turn him over to the German Station and go look for another agent.

Then, as Dieter went eagerly on, van Claire began writing his contact report in his head. Phrases like "Evidence of new Soviet penetrations in sub-Saharan Africa" and "Danger to America's cobalt supplies in Katanga Province" cropped up. Maybe he could perfume the pig and turn this into something that would garner an attaboy from the Deputy Director. He looked back at Dieter and tried to pay attention to what he was saying.

Dieter, who prided himself on not standing behind the door when they were passing out the brains, was aware that he had less than Navarre's full attention. He stopped talking.

Fully back in the room now, van Claire/Navarre leaned forward and tried to look eager. "Yes, please go on." Dammit, now his underwear was getting soggy.

"Sir, I have a Soviet with a great deal of inside information who is ready to defect."

The words "Soviet" and "defect" in the same sentence had a magical effect on van Claire. "Who is he and what does he know?" Now he was paying attention, by God. He became Henry Navarre at his most avuncular.

Dieter told the story quite well. He laid out the whole scenario as he had seen it: Ivan Goshkorow had been the man who had prepared the spread sheets, written the briefing papers, assembled the documents, and knew all the players on both sides. He had the whole Soviet financial and operational plan for sub-Saharan Africa in his head or at his fingertips. Because he was so inconspicuous, and so much the *Dienstmädchen für alles* who was always at hand, always knew what to do, the Soviets had completely ignored the basic intelligence rules. There had been no separation of functions, no need-to-know rules applied in his case. Little Ivan had seen it all.

"And he can bring it with him, sir." Dieter concluded. "He actually has free run of the place. He has extensive notes. He can stick them in his pocket and meet us in Frankfurt ready to go. He has no family left, which they have forgotten, or they would never let him leave the Soviet Union to come here. But they will remember eventually, so next week may be our only chance to get him." He paused and swallowed. "*Our* only chance?" What am I, a CIA officer now? "Um, I mean your only chance." He sat back and waited. If ever an agent should be showered with moist kisses, it was now. He looked at Navarre expectantly.

Instead of being jubilant, Henry Navarre looked slightly disappointed. "But he's only a clerk," he said, sounding almost petulant.

Dieter was confused. "So what, sir? He has the keys to the castle."

Van Claire got control of himself and smiled and patted Dieter on the shoulder. He forced his dreams of bringing home a top-level KGB officer to be paraded before the top men in the intelligence world to dissolve into a pleasant daydream that he could use to get to sleep on the plane on the way home. Actually, for a first meeting with a new agent, this INGRESS affair was a very successful outing. The agent, INGRESS, should be praised. He set about praising the agent.

"You have done a very superior job, Dieter. Very superior. I shall apprise my people of this, and I daresay you can expect an augmentation of your consulting agreement as a result. Now, let's work out the details of our next meeting and what we are going to do about getting Mr. Goshkorow a new home." They spent the next twenty minutes working out a detailed plan. A critic would note that field agents should not spend inordinate amounts of time chatting with each other in public places. But both Dieter and van Claire could be forgiven, since neither of them had had much field experience.

They shook hands on parting, Dieter going one way and van Claire the other. Dieter didn't notice van Claire nod to the two fishermen. They waited until van Claire was well past them, then took their poles and followed him. The two men, both retired D.C. policemen now working for the Office of Security, cursed van Claire softly as they moved out.

CHAPTER EIGHT

Van Claire had to sprint to get to his meeting with CITADEL. He had already checked out of the *Vier Jahrenseit*. The hotel cost far in excess of what government per diem payments allowed. Clay spent a good deal of time developing reasons that would appease the bean counters and have them reluctantly pay the higher rates. Since no really good story occurred to him, he decided to leave it to his secretary to figure it out. She could always talk to Grant Natz if need be. He certainly knew to beat the travel people out of every last dollar.

He had thought long and hard about how he was going to present INGRESS's information to Headquarters. The obvious thing would be to drop in on Frankfurt Base just down the street, or go up to Bonn after his meeting with CITADEL and crank out a cable about Goshkorow. He could dictate a long dispatch on the contents of the seminar that INGRESS had provided — page after page of meticulous, tiny handwriting — but that would take him days. Besides, that was the stuff they hired junior officers to do. Even worse, the German Station would then be privy to the operation and would undoubtedly try to muscle in and get a piece of the action. They controlled the Cable Secretariat in the embassy, so they might even write up his information in a way that deflected credit onto them. His face reddened at the thought. All right, decision time. He decided.

He would take it home and have Grant Natz do it. That asskissing son of a bitch would be grateful to be a part of the operation. As to Goshkorow, how was he going to handle him? The man might have useful access to all those African operations, but the fact remained that the man was a damn clerk. The way INGRESS had described him, Goshkorow was a GS-9 or a GS-11 tops. He'd either have to pump up Goshkorow's status a bit or downplay his rank. Which should it be? He decided to slide down to the bar and have a drink. He'd heard these Europeans drank a lot of champagne. He might as well join them.

The meeting had gone well; he was ready for Koblenz and CITADEL. He felt fit, rested, and ready, to borrow a phrase from Richard M. Nixon, a man he greatly admired. He wished CITADEL would quit dancing around and tell him his goddam name so he could establish just how high up in the KGB hierarchy he was. On the other hand, considering the business they were in, CITADEL might just lie to him.

Van Claire and his two security men hopped the ten thirty a.m. express for Koblenz. As usual, he didn't speak to them, so they sat silent too. When they got to Koblenz, van Claire left the station for the three-block walk to the promenade along the river. It had stopped raining, but the sky lowered. The two bodyguards followed at thirty yards. They were dressed in German clothing bought at a down-market store in Bonn. They now looked like two D.C. cops wearing German clothes. But then they hadn't looked like fisherman three hours ago either.

A middle-aged man appeared, apparently out of nowhere, and fell into step beside him.

"Good morning," the man said in American English.

Van Claire just nodded. "You have a name?"

"Soon."

Van Claire, his hands behind his back, made shooing motions to the two goons, who fell back.

"Put your right hand in your coat pocket," CITADEL said. It wasn't quite an order, but van Claire bridled a little. But he did put his hand in his coat pocket. What the . . . ? There was a small envelope there. He hadn't put anything in the pocket. He looked sideways at CITADEL. This guy's a reverse pickpocket. He was suddenly a little nervous. This guy seems to know a lot of tradecraft.

"There's five rolls of microfilm in there, encompassing about 500 pages of documents. Do you read Russian?"

No, of course he didn't read Russian. He was a senior executive, not some Russian émigré sitting in a cubicle. "What does it say?"

"It deals with the organization and structure of the KGB, some forward-planning papers for the coming year, and three hundred pages of information on our sister service, the GRU, which they would rather you didn't have. That should do in lieu of my name."

Oh my sweet Jesus, I have hit the jackpot. The president is going to give me a medal. In secret of course, but everyone in Operations will know about it. Van Claire's chest burned. He could feel the President's fingers fumbling at his suit jacket as he held the medal in his other hand. "Thank you."

He suddenly realized they were walking along rather rapidly. He glanced to his right again. CITADEL was red-faced and sweating. "Slow down a little, the Olympic trials aren't until next year." He looked at CITADEL again. "Is something wrong?" CITADEL slowed but said nothing.

There was a long silence. Then, very quietly, "Yes, something is very wrong for you and for me."

More silence.

Finally van Claire could stand it no more. CITADEL wins this little game and I will speak first. "Well, what is it?"

"I have just heard, very indirectly, an inference that we have a penetration of your Headquarters. A very senior one, if the whisper is to be believed."

Van Claire almost stopped. My God, Angleton was right. I thought that was all just crackpot paranoia. I think I'd best take this straight to Angleton when I get back. No, no, that won't do. The Deputy Director will be furious if I go around him. Perhaps this is big enough to go directly to the Director himself? No, no. Follow the chain of command. Otherwise I'll be Chief of Station in Ouagadougou. End my career in a one-man station in the middle of Africa watching the locals eat each other. But if it worked, then I would rise above the squabbling gray heads, the men throwing elbows under the basket and cursing each other in gentlemanly tones, and perhaps become the Deputy Director myself. That would be fine, very fine.

"What's his name?"

"If I knew that I would come with you right now and we would go back to Washington together. I am working on it."

Van Claire was about to say something to urge him on to try harder to find out the name, that this was of the utmost importance. Then he didn't. It was obvious to both of them — hell, it would be obvious to the newest trainee — that the name of the KGB penetration of the CIA was worth a king's ransom. Phrases like "utmost importance" were briefing-room language anyway. Out here it would sound kind of, well, pompous.

"Do you have the means to obtain the name?"

"Perhaps. It will take skill, and luck and patience." CITADEL smiled a little. "Are you good with patience, Mr. van Claire?"

"I am not. I'm an 'action this day' type."

"Mr. Churchill's words, I believe. 'Action this day' got him into a lot of trouble over the years, I believe. But you think you are a Mr. Churchill type?"

"Of course not." Actually, van Claire did, a little, but only when he was composing himself for sleep. "So you can't give me an estimate of how long it will take you to get" — and here he almost said "ascertain," but that also sounded a little pompous and he was anything but that — "the name?"

"Ahh, that leads us to the bad news for me. I do not know how much time I might have. The same breezes that whisper of your penetration talk of some people beginning to wonder about me."

"About you? What about you? What people?"

Now CITADEL stopped. He stood, red-faced and sweating, and looked at van Claire. "You know I talk to you because I think the . . ." He paused. "How do you say it — the vultures are circling. I have indications somebody suspects I am meeting you today. Not you specifically, but some American agent."

"Today? Not the other time?"

"No, thank God." He paused again. "Good communists should not enlist God to help them." He smiled ruefully. "Today I leave the office; I go through the usual drill to clear my tail. I think I see someone, and then I don't." He stopped. Then, sounding miserable, he said, "Then I am almost sure I see someone."

"What did you do then?" This time van Claire didn't have to try to sound concerned. He *was* concerned. Shit, are we going to lose the best thing that's happened to CIA in ten years?

"Oh, I shake off the tail in a way that makes him think it is an accident or his fault. I know how to do these things."

Yes, judging from the way you appeared out of nowhere today and slipped the microfilm in my pocket, you do know how to do these things, van Claire thought. I'd really like to learn some of this stuff myself. "So you're OK?" *Please* say you're OK.

"I think maybe I come with you right now. It is the only safe thing to do. You can take me with you today? I have already brought you a great deal, and I have ten times that much in here." He tapped his forehead.

Yes! Take him with you. Return to Washington and the cheering crowds.

No! He doesn't know the name of the penetration at Headquarters yet. They'll hang you if you let him walk away without finding out who the mole is. Besides, you don't even know what CITADEL's name is. He could be another phony, like Frankfurt. The microfilm might be blank. Not yet. You have to establish his bona fides.

"What is your name? What is your rank? Where and in which Directorate do you work?"

"I'll tell you on the plane."

"What about your family?"

"My problem, not yours."

Jesus, van Claire thought, what a hard-bitten prick this guy is. His family would pay for his defection. "Let's not be premature. Do you have any options?" Somewhere long ago some instructor had said something about not letting the agent get control of a meeting, but van Claire just couldn't think of anything else to do except ask. Two meetings in one day were two much. I shouldn't have tried to jam things together like this.

"I have one chance. If I am under suspicion, if I get confronted, I tell them with great excitement that I have met you by chance and that you are suggesting you will help us out in return for as great sum of money."

Van Claire bridled. What, now I'm the defector? Well, why not play the game? The double game! It would be a classic case, one that the instructors would teach at the Farm for a generation, a prime example of espionage as blindfolded chess.

"Explain yourself."

"Things go two ways. If I am confronted, I say I have met you in a chance encounter and you pressed yourself upon me and suggested that you were willing to serve as an agent in place. As evidence of your bona fides you gave me something very valuable."

Van Claire was startled."Huh? Like what?"

CITADEL looked at him imploringly. "I don't know: the name of an agent, an operation, the CIA Headquarters telephone book.

Something that will save my life." He paused. "Or at least save it long enough for me to discover who your penetration is. The whisper says he was a member of your . . ." He paused, looking for a word. "*Nomenklatura*," he muttered.

"A supergrade?" blurted van Claire, excited now. He had been idly thinking that even Headquarters wasn't dumb enough to publish a phonebook. The traitor was a supergrade! A GS-16, GS-17, GS-18 traitor. Wouldn't Angleton's eyes light up when that name crossed his desk?

They walked on in silence, CITADEL sweating and nervous, awaiting van Claire's next words. Van Claire was thinking furiously. The case officer side of him argued against telling this guy anything. CIA was buying, not selling. What if this business of being under suspicion was a cock-and-bull story designed to elicit information he had no business disclosing? Shut up. Challenge him. Do something.

The Headquarters executive side of him was calculating just as rapidly. This guy is about to dissolve in a puddle of fear. If he didn't really believe he was on the verge of being discovered, he was sure one hell of an actor. And the potential reward: the name of a traitor in the heart of the Clandestine Service. America was in danger and it was his duty to do something about it.

"What if you're wrong? What if you're just being a little more paranoid than usual?" It could be that; all agents were paranoid. It was like the old joke they told the trainees: "You're not being paranoid, gentlemen, somebody probably *is* following you."

"Then I tell no one, ever, what you told me. My goal is to be a senior contract employee of CIA, living somewhere warm and safe. I would never endanger this dream, nor permit anything bad to happen to the great man who is making my dream possible. That great man is you. You hold my life in your hands. I would be insane to betray you."

Clay van Claire felt his insides tying themselves into little knots. Finally an unheard voice, his own probably, said to him, "Make a decision, you putz."

"Speaking hypothetically, what if I gave you the names of the entire CIA hierarchy? I could list . . ."

CITADEL's voce was high-pitched, almost squeaking. "You think we don't know? The Deputy Director is Tom Kamarassines, Cord Myer is the head of Covert Action, and James Angleton is the head of Counterintelligence. The Chief of Station in West Germany is . . ."

Van Claire made placating motions with his hands "OK. OK. I hear you."

"Philby even gave us their red-line phone numbers," CITADEL finished.

They walked on. Christ, I don't know anything that couldn't be traced back to me if this guy double-crosses me, van Claire thought. Nothing that would be good enough to convince his bosses that I'm selling out. Except . . . of course . . .

I know, van Claire thought, INGRESS's little man. Nobody knows about that except me and INGRESS. It would be a shame to waste a penetration of the Soviet Trade Ministry, with all that good stuff about arms trade to Africa and their plans to get their hands on Katanga's cobalt. But still, who gives a shit about Africa except Africa Division? And the guy is only a clerk. He took a deep breath. He had decided. This was the right thing for him to do, for him and for his country.

"Did you know we have a man in your Trade Ministry who's giving us most of the details on your operations in Africa and is about to defect with the rest?"

CITADEL just plodded along beside him, silent and sweating. Finally, reluctantly, he said, "It might be enough. What sort of things did he tell you?"

Van Claire gave him much of what he could remember of his meeting with INGRESS. It was only this morning but he'd forgotten half of it already. He should have taken the time to have written in down, but today he hadn't had any time. Damn, lesson learned.

Finally, almost as an afterthought, CITADEL said, "What is this man's name, anyway?"

Van Claire gulped. Christ, he'd forgotten. No, wait he had it. "Goshkorow. Ivan Goshkorow."

"And he is the head of this trade delegation?"

"Um, no. He did all the arrangements though — prepared the charts, did the spreadsheets, and assembled the documents."

"Huh, a clerk," CITADEL said dismissively. "Well," reluctantly now, "perhaps that will be enough."

CITADEL looked at his watch. "I am, as you say, pressing the luck to be with you this long. We must part. If things go very badly, Ivan Goshkorow may save my life and our operation. If things go well, I forget all about him. In either case, I will redouble my efforts to chase the whispers and see if I can find out who our agent in your Clandestine Service is."

Van Claire was about to remind him that the Clandestine Service had been renamed the Deputy Directorate for Plans when the case officer side of him told him to shut up. He and CITADEL walked on, making plans for their next meeting, and CITADEL thanking him profusely for possibly, or maybe probably, saving his life.

They parted at a point almost back to where they had started, CITADEL suddenly stepping up and embracing van Claire, to the embarrassment of them both. Van Claire turned back towards his two guards to retrace his steps to the train station. CITADEL turned in the other direction and just seemed to disappear.

Van Claire was still thinking furiously. I am sure I did the right thing, he told himself. The security of the United States was at stake and a decision had to be made. And I made that decision. I think, though, that now I will go to ground, probably at the poshest hotel I can find, and think and think and think and think. I must be sure that my skirts are clean, that nothing embarrassing can be traced back to me. He looked back at the two men plodding along dutifully behind him. I'll send them home today, he decided. In the end I'm not sure it was a good idea to have them here. Then he forgot about them.

I have to decide just how I'm going to present the CITADEL material to Headquarters. Should it just be as modestly stated contact report, or do I pull out all the stops and have my staff and Grant Natz put together a real dog-and-pony show? No, I can't do that; it would expand the bigot list. I . . . hell, I need to sit it in a very comfortable armchair and sip a little champagne and sort this all out.

And stop feeling guilty, he told himself. Goshkorow's only a damn clerk. Besides, the old bastard was turning traitor. Serves him right if he gets caught.

CITADEL didn't even glance over his shoulder as he slipped away from van Claire. That went well, he thought, very well. He was eager to get back to his hotel; the set of heavy wool underwear and the thermal warmers stuffed under them next to his skin had induced a convincing sweat, but now they were driving him half-insane. He smiled: Handling van Claire was easy.

It had gone better than he had planned. He never expected van Claire to take him up on his offer to defect today. In the unlikely event that he did, CITADEL had another story ready for why he suddenly couldn't. He worried about Moscow adding the mole story. They were ending up with a three-headed operation: planting the name of a fictitious mole, spreading disinformation, and milking van Claire. The three were incompatible and were bound to blow up pretty soon. And guess who would be blamed?

He frowned: the would-be defector's identity had, by standing protocol, to be transmitted to Moscow immediately. That would have been a real coup for CIA: Goshkorow was the perfect spy — the clerk who knew everything, the man nobody noticed. But that vicious peasant Komsomol . . . he hoped Komsomol wouldn't lash out or otherwise do something stupid. This hand had to be played carefully.

CHAPTER NINE

The next afternoon Dieter, unsure of himself, gave in and went back to the conference center. He knew he should stay away from poor Goshkorow, but he worried about him. The guy was so forlorn, and was now so dependent on him. Why couldn't Henry Navarre just have said, "Well, bring him along then and let's get over to the embassy," or whatever it was the CIA did when they whisked defectors off to safety? I suppose they had to be cautious. They must have twenty or thirty people a day showing up at embassies around the world claiming to be secret agents or the local dictator's right-hand man and demanding money and Cadillacs in return for their secrets.

And he had read in the German newspapers when he was young about the Americans buying the services of Ukrainians who claimed to have an army of nationalists ready to rise and chase the Red Army out of Kiev if only they had boots and weapons. Apparently the Americans had bought a lot of boots for feet that didn't exist. So they had gotten burned and had learned to be cautious. Still, this was different: he had stood witness for Goshkorow as being real, and had brought the documents to prove it. But then he was new, and he supposed the Americans weren't sure of *him* either. Upon reflection, he wondered how experienced Henry Navarre was at all this; for all his silver hair and expensive suits, he seemed kind of indecisive and uncertain. But then what did he know? So he decided to check on poor Ivan one last time.

The entrance hall to the conference center was gloomy and ill-lit. He had entered it from the three-story-tall foyer. The foyer was ornate and complete with chandeliers; the hallway was narrow. The light switch in the hall was on a timer, like all European hallways. The timer often turned off the lights too soon, so half the time you ended up in the dark before you had reached the door you wanted. Somehow it didn't seem to bother other people, but he found it annoying. There: it happened again — the damn light went off. Squinting and using his hands, he found and opened the door to the room where odds were Ivan, if he was around at all, would be packing up the last of the conference materials.

He stopped short in the doorway. There was Ivan, sitting at a table, staring straight ahead. Standing over him were two of the goons who had been shepherding the African delegates yesterday. They towered over him, looking menacing. What were they doing? Dieter's eyes, never that good, were slow in adjusting to the light. He was half-blinded by the glare in the conference room. Something in one Russian's hand flashed, like metal or glass catching the light. What was it? What were they doing? One of the Soviets looked up. Was the Russian looking at him?

In that moment, Dieter was terrified. Nothing was obviously wrong, nothing was moving, but somewhere inside him a great fear roiled up. He quickly stepped back, closed the huge door, and turned and ran, stumbling, down the very dark, almost black corridor. More by luck than anything else he came up against the door to the foyer. He opened it and ran across the big room and out the door. He did not notice the young German woman carrying a stack of papers, the receptionist who was just going into the management office on the other side of the hall.

Dieter stumbled down the front stairway. It was made of granite slabs designed by the architect to be wide enough so that you could not walk down them like regular stairs. You had to skitter-step your way, looking down to make sure you didn't end up flat on your face. He made it down to Goethestrasse, turned left, and red-faced and gasping ran as fast as he could for the intersection. He was past the point of rational thought.

The Soviet who had been standing on Goshkorow's right blinked, saw Dieter appear suddenly, and then saw him disappear even more suddenly. He put what looked like a child's water pistol back in his pocket. As he stepped back, Goshkorow's body fell forward and his face hit the table. The goon turned to the row of telephones on a credenza against the wall, picked one up and dialed a three-digit number.

"Front desk. Ursula speaking. How may I help you?" said a young woman's voice in German. Haltingly, the Russian said, "Is Herr Arbarkian from the conference perhaps there?"

"*Ja, mein Herr. Einen Augenblick, bitte.*" A pause.

Then Arbarkian came on the line. "Yes?" Arbarkian had been sitting at a vacant desk, ostensibly doing conference paperwork, and waiting for the call. He spent his waiting time cursing that fucking Komsomol, always seeking instant revenge. Why did Komsomol have to be so bloody-minded? He was ruining the whole operation. At the same time he engaged in light conversation with the earnest (and weren't all Germans earnest?) young German woman, trying to be someone pleasant and easily forgettable.

"There is a problem."

"The other matter has been taken care of?"

"Yes."

"I'll be right there."

He turned to the young woman with a look of great concern. "One of my colleagues appears to have taken ill. We may require medical assistance," and rushed off.

Only one goon was still there, the one who had looked up when Dieter had opened the door. Goshkorow was still slumped face down on the table.

"Lay him out on the floor. When you hear people coming start giving him artificial respiration. There was a problem?"

"A man came in just as I got him." The goon made a gesture like squeezing a hypodermic needle. "Then he closed the door and went away."

"Who? What did he see?"

"It was a fat young man from the conference. A reporter I think; he sat with the reporters. I don't know whether he saw, but . . ." The man shrugged his shoulders.

Shit! Another problem to solve. "I will find out who he is. Get ready."

He ran to the door, and then down the hall Dieter had used, and burst out onto the foyer, He wanted to be sure and to be breathing hard when he talked to the young woman.

"My associate. A heart attack I think. Can you call an ambulance, please? Hurry."

It took eight minutes before they heard the hee-haw of an ambulance siren. It took two more minutes before uniforms appeared in the foyer. There were three of them, two carrying a stretcher. When they rushed into the conference hall the goon was bent over Ivan Goshkorow, gamely giving him artificial respiration. The medics pushed him gently aside, very gently when they felt the hard pack of muscle under the goon's gray suit, and examined Goshkorow.

"Heart attack?" asked Arbarkian, planting the seed.

One of the attendants nodded. "Probably." They lifted the obviously dead Goshkorow onto the stretcher.

Arbarkian followed them out into the foyer. He went into the office looking sorrowful and said, with a sad smile, "I'm afraid our dear colleague has died. Heart attack, they say."

She nodded. "I'm so sorry. Is there anything we can do?"

"No. Except . . . he was friendly with one of the journalists, a rather stocky young man . . ."

"Oh, I saw him just now. He was leaving the building just before your colleague called. He must have been in a hurry. He was running. Oh, he was so close to being with his friend when he . . ."

". . . And yet so far, "Arbarkian said solemnly. "I should contact him. Do you know his name perchance?"

"Oh, yes," she said, pleased to be so knowledgeable. "He's Mr. Volkmann of the *Frankfurter Allgemeine*. Dieter Volkmann, that is." She opened a file. "Here's his registration form." She handed it to him, then came around and looked over his shoulder. "Here it is: he's staying at the Gasthaus Stuebli on Turnaurstrasse."

"Thank you, you are most kind. And most efficient," he added. She preened. Germans like to be called efficient.

He went back to the conference room where the goon stood waiting.

"They told me he went running out of here. We have to assume he saw something. He may or may not involve the police. If the police come, I will deal with it." God knows how, he thought, but I'll think of something. "But let us assume he did not. I want him dealt with. That is regrettable but we have too much at risk to have him running around making accusations. I want somebody at his hotel right now." He gave the goon the *Gasthaus* address. "Cover the American Consulate here, and their embassy in Bonn. His registration form says he comes from the University of Luxembourg, so put a couple of people in Luxembourg City too. He just came from there. He may go back, you know, like army deserters always go home to Mama. Do we have enough people to cover the airport and the railroad station?"

The goon looked away into the middle distance. He was counting. "Thin coverage in Frankfurt, but maybe enough. The Bonn embassy has plenty of people; they can do Luxembourg too. I will see to it." He walked away, moving fast.

"Slow down! " Arbarkian snapped at his retreating figure. "Drag your feet. You're in mourning."

Gasping, Dieter rounded a third street corner and wheezed to a halt. He stood bent over, his hands on his knees, and took almost two minutes to regain his breath. The absolute terror had receded, but he was still very frightened. He turned into the first café he saw and plopped down on the first chair inside the door.

"*Schnapps, bitte*," he said to the man behind the bar.

There was silence. Dieter looked up. The man, frowning, pointed to a sign in white letters on the door: ALKOHOL FREI. Oh, Christ. One of the several dozen alcohol-free cafes spread around Frankfurt. God spare me from teetotalers, especially today. He raised his hands in apology and defeat.

"*Entschuldigen. Kaffee bitte.*" He hated coffee.

Sipping at the coffee, Dieter tried to make his head stop swirling. Think, man, think. What should I do? They were killing Goshkorow! Or were they? They were standing over him in a menacing way, but those KGB goons would look menacing sitting in a bathtub playing with a rubber ducky. Goshkorow was sitting, looking straight ahead; his eyes were open. He wasn't dead. Yet, anyway.

I must call the police. They can deal with this. And tell the police what? That I saw two security guys crowding a colleague? He could hear the German cops now:

"What did you see, Herr Volkmann?"

"Well, I saw these two men standing over Mr. Goshkorow."

"And then what, Herr Volkmann? Did they strike him?"

"No, but . . ."

"Was Herr Goshkorow sitting up or lying down?

"Well, sitting up."

"Were his eyes open?"

"Yes, but . . ."

"Herr Volkmann. You want us to go to the trade center and arrest two men for standing close to a colleague. Is that the sum of your complaint? Do you really expect us to do this? Have you taken drink this morning, Herr Volkmann?"

He could hear it all now. So no, no police. But who? He had no way of contacting Henry Navarre immediately. He could, of course, leave a note in his mailbox at poste restante. But what good would that do: when would somebody pick it up? His next meeting with Navarre wasn't for a week. Well, he could leave a message; that would at least be doing something. And the cops could be right; he hadn't seen anything after all.

But he had, dammit. That sudden premonition of horror. He had felt that once before when a retreating squad of SS had come through his village in the spring of 1945, and a ten-year old Dieter Volkmann had peeked cautiously out of a basement window of a burned-down house. The SS had pushed three sad-sack *Landsers*, in uniform but with no weapons, and two terrified *Hitlerjugend*, boys not five years older than he, up against a wall, and, without hesitating, machine-gunned them. There was blood and screams and then silence. The SS had put up a crudely lettered sign saying "Deserters" and left. Dieter had had the same feeling of horror this morning. He just *knew* those two goons were going to kill poor Ivan.

Should he have confronted them? He would have been killed himself. Or if he had been wrong it would have raised a stink. Dieter's reputation would have been damaged, and Ivan, having had attention called to himself, would be whisked away behind the Iron Curtain and never allowed to come to the West again. Either way, it was a losing proposition.

But what should he do now? If the goon had really focused on him, seen him, remembered his face, and then had killed poor

Ivan, then they would have to come looking for him. If they hadn't, and it was a tempest in a tea pot, then things were back to normal and he could go back to be acting normal. Think, Dieter, think.

He stood up and gave the barman a smile. Laying a coin on the counter, he asked if there was a phone he might use for a brief call. A local call, of course. There was such a phone. He checked his notebook and called the exhibition center. "Good morning, and I am sorry to disturb you, but I understand there has been an incident and hope it did not involve one of my colleagues." Then, "Oh, some poor man had a heart attack and died? How tragic. Oh my goodness, it wasn't Henry Jalonichek was it?" Finally, "Oh, it wasn't, it was a Herr Goshkorow?"

"Poor man, but I am so relieved it was not my friend, although of course I feel sorry for the poor man who died. Thank you so much. Goodbye." He hung up and felt awful. His first feeling was relief that he had been right all along. His second feeling was a tremendous sadness that poor Ivan was really dead. Then the fear came back.

One thing was for sure: he had to get away from here. And go where? The *Frankfurter Allgemeine* would be less than delighted if their new correspondent came running to them with a problem they couldn't solve. If, that is, they were any more believing than the German police might be. The German police? Judging from what the woman at the conference center had said, everyone was assuming it was a heart attack. How had the goons done it? He remembered something glass or metal in the goon's hand. Was it some secret poison? He had read about things like that. The KGB had killed some Ukrainian nationalist in London using some poison that dissolved in the bloodstream or something and was undetectable after a few minutes. Was that true? Had he read it in a real paper or in one of those tabloids that made things up?

If he went to the police and told his story and they had only evidence of a heart attack, he might be charged with making false accusations. Worse, he and the Russians would be brought together for a confrontation and that would be the end of his being a Moscow correspondent for anybody. That wouldn't do.

Get control of yourself, Dieter. What are you going to do next? How about something simple like go get your suitcase from the guesthouse and get out of town? And go where? How about the American Embassy in Bonn? They could contact Henry Navarre for him. But was Henry Navarre really an American agent? What if he really was a member of some economic institute in New York and only a stringer for some intelligence agency? What if he didn't work for an intelligence agency at all?

Then worse thoughts struck him. What if Henry Navarre was the one who had betrayed Goshkorow to the KGB? But why would he do that? But who else could have done it? Or had Goshkorow not been exposed at all? If the goons had just frightened him by accident and he really had had a heart attack, then what? Christ, this is getting worse and worse. Go get your suitcase.

He thanked the barman too profusely and went out of the café, peering up and down the street before moving off. Stop that, dammit, he told himself. You're acting like a suspicious character on a TV show. He walked the six blocks to his hotel in his best imitation of a normal person.

When he was close to the hotel, he slowed down and began looking around. There were passersby; all looked German. There was no one sitting in any of the parked cars. It was only when he was fifty yards from the entrance to the *Gasthaus* that he saw what could only be a goon leaning against a wall, holding a newspaper halfheartedly open. Thank God the Soviets were not subtle. The stocky build, the cheap gray suit, even the bulge in the suit pocket were too familiar.

Dieter immediately about-faced and walked off rather too rapidly. He had his passport and his wallet. It was time to get out of here. And go where? Let's try for the American Embassy in Bonn.

There was a consulate here in Frankfurt, but he didn't know if the CIA had anybody there. Now, how do we get to Bonn? Renting a car in Europe was a relatively new idea, hard to find, and took mountains of paperwork. Dieter had no interest in leaving a paper trail. It was about two hours by fast train, maybe twenty-five minutes more on a local. The Soviets would certainly have somebody at the railroad station. Dieter thought a moment. He didn't know Frankfurt all that well, but there was a lot of public transport, and it was frequent and regular. A stop at a newsstand and Dieter had a map of Frankfurt, which of course included all the bus, trolley and ferry routes. The *Kursbuch* for the German national railroad system had an equally extensive list of timetables, maps, stations, fares, and lots of information Dieter didn't care about at the moment, such as how to ship your bags ahead of you or where to board a train with a baby carriage.

Dieter consulted the materials he had bought, made notes in his pocket notebook, and then dumped the material in the trashcan next to the bench. In West Germany, there is a trash bucket everywhere, and heaven help you if you don't use it. He wrote a note and walked the short distance to the post office and left it in his post restante box. Then he started heading west, walking almost a half-mile before getting onto a trolley. The Russians would need an entire airborne brigade to cover that many trolley and bus stops, so he felt safe. He rode the trolley out to Bärsgarten and took a local train, which got him into an eastern Bonn suburb by three thirty p.m. Bonn was a small city too, much smaller than Frankfurt, and it was only three-quarters of a mile to the American Embassy, which was another ten minutes by trolley.

A cautious approach to the American Embassy was cut short by the sight of two men in a car, obviously not waiting for Godot. The shaved heads and gray suits told him who it was. There was another one sitting on the bench by the bus stop across the street. Would either of them try to prevent him from going into the embassy?

And if he did make it in, and the Americans had never heard of Henry Navarre and had gently ushered him out, the Soviets would be right there waiting for him.

He about-faced again and bought another street map and took a bus to Bonn-Bumpliz and another local train to Koblenz and changed for Luxembourg City. He got off the local at 5:10 and immediately felt better. He stopped at the PTT office and went to a public phone. Whether or not Sam was somehow involved with Henry Navarre, he was an American who had been around a while and was a trusted friend. Sam could get into the American Embassy for him while he hid out in one of the cheap hotels by the railroad station. He called Sam's number; no answer. Damn. He went through the side door into the hallway leading to the first- and second-class restaurants that occupied the left wing of the railroad station. The station had been built in the eighteen-eighties out of reddish-gray sandstone and was quite impressive in its belle époque way. Dieter collapsed onto a wooden bench in the second class and said the words he'd been dying to say all day: "*Ein Bier, bitte.*"

It was growing dark when Sam got back from the swim club. He and Charlie had been hiking in the hills and then did some target shooting. As usual, Sam blew the black out of every target while Charlie was having trouble holding a group. When he finally did manage to place his shots closely together, his group was at ten o'clock in the three ring.

Charlie, fortunately, didn't care. He was burbling with good humor. He said he had been to a conference in Bonn last week, and what a nice town Bonn was. He said he appreciated how much the U.S. government was doing to try to promote American businesses abroad. Between curses at some of his errant shots — one actually missed the target entirely and sent up a puff of sawdust off to the right — he made patriotic noises.

Sam had to bite his lip to keep from laughing. It wouldn't take a clinical psychologist to figure out that Charlie had gotten himself recruited by the Agency. Clearly, Charlie was damn pleased about it. Good for you, Charlie. Let's hope Charlie doesn't start meditating about how, or who, had brought him to the Agency's attention. They finished shooting, had a beer at the club's little café and talked idly about the hike and how European Marlboros were a poor imitation of American tobacco.

Charlie dropped Sam off, since Anne had taken their little Volkswagen bug and gone off with Angelica from next door and the four kids to some festival.

Sam had brought the .45 home with him in an ammo box along with the cleaning gear. Tonight would be a good time to clean it, since the twins wouldn't be around to help. He had just laid the cleaning gear and the pistol out of the table when the phone rang. It was six p.m. It might be Anne. She and Angelica usually didn't keep the kids out this late.

"Six four six nine," Sam said, imitating the way the Germans answered with the last four digits of their phone numbers."

"Sam, Sam, thank God you are back!" It was Dieter's voice. He sounded scared and half in the bag. He had had time to get panicky again.

"Dieter, it's great to hear your voice. You must be in town; there's no operator connecting us. Where are you? How was Moscow? How's your new job?" Sam was delighted to hear Dieter's voice. He really missed his friend.

"Sam, listen to me: I am in terrible trouble. You must help me. I must talk to your Henry Navarre. He must help me. I gave him Ivan Goshkorow. I have to talk to him now."

"Dieter, what the hell are you talking about? Who's Henry Navarre? Who's Ivan Goshkorow? What are you so upset about?"

Dieter was clearly flustered and sounding increasingly panicky. "Sam, the Russians. They're going to kill me! I will explain all. I am at the railroad station. I am going to the Gambrinus now. Meet me there. Do this, Sam. You must meet me."

"Yeah, yeah, sure, of course, Dieter. I'll take off for Gambrinus right now. Calm down, buddy; it's going to be all right. We'll have a beer . . ." Sam was talking to the dial tone. Dieter had hung up. He hung up too and looked out the French doors at the city skyline. What the hell was this? Dieter, here? The Russians are going to kill him? Is he nuts? He bit his lip. Dieter was excited — scared — but not nuts. God knows what had happened, but maybe the Russians *were* going to kill him. Two years of CIA training had left Sam in no doubt that the KGB was an extremely nasty organization. It might well be that Dieter had run afoul of them in Moscow.

What to do? Another bit lip. Staff Sergeant Mills' voice from officer training came back to him: "When it hits the fan, young gentlemen, don't just stand there with your thumb up your ass. DO SOMETHING!" Staff Sergeant Mills had shouted the last part.

Sam did something. He scooped the pistol off the table, loaded a clip with ammunition, jammed the clip in the .45, flipped the safety on, and stuffed the pistol in the back of his pants. He pulled his shirttails out to cover the pistol and went pounding down the six flights of stairs.

Dieter, panicky again, hung up. He sat there for a moment, unable to do or think anything. Then he gathered himself and, his mind made up, walked quickly out of the second-class restaurant into the Place de la Gare and marched off towards Rue de Bec and the Gambrinus. He was almost speed walking, and the goon was watching the railroad station entrance, not the door to the restaurant, so he almost missed him. He finally saw Dieter's broad bottom disappearing around the corner of the Rue des Bec in time to throw away his cigarette, bark a warning to his partner and take off at a run.

Sam came storming down the stairs onto the Cote de Eich and sprinted down to the walkway along the Old City wall. Then he ran along the Rue de Fosse to the Rue Notre Dame. His breathing was adjusting to the pace and he wasn't gasping any more. Thank God for those long morning runs. Plus he had quit smoking again on Tuesday. He wished he could move faster, but he was still wearing the old Marine Corps boots he had used for hiking in the mountains with Charlie. That was slowing him down a little. It had been almost a half-mile now and he still had to get across the Rue de Strasbourg to the Gambrinus.

He made the last turn and burst into the Gambrinus. It was, as always, dimly lit and smoky. The usual customers were sitting at their usual tables, drinking beer and schnapps and smoking. A scattering were eating an early dinner. At one *Stammtisch* down front there seemed to be some sort of reunion going on. The group was being noisier than usual and some guy with a camera and a flash was taking pictures. The flash went off again as Sam came in, so that he couldn't see. He stood there panting, waiting for his eyes to adjust.

Then he saw Dieter sitting at his usual table, back in the far corner. For a big guy he looked small and frightened. Dieter didn't see the two guys with cropped heads and bad suits coming up on him from behind, one on each side of him.

"Hey you!" he yelled in his parade-ground voice. "Stand away from that man! Stand away!" Even as he yelled, Dieter pitched sideways and half fell out of his chair. The goon on the left looked up, dropped whatever he had in his hand, stuck that hand in his pocket and pulled out a very substantial pistol.

Sam saw the pistol. He came to an abrupt stop, raised his pistol and fired. The sound of a .45 going off in a crowded room was equivalent to the explosion of an artillery round. There was a big muzzle flash in the darkened room and, incongruously, another flashbulb going off.

The goon was blown over backwards, blood and bits and pieces of his insides spraying against the far wall. The other Russian had his pistol out now, and was raising it as Sam charged him, knocking him down. Sam was up first, and as the Russian rose to his haunches Sam gave him a tremendous kick in the face. The Russian went down again and lay still.

Sam crouched over Dieter. "Dieter, it's me. It's going to be OK, honest. Dieter, talk to me." But Dieter didn't. Dieter was dead. Sam, stunned, stood up, ejected the magazine and racked the slide back, ejecting the round that was in the chamber. He laid the pistol and magazine on a table and looked over his shoulder at the crowd, now mostly standing, open-mouthed.

"*Rufen Sie die Polizei an, bitte*," he said. I think I have that right, he thought. *Anrufen* is to call.

He was sitting on the stone floor with Dieter's head in his lap when the two policemen ran into the restaurant.

CHAPTER TEN

Sam sat on the hard bed and inspected his cell. Never having been in jail before, he couldn't tell whether its guidebook rating should be better or worse than average. Probably better, he suspected. He was in the basement of the gendarmerie headquarters, a block from the Hotel de Ville and the Cathedral, in a late medieval stone building. There was the one bed, one locked oak door, one 40-watt light bulb in the ceiling some eleven feet up, and a hole in the corner that he presumed was the toilet. It smelled that way, anyway. The British guidebooks talked about better hotel bathrooms being "en suite," so he guessed that gave this place an extra star. He lifted the edge of the inch-thick mattress and saw a stone slab. Oh well, no worse than sleeping on the ground out in the boonies.

He leaned forward, put his forearms on his thighs, clasped his hands and looked at the stone wall. Well, you sure screwed the pooch on this one, my boy. He never knew why Marines said that or what it meant, except the meaning was that you had fouled things up royally. You might have called the cops instead of running over there and playing G. I. Joe. But that wouldn't have saved poor Dieter. His halting German, working past the cop's initial disbelief that some idiot was trying to convince them that a murder was going to take place at the Gambrinus — that would have taken all evening. No, his had been the best plan that wouldn't work.

He switched to looking at his folded hands. Poor Dieter. What in hell had Dieter done or seen that would drive the KGB to commit murder in a public place? He assumed it was the KGB, anyway. And the murder itself. It was taking place very quietly until he came along, and the killers might have slipped away unnoticed. How did they do it? Did they stab him or something?

Oh God. Anne and the boys were going to come home to an empty apartment and wonder where he was. And then what would happen? Angelica next door or the newspaper or somebody else would tell her that her husband was in jail on a murder rap. What was she supposed to do? For damn sure the Agency wasn't going to help. Harvey Masters had told him that the first time he had gone to Frankfurt: "Be very careful, Sam. You're under cover here, and you haven't been declared to the Luxembourg or German governments. You get caught and you're on your own, I'm afraid." Harvey had gone on to explain that the good news was that European jail sentences were much shorter than in the United States. The bad news was that there was no time off for good behavior. You behaved well in jail or you didn't get out on time.

For that matter, what was he being charged with? When the cops had come into the Gambrinus they had come in with their pistols out. But when they saw everybody including him was unarmed they put the guns away and made their way over to him. The moron with the camera was still taking flash pictures until the cops made him stop. Everybody was crowding around the cops, shouting their version of what had happened. They were Luxembourgers after all; there would be no skulking or avoiding contact with the police. The cops shooed everybody away from Sam, who was still sitting on the floor with Dieter's head in his lap, next to the other two bodies and the pistol lying on the table.

One cop had lifted Sam by the arm. He had even let Sam wipe the tears from his eyes before taking him by the elbow and walking him to the door, down the granite stairs, and into the back seat of a police car. There was no drama, no handcuffs. The police car was a tiny Citroen, not the 2CV but the next tiny size up. At the prefecture there had been some milling around, and Sam had been put in a small room where two plainclothes cops had tried to talk to him, first in German and then in French, which hadn't worked. Not many people spoke English in Luxembourg, or in West Germany for that matter.

What to do? The old Agency adage was: "Deny everything, admit nothing." Some people thought that was a joke, but it wasn't. It wasn't in this situation anyway. He didn't know anything about the Luxembourg judicial system. Did he even get a lawyer? What would he do with a lawyer? He'd have to lie to the lawyer from the start about why he came charging into the Gambrinus. This would not be a good start for the kind of close, trusting relationship a criminal needed with his lawyer. Not if the lawyer was going to try extra hard to get him off. And what was the lawyer going to get him off of? Even if they dropped the murder charges, if that was what the charge actually was, and called it self-defense, he still had the small problem of explaining what he was doing running around Luxembourg with a .45 stuffed in his pants. He went back to looking at the wall again. One thing was for sure, he thought. He was going to begin and end his Agency career as a second lieutenant spy.

Anne and Angelica got back with the kids around 7:30. It was unusual to let the children stay up this late, but there had been a pageant in a nearby town, and a children's choir, and a dinner for a moderate price in the hall of the Maison de Ville. It had all been very charming and the children had been trying to repeat the songs until they fell asleep in the back seat, clustered together like puppies.

Anne was surprised that Sam wasn't home, but not alarmed. He often went off prowling around town, burning off excess energy, lost in his own thoughts and forgetting what time it was. She put the children to bed. It was quiet. It was always quiet in Luxembourg. She heard the elevator stop at their floor. That was probably Kurt getting off his shift. She was just getting into an old Helen MacInnes novel when she heard a soft double knock on the door. That was undoubtedly Angelica. She opened the door, smiling and curious to learn what Angelica had on her mind.

Angelica had a woebegone look on her chubby but beautiful face. She rushed in and wrapped her arms around Anne. Anne was startled. The Luxembourgers are not a huggy, kissy people, and certainly not with foreigners.

"Angelica, what . . . ?"

"Oh, Anne, Sam's been arrested. He's in the prison. And your friend Dieter is dead."

Dieter, dead? Dieter, the jolly Bavarian who was whirling the twins around this living room three weeks ago? Anne, who secretly considered herself a pillar of WASP reticence, burst into tears. Angelica stood patting her back and making the soothing noises that everybody knows doesn't do any good, but makes people feel like they are at least trying.

Anne got control of herself and stepped away from Angelica. "Oh, Angelica, what are you saying? Did Sam kill Dieter?"

"Oh no, no. Kurt says he can't tell me much because he's a policeman and all that." She paused. "And he's so dutiful anyway. Sometimes I learn more from the newspaper in the morning than he told me the night before."

"I have to go see Sam."

"I'm not sure you can. It's a real mess and Kurt says the *Surete* is trying to sort it out. The Prefecture of Police has put a clamp on everything and they're not saying anything. But all the people in the Gambrinus are free to talk to anybody they want to. Kurt says the crowd said . . . well the crowd said a lot of things, but on average they said that it seems Sam burst in and yelled something in English at two men in the back of the room with Dieter. One man pulled a pistol and Sam shot him, and then he kicked the other one in the head. And somehow Dieter was dead but nobody shot him. The crowd thinks all three men are dead but they're not sure about the third one.

"Anyway, Kurt says the way it works here is the criminal police work for a magistrate who reports to the public prosecutor. The magistrate can have people arrested and interrogated." She stopped and held up a finger in a schoolteachery way. "Interrogated in Luxembourg means you get questioned by policemen, not like they hit you with chairs until you confess or something." She paused for breath, and then went on. "And people of 'special interest' can be held" — she paused — "held incommunicado. How do you say incommunicado in English?"

"Incommunicado will do just fine." Anne thought that Kurt had said quite a lot for a man who wasn't supposed to say anything. Bless Kurt: He's being nice. He knows he's telling me through Angelica more than he's supposed to. The initial shock had worn off and she was trying to put things in order. What do I tell the twins? What do I do if a reporter comes to the door? Should I call Harvey Masters or the Chief of Station in Bonn? Am I going to collapse in a puddle right here on the living room floor and just sit and cry until all of this goes away?

No, I am not, she decided. She thanked Angelica profusely, walking her to the door and asking her if perhaps Angelica could watch the boys tomorrow morning while she tried to go see Sam. Of course Angelica would; she'd do anything Anne wanted. After the door closed Anne looked at the telephone and thought about calling Harvey. To what end? Harvey was a nice man and he'd be sympathetic, but he couldn't *do* anything. If this was somehow a

CIA operation that Sam hadn't told her about, which was most unlikely, Harvey still couldn't do anything. What was he supposed to do? Borrow the embassy Marine guard and bust Sam out of jail? Have the ambassador call the investigating magistrate and tell him it was OK, it was an approved CIA operation? That would go down well with the determinedly neutral Luxembourgers. No, I think that no matter how much they'd like to, Harvey and the Chief can't do anything for us. And, given what Sam had said about Grant Natz and Headquarters, Headquarters wouldn't touch us with a barge pole. You're on your own, Anne.

Chief of Station West Germany heard all about it the next morning in an excited but guarded phone call from Charlie Berringer. Charlie was now code-named CHECKBOOK and a CIA asset newly recruited by the Chief himself. Chiefy had a slight champagne hangover from last night's dreary do at the Spanish Embassy, and was not one for 8 a.m. telephone calls anyway.

"Good morning, Charlie." Charlie, please remember you're on an insecure line. Watch what you're saying. He wished he could say that out loud.

But Charlie hadn't made it to a senior position in a big company by being dumb or careless.

"I thought the embassy might like to know that there was an incident last night which may involve an American citizen here in Luxembourg. There's gossip all over town but the police aren't saying anything except that the matter is being investigated. The one thing there appears to be a consensus on is that there was a shootout in a local restaurant last night around seven."

"Did you say a shootout? In Luxembourg?"

"I know it sounds crazy, but that seems to be what happened. And it might involve a friend of mine, an American named Sam Carpenter."

Oh shit oh dear. Not Sam. Please not Sam. Well, at least Charlie was being very circumspect about this. "You said, 'might involve.'"

"Yes. The talk is a man burst into a local restaurant and shot three people. The Luxembourg cops are sitting on it and not saying anything except the case is under investigation. But the rumor mill says the shooter had a buzz cut and was wearing combat boots and yelled something in English before he started shooting. Sam's got the only buzz cut I've seen in town, and he was wearing combat boots yesterday to go hiking with me, so I'm assuming it's him. I called his apartment but the phone's off the hook. I'm going to go over there and beat on the door. His wife, her name is Anne, and their two little kids will need some help. Anyway, I thought I'd give the embassy a heads-up. I don't know the rules about Americans overseas. Can you do anything for him? Can you bail him out or get him a lawyer?" Charlie didn't say it out loud, but he was asking if the CIA was going to do anything.

When Charlie got recruited, he had talked at length about ITT's overseas operations. The Chief was most interested, particularly when it turned out that Charlie had been sent to Luxembourg to replace the German manager, who had gotten a little too casual about what he was selling and to whom he was selling it. It seemed one of ITT's subsidiaries made semiconductors and they had sold it to somebody who sold it on to the Russians. There would be no more of that under Charlie's reign.

But then Charlie had turned to talking about Sam. He thought Sam hung the moon. Sam's virtues as a financial investigator were extolled, and the Chief learned all about the scam in Charlie's office that Sam had uncovered. Sam, said Charlie, would make a great CIA agent. The Chief had heard him out, wondering whether Charlie knew something and was pulling his leg or whether this was just another situation in the Alice in Wonderland world of clandestine operations. He decided it was the latter, or at least he hoped so.

Charlie must have wondered if Sam was a CIA talent scout or something, since his recruitment had come not all that long after Sam had shown up in Luxembourg. But to turn around and talent-scout Sam? Oh dear, what a tangled web we weave, when first we practice to deceive. Who wrote that anyway? The Chief could feel his headache starting to throb. It was aspirin time.

"Um, thank you for letting me know all this, Charlie. I'm not sure there's anything anybody can do at this point," He trusted that Charlie would read between the lines and understands that the Agency wasn't going to get involved in this. "Perhaps the embassy can send a consular officer to visit him when it's allowed. Although I'm afraid that about all he can do is inquire whether he's been well-treated and pass messages to his family."

Charlie, wishing he had heard something better, thanked the Chief and rang off after telling him he was going to go over to Sam's and get Snow White and her kids away from there before the reporters showed up. Charlie's wife, Barbara, had been drooling for an opportunity to spoil the twins anyway. Thank God, the Chief thought. I'm sure Anne would be discreet, but what if she was upset and incautious? He went in search of an aspirin and decided to talk to Harvey in Frankfurt. What were they going to tell Headquarters? Or, if and when this hit the newspapers, what was Headquarters going to tell them?

By noon, the *Luxemburger Wort*, the city's principal newspaper was on to the story. By early afternoon they had discovered the names of a number of diners and drinkers at the Gambrinus the night before. More important, the photographer had developed his pictures and announced they were for sale. By mid-afternoon stringers from the major German, and then two hours later French and Belgian papers, were in town. So was the Bonn bureau chief for the *International Herald Tribune*. The best story that any of them could put together was that a young man holding a pistol, which most noted was pointing at the floor when he ran in, yelled something in English at three men in the back of the restaurant. Two of the three men were standing up, and the one on the left started to pull a pistol out of his pocket. The young man then raised his gun and shot him. Then the young man charged into the other man who was standing up, knocked him down and kicked him in the head. Almost without exception the eyewitnesses winced when they talked about the kick. It must have been a very hard kick.

The eyewitness accounts got muddled after that, as everybody had stood up and crowded in to see what was happening. Being Luxembourgers, it never occurred to them to dive under the tables or flee. It appeared to the reporters that, judging from what those in the front row had seen, nothing much more happened until the police came and took the young man away. The young man had been, variously, either bent over the body of one of the victims or holding the victim's head in his lap or just standing there. Those in the back row thought they heard scuffles as some brave men in front of them wrestled the young man to the ground and subdued him. They all agreed the ambulance came just after the police, and three men were loaded into the ambulance and taken away. They all looked dead to the crowd, but no, they didn't know for sure.

Half the crowd knew who one of the dead men was. He was Dieter Volkmann, a confirmed Gambrinus beer drinker who had recently been awarded a *Doktorat* by the university and had gone off to Moscow as a foreign correspondent. Dieter had shared that news with the Gambrinus crowd, several times in fact. That perked the stringers' interest. It added an international flair, and the word "Moscow" always got everyone's attention. The last murder in Luxembourg had occurred eleven years ago when two drunken farmers went after each other with pitchforks. This one was much more interesting.

But what was the story? Who shot whom and why? The *Surete* would absolutely not say anything except that "the matter was under investigation." Several in the crowd thought that the shooter was an American. Two had seen him in the Gambrinus before with

Dieter. Perhaps a fellow student? There was a rush to the university. The registrars, thrilled at the attention and unimpeded by privacy laws (in Luxembourg only bank clients had privacy), told them there were only two Americans registered there. There was a woman studying Latin derivations of early French colloquial speech, and a Sam Carpenter. The pack called Sam's telephone number endlessly. They knocked, and then hammered, on his apartment door. No answer. They were frustrated.

What frustrated them even more was the question of the identities of the other two men. The rumor was that they were just *Gastarbieter* — guest workers — mostly Italians who did the work the Luxembourgers didn't want to do. They dug the ditches and mucked the drains and worked in the steel mills down south by the French border. They went largely unnoticed except to be looked down upon by the mistrustful Luxembourgers, who were proudly xenophobic.

As the obstacles to finding out the whys and wherefores mounted, the story was starting to lose its allure. It might have been relegated to a box on page three if it hadn't been for the pictures. Or, to be more accurate, The Picture. The photographer at the fraternity reunion had been barely more than an amateur and his speed and aperture settings on the Nikon camera had been uncertain. A lot of the pictures were consequently blurred and some were out of focus. But by luck and the grace of God, one shot was spectacular. It showed a back-lit Sam, looking clean-cut and very military, standing in the middle of a crowd with his big pistol extended and clearly about to shoot somebody. It was very dramatic. The *International Herald Tribune* outbid the Europeans. The other papers had to settle for a notice in italics under their articles saying, "*Photo courtesy of the International Herald Tribune.*"

"Did you see this? Did you see what that idiot did?"

Ross could hear Grant Natz's voice, loud, shrill and petulant, coming down the hall toward him. In a moment Grant appeared in the doorway of Ross's tiny office, waving a newspaper. He was pointing at a black-and-white picture above the fold.

Squinting, Ross could see that it was the *International Herald Tribune*. Good lord, Natz must have policed it off the floor of the executive men's room, Ross thought. EUR doesn't subscribe to any newspapers, and certainly not the *Herald Trib*. This must be the airmail copy that was flown in overnight for the DDP. So our boy Grant had latrine duty this morning. How fitting. Grant Natz squawked again: "Did. You. See. This?" Ross squinted some more. Oh, he means the picture. He realized what it was. His Army training kicked in.

"Yes. Somebody's firing a pistol from the Olympic firing position. Good form: arm straight, back straight, standing at right angles to the target. Right out of the book. Why?"

"Why? Why?" Speechless, Grant Natz thrust the newspaper at him.

Ross looked more closely. "Jesus, that's Sam." He scanned the article, incredulous. The phrases jumped out at him: "First shots fired in peaceful Luxembourg since WW II" and "the assailant, possibly an American student at the University of Luxembourg, was being held by police last night after allegedly shooting and killing an unknown man and seriously injuring and possibly killing another," and "a third man was found dead at the scene," and "from a photograph taken by a participant in a Luxembourg fraternity event." The rest emphasized what a small, peaceful city Luxembourg was and how rare any sort of violent death, particularly one by gunfire, was. What in hell was going on? Speechless, Ross handed the paper back to Natz.

Then his voice came back. "Do we know any more?" He had heard a rumor that Bonn had sent in a cable yesterday that had Grant running across the hall to the Director of Europe's suite.

Grant just glared at him. "Do *we* know any more? Do *you* know any more? He's your Boy Wonder."

Ross was about to tell him he had no idea. Hmm, now Sam is now *my* boy wonder. Thanks a lot. Over Grant Natz's shoulder he could see the Branch's Chief secretary approaching, holding what was probably the morning's cable traffic. "Maybe we have an answer here."

They did and they didn't. On top was a cable from Bonn providing a digest of the early-morning coverage in the European newspapers. The final edition of the *Herald Trib* identified the "unidentified third man" in the earlier edition as Dieter Volkmann, a German economics correspondent. A German tabloid, *Blick*, said Volkmann had been in Moscow recently and suggested in a barely non-libelous way that the two unidentified men might be Soviet agents. This in turn let them raise speculation as to who might be the employer of the unidentified American, if he were in fact an American. They didn't quite say CIA.

A second cable referred to yesterday's report from CHECKBOOK, the ITT guy, which had more or less confirmed that the shooter was Sam. CHECKBOOK advised that Sam's wife and kids were safely sequestered from the press in CHECKBOOK's ski chalet in the Ardennes. CHECKBOOK had no new information. The Station Chief also wanted to know the disposition of the original request for an approval to recruit Volkmann, and asked Headquarters to shed some light on the case. The Germans were sure to be asking, at least informally, just what this James Bond crap was all about. The station chief pointed out that while the Germans were our dear friends and all, they could get very pissy very quickly if we got involved in possibly shooting their citizens. Headquarters was urged to hurry its response.

"The INGRESS operation is code PURPLE," said Grant Natz, waving the cable. "I want Carpenter fired right now. We have to be able to tell the Germans that Carpenter is not an Agency employee. Call personnel and get the papers moving." Grant Natz stomped off.

Ross was so surprised that he just stood there. The fool was going to abandon Sam and leave the West German station chief hanging without an explanation? Was whatever INGRESS had been doing so important that Headquarters was willing to risk a very good liaison relationship with the Germans? Was CIA willing to treat The BND in the same suspicious, hands-off way they expected the Germans to treat the Soviets just to protect the INGRESS operation?

For that matter, it didn't take a PhD from MIT to figure out that Sam thought he was about the U.S. government's business when he went charging into that restaurant. Since he was under cover he was on his own, but the Agency had many options for dealing with problems like this. This is why they spent so much time and money to establish close and friendly liaisons with other intelligence services all over the world. Depending on the circumstances, something often could be worked out when an Agency officer ended up in hot water overseas. This could be one of those times.

What to do now? He would dearly love to cable Bonn, copy to Frankfurt, and tell them what Grant Natz had just said and done, but Grant would never sign off on the cable, and if he sent it himself he'd be fired too. On the other hand, he really didn't need to. The Bonn Station was on the hot seat, and they'd be demanding an answer within hours, so Ross putting his head on the chopping block wasn't really necessary. Ross considered doing so anyway. He'd had a bellyful of this place. Then he thought he might do better by Sam if he went downstairs and gummed up the works, delaying Sam's firing or even getting it cancelled.

Ross knew Agency employees were unlike the rest of the federal government. Firing a GS-13 in the Department of Agriculture could take years, even if the employee had done something dreadful. Even then a firing could be overturned if an administrative law judge found even a comma out of place in the trailer truck full of documents generated by the dismissal process. A CIA employee, however, was an at-will employee, which meant he or she could be fired anytime the bosses felt like it, and with no reason given. Over the years plenty of people had been. This system had the salutary effect of making CIA staffers damn careful what they said to the boss.

Ross decided to head for Personnel. After all, everybody told him he was no good at Headquarters work, so why not screw up Sam's firing and prove it?

His spirits lifted, Ross headed for the elevators. He wasn't so sure that Grant Natz had the authority to fire anybody. But it would be better for him to visit Personnel than Grant. An angry Grant might actually get results. Ross had gotten Personnel's red-line phone number and called. Personnel didn't know what to do. That wasn't unusual. They insisted Ross come down and meet with them. He should be prepared to explain everything about the case, and in detail. Ordinarily Ross didn't get along well with support people in general and personnel officers in particular. Back when he was in the Army he had a wooden sign on his desk that said, "Resist the Tyranny of Clerks." Today, however, he was willing to sit down and chat with the Personnel pukes and fill out forms until both he and Sam were old enough to file retirement papers. The elevator came and he got on, wishing he had one of those pillows you sat on during long meetings.

The Chief of Station, Bonn, waited, very patiently in his estimation, for four whole hours before he permitted himself to lose his temper. It was purely by the grace of God that the Germans hadn't been on the phone already. Who would be calling? Foreign Ministry or the BND? It didn't make much difference. The Foreign Ministry would be smoother, while the BND less so. Much less so, probably. He wrote a cable.

REQUEST IMMEDIATE RESPONSE MY B32467 OF TODAY. ARE WE IN OPERATIONAL RELATIONSHIP WITH INGRESS? IS/WAS DOUGLAS S. WINTHROP (Sam's dispatch pseudonym)

FALLBACK CONTACT FOR INGRESS? WHAT WAS INGRESS DOING IN LUXEMBOURG? IF NECESSARY OR ADVISABLE MAY WE ACKNOWLEDGE WINTHROP AS CIA OFFICER? EXPECT QUERIES FROM GERMANS. NEED RESPONSE NOW.

That sent, he waited again. This time the response was prompter:

IN THE INTEREST OF PRESERVING LIAISON RELATIONSHIP WE ARE TERMINATING DOUGLAS S. WINTHROP TODAY, CONSEQUENTLY YOU MAY TELL GERMANS WE HAVE NO RELATIONSHIP WITH HIM. REGRET INGRESS CLASSIFIED PURPLE LEVEL THUS WE ARE UNABLE TO COMPLY WITH YOUR REQUEST FOR INFO.

COS Bonn shook his head as he read it. "Why, you clueless little prick." The cable had the fingerprints of Grant Natz all over it. But the Chief had the right to use a private channel to communicate directly with the Deputy Director, bypassing even his immediate boss, the Chief of Europe, and of course, Grant Natz, the despised GS-15 branch Chief. So he did:

DEAR TOM, I NEED YOU TO INTERVENE IN CASE OF INGRESS MURDER/DOUGLAS S. WINTHROP DISMISSAL. CLASSIFICATION LEVEL PURPLE OR NOT, I NEED TO KNOW ENOUGH TO DEAL WITH GERMAN LIAISON REQUESTS. I ASK YOU TO PROVIDE ME WITH SUFFICIENT INFORMATION TO DO THAT. I QUESTION TERMINATING WINTHROP WHILE IT STILL UNCLEAR WHETHER OR NOT HE WAS ACTING OPERATIONALLY. IN ANY EVENT IT IS DEEPLY UNWISE. ABANDONING CAREER OFFICERS IN THE FIELD WILL HAVE A DISASTROUS EFFECT ON EMPLOYEE MORALE. BEST TO KATIE AND THE KIDS.

The Deputy Director for Plans read all mail on his personal channel immediately. Forty-five minutes later Bonn had a response:

CASE OFFICER FOR INGRESS IS AUGUSTUS C. HETHERINGTON (Oh, shit, thought the COS, it's that pompous ass van Claire) WHO IS CURRENTLY IN TRAVEL STATUS. I WILL

DEBRIEF SOONEST. I HAVE REVIEWED INGRESS FILE AND SEE NOTHING IN IT WHICH MIGHT HELP BUT AM POUCHING YOU A COPY OF THE FILE TODAY. IT IS NO LONGER CLASSIFIED PURPLE. AS REGARDS WINTHROP, HE IS STILL ON ACTIVE DUTY AND I AM TAKING STEPS TO DEAL WITH THIS MATTER. BEST WISHES TOM

Twenty-three thousand feet above the Atlantic, the Boeing 707 had just cleared the French coast and was climbing to cruising altitude for the run to Washington. Direct flights from Paris to Washington were new and in great demand, so the plane was almost full. This was most unusual; transcontinental flights were rarely more than half-full, so that any number of passengers could lie down across three seats and sleep most of the way. Clay van Claire was squirming in his middle seat, still seething with rage. He had been in a near-jubilant mood when he had arrived at Orly that morning. A day ago, flush with victory after his meetings with CITADEL and INGRESS, he had taken a plane from Bonn to Paris and treated himself to a night in the Georges V — well, the Agency was going to treat him. He'd had somebody from the Paris Station come by and brief him on the current European situation. He didn't care, but it gave him an operational meeting he could use to justify staying at the Georges V, which cost almost precisely four times the authorized federal per diem rate. His secretary would use the DDP's name to bully Travel into paying up. He'd intended to do the same thing to fly first class home, only to find that some damn Saudi princelet had reserved the whole first-class section, and here he was stuffed into an economy seat. No amount of raging at the Pan Am desk clerks had produced a first-class seat. The vindictive bastards had even stuck him in a no-smoking seat, so he had to go stand by the toilet when he wanted to smoke.

Fuming, he dragged out the *Herald Trib* he had bought at the airport and scanned the headlines. De Gaulle was making an ass of himself again. There was nothing new in that. Hmm: murders in Luxembourg. That's unusual. He read on. The picture of some kid with a gun was dramatic, but so what? He was just losing interest again when the name Dieter Volkmann jumped out at him. What? What? He read the article again, very carefully and twice.

He tried to recline his seat, but the Pan Am clerk at Orly had put him in the last row. The thigh of the fat woman in the aisle seat pressed against him. He turned to glare at her and she glared back. He backed off from saying anything. All he needed was a sidebar in the *Post* saying "Senior State Department officer in scuffle on Paris flight." He hated middle seats. He hated the Pan Am desk clerk.

Back to Dieter Volkmann. What did this mean for him and the INGRESS operation? The article said, or implied anyway, that some American did it. Who? Why? Did he even care? One way or the other, the INGRESS operation is obviously over. I have the data he gave me and the name of that Russian clerk who wants to defect, assuming CITADEL keeps his word and doesn't rat him out. But he won't unless they put the screws to him. He sat back and tried to concentrate on thinking for the next hundred miles, trying to ignore the fat thigh pressing into his. The stewardess came by taking drink orders. That irritated him too. He had read that the airlines fired the stewardesses when they turned 30, so that the cabin crew was always young, chirpy and slightly sexy. This stew was pretty battle-worn and looked at him and took his order with polite disinterest. In first class they'd at least pretend to flirt a little. He hated Pan Am: he'd fly TWA next time.

Another hundred miles passed before he made up his mind. There would be an Agency inquiry into INGRESS's death. He would be nagged about INGRESS's state of mind, apparent mental health and whatnot. They'd want to know if INGRESS complained about enemies. Had his own tradecraft been deficient? Had he been observed meeting INGRESS? Was this all somehow his fault?

Internal Security and Counterintelligence had to blame somebody when things went wrong with an agent, and the case officer was the obvious target.

And then there was the matter of Goshkorow. Clerk or no clerk, he had given his name to CITADEL. He hated to admit it to himself, but CITADEL now had leverage on him. He had, even if for noble purposes, exposed a would-be Soviet defector to the KGB. CI staff would be really shitty about that if they found out, his arguments about operational necessity notwithstanding. He could be disciplined, or fired, or maybe even prosecuted. No, they'd never risk the public disclosure of the operation. Or would they? A wave of something very much like fear ran down van Claire's spine, causing him to forget all about the cramped seat and the interfering thigh.

Another hundred miles. And then . . . he had it! He smiled, which made the fat lady next to him unhappy. She wanted him to be as uncomfortable as she was. He nodded his head. The joke was that for every problem there is a solution which is simple, obvious . . . and *wrong*. Well, in this case there was a problem that was simple, obvious and *right*. He'd simply report that INGRESS had failed to show up for the meeting. There would be no inquiry, no reason for them to interrogate him. The two security guards didn't know who he was meeting with, and this operation was classified PURPLE, so the investigation would never go outside the Clandestine Service anyway. Certainly not down to them interviewing Office of Security people. He was home free. And best of all, no one would ever know that he had told CITADEL about Goshkorow. Ahh, a happy resolution to a knotty problem. He settled back in his seat as best he could and even smiled at the fat lady, which she found disconcerting.

Gregor Arbarkian had known something was wrong when the team assigned to Luxembourg failed to check in at the appointed time. Damn. Things were going so smoothly with Clay van Claire, the pear-shaped CIA fool who thought he was James Bond. Arbarkian had already decided to accelerate the operation before CIA analysts began to unravel the carefully manufactured documents the KGB had assembled for this operation. And that did not include the intricate fabrications woven into the various narratives. If, as he hoped, they would be stupid enough to act on the fabrications. Arbarkian could only smile as he thought of the damage that would do. In any event, with luck Arbarkian hoped to have cleaned out the CIA's pantry of secrets by then.

He cursed Komsomol, his new area Chief. That stupid, bloody Russian peasant. He ran intelligence operations like he was driving a steamroller. When news of poor Goshkorow's proposed defection reached Moscow, courtesy of van Claire, Komsomol had erupted in rage and demanded Goshkorow's immediate execution. Nobody, including Arbarkian, dared argue with Komsomol when Komsomol was in the midst of one of his tantrums — it would have been like telling the Emperor Nero to stop playing with matches — and so the order went out. Arbarkian was bitterly disappointed.

Arbarkian was from Marnculi, a town on the Georgia-Armenia border, where people ran clandestine operations and smuggling routes with skill and style. They saved the killing for wars and blood feuds. But where money and intrigue were involved, manipulation and bribery were the keys. Komsomol and the other Russian oafs who were now running his department always reacted to any setback with instant rage and a desire to punish everyone connected with the mischance, innocent and guilty alike, immediately and without regard to consequences. The fools.

But what is done is done, and so Arbarkian set about cleaning up the mess. Because Komsomol demanded instant action, he had had to use embassy security people instead of bringing in a trained assassination team to dispose of Goshkorow. But the security goons were clumsy, and that German reporter had seen them, and so the German had to be dealt with. Now something had gone wrong in Luxembourg. But what, exactly, had gone wrong?

To his irritation, Arbarkian learned about his broken operation not from clandestine sources, but from page 1 of the capitalist propaganda rag the *Herald Trib*. How unprofessional. Also, how inconclusive. Three men killed, including the German. Well, at least the German was taken care of. To a degree, the loss of both of his subordinates came as something of a relief. Arbarkian assumed the two had had the sense not to be carrying any identification. If so, they would not be identified as Soviet Embassy personnel, or even as Russians. They were just two dead men in their early thirties, nationality and motivation unknown. And who was the shooter? Here was yet another matter to be dealt with. The KGB, all the way back to the days when it was the czar's Okhrana, prided itself on always getting captured agents back, by rescue or exchange of spies. It was also a point of honor to avenge its dead. Komsomol and his buddies would fix on that point soon and come baying after Arbarkian to get on with it. Damn. Double damn. Here was a carefully designed operation, quite sophisticated and starting out quite nicely, turning into one of those gunfights they always have in those capitalist Western movies. Whoever the shooter was, he was a dead man. Arbarkian hoped he wouldn't have to do it, but somebody would.

In the end, it was decided independently and on two continents that it was time to pay attention to something else. The newspapers left off trying to update the shooting story, interesting as it was in the beginning, because there were no new tidbits to report. They rushed elsewhere to cover something that was, in fact, new news. No foreign paper had the time or resources to have reporters hanging around a one-horse town like Luxembourg City waiting for the story to break, and the local papers knew from bitter experience that they weren't going to hear anything more until the gendarmerie were damn good and ready to tell them.

But there was no news on the Gambrinus murders because the Luxembourg gendarmerie didn't quite know exactly how to find more evidence. So they had taken to sitting in their offices, alternately plodding and pondering. The investigating magistrate and the public prosecutor were dying to get moving, but knew better than to hurry the cops, who got mulish when pressed.

Moving up the line, the executives in the Duke's entourage were all for nothing happening. In Bonn the silence was also appreciated. Why kick the hornet's nest about Dieter Volkmann? In turn this meant that Chief of Station's blood pressure returned to normal when his German opposite numbers never called to ask embarrassing questions. He had to content himself with the Deputy Director's second private message describing in lip-licking detail the ass-chewing he had administered to Grant Natz, who was going to be on the next plane to Vietnam. He also promised to debrief van Claire pronto.

The Soviets, always ones to hide in the bushes and wait for unwary people to come by, remained unaware that one of their employees had been discourteous enough not to die.

CHAPTER ELEVEN

Kurt Baeriswyl was sitting at his desk in the *Surete's* counterintelligence section. It consisted of two tiny rooms on the third floor of the ancient stone building across the square from the Maison de Ville and the Cathedral. Neither room had a window, but the seventeenth-century building had eleven-foot ceilings and rococo plaster crown moldings of intricate detail. Kurt was an *Inspektor* of the *Verkehrsbrigade*, the traffic police. Somehow in the last hundred years counterintelligence had become attached to the traffic police instead of the *Surete*. Kurt was not busy: the Soviets seemed to run their operations elsewhere in Europe. The Americans weren't in evidence. Surprisingly, nobody seemed to be taking much interest in the Hochmann AG facility about three miles out of town. One would think their polymer and crystallography work would be of interest to somebody's creepy crawlies.

Still, getting an open *Inspektor* spot was a step up and made Kurt the equivalent of a first lieutenant at the early age of 24, so he had grabbed it. The Luxembourgers are remarkably frugal in paying their civil servants, so an *Inspecktor* wasn't making much more money than a grocery clerk. But he missed being a highway patrolman. The Duchy's police had three VW bugs with Porsche engines slyly slipped inside. It always amused Kurt no end when some speeder looked in the rearview mirror of his Mercedes and saw Kurt in a VW police bug with flashing lights tailing him at 170 kilometers per hour and waving him over to the side of the road. Kurt missed the adrenalin, but Angelica was still wearing her school clothes because that was all they could afford. The promotion had been badly needed. Oh, there was some money from FC Luxembourg, the city's semi-pro soccer team, but not enough to make much of a difference since he hurt his knee (again) and wasn't playing much. An otherwise good halfback with a limp is not in great demand, even down in the semi-pro leagues.

Kurt was still a little uncomfortable about telling Angelica about their next-door neighbor being locked up as the chief suspect in last night's shootout. It was strictly against orders, but Anne was so nice, and she needed to know more than he needed to obey orders. Besides, Angelica would skin him if he hadn't told her. He was still thinking about it when there was a perfunctory knock and his boss walked in. Chief Inspector Furtwangler was, unfortunately, a typical senior Luxembourger official. Everybody had been desperately poor during World War II. That generation had come out of the war wary, bitter, distrustful, and parsimonious. They were well aware that they had had to play footsie with the Nazis to a far greater extent than they were willing to admit to themselves. To make up for it they focused on palliatives like naming at the main street in Luxembourg City Rue Franklin Delano Roosevelt. All of this trying to forget led the older generation of Luxembourgers to tend towards being judgmental, abrupt in conversation and, well, generally testy. The Chief Inspector was no exception.

"Baeriswyl, I'm loaning to this shooting investigation. Your English is adequate, is it not?"

"Barely, Chief Inspector."

"Well, it will have to do. Get downstairs and report to Deschamps." The Chief Inspector would not refer to his opposite number in the *Surete* in any other way. Kurt's Chief Inspector was a German Luxembourger, and Deschamps was a damn Frenchman from down near the border. The airy fop wasn't even a city *Luxembourgoise*, for heaven's sakes. "And don't forget your kepi."

No, Kurt wouldn't forget his uniform cap. It was the same instruction every senior Luxembourg policeman said to every junior Luxembourg policeman every time he had the chance. Nobody knew why; it was just a habit that had sprung from somewhere.

"Yes, Chief Inspector." The Chief turned around and left without another word of explanation or encouragement. Kurt picked up his kepi, checked to see that his uniform was properly aligned, tapped his holster flap to make sure it was secured, and headed downstairs. He hoped this would not turn out badly. His English was not a great deal better than his next-door neighbor's sputtering German, but it would have to do. As far as he knew almost nobody in the Luxembourg police spoke much English beyond "Show me you driver's license, please," which they read off a card they carried.

Chief Inspector Rene Deschamps was tall, thin, and haughty, and hoped that he somewhat resembled a younger Charles de Gaulle. He addressed Kurt as he walked in the door. "You can use that desk in the corner there. Your task will be to interrogate the American. This is all very closely held and you will discuss this case with no one outside this office. Understand?" The language had switched to French and would stay that way.

"Yes, Chief Inspector." Interrogate Sam? He better tell the Chief that Sam was his neighbor. Wait: the Chief already knew. Deschamps was the one who had given him the commendation for his part in the case of Charlie Berringer's embezzling office manager. Well, if he doesn't care, then neither do I. And as for not discussing the case, well, that advice was coming a little late. Let's just shut up and sit in the corner and open our ears.

Ignored, he sat in the corner while Deschamps and the three *Surete* investigators, who together were almost the entire officer corps of Luxembourg's tiny police force, wrestled with what they were going to do with the case. By lunch he had learned some interesting things. Eleven witnesses had, surprisingly, generally agreed on several points. The unknown man standing on Dieter's right had pulled a pistol out of his pocket before Sam had raised his pistol and fired. Hence, Sam had arguably shot the man in self-defense. Similarly, the other man was also pulling a pistol out of his pocket, which presumably was why Sam had knocked him down and kicked him in the head. Again, arguably, a case could be made for self-defense.

Plus, the man Sam had kicked in the head wasn't dead. He was in some kind of coma, lying in a bed in the hospital just up the street. If and when he ever came to his senses he would be most useful in helping the *Surete* figure out what had happened.

But nobody knew what to do about Dieter Volkmann. Dieter was dead but there were no marks on his body. Well, there was one. He had been given an injection. The glass thing everybody had seen the first man drop when Sam came bursting in the door was a broken hypodermic needle. Clearly, that was what had been used to kill Dieter. But what had been in the hypodermic, and what was now in Dieter? The police lab tech had been absolutely bewildered when confronted with this. Yes, he was familiar with blood stains and semen samples, but poisons?

Deschamps and the three senior investigators decided that what would break the case would be Kurt's interrogation of Sam. Why had Sam suddenly arrived at the Gambrinus just when the two men were busy killing Dieter? Why, for God's sake, was he carrying a gun on the streets of Luxembourg? They talked as if Kurt wasn't there. Kurt also realized that the responsibility for solving the case was being firmly dropped in his lap. If the Luxembourg *Surete* couldn't break the case, it was going to be all Kurt's fault. Shit. Being the junior lieutenant really sucked.

As they broke for lunch, Kurt ambled over to one of the senior investigators and murmured, "You know, *Monsieur le Capitan*, the Hochmann AG plant here employs hundreds of the best chemists in Europe; I bet they'd know what was in the hypo and the victim." The captain didn't even glance at him as he rushed out the door to catch up with the Chief Inspector. Kurt had thought about going to the Chief directly, but figured that since he wasn't going to get the credit anyway he might as well make a few brownie points with his senior colleagues.

Then he had another idea. He was quite pleased. He never thought of himself as the imaginative sort, but actually working on an investigation seemed to stimulate the little gray cells, as Hercule Poirot would say. Kurt had read many Agatha Christie novels as preparation for his duties as a policeman. He sidled over to another of the captains and said, "I wonder if it would be profitable to make inquiry of the four countries bordering Luxembourg as to whether any foreign nationals were reported to be dead of unexplained causes on the days around the time this business took place." The captain departed with equal speed.

After lunch Kurt was directed to an interrogation room on the third floor. He arrived to see Sam, rumpled but undamaged, sitting in an upright chair by the small oak table. It was set in the middle of the tall but otherwise small room. One of the three senior inspectors was sitting in a more comfortable-looking chair over by the wall, smoking and looking impatiently for Kurt to begin. Kurt was carrying a Uher reel-to-reel tape recorder, the *Surete's* newest acquisition. Kurt was one of few people who knew how to operate it, and he not all that well.

Sam, who usually sat straight up, was slumped slightly, but he straightened up, surprised, when he saw Kurt. Kurt gave him a slight "no, no" turn of the head, raising his chin towards the captain as he did. Sam got the message and slumped again. This is not so odd after all, Sam thought. You have to remember this small city is the size of an American town. What is coincidence in the city is customary in the small town, where after a while everybody recognizes everybody else. Sam wondered whether knowing Kurt would help or hurt, or whether it would make any difference at all. Then he decided to give up thinking about it. At the Marines' Basic School for officers, they always told them: "Gentlemen, don't fight the program. Just follow the school solution." Well, what was the school solution for this?

Kurt gave no indication that he had ever seen Sam before.

"Nobody in building speaks English except you and me, and me not so good." Actually, almost nobody in town spoke English except Angelica. His wife, a natural linguist, had picked it up working in a travel agency before they got married. He opened the carrying case and started pulling out reels of tape and a power cord. "We record this, but I am sometimes having problems with machine so maybe not everything gets recorded. Tell me what happened."

"Can I ask a question?"

"Don't expect answer."

"Does Anne know where I am? Is she all right? I mean you haven't arrested her or anything?"

"She and kids are with Charlie and Barbara."

"Please tell her to go home."

Kurt nodded. "Now talk into machine and tell me what happened." He turned the tape recorder on.

So Sam did. He gave the tape recorder a nearly word-for-word recital of what Dieter had said, omitting only the part about "But I gave Henry Navarre Ivan Goshkorow's name." It was little enough, so it didn't take long. He did leave in the part about Dieter saying the Russians were the ones who wanted to kill him, though. If the Luxembourg cops wanted to go after the KGB, then bless them.

"So those two guys you finish off are maybe Russians?"
"Could be."
"KGB?"
"How would I know?"
"Why you have the gun?"
Sam explained about Charlie and the range.
"Why fighting boots?"
"They're called combat boots." Sam said. He explained about hiking in Schwarzenberg.
"Why not call police? Why not knock on door, tell me?"
Sam explained some more. They both knew Kurt wouldn't have been home at the time, but that needed to be explained to the tape recorder. Now they would be reminded that Sam and Kurt were neighbors, although nobody seemed to care.

Kurt went on for an hour. Sam repeated his story three times, Kurt waiting for a discrepancy and finding none. Finally, Kurt said, "OK," and began shutting down the tape recorder.

"One more question?" Sam asked.

Kurt looked at him. "Try."

"What happens now?"

"I don't know. Magistrate reads interviews, goes to public prosecutor; they decide. I think you defending yourself. You got problem with having gun. Maybe magistrate more interested in other guys."

"Why did they kill Dieter? Who are they? KGB?"

"Is none of your affair, Samuel. Go sit in cell. Hope for best."

Kurt unplugged the Uher, nodded, deferentially he hoped, at the slouching captain, and left the little room.

Early next morning, as Sam was finishing his breakfast after his third night in jail, Kurt and his superiors were rehearsing their eight a.m. meeting with the supervising magistrate. This was a big deal for Chief Inspector Deschamps. He and the magistrate were not friends, and neither one was friends with the public prosecutor, so they all wanted to win and the others to lose.

Deschamps started. "So, the story we have assembled to date is that Monsieur Volkmann was a student here at the university. He was friends with Monsieur Carpenter. A month ago he was awarded a *Doktorat* in economics. He gets a job almost immediately with the *Frankfurter Allgemeine* and goes to Moscow as their foreign correspondent." He knew the correct title was "economic correspondent," but "foreign correspondent" was more dramatic.

"Then we know nothing until four days ago when he suddenly turns up here in Luxembourg. He calls Monsieur Carpenter and tells him the KGB is going to kill him. Monsieur Carpenter is to hurry to the Gambrinus and meet with him and tell him what to do. Monsieur Carpenter has been hiking and target shooting with his friend Monsieur Charles Berringer, who is the head of the ITT company operation here in Luxembourg." Here he nodded his head appreciatively at one of the captains. "Monsieur Berringer confirms the story, thus accounting for why Monsieur Carpenter was wearing heavy boots and in possession of a pistol."

The Chief Inspector looked down at his briefing notes. "Monsieur Carpenter says his language skills were not sufficient to notify the police. He is very alarmed for his friend's safety so he rushes to the Gambrinus to protect his friend. Upon entering the restaurant, he sees Monsieur Volkmann in the back of the restaurant being menaced by two unknown men. He says, 'Stand away from that man.'" He stopped; "Is 'stand away' the correct translation?" He looked at Kurt accusingly.

"Monsieur Carpenter was in the U.S. naval infantry. It is a naval term meaning get back," Kurt said.

The Chief inspector continued. "Instead both men start to pull out pistols. Monsieur Carpenter shoots one and kicks the other in the head. Monsieur Carpenter says this was in self-defense since the two men clearly intended to shoot him."

The Chief Inspector looked around the room. He was practicing a dramatic pause while the magistrate absorbed all this. He continued: "The identity of the two men is still in question. They have obvious Slavic features: the cheekbones and the broad foreheads and all that. They were carrying no identification. Both bodies had old scars indicating previous combat or fighting. Plus . . ." — here another pause and another nod towards one of the captains — "the Hochmann AG staff has confirmed that traces in the broken hypodermic and Monsieur Volkmann's body indicate a very complicated chemical substance which produces a similar effect on humans as a very big heart attack. Were it not for this contretemps and the hypodermic needle, Monsieur Volkmann's death would have been assumed to have been a heart attack. Hochmann says the chemical is very subtle and would not be noticed unless they were specifically looking for something."

Another meaningful pause. "And finally, I have received answers to Letters Rogatory to adjoining countries. On the same day as this incident, five other foreigners died, four of whom were in West Germany. Three were *Gastarbieter*" — this said dismissively: who cared about dead Italians? "One English tourist who fell into an Amsterdam canal" — he almost said "again" — "and a Soviet official in Frankfurt who died of an apparent heart attack."

He looked around the room triumphantly. "I emphasize apparent. Obviously, this is part and parcel of the same conspiracy. Based on my investigation" — and here he drew himself up to his full, almost as tall as Charles De Gaulle, height — "we have uncovered a major Soviet espionage operation and assassination campaign which the American CIA agent attempted to break up in a most violent and crude manner. And they did it here." He jabbed at the floor. "Here in our Duchy, callously violating our sacred soil, endangering our citizens, bringing murder and gunfire to our peaceful streets." He looked proudly at his subordinates.

"I shall propose that all declared and suspected American and Soviet intelligence officers be declared persona non grata and publicly expelled from Luxembourg, including our American in the cell downstairs after he serves a term in prison. That should create enough of a stir to deter them from trying anything like this again!"

Jesus, Kurt thought, he's really gone off his trolley. Talk about jumping to conclusions. The bits and pieces of evidence were like toothpicks trying to hold together a fat pork roast of conjecture and hyperbole. And the Soviet and American embassy staffs are tiny. Do they even have KGB and CIA agents here? We certainly don't know. But who knows: maybe the magistrate and the public prosecutor will want their fifteen minutes of fame too and will jump on the Chief Inspector's bandwagon. The "everybody gets to be famous for fifteen minutes" he vaguely remembered as having been said by Andy Warhol in Stockholm a couple of months ago. Already everybody in Europe had repeated it to each other so often that the phrase had been beaten to death. And "based on *my* investigation" could backfire if his bosses didn't buy it. Ah, the dangers and excitement of high office.

The Chief Inspector looked proudly at his men. "Captain Chambre will accompany me to the briefing." Captain Chambre was the most senior of the captains. The rest of us will be permitted to remain anonymous, Kurt thought. Oh well, at least the two captains who had claimed credit for his ideas were also relegated to the children's table. Too bad; it would be most interesting to see how the Chief Inspector's meeting goes.

Less than a half-hour later the Chief Inspector and Captain Chambre returned. Their heavy footsteps could be heard in the stone corridor, and then a *click* followed by a slam as the Chief Inspector went into his office. A lower-ranking slam indicated that Captain Chambre had also returned.

"Well, looks like the war with the Americans and the Russians has been put off for now," the captain who hadn't been afforded an opportunity to claim credit for Kurt's ideas said brightly. "Who's for lunch?"

Inspecteur Rene Deschamps sat in his office and glowered. Everything had been proceeding superbly until the very end. His boss, his boss's boss, and two tough-looking middle-aged men, probably from the Duke's personal staff, were present. Deschamps had beamed: excellent, his work would become known at the highest level.

After a nod from his boss, Deschamps launched into the briefing he had rehearsed at eight that morning. Things seemed to be going smoothly, even getting Deschamps laudatory nods for having consulted Hochmann AG and sending the Letters Rogatory. One of the tough men even muttered "not bad" loud enough to be heard. But when Deschamps launched into his recommendation to expel the known KGB and CIA officers as persona non grata, things went downhill.

"A moment, Chief Inspector. I have heard no evidence that the Russian in Frankfurt — Goshkorow you said he was? — was poisoned, or that it was the same poison used on Monsieur Volkmann. Did I miss something?"

There was an awkward pause. When it become clear that Deschamps was not prepared to either bring forward the requested evidence or even answer the question, one of the tough-looking men spoke up.

"*Monsieur le Inspecteur*, you say these two men looked Russian. Do you have any further evidence that they are Russian? And how do you know they are KGB? And how do you know Monsieur Volkmann was an agent? How do you know he was an American agent and not a KGB agent, assuming of course that he was an agent at all? And if we do not know the answers to this, how do we know Monsieur Carpenter is a CIA agent?"

There was another long, miserable silence. Deschamps could hear his career being carried to the window and defenestrated. It was four floors down to the courtyard.

Then the second tough-looking man spoke. "Let us assume that this was an intelligence operation gone wrong for whatever reason. If indeed the second man is a KGB employee, are his masters aware that he is still alive?" He looked at Deschamps.

"No, sir."

"Might we assume that there is a possibility that someone might wish him to remain permanently silent?"

"Yes, sir."

"Is he under guard at present?"

"No, sir."

"Might I suggest that would be a good idea, at least for the moment, until we get this sorted out?"

"Yes, sir." Deschamps glanced at his boss, who nodded. "It will be done immediately, sir."

"Thank you, Chief Inspector." Turning to Deschamps' boss, he asked, "What do you plan to do with the American?"

"Actually, I was going to ask you about that," the boss said. "Charging him with murder seems a bit much. Manslaughter, I suppose." The boss was clearly uncomfortable at not being definitive and in charge. Hoping to relieve the tension, someone murmured, "How about wrongful discharge of a weapon in a public place?"

That brought no hoped-for laughs, no smiles, no nothing.

"I think this requires His attention," the man from Duke's personal staff said, and they delegated the problem upwards.

CHAPTER TWELVE

Feeling just marvelous after a good night's sleep, and still treasuring his snotty remark to the stewardess as he deplaned, Clay van Claire arrived at the office the next morning. His briefing on the CITADEL meeting was already written in his head. His secretary stopped him as he walked in the door.

"Oh, Mr. van Claire, the Deputy Director wants to see you immediately. He's waiting for you."

The usual stab of fear at being called before the boss was replaced by a warm glow today. I am CITADEL's case officer. I have a penetration into the KGB. I, dammit, am as close to being King of the Hill as you get around here. He tried not to strut down the hall to the boss's office. His secretary looked up, gave him the minimum required smile, and walked him to the door. She spent a lot of time in the cafeteria telling her friends what an asshole he was. She knocked once, heard a voice say "come" in the British fashion, and gestured him inside, closing the door after him. She had tried not to let her dislike show. She had failed. Van Claire noticed. Someday, missy, someday . . .

The boss was enveloped in a cloud of cigar smoke, as usual. Without looking up he said, "Pull up a chair, Clay. What's this about INGRESS being classified PURPLE?"

Van Claire was taken quite off-guard. He'd expected to be debriefed on his meeting with CITADEL, to be followed by a shower of moist kisses. "Um, oh, I'm not aware that it was, Tom." He had taken to calling the Deputy by his first name since CITADEL had come along. Perhaps that was unwise this morning; perhaps he should revert to "sir."

"Your agent is dead. Any idea why? What did he say at your meeting last week? I haven't seen the contact report."

"Uh, there isn't any contact report, sir." It *was* time to go back to "sir." "He didn't make the last meeting."

"What's the fallback when that happens?"

Van Claire swallowed. Was there supposed to be a fallback for a missed meeting? He tried to remember back to his training days many years ago. "Uh, he didn't activate that either, sir." That sounded good, whatever it meant. He'd have to remember to set up a fallback at his next meeting with CITADEL.

The DDP looked at him a trifle suspiciously. "Take the PURPLE classification off this operation, please. I've sent a copy of the file to Bonn. Do you have any idea what INGRESS was doing in Luxembourg?"

"No, sir."

"Do you have any idea how Sam Carpenter got mixed up in this?"

This time he could tell the truth. "Carpenter was the one who originally spotted him; maybe INGRESS figured that out and went to him for some reason when he couldn't make the meeting with me." On second thought, that sounded eminently reasonable. It could even be what actually happened.

"Do you have any idea why they — they being the KGB, we assume — went after INGRESS?"

"Absolutely none, sir."

Another horrible thought swept over him: the poste restante box in Frankfurt. What if INGRESS had left him a message about why he was in trouble? Might that refer to their last meeting, the one he just told the boss never took place? What if Frankfurt Base empties the box for some reason? No, they wouldn't do that: it's PURPLE and they can't go near it unless I say so. But the boss just said to take the PURPLE restriction off. Shit, I think I'll just drag my heels and not do that until I can get out there and check it. I'll do it when I go to Koblenz for the next meeting with CITADEL.

He looked up to see the boss squinting at him quizzically. "Clay, are you all right? You look like you're working on a kidney stone."

"Sorry, sir, I was just trying to think what INGRESS might have done in Moscow or Frankfurt to get the KGB on his neck. I'd just recruited him; he was going to be reporting on his meetings at the two trade conferences. He obviously must have seen or done something, but I'm afraid we'll never know what it was."

The DDP looked at him again for a while and then sighed. "Enough of that for the moment. Tell me about CITADEL."

Relieved, van Claire launched into his carefully memorized briefing of his meeting with CITADEL. It took him twelve minutes to recount a blow-by-blow description of the meeting, less, of course, the Goshkorow business and the German engineer.

"That's extremely valuable information, Clay, and I'm sure Jim Angleton is going to be delighted to be finally vindicated, although I'm not sure any of us are going to be happy if we actually have a traitor in our midst. But I'm a nasty, suspicious old man, Clay, and the KGB has been dangling suggestions of us having our own Kim Philby since the end of the war."

He stopped for a minute, and then continued, "I want you to start testing the stuff CITADEL has given us. Have you done any to date?"

"Oh, no sir, we were afraid to let anyone outside the bigot list see the material for fear the traitor would get wind of it and blow CITADEL to the KGB."

The boss looked at him curiously. "You don't have to identify the source to test the material. I want a plan on my desk by tomorrow to go to the Germans and tell them about this agent the KGB has on Willy Brandt's staff. Now if you'll excuse me, I have to go up to the front office and curtsey to the Director."

His boss looked after the departing van Claire and bit his upper lip. Those stories about the INGRESS mess don't pass the smell test. I don't know why van Claire has risen to such high estate. In my opinion he's one of those "often wrong, never in doubt" types who aren't nearly as smart as they think they are and often screw things up royally. And why hasn't he tested the CITADEL material? I think I need somebody to run some checks on this. Van Claire may have high-level sponsors, although God knows why, but he's going to have to do better than this if he wants to stay on my staff. He wondered who van Claire's current rabbi was — rabbi was the State Department term for someone's high-level sponsor — and just what it was he saw in his protégé.

Then he remembered: van Claire was one of Bissell's boys. He had somehow survived the housecleaning when Bissell had screwed up the Bay of Pigs operation and gotten fired for his blunders by President Kennedy himself. Allen Dulles went too. It was the first and probably the last time that anyone except the case officer was punished when an operation blew up. Van Claire worried him; the story about INGRESS didn't ring right. And the CITADEL operation was a little disturbing too. Why hadn't they tested the stuff CITADEL was giving them? Was CITADEL the most extraordinary piece of good luck the Agency had enjoyed in years or was it a clever Soviet dangle, using the not-so-clever van Claire as the messenger?

Much as he would have liked to get into this game himself, his operating days were over. He thought a while. Harvey Masters was due on home leave soon. He could fly him home, brief him, get a couple of people poking around here. Harvey could go back and forth to West Germany if needed and do it without attracting any attention. He was a good man, highly educated, a linguist, an intellectual, prickly, and unlucky. He'd never drawn the high-visibility cases that brought him to the attention of senior management. And, let's face it, Harvey was a Jew. The people who controlled much of the Agency were anti-Semites, born and bred. Harvey was going to retire as a GS-14 and that was that. The DDP smiled. Maybe this would give Harvey a chance to get even.

He pushed the buzzer for his secretary. "Margaret, we need to send a private-channel cable to Germany asking them to let Harvey Masters start home leave early and have him call me at home as soon as he gets to Washington. Would you draft that please, and make sure to give him my phone number? And get me the 201 file on a CT named Sam Carpenter, please. Could you get the 201 without our fingerprints on it?" Of course she could. "Oh," he added, "please make sure your friend and admirer Clay van Claire is unaware of all this, if you please."

Margaret drew herself up to her full five foot ten and said, "Tom, I'd rather die than tell van Claire his fly was open."

Van Claire left the meeting in a highly nervous state. That hadn't gone at all the way he had hoped and planned. Why was the boss so suspicious about CITADEL? My God, CITADEL was the best thing that had happened to CIA in the last ten years. I bet the boss thinks I'm aiming for his job. That's it: he's afraid I'm going to parlay this into a *coup de espionage* so big they'll ease him out and bring me in as the Deputy Director. Well, that could certainly happen. He liked that idea. His thoughts turned to how soon he could meet CITADEL again and how soon he could check the poste restante box in Frankfurt. The more he thought about it, the more unlikely it seemed that the panic-stricken INGRESS would have had time to drop off a note on his way to Luxembourg.

When van Claire was leaving the office for home, it was mid-afternoon in Frankfurt. A bored detective in the Frankfurt city police had seen the Letter Rogatory about deaths of foreigners in West Germany two days before and had gotten curious. His department had only done what the letter asked and had reported Goshkorow's death by heart attack. Curious and with time on his hands, he had gone over to the conference center and struck up a conversation with the nice lady at the reception desk. She was just as chatty and forthright with him as she had been with everyone else inquiring about poor Mr. Goshkorow's death.

"Oh, it was all so sad. I was sitting right here when that nice Russian gentleman came rushing out of the main hall and said to call an ambulance, that Mr. Goshkorow had had a heart attack. No, wait, he only said a colleague was sick. We didn't know that it was Mr. Goshkorow then, or about the heart attack. And, it was just the most amazing thing, that nice German newspaperman, Mr. Volkmann, had just come by. And wasn't he the one who got killed in Luxembourg? My goodness, what a coincidence. You just never know what is going to happen next. Anyway . . ."

The detective literally ran back to Headquarters. He'd been drinking a lot of beer lately and hadn't had much exercise since last year's two-week annual Army training for the reservists. Actually, a lot of that time had been spent sitting around drinking beer too. In any event, he was wheezing alarmingly by the time he reached the inspector's office.

The inspector listened to his tale with great interest. When he finished, the inspector said: "You know, Weissendorfer, I've always wondered how layabouts like you end up being the chief of police, and now I know. It just proves God has a sense of humor. He picked you to get off your lazy ass and come up with a big fat clue in the biggest murder case in umpteen years. Christ, I'll be saluting you by this time next week." He stood up. "C'mon, let's walk this up the line."

It took until close of business for the inspector and the detective to be shown into the office of a very high personage indeed, who listened to their story with grave attention. "Most interesting," he said, "most interesting. The question is, what we shall do with it? It is now at once a part of a murder investigation. It is also part of a possible, maybe probable, foreign intelligence operations here and in Luxembourg. In whose inbox shall we drop this little morsel, and who will be most grateful to receive it?"

He looked at them benignly. "You two are street cops. You don't understand that this is going to set off a jurisdictional dispute that is now a couple of hundred years old. Who gets it? The cops or the spies? Us or Luxembourg? They will all want to have a secret to themselves. You did a very good job. After the high-level pissing contest is over they'll get together and make a case and kick half the Russians in West Germany and Luxembourg out. Maybe some Americans too. Go home and wait for your rewards. It might be tomorrow, it might be a month. It depends on which bureaucracy wins and by how much."

In Moscow a very murderous bureaucrat had been raging at Arbarkian for over an hour. Ivan Komsomol looked a bit like Nikita Khrushchev, who in turn looked like half of the peasant population of Russia. This was odd, since he was a Ukrainian, but the broad forehead, small eyes, cheeks a nice alcoholic's red, and fat body disguising quite a fair amount of muscle spelled Russian peasant. He had berated Arbarkian for using KGB security personnel from the embassy to dispose of both Goshkorow and Dieter Volkmann. Those security men were untrained in the niceties of doing a discreet execution. And why hadn't Arbarkian followed up in Luxembourg to find out what the hell had happened? And why was there no operation in train to get revenge for the American's killing them?

Oh God, Arbarkian thought, I'm going to have to go to Luxembourg and set this up myself. Dammit.

Then Komsomol switched to van Claire, code-named WALRUS. Why hadn't Arbarkian pushed harder to get more information out of him? Arbarkian sat there and took it. He alternated between fear and loathing. The fear was genuine. It had happened years ago, back when things were looser under Beria: Komsomol had, so the stories went, once lost his temper so badly that he had pulled out his pistol and shot a captain right in the middle of argument. Arbarkian bit back a smile. Imagine going back to your office after that and having your secretary say, "Anything interesting happen at the staff meeting today?"

But Komsomol was so damn unreasonable. Arbarkian had no choice but to use the goons at the embassy. The orders were to do it right now. Who else was he going to use? All the people who did that sort of thing were out in training camps in the Caucasus. Going through the paperwork to get them to Frankfurt would have taken a week. And couldn't Komsomol have just waited until Goshkorow came back to Moscow with the trade delegation? Oh no, when Komsomol said "now," it was right now. It wasn't his fault.

And hurry up the WALRUS operation? They had been planning and designing this operation for a year. If it worked, it might go on a long time, collecting great amounts of valuable data from the blundering WALRUS. He had already given them Goshkorow and the German engineer. WALRUS seemed to hand out agents' names like potato chips at a party. Didn't he realize he was condemning these people to a most unpleasant future? Was he naive or some kind of sociopath? Maybe a bit of both, if the CIA's high bureaucracy was like the KGB's. But Komsomol was going to ruin it all if he kept pushing so hard.

Well, orders were orders, so let's get on with it.

CHAPTER THIRTEEN

Sam Carpenter was doing sit-ups when they came for him. In the nine days he had been here, he had done 10 sets of a hundred sit-ups every day. That was coming up on 9,000 sit ups. He had also done 10 sets of 30 push-ups a day, so that was 2,700 push-ups. He would have been more pleased with this except that he had done it because there wasn't anything else to do. He got a modest meal three times a day. It was always muesli in the morning, bread and cheese at one p.m. and something greasy for dinner. The Luxembourgers were conservative about toilet paper, and it had taken some impassioned speeches in broken German to snag a second roll six days into his imprisonment. The rules said one roll a week.

They hadn't been mean to him. It just seemed that if you were a prisoner in a Luxembourg jail you just sat there, or lay on your bed, until they decided to let you out. Sam had taken to rereading books in his head, since there were no actual books on offer. At night he concentrated on not thinking about Anne and the boys. He dearly wished his religious education had taken hold. If this wasn't a time for earnest prayer, then what was? He knew that they would eventually put him on trial, but waiting was most certainly not his long suit. When he got jumpy, and was tired of push-ups and sit-ups, he ran in place. He must have run to Cleveland and back in the last nine days.

The sound of the door being unlocked surprised him. It wasn't mealtime, which was the only time they came, except once. That was at the end of the first week, when they let him take a shower. Living in Luxembourg, he had learned that the Luxembourgers, while a neat and tidy people, weren't heavily into bathing. Getting on a bus or train meant entering something that smelled like a cattle car. Even the otherwise dainty Angelica next door used a cheap and heavy perfume to cover the smell of sweat. You got used to that too. Women didn't shave their armpits. Men didn't seem to bathe. You got used to it. Viewed in that light, a shower once a week was a sign of enlightened prison management. He wished his jailers were readers though.

The guard beckoned him with a finger. A week of silence, broken only by impassioned arguments for a roll of toilet paper, hadn't improved Sam's German any. He was still in the clothes he had been arrested in. He followed the guard down the hall, noting that the other cells seemed to be empty. Except who knew? You don't make much noise sitting in a cell looking at the wall. The guard went up two flights of stairs, never looking back to check whether Sam was following him. Well, he would be following him, wouldn't he? Who wanted to stay down there?

The guard waved him into a room that looked like the one he had been questioned in. As a matter of fact, it was; he recognized a black boot smear in one corner that some poor *Gastarbieter* had failed to scrub off. Sitting behind a desk was a very official-looking man in uniform who looked a little like Charles de Gaulle. Behind and to the left of De Gaulle was Kurt, looking angry. Why was he angry? Was he mad at me or at what they were going to do to me or was it something else? The guard pointed at the chair in front of the desk and Sam sat down.

Chin up, Lieutenant, he told himself. I don't think you're going to like this but let's try to look squared away. Charles de Gaulle started talking in French. Well, Sam thought, what's the difference? French or German, it was all Greek to him. He paused. No, that wasn't funny. Nice try though, considering the circumstances. Sam wished de Gaulle would shut up and let Kurt tell him what they were going to do to him.

Finally it was Kurt's turn. He spoke in a neutral voice. "You are being released conditionally on . . ." Kurt was struggling. "*Sie werden auf Bewährung entlassen.*" He hesitated. "Parole with conditions."

Sam could have jumped up and kissed him and Charles de Gaulle too. Parole! Hot shit. He was afraid he'd never see Anne and the kids again. Oh joy and rapture unforeseen. He'd always liked "HMS Pinafore." He forced himself to pay attention to Kurt ". . . surrender your passport, *carte de sejour* and driving license." Finally, Kurt finished. "Sign these documents and you may leave." Why was he being so abrupt? Does he really think I killed those guys in cold blood? Sam signed the documents and sat up straight, waiting to see what happened next. The Luxembourgers looked at him expectantly until Kurt jerked his thumb towards the door. Sam stood up and the guard opened it.

Outside, the late November sun was blinding. He was standing next to the plaza by the Maison de Ville and the cathedral, which were sited on the bluff above the river. Home was three hundred meters away. He started walking that way, then walked faster, and then broke out in a flat run. He ran up the Rue de St Esprit and stormed up the flight of 47 steps to the door of his apartment building. He skipped the ponderous elevator and ran up the six flights of stairs, his boots pounding on the granite.

Anne must have heard him coming because she was standing in the door as he came to the landing. He grabbed her and held her, lifting her off the floor.

"Sorry," he gasped, heart pounding, breathing the hint of perfume in her hair. "I got held up at the office."

She was crying, and he couldn't talk because he was feeling choked up himself. They stood that way for a long time until a small voice said, "Johnny, Daddy's home," and two small figures appeared and hugged his legs.

Finally Anne took her head off his chest and looked up at him. "I was really scared, Sam." They both started laughing, the nervous, rather high pitched-laughter that marks a release of tension. Then it turned into real laughter when little Sam, wrapped in his father's bear hug, said, "You stink, Daddy."

They were just going into their apartment when the other door on their landing opened and Angelica peered out. She instantly gave a delighted smile. "Sam! They let you out. Oh, I am so pleased." Then her beautiful face turned severe. She frowned. "Kurt didn't tell me. I must go." The door closed.

"I think Kurt's in for it," Sam said.

"Well, he damn well ought to be," Anne said in wifely solidarity.

Sam headed straight for the shower while the kids bounced around the living room and Anne just stood there looking thoughtful. He came out a precise four minutes later, dressed in clean clothes in colors only ex-military people think civilians wear.

After dinner, and after the beddy house bells, they sat in the living room and worked on what to do next. "I've got to get ahold of Harvey Masters," Sam said. He told her Dieter's last words: "But I gave him Goshkorow."

"Who is Goshkorow, Sam?"

"Damned if I know, sweetie. I don't know if that's what got him killed either."

"Sam, stop right now and tell me the whole story."

So he did. The telephone call, why he had a weapon, what he remembered of the fast sequence of events at the Gambrinus. The two men he'd killed.

"Only one, actually," Anne said. "The one you kicked in the head is in the hospital. He's still unconscious. It's supposed to be a big secret, but you know Luxembourg. Angelica told me. She says Kurt's not telling her anything but everybody else in town is. They even have a guard on him. That's supposed to be a secret too." She paused. "I sound so callous. But somehow I just can't believe that my mild-mannered husband is running around killing people."

"Neither can your mild-mannered husband," Sam said ruefully. "But that's a piece of good news at least. I didn't kill two people. I only killed one and just turned the other one into a vegetable. Whoopie."

They went back to talking about that night at the Gambrinus.

"Do the cops know who those two guys are?"

"The *Surete* hasn't announced anything but everybody says it's the KGB."

"And how did everybody reach this conclusion?"

"Well, *Luxemburg Wort* published a long article citing interviews with people who were at the Gambrinus. Most of the people agree that the two men must have killed Dieter just as you came in the door. And since Dieter was the Moscow correspondent for his newspapers then the killers must be Russians."

"I wouldn't call that evidence. More like idle speculation."

"Well, it gets better. Angelica says the guy in the hospital has started babbling in Russian."

"How do they know it's Russian?"

"Somebody saw a professor of Russian studies from the university coming out of the hospital one morning a couple of day ago. That started this rumor that they've got Russian speakers listening to what he's saying."

"Either that or the professor is visiting somebody in the hospital."

Anne wanted to hear more. She walked Sam through the Gambrinus shooting again, and then asked an obvious question:

"Weren't you scared?"

"Later, not during."

"Why is that?"

"When he started pulling a gun out of his pocket all I could think of was 'round in chamber, safety off, sights on middle of target, hold 'em and squeeze 'em.' You know: USMC robot drill."

She wasn't sure she liked that. "And Dieter was already dead?" Anne sighed a great sigh. "Poor Dieter. I liked him so much. Do you remember him swinging the twins around the day he got his *Doktorat?*"

"Painfully. Let's change the subject. Maybe we better read the paperwork they gave me. I may have to go down there and make Charles de Gaulle's breakfast or something as a condition of parole."

They started reading the forty pages of documents Sam had been handed as he went out the door. Actually it was only twenty pages, since it was the same information, once in French and once in German. Anne went to work on the French while Sam went after the German.

"Crap," Sam said. "I can't leave Luxembourg. If we do for any reason I go right back to jail. "Does Harvey even know I was in jail?" Sam asked.

"Dolly, everybody in Europe knows you were in jail." She got up and took a pile of newspapers from the dining room table. "Here: read 'em and weep. Or maybe you'll like them. A couple of papers thought it was like a movie. You know: James Bond shoots the creepy crawlies."

"Oh, Christ, *Bild* says it was a KGB operation and CIA, which means me, broke it up."

"That ought to do your career some good."

"My career is over, maybe retroactively if Grant Natz has anything to do with it. Would you like to be married to a bank teller?"

"You'll be a very studly bank teller. Why can't you just call Harvey and tell him about Goshkorow?"

"When we first got here Harvey told me there's so many taps on his home and embassy phones that he can hardly hear who's calling. Plus, since they let me out of jail for reasons they aren't explaining, I assume our phone is tapped."

"Write a letter?"

"Harvey says the German won't admit it but they have a mail cover on everything going into the consulate or his house. Besides, how do I address it so the State Department mailroom doesn't read it first and say, 'Oh, this one's for the CIA guy'? It's the same with the embassy in Bonn. The State Department hates having us spies in the same embassy with them, so anytime something like happens it's all over the building in twelve minutes, including the local hires."

"OK. Back to square one. We'll think of something."

Sam sat there and had a chat with his brain. OK, brain, I know you've had a hard nine days and you don't want to do anything but sleep, but how about helping out a little here? His brain obviously heard him, for he found himself saying, "Of course, Charlie gets to be mailman."

Anne looked surprised. "Charlie? But he's not supposed to know that you're a . . . whatever it is you are now. And you're not supposed to know that he's been recruited. Well, at least the way he's been acting, we assume he's . . ." Anne threw up her hands. "The spy business is too complicated for human beings. Anyway, you know what I mean."

Sam realized his brain had let him down. "Yeah, I can't use Charlie except as a last resort. Let me see if I can sneak up to Frankfurt. This isn't Russia. There aren't that many Luxembourg cops and it's not like there's one standing on every corner with my picture in his pocket. Maybe there's a routine stakeout of Harvey's house or the consulate or the embassy in Bonn at the most. If that doesn't work, then we turn to Charlie. I mean, Charlie's a really sharp guy, but this spy bit has got him as excited as a five-year-old in a toy store. I think it's all he can do not to get somebody to silkscreen him a T-shirt that says, 'Don't ask me if I'm a CIA agent.' If we have to use him to get the message to Garcia it's all over anyway."

"A message to Garcia? What's that about?"

"Oh, it's one of those adventure stories set in the Spanish-American War. You know, plucky chap overcomes all obstacles to get a message to a Cuban insurgent general for the U.S. Army. It was reading that kind of stuff when I was ten that gets me into messes like this."

"My mother told me not to marry a Peter Pan type."

"She was right."

Then they turned to what on earth they were going to do next. Anne had already talked her parents and Sam's into not appearing on their doorstep, ready to rescue their babies and grandbabies. Not yet, not yet, was her message: I'll let you know when we need help. She knew if she'd just come out and said "no" all four of them would have been on the next plane. Plus the university had sent a sniffy letter saying that students who were in jail were obviously not in class, and what did he intend to do to rectify this situation? *Beheben* was the German word for rectify, and it was sprinkled liberally throughout the letter. Hypocrites, Sam thought. They don't give a damn if you show up or not until you embarrass them. Then all of a sudden it's a big deal. He had to do something though: if the university kicked him out he'd lose his *permis de sejour* and then he'd be between a rock and a hard place. The immigration people would want to deport him and the cops would want him right here where they could keep an eye on him for some unspecified reason. Cheez.

Plus, there was the 800-pound gorilla in the room. Why had the cops let him out on parole or bail or whatever his status was?

The next morning Sam was out and about at a much earlier hour than he generally preferred. He shivered as he remembered those

O-dark-hundred wakeup calls in Officer Candidates School where the friendly drill instructor flipped on the lights, turned over a couple of double-decker bunk beds with sleeping men in them, and announced, "Wakey wakey, girls. Outside in utilities and a light marching pack in four minutes." Then they ran around the parade ground for an endless amount of time in the dark. Why, he asked himself for the thousandth time, did I ever volunteer to do that?

He was wearing dungarees and a woolly pully, the British Army dark-green pullover wool sweater with a cushion sewn in the right shoulder to help absorb the impact from firing a rifle. It had been quite popular with Marines a couple of years ago and was now a hot item for fashionable young Brits who otherwise wore Carnaby Street clothing. That and a watch cap and he would be practically invisible in low-light conditions. He had a reversible light raincoat from his surveillance team gear wrapped up tightly in his hand. He had trotted in the dark to the first town east of Luxembourg, where the milk train stopped at 3:20 a.m. At least he had gotten out of Luxembourg City without getting caught. Let's see if I can get home too, he thought. He pulled the watch cap over his eyes and tried to doze until the train reached the border. Once again, off the train and through the unguarded woods and into West Germany. The Luxembourgers and West Germans were pretty perfunctory about guarding their mutual border.

By five a.m. he was on the fast train for Frankfurt. It was an overnight sleeper that started at Hook of Holland and ended up in Vienna. He was again sitting in a first-class car, one of the few that weren't sleeping cars. Harvey had told him to always go first class: the police, Harvey said, always gave first-class passengers a more cursory inspection and more often the benefit of the doubt, even though there was no reason to. It was the human condition, he supposed.

In Frankfurt he took a bus heading in the direction of Harvey's house in the suburbs. He got off a half-mile away and began a circuitous route to Harvey's house. There were narrow, tree-lined streets with a sprinkling of cars parked on them. The area was hilly, and the streets curved a lot as they climbed the hills. The houses were small-windowed and shrouded in shrubbery. It provided great cover. The Agency had provided reasonably good surveillance training, and God knows he'd spent a lot of time snooping and pooping through the woods in the Marines. Five minutes later he was satisfied that nobody was watching Harvey's house. Nobody seemed to be in it either. The house was dark and Harvey's government car and Charlotte's green Ford were gone too.

Time for Plan B. Anne and Alicia had become friendly during their surveillance training runs with Harvey. Anne had collected Alicia's address for her Christmas card list. Sam had been standing there at the time and had asked where her apartment was. The name Leopoldstrasse had stuck in his memory, as most things did. He looked at the Frankfurt street map he had brought with him. He calculated he ought to be able to get there before Alicia left for work, assuming she was in town. If Harvey had gone on home leave or something maybe she had too, in which case he was screwed. He had no Plan C for Frankfurt except to try to sneak back into Luxembourg without the cops noticing.

Another bus, another careful prowl, this time around Alicia's neighborhood. There was no evidence that anybody was taking an interest in her building. A number of people were marching German-like to bus stops. Since it was now daylight and he was out in public, the watch cap was back in Sam's pocket and he was wearing the raincoat tan-side out. He looked, he thought, more or less like everybody else. He was shielded by a bus shelter when Alicia came out of the apartment building and headed the other way. He followed, intending to catch up with her.

She surprised him by stopping at a street corner while he was still thirty feet behind her, turning around, and saying, "Good morning, Sam."

Sam stopped short. Then he closed up to her and said "How did you do that? Do you have eyes in the back of your head?" She shrugged. They crossed the street together and headed for a trolley stop. There was a small café there, already open of course, this being West Germany. They stepped in and ordered coffee. German coffee was strong and good.

Sam got right to it, "Alicia, I've got problems . . ."

"I know," she said. "They have newspapers here. Nice shooting, Tex. I imagine you want Harvey. He's on home leave. At least I think it's home leave. He blew out of here the day before yesterday in a big hurry. Charlotte went with him, so maybe it is home leave. Weird way to go about it. But tell me more about the shootout at the O.K. Corral. Gee, I wish I'd been there." Her plain face was lit up. She was clearly really into the boom and bang side of the intelligence business. He didn't have the heart to tell her that the last CIA-KGB brawl was in Vienna in 1946. She was twenty years too late. Well, wait a minute. If those two guys I tangled with were KGB . . .

"Alicia, I need to send a cable to COS Bonn. Will you do that for me?"

She looked at him for a long time. "You know, you and Anne and Harvey talk to me like I'm a real human being. You officers don't know what it's like being a secretary. It's like we're a piece of office furniture, there to be used when you want to and ignored the rest of the time. We girls talk and we think we know what the Negros back home feel like. So yes, that's totally illegal and I'll be in deep trouble and probably get fired and I'll send your damn cable anyway." She looked like she was trying not to cry.

"Please don't cry, Alicia. You're not going to get fired. You're right: I'm the officer, even if I'm just a lousy second lieutenant. You will be following my explicit orders. It's all my responsibility. If it hits the fan it'll all be my fault. OK?"

She was back to being her enigmatic self. "What does 'hit the fan' mean?"

"Um, it's a rather crude military term."

She nodded; now she got it. Alicia reached into her large purse and took out a steno book. "Start dictating, Lieutenant. Remember I can do 120 words a minute." It took him three minutes to cover the whole thing. Alicia told him how to she was going to put the addressee slugs on it, and the routings, in a way that would get it to Bonn and the CI staff at Headquarters but not EUR or anywhere else in the DDP.

"That's perfect, Alicia. Thank you very much. How do you learn stuff like that?"

"The galley slaves murmur among themselves when the overseer is off getting his whip winterized."

They exchanged phone numbers and ways to get ahold of each other through letters and newspaper ads. They picked some stock phrases to use in telephone calls to disguise what they were actually telling each other. Sam was back in Frankfurt in time for the ten a.m. train. Anne was going to pick him up just over the Luxembourg border at three p.m. It was in the Duchy of Luxembourg, and if the cops had intended him to stay within the city limits of Luxembourg, they hadn't put it in writing.

Anne dropped Sam off in front of the Maison de Ville. He went in and made his daily check-in with whoever was on the front desk of the *Surete* office at the moment. That person checked him off a list and nodded in dismissal without asking for identification. That was just as well, since Sam didn't have any. The last he had seen of his passport, *carte de sejour* and driver's license, they were being swept into a brown accordion folder by Charles de Gaulle. The cops' method of counting noses could come in handy, he thought. *Maybe Charlie could check in for me in a pinch.*

He came out the front door and started walking towards Charlie's office. Charlie had skipped the Beaux-Arts office buildings on the rue de la Reine. Instead he had renovated a series of rooms in a picture-postcard seventeenth-century building on the

Rue de Bec, which was smack in the middle of the Old City. Sam hadn't gone twenty steps when, surprised, he ducked into a shop. He closed the door, turned, and looked out the window. He had seen the man just coming out of the Hotel le Royal before. Where was that? The man was middle-aged and well-dressed, at least by German standards. He looked kind of Armenian or something. That was it: he and Anne had seen him walking along the waterfront in Koblenz last month. He was with the pear-shaped guy whom Sam had also seen somewhere before.

Sam didn't believe in coincidences anymore. He turned to nod at the shopkeeper's cheery *"Bon jour, Monsieur,"* asked for something the shopkeeper didn't have, expressed sorrow and despair when the shopkeeper didn't have one, said *adieu*, and was back out of the shop in under eight seconds. Let's see how good we are at one-man surveillance, Sam thought.

The Armenian-looking guy walked around town as if he hadn't a care in the world, and was certainly not worried about being followed. He went to the offices of the *Luxemburger Wort*. OK. So he's another journalist checking stories. Maybe this guy really is just another journalist. I'd believe that except for that Koblenz meeting. He and Pear-Shaped were talking serious business in the middle of a well-known Soviet stomping grounds, so pardon me for being suspicious.

Then the man went to the university, first to the registrar's office, then the Journalism Institute. Sam felt a sudden chill: the man was tracing him. Still, the guy was doing what any reporter coming late to a story would do. He was retracing the steps of the early birds. Let's not jump to conclusions here. Sam was by now sick of sitting in cafes sipping coffee, although thank God Luxembourg was littered with cafes, trattoria, *Weinstubes*, and restaurants with outside tables. It made tailing people easy, and lurking almost respectable.

Then training and common sense kicked in. C'mon stupid, look and see if *you've* picked up a tail. It sounded ridiculous, but then being on parole for a murder rap didn't feel all that real either. Tucking a coin by his saucer, he slid out and around the side of the building where a *Gasse* led behind two ancient buildings and around to Place d'Armes. He moved briskly down the alley and slowed when he reached the Place. There he walked over to a nearby newsstand and began inspecting a carrel of newspapers, stepping around it and looking down the street as he did.

There he was! The tail might as well be carrying a sign. He looked so much like the three guys he and Anne had seen in Bonn only a few weeks ago that he wanted to laugh. It was a young guy, square-shouldered and wearing the same kind of cheap suit and earnest expression as his colleagues in Bonn. Only instead of following a colleague with a funny hat he was following — well, who was he following? Me or the Armenian? As he stepped away from the carrel he noticed that it consisted of dozens of Italian newspapers. Oops. Bad tradecraft.

He waited. The earnest young man was not looking around for him. Instead his eyes were on the Armenian-looking guy. The Armenian-looking guy walked around the far edge of Places d'Armes and turned into the Rue du St Esprit. Jesus! He's heading for my place, Sam thought. If he gets near Anne and the kids I'll tear his head off. If he turns out to be the cultural editor for the *Los Angeles Times* they can just add it to my charge sheet. But I bet he isn't. Sam turned around, sprinted back down the *Gasse* and headed for the promenade along the Old City walls. He'd beat the man back to the apartment and be waiting if he showed up. All that running was going to come in useful for something besides killing time after all.

Sam's apartment building was cut into the side of a hill. The best side, the one with the balconies, looked across the Rue du St Esprit to the Old City. You had to climb the 47 steps to the first landing to get to the front door. It was around in back on the ground floor, with seven stories of apartments, two to a floor, above it. The basement carried the posher name of *rez-de-chaussee*, which it wasn't, since it was above the street on one side and below it on the other. In a helpful gesture to Americans, the second floor was numbered the first floor in Europe.

The Armenian was just coming up the Rue du St Esprit when Sam popped into the apartment, said, "Hello everybody," to Anne and the twins, and disappeared into the bigger bedroom. He came out a minute later with his camera and a box with a 250-millimeter lens in it. Unscrewing the camera's lens, he inspected the camera body, checking to see there was film in it. Next he screwed the big lens in and went rooting in the hall closet, the camera in one hand. Anne stood looking quizzical. The twins hoped Daddy was bouncing around like this preparatory to doing something goofy that would make them laugh. He did this a lot, after all.

Sam said, "All will be explained," over his shoulder, screwed the camera to the tripod he had found in the back of the closet, and went out onto the balcony. The Armenian was just turning towards the stairs. Sam turned and went into the back bedroom. It had a more mundane view of the parking lot. He extended the legs of the tripod and set the camera up facing out the window and down. The twins, disappointed that Daddy wasn't doing something goofy, rushed over to see if they could help knock the camera over. Sam mouthed "chocolate" at Anne while he fended off little hands. Anne got the message.

"Chocolate, chums," she called, heading for the kitchen. The twins shot out of the room. Sam stood at an angle to the window. He had long ago checked his windows from the street at all angles and most light conditions. The view was always obscured by reflections. He waited and, sure enough, the Armenian-looking guy, clearly huffing and puffing, appeared at the top of the stairs. He ostentatiously consulted a map. Click. Shutter speed 1/60th. After all, what tourist would be wandering around this almost blue-collar neighborhood? Click. He squinted at the map and made a note — license plate numbers, I betcha, Sam thought — and then wandered up to the connecting street. There the square-shouldered cop, who had obviously come up the other way, had no choice but to march straight past him and off to the intersection with the Rue du St Esprit, a hundred yards away in the wrong direction. Click. Rookie, Sam thought. He bundled the camera and lens back into their places and barreled out the door. Anne's "You haven't explained all, dear" was almost inaudible as he ran out.

The elevator was just stopping on their little landing as Sam came out his door. The heavy elevator door swung open and Kurt came out, home for lunch. Walking back and forth from the *Surete* didn't leave Kurt much time to eat, Angelica had explained to Anne, but it was *sparsam* . . . she had hesitated. "Thrifty?" Anne guessed. "Yes," Angelica had said, nodding. That was exactly the right word. Kurt held the elevator door for Sam and, as Sam smiled his thanks and stepped in, patted him on the shoulder. Sam was confused. The angry Kurt at the *Surete* had been replaced by a Kurt who had given him a friendly pat on the shoulder. His expression had been — what? Sympathetic, empathetic? Certainly not angry. What was that all about? And Anne had said that Angelica had told her that Kurt was still in a foul mood, storming around their apartment. He had even growled at one of his children, an unprecedented event. His daughters normally treated Kurt like a stuffed animal. They usually climbed all over him and tickled him when he was trying to watch a soccer match on television.

Sam caught the Armenian again walking up the Rue de Hopital to, well, where else? So the Armenian had heard the story about the other Russian not being dead but in the hospital instead. That was not good news. After that, things were uneventful. The man came out of the hospital after a long twenty minutes and walked back down into the Old City to the Hotel Le Royal. When one of Luxembourg's few taxis pulled up to the hotel entrance ten minutes later, Sam made a quick guess and started walking fast towards the railroad station.

Sure enough, the taxi appeared at the *Hauptbahnhof* just as Sam slid into the second-class restaurant on the ground floor of the station. The Armenian looked at his watch and walked into the first-class bar-restaurant. Since the train board had showed expresses going in each direction, both arriving in the next twenty minutes, Sam snuck into the station and bought a first-class round-trip ticket to Frankfurt, and then a first-class ticket to Bonn. The clerk frowned. Sam gave him his friendliest smile. "*Mütti*" he said, pointing towards Bonn. "*Tante* Edna" he said, pointing toward Frankfurt. Mommy going in one direction and Aunt Edna in the other sounded reasonable to the clerk. He smiled back and forgot all about him, which was what Sam had in mind.

If he goes beyond Frankfurt or Bonn I'm screwed, he thought. I don't have a passport so I can't leave Germany, not on a train anyway. He slumped over a coffee in the second class, waiting for the Armenian to finish his drink and go wait for his train. At least it was almost five p.m. and a lot of people were traveling, so he could stand on the platform in the middle of a crowd. There! The Armenian was walking out the door as the station loudspeaker announced the arrival of the *Schnellzug* for Koblenz. The Armenian went down the underpass and up the right side set of stairs towards the first-class end of the platform. Sam turned left towards second class.

The train, as almost always was the case, was within ten seconds of being exactly on time. It would stand in the station for precisely ninety seconds before departing. It was assumed that the lame and the halt were going to move out smartly if they intended on traveling. Sam got on the first car of the second-class section, which was coupled to the last car in first class. He didn't see anyone who looked like a cop on the platform, so maybe he had been overcautious this morning. Or was he just lucky now? He hadn't seen the square-shouldered cop again. Where had he gone? Had he broken off pursuit when the Armenian got to the station, or had he been shaken before, when the guy had taken a cab? Well, another of life's little mysteries.

The next stop would be Koblenz, where he would change trains to go either north to Bonn or south to Frankfurt. What to do in Koblenz? He was lucky not to have been spotted so far. Well, maybe not so much. Sam knew every alley and *Gasse* in Luxembourg, and could almost always stay out of sight. And guessing where somebody was going and being on a stakeout when he got there defeated most countersurveillance methods too. So it hadn't all been luck.

Still, he wasn't going to get away with that in Bonn or Frankfurt. Neither the Soviet Embassy in Bonn nor the consulate in Frankfurt was far from the train station — he'd scouted both as part of his surveillance training — so he'd just take a chance. He would dive off the train when the Armenian got off and try to get there ahead of him. If the Armenian instead went to a hotel or the airport or any of a thousand other places he might go, then, well, he was screwed.

At Koblenz, Sam couldn't see through the crowd, so he stepped off the train and stood looking at the two connecting trains. Which one? He wait for agonizing seconds trying to spot the Armenian. There he was. The Frankfurt train. He ran for it. The train gave a blast as the air brakes released before the steps lifted and the automatic doors snapped shut. Sam just made it. He decided that in Frankfurt he'd be off the train as the doors opened and run around the back of the station. Then he would head for the Soviet Consulate and hope for the best.

The train arrived on time, of course. Sam was out and running just as the doors hissed open. People run in stations all the time, but not in the streets of Frankfurt after dark. So Sam walked at a forced march pace for the half-mile to the Soviet Consulate. His reversible raincoat was turned to the black side and the watch cap covered most of his head. He sidled into a gap in an eight-foot-tall row of hedges across the street from the consulate and waited.

After five minutes he decided he was a damn fool. Of all the places the Armenian might go, this wasn't one of them. It was getting time to try again to slide back into Luxembourg without the cops noticing. Then he saw the cab. It drove past his hedge and stopped in front of the consulate. The Armenian got out and paid the driver and walked up to the door. He pushed the annunciator button and said something into the microphone. After a minute's pause, the door opened. Journalist my ass, Sam thought.

It was well after midnight when Sam slipped into their apartment. He tiptoed in and was heading for the bedroom when he saw a note on the side table. It was just light enough to read Anne's writing: "My friend Alicia called and said she was passing though and would come to visit me tomorrow. You got the kids." So, Alicia had gotten her cables through and was coming to town with instructions from either the COS or Harvey or both. Hot damn, the game's afoot, Sherlock!

CHAPTER FOURTEEN

Harvey had no intention of landing running when he got to Washington. Landing running was for amphibious assaults. Harvey agreed with the KGB: intelligence operations were best conducted by hiding in the bushes and watching what the opposition was doing. He and Charlotte had parted at Dulles airport. She was going on to visit their daughter in Cleveland, where he would join them as soon as he could. Assuming, of course, that he ever could. God knows what the Deputy Director had in mind. He walked her to her connecting flight, which itself was a rare piece of luck for them.

Dulles had opened six years before to great fanfare, with President John F. Kennedy himself doing the honors. It had since taken on the aspect of a beautifully designed abandoned warehouse. Eero Saarinen's terminal building stood almost empty. So did the six-lane divided highway connecting Dulles to Washington. Dulles was the butt of a thousand jokes, some bitter, about the government having come up with a solution for which there was no problem. There could not have been more than a couple of dozen flights a day out of Dulles, in contrast to the always-packed National Airport downtown, whose control tower you could almost see from the Capitol steps. But the Lufthansa clerk in Frankfurt had sworn there was a connecting flight to Cleveland that night and, being German, he was right.

Harvey started to wipe Charlotte's lipstick off his mouth, and then decided he wanted a souvenir and stopped. He headed for the rental-car counter. No self-respecting Washington taxi would deign to drive all the way out to Dulles. Local taxis in the barren Virginia countryside were unheard of. Most of the land around there looked like it had when Mosby's Raiders swept through towards the end of the Civil War. The vehicle of choice out here was generally a worn pickup truck with a gun rack, and, the wise guys said, a bumper sticker reading, "Guns don't kill people: I do."

The rental was a Plymouth with jet-fighter tail fins. He headed down the empty expressway toward the city. Like many Foreign Service officers on home leave, Harvey would stay at one of the short-term rental apartments clustered around the new State Department building in Foggy Bottom. From there he could either drive out to Headquarters or take the Blue Bird shuttle. All things considered he would just as soon skip the Blue Bird. For a supposedly clandestine organization, the Agency support people could be pretty dense. The Blue Bird shuttle, named after a Southern bus-building company, ran in a loop from Headquarters to New State (which was an affectation of old-timers. Old State was the executive office building next to the White House, which hadn't housed the State Department in over a century), to the supposedly secret listening and observation post catty-corner across Sixteenth Street from the Soviet Chancellery, to the drab concrete office buildings the Pomponio Brothers had built in Rosslyn, just across Key Bridge from Georgetown. As a result Rosslyn became known as "CIA City," and Agency employees seen entering or leaving the Blue Birds were subject to amused comments from friends and colleagues who had seen them and who made cracks about how they thought they were Air Force civilian employees — ha ha.

Harvey checked into his slightly battered efficiency apartment, got a parking pass for the small lot behind the building, and called the number he had been given. It was a Maryland area code.

"Hello," said a polite but neutral voice on the third ring.

"This is Harvey Masters."

"Oh, Harvey, of course. I've been expecting your call. It's Tom K. here."

Wow, Harvey thought. The Deputy Director's home phone number. I'm getting up in the world.

"I had wanted you to drop by as soon as you came home, but decided it might not be helpful for us to be seen together at Headquarters."

Ah, so it was going to be like that. Harvey hoped this was a secure line. Well, hell, it was the boss's home phone. It better be. "Yes, sir."

"Would you check in tomorrow and go to room 2C34? There'll be a packet there that will explain all." There was a hesitation. "Well, as much as I know anyway. Bill Hood or his people will get you everything you need."

"Yes, sir." Wow. Bill Hood. Another OSS type. He and Harvey knew each other.

"I'm sorry to drag you over here on such short notice, but I needed a grown-up with an outsider's viewpoint. As you may have already gathered, we may have a little tong war developing here, so keep your head down, please."

"Yes, sir."

"Thank you, Harvey. I realize this is all quite unorthodox, but that is precisely why we're doing it this way. Good night."

"Good night, sir."

The next morning Harvey, who had no Headquarters identification, parked in the visitors' lot right outside the front door. Inside he was given a visitor's pass and an uncomfortable plastic chair to sit on while he waited for an escort. Harvey, who had been back to Headquarters many times, had provided himself with a book to read. He was just settling into it when a familiar voice said, "Harvey!"

He looked up. Well, a nice surprise: it was Ross Callahan, the German Deputy Desk Chief. He was afraid it would be Grant Natz. No, that's right, Grant's been sent to the CIA's equivalent of the Eastern Front.

"Hello, Ross. Are you my babysitter today?"

"Nope. You're my new boss. And I'm your entire staff. Shall we adjourn to your office? We have to get you some ID first, of course."

Ross walked him over to the personnel office. The personnel people took his picture and gave him a laminated ID card with a cord to hang around his neck, just like everyone else wore. Harvey's, however, had a series of letters around the edge of the card, seven in all. Personnel went on at irritating length about the vast access these little letters gave Harvey to staff and documents of enormous secrecy. They also gave him an off-pissing security lecture about how he should protect the vital information that he might be entrusted with. Since they were barely cleared to read the cafeteria menu, it came across as unnecessarily condescending.

Freed eventually, they headed for room 2C34. "2C34 is Counterintelligence staff territory, isn't it?" Harvey asked.

"Yes indeedy."

"They tell you what we are supposed to do?"

"Nope. I'm just supposed to do what you tell me."

Harvey snorted. "I wish I knew what to tell you."

Room 2C34 was an off-white room with five gray metal desks and two four-drawer safes. It was otherwise empty. Ross had the combination for the safe nearest the door and started spinning the knob. "Twice left to 34, once right to 12, one left to 19." He opened the safe. There was one thin tan manila envelope in the top drawer. There was nothing else in the safe. The writing on the envelope said, "EYES ONLY HARVEY MASTERS" and was double-sealed. In earlier days, it would have said, "EYES ALONE," an MI6-ism that was dying off as the older OSS guys did.

Harvey started tearing the envelope open. "Well Ross, let's see if it's a letter bomb."

It wasn't, but it was, Harvey thought, mighty interesting. The top sheets were a letter to him from the Deputy marked "TOP SECRET." There was, Harvey noted, no "EYES ONLY" restriction. He put his feet up on the desk and started reading. Ross, having nothing else to do, put his feet up on another desk and contemplated taking a nap. He and Maria had suddenly gotten carried away last night and then again this morning. He was feeling like Mel Brooks' 1000 Year Old Man. Some spark had set them off after dinner. It had progressed from comfortable warmth to an easy intimacy to a sudden KABOOM! He was too old to fall in love again, but this sure was a damn good imitation.

Ross wondered how closely Harvey was going to hold this operation. Harvey had a good reputation, but he was known to be a member of the intelligentsia. Ross was just a street guy. He leaned back a little further to think about it. Then a voice woke him from a half-doze.

"Ross, read his." Harvey was handing him the DDP's instructions. Wow, I get to sit at the adult table, Ross thought. He started reading. It was quite straightforward: the boss was uncomfortable about how the INGRESS operation had been handled and was even more uncomfortable that the CITADEL material hadn't been tested. The Deputy gave then a twofold mission: develop a detailed history of the INGRESS operation and come up with a plan to test the CITADEL material without loosening the bigot list restrictions too much. They could use whatever resources they needed.

Then they read the rest of the package. It contained a copy of the same INGRESS case file that the boss had pouched to Bonn, plus the briefings the boss had been given on CITADEL by van Claire, and van Claire's two-page précis of the hundreds of pages of documents CITADEL had provided.

The last documents were administrative. They were to be known as TEST GROUP B, and given an appropriations code to charge expenses against. There was also a memorandum authorizing them to speak with any CIA employee up to the level of their clearances, which Harvey had already noted were very high indeed. All employees were instructed to tender their complete co-operation. The memo ended with the traditional injunction, "Fail Not!" and a scrawled signature.

"Jeez," Ross said, scratching his head. "I think this even gives us permission to bang his other secretary, the one with the giant boobs."

Harvey looked at him. "Judging by your appearance I would guess you are currently incapable of molesting anyone. What is your appreciation of the situation?"

Playtime was over. Ross put his feet down on the floor, sat up straight and started: "The only thing that ties these operations together is that van Claire is the case officer for both. The INGRESS operation is over and the agent is dead. We need to know how and why INGRESS got dead and what in hell Sam Carpenter is doing mixed up in this. But that all comes second." Sorry, Sam.

"First, CITADEL is ongoing and is potentially either enormously rewarding or enormously dangerous. So I think we need to focus on CITADEL and move quickly if this thing turns out to be a dangle. The Deputy's support and our being housed within Counterintelligence staff areas are advantages. The disadvantages are obvious. You're not senior enough to browbeat the Brahmins, and I'm just a street guy who will be absolutely no use to you in a Headquarters investigation.

"Finally, we neither of us know how the boss's staff set CITADEL up. We need somebody senior to help and we need to get our own researcher/administrative officer." He paused. "I've got the researcher in mind."

"And he is?" Harvey asked.

"She, boss. Maria DeAngelo. She's an assistant on the German Desk, and what she doesn't know about the workings of Europe, the Soviet Bloc and the old East Europe divisions isn't worth knowing. She also knows staff and the admin stuff."

"She have anything to do with you arriving today looking like something the cat dragged in?"

"That's purely a coincidence. No, really, Harvey — boss, sir — she's the real deal. We need her."

Harvey looked at him and rubbed his eyes. He sighed. "I can't think of a more stupid way to recruit people for this little squad than picking a street goon's girlfriend as our Headquarters anchor, but OK, get her up here at lunch; let me talk to her. If I like her, she can cut her own orders detailing her over here." Then he smiled grimly and looked around the barren room. "But no sex at the office."

Maria DeAngelo arrived promptly at noon. She walked to the chair directly opposite Harvey, sat down, pulling her skirt towards her knees, folded her hands in her lap, looked directly at Harvey and smiled. The usually unflappable Ross dithered, and then sat down in the corner. "Good afternoon, Mr. Masters. Ross tells me you're looking for a researcher and executive officer." Harvey smiled back. An intelligent, good-looking woman with fine eyes and what his wife, Charlotte, would call a zaftig figure.

"Yes, Miss DeAngelo. Could you tell me something about yourself and your background and skills?"

"Certainly. I'm 37 years old and have been at CIA since I graduated from GW. Sorry, George Washington University downtown. In the 16 years I've been here I have advanced to the lordly grade of GS-9, which is as far as I'm going to get. I know my way around every research resource in the Agency and know how to make the administrative apparatus cough up what I need to know. I am a loyal CIA employee even if I hate the way you people treat women. In answer to your raised eyebrow, yes, I have a relationship with Ross Callahan and would go to great lengths to ensure that no ax chops off his thick Irish head."

"Thank you. Do you know anything about this little unit we are establishing?"

"No, I know nothing. But I know you and Ross."

"Me?" Harvey said.

"Code-named GRUMPY WOLF, you were real OSS. Almost got caught by the Gestapo near Louvain in 1944. Transferred to CIA in 1947, did good work in the old East Europe Division, got caught up the pissing contest when they melded the hardcore ex-OSS, émigrés and Jews from East Europe with the WASPS from West Europe Division. You lost, and became a terminal GS-14. Your secretary, Alicia, thinks you're the nicest man who ever lived except her father." She stopped.

Harvey was quite surprised. "How do you know all that?"

"The secretaries and assistants at Headquarters are like the Negro servants downtown. We are neither heard nor seen, but we're there all the time and hear and see everything."

"Oh, you'll do, Miss DeAngelo. You'll most certainly do. Welcome to our little group, and call me Harvey, please. Before you sign up though, let me warn you: I think this is a suicide squad. Whatever we do or don't do here, we'll make important people angry with us. And if we find something very bad, the big boss is just going to sigh sadly and wave goodbye. Are you still sure you want to join?"

Maria crossed what turned out to be rather admirable legs and smiled generously. "Harvey, all three of us are shark bait anyway. What have we got to lose? Oh, and call me Maria, please."

The door opened, there was a polite cough, and a gloomy man in an expensive charcoal-gray suit slid into the room. He was well over six feet tall, quite thin, and pale-faced. He gave a courtly nod and said, "Gentlemen, pretty lady, I am Craig Withers. Bill Hood sent me down to greet you and to offer my modest services. May I?" He nodded towards a chair, swooped around it and seated himself quite elegantly, pulling his trouser legs up slightly in the same manner as Maria had pulled her hem down. He smiled what was meant to be a benevolent smile at them, although to Ross he looked like a vulture settling down over a nice fresh road kill.

Harvey knew who he was. A bit of a legend, Withers was known in CIA operational circles as The Abominable No Man. His doubts and arguments had cancelled dozens of operations. His critics said he had done more to bring CIA operations to a halt than all the efforts of the KGB put together. His supporters — and a lot of them peed in the executive washroom — said he had killed more nitwit operations than could be believed. They swore that there never would have been a Bay of Pigs if Craig hadn't been off having his appendix removed when the vote had been taken to proceed.

Craig crossed his legs female-style, the knees close together. He continued: "Harvey, your reputation precedes you. But I don't believe I know this gentleman or the lady."

Introductions were made and Harvey was left to wonder just what kind of a reputation had preceded him. Then Craig Withers continued: "Bill was a bit vague as to what you are up to, except that it involves peeping into Clay van Claire's undies and rushing upstairs to tell the Deputy Director what you saw. I certainly would approve of such an undertaking." He nodded at Maria. "I assume the pretty lady is your administrative officer." He beamed at her. "If you would be so kind as to accompany me across the hall, we have a couple of cables with Counterintelligence slugs on them which have been looking for a home. They came in last night. I shall introduce you to our representative on the Cable Secretariat whilst you get settled in." He rose gracefully, knees still together. He nodded benevolently again and left, Maria following him.

She was back ten minutes later, slamming the door with unnecessary force. "That old pervert goosed me as I was leaving," she said. She glared at Ross as if it were his fault. "And don't you get all Sir Galahad about it. All you operations officers treat the secretaries and assistants like you're drunken sailors in an Okinawan whorehouse." She extended three cables to Harvey. "You'll want to read these, boss. All is explained." She hesitated. "All is explained enough to make things even more complicated."

Harvey, with Ross looking over his shoulder, read the two cables. The first was from Frankfurt, sent by Alicia of all people, and . . . he hesitated at an unfamiliar dispatch pseudonym, and then said, "My God, that's Sam."

"You were expecting somebody else?"

"I thought he was in jail."

"So did we all. And what is Alicia doing sending cables on her own hook?"

"Breaking all the rules. And she's such an orderly little soul. Sam obviously put her up to it."

"Back to business. Who's Goshkorow? And Sam says INGRESS said, 'But I gave him Goshkorow.' Who's him? Van Claire?"

"So it would seem."

"But the stuff the Deputy gave us says van Claire claims he never met INGRESS a second time."

"Clay van Claire would never tell a lie."

"Yeah, right. But why lie to the Deputy Director?"

"Because he thought he could get away with it. But what's he trying to conceal?"

"That he knows about Goshkorow, whoever Goshkorow is."

"Oh shit, oh dear. I see what Maria means; every explanation makes things more confusing."

The second cable was from Bonn. The Chief said that he was aware that Alicia had no business sending cables and thought she ought to be commended for it. Why and how Sam got to Frankfurt was beyond knowing at the moment, but he had obviously come looking to report to Harvey. The COS had subsequently told Alicia to close Frankfurt Base down, go to Luxembourg, debrief Sam from the beginning, and take Sam a present. Then she was to get back to Bonn and tell him all. The Chief also said that he had received notification from the Deputy Director that Harvey was setting up a unit at Headquarters to do he didn't know precisely what. Bonn would be happy to cooperate, but he didn't want any of his station officers risking their careers by getting involved in a Headquarters tong war. Consequently he would handle the German end of this investigation himself. He awaited instructions.

"The first thing we have to do is empty that dead drop," Harvey said. "I shouldn't have paid any attention to the PURPLE restriction and done it myself the day after INGRESS got killed."

"You think there's anything in it?"

"Don't know. But INGRESS was supposed to have been at a trade conference in Frankfurt the day before he turned up in Luxembourg. And suddenly two guys showed up in Luxembourg and killed him."

"Do we know how or why yet?"

"Not why, but the press reports were talking about the witnesses seeing a broken hypodermic at the scene, and nobody said INGRESS was shot. My guess is Sam broke up a quiet KGB assassination."

"So INGRESS knew something the KGB didn't want INGRESS telling anybody. INGRESS told Sam it was about somebody named Goshkorow."

"Whom van Claire says he didn't know anything about."

"You think there's anything in the drop? Where is it?"

"It's a post restante box in the main Frankfurt post office. Let's tell Bonn to empty it before somebody else does."

"Cable will be ready in five minutes," Maria said.

"You saw the rest of the stuff the Deputy gave me. Van Claire changed his mind and is pushing through the release of intel that that aide to Willy Brandt is a Stasi agent. He's meeting the bigot list committee to tell them it's going out today."

"That's not much of a bigot list if we know about it."

"The boss unilaterally expended it. He's number one on the bigot list."

"Gee, Headquarters is a wonderful place," Ross said.

"Yeah, well, you'll have to leave it for a while. I want you in Bonn to nose around and see what the reaction is. What's this Kirst guy's access to classified material? What has he done to make him recruitable? Most important: is he really a Stasi agent? You know the drill."

"Indeed I do." Ross turned to Maria. "Dolly, will you cut me orders and get a plane ticket for Bonn and send a cable to Chief of Station Germany telling him I'm coming? Oh, and give him a précis of what this is all about?"

"I can. Well, I know the people who can, which is much the same thing. I bet you and Harvey and the Deputy don't, though." She paused at the door. "You know, until just now I was wondering which set of restrooms Withers uses." Then she was gone.

Harvey looked after her admiringly. "She's really something, Ross. Nice find."

Ross nodded. "You don't know the half of it. I assume I tell my German Station contact everything we know?"

"I think Chief of Station will want to handle this himself. Partly because he doesn't want his troops dropped into this can of worms and partly because he'd like to do van Claire one in the eye."

"I have a good feeling we're going to get this mess sorted out. Or is it a bad feeling?"

"Both is good. Oh, we'll figure it out. It's just that when we do and we come running home to tell Mother, will Mother really want to hear about it?"

CHAPTER FIFTEEN

Upstairs, Clay van Claire was in a hurry to get to Europe too. He'd gotten an urgent signal from CITADEL. It was a simple matter of a personals ad in the *International Herald Tribune*, suitably worded. CITADEL said that the old ways were the best. Van Claire shrugged. This tradecraft business was a lot of crap, in his opinion. All that holding agents' hands and listening to them whine about how hard it all was and meeting in inconvenient places took up time. In his view a carefully designed series of briefings was what got operations off to a good start and kept them there. With everything proceeding smoothly at Headquarters, the fieldwork could be done by practically anybody. Still, being the case officer for CITADEL gave him the luster that some people accorded skilled field operatives, and also a lot more control.

Today's briefing would be tricky and would require all of his skill and finesse. The DDP was pressing for field tests of the CITADEL material. The bigot list had been amended once again, which was probably a no-no, so that it now consisted of himself, that creep Withers from Counterintelligence, the Chief, Europe,

Rogers Cline from Soviet Bloc, and the Deputy Director himself. The Deputy, thank God, wouldn't be there today. He ran through the briefing points in his head and then went into the conference room, taking solace from the picture of Allen Dulles hanging on the wall. Allen knew how to run a briefing: van Claire had sat and listened in the back row when Dulles had gotten some outrageous stuff nodded through committees without a question.

The three men already sitting there looked at him expectantly. They had been told this was a meeting of considerable importance.

"Good morning," he said briskly. "Let's get right down to business. Today we are releasing the name of the Stasi agent on Willy Brandt's staff to the *Bundesnachrichtendienst*, the BND. I am meeting with the BND station Chief in Washington" — he paused to look at his watch — "in one hour. We expect that this will be the cause of some commotion in Germany, but that can't be helped. It will, we expect, earn us the undying love of both the BND and the Christian Democrat wing of the government. It will also give Willy Brandt and the Socialists something to chew on when they continue their insistence on sucking up to the Soviets. This ought to give them the impetus to keep their skirts clean." He paused for comment. He had deliberately kept saying "we" rather than "I" in the clear expectation that the listeners would get the hint and understand that "we" was van Claire and the Deputy, standing shoulder to shoulder, bound together in total agreement.

Chief, Europe was looking dubious. "Are you quite sure, Clay? This Hans Georg Kirst, the supposed spy, is well-known as a staunch supporter of the U.S., just like his boss. Have you coordinated with State on this? They think highly of Willy Brandt too."

Van Claire looked at him. "I don't think it would be wise to cut State in on a very delicate operation like this. They have no understanding of the danger CITADEL is in, and how an indiscreet word at a cocktail party could destroy a high-level penetration of the KGB."

The Chief looked unappeased. Van Claire went on: "We should not underestimate our opponents. Of course the KGB is going to go after what would appear to us as being the least likely candidate for recruitment. They are clever bastards. Finally, we must remember that this is on a bigot list because we have a traitor out there," and here he waved in the general direction of the rest of the building. "Our primary mission is to discover who he is. If we have to break a little furniture in the process, well, so be it."

Europe sat silent. They all knew that the opportunity to uncover the traitor was the trump card.

There was another throat being cleared. "We're, ah, not releasing this information a couple of months before the elections in the hope of keeping the right-wingers in the chancellorship and keeping Willy Brandt and his Socialists as the junior partners in a shaky coalition, are we? I thought that was a no-no these days."

"Certainly not," van Claire said, too fast. "The only reason we are doing it now is for pressing operational reasons. Besides, we are releasing this information on a top-secret basis only to the BND, who I trust are also professionals and will use it solely to permit the BfV to start an investigation to see whether a criminal case can be mounted. The BfV, the *Bundesamt für Verfassungsschutz* is . . ."

"The new Gestapo."

"I was about to say, the West German FBI can be counted on to be professional."

"C'mon Clay, that's bullshit," Rogers Cline from Soviet Bloc said. "The BND and the BfV will have a contest to see who can leak it first. They're desperate for some credibility. Every week it seems there's another Stasi agent or ex-Gestapo type surfaced as one of their employees. Those guys would kill their own mothers for good press." He paused, "Hell, some of them probably have killed their own mothers."

"Do you really want those remarks in the minutes of this meeting?"

Cline waved his hands in a backing off gesture. "Just an observation. You needn't make a federal case out of it."

"Clay," said Craig Withers in his most soothing tones, "do we have any corroboration of these accusations?"

"Just how many KGB agents have we recruited lately?" Clay asked. "The answer is precisely one. My guy: CITADEL."

"Now Clay, I hadn't known you had recruited him. I thought he was a walk-in. May I offer my congratulations? I ask again: does CIA have any independent information that this" — and here he peered at his briefing sheet — "Hans Georg Kirst is a Stasi agent?"

"I've answered that question, Craig. We are not working for the FBI. Let me remind you that the Central Intelligence Agency is not a law-enforcement operation. We are not required to follow the Rules of Criminal Procedure. The evidence gathering is for the Germans to do. That is what the BfV *does* for a living. Are there any further questions?"

"Just the one unanswered one," Withers continued.

"Do you claim that it is not the mission of CIA to collect and disseminate intelligence of value to us and our allies? Do you propose to let a traitor sit in the office of Willy Brandt, our strongest supporter in West Germany, and sandbag him by not telling him he's being betrayed? Is the role of CI Staff solely to say no to everything and never tell anybody anything? That means you're defining our mission as to do nothing. If our purpose is then to do nothing, why should CIA exist at all?"

"Just the unanswered question please. You're really not going to answer, are you?"

Van Claire had had it. "Meeting adjourned." Clay was most unhappy. Shit. I needed an Allen Dulles show today and all three of them are dragging their feet. Could somebody have put them up to this? No: nobody else knows. He looked at his watch. Time for lunch with the BND guy and then off to the airport. I wonder what CITADEL's in such a hurry about?

Lunch with the BND went better, but it was not what van Claire had expected. The BND guy, not surprisingly, had wanted to meet at the Rathskeller, a real German restaurant on Sixteenth Street. Clay had insisted on the Rive Gauche. If the Kennedy clan had made the only French restaurant in Washington into the family mess hall, then it was good enough for van Claire. Besides, the maitre d' was good at fawning, which ought to impress the BND guy.

The BND guy looked more like a mathematics professor at a second-string university than a German intelligence officer. Clay was not impressed, but forged on anyway. The German had looked a little wary of the menu and raised an eyebrow at the New York prices on the entrees, but he ordered politely and did an excellent job of executing the liaison niceties. There were the usual expressions of warm feelings between the two services, a general admiration of their mutual intellectual abilities, and a fine appreciation of the close and enduring relationship between West Germany and America, World War II notwithstanding.

Clay cut to the chase as the entrée plates were being cleared. The German waved off dessert, patting his tummy in mock despair. Clay put his elbows on the table and leaned forward. "I greatly regret to have to tell you that we have it from an unimpeachable source that Herr Hans Georg Kirst of your *Auswärtiges Amt*, your State Department, is an agent of the Stasi."

The BND guy slid past the insult of having his own language translated for him. It was mistranslated to boot: *Auswärtiges Amt* is foreign ministry, not state department. Nor did the revelation of a spy in his midst seem to bother him. In fact, he sighed in relief.

"Ah, thank God. When you called we thought you were going to tell us you found another Nazi. So Hans is a Stasi agent? I would have thought that most unlikely. He is so pro-American, you know, and the Socialists criticize him and his boss for being that way. Can you tell me more? It would be most helpful to the BfV." Since the Germans most desperately did not want another Gestapo, the

BfV was so designed as to be almost useless. There were so many internal and external controls that the employees spent most of their time investigating one another for having violated someone's constitutional right not to be arrested for anything. They were very good at leaking stuff though, and both van Claire and the BND guy knew it.

Both knowing what was going to happen next, they solemnly shook hands and parted. But not before the German had to sit and watch van Claire work his way through a very expensive and very good dessert.

Clay made it to the airport in good time, having spent the afternoon and early evening at the office. It was well after dark when he left his car in the vast, empty parking lot next to the ethereal terminal. He cursed when he looked at his tickets though. Damn it, they were for Bonn, not Frankfurt. Well, Koblenz was only two towns down the Rhine from Bonn, and Frankfurt was two hours from Koblenz, so ticketing him through Bonn was logical. But he had to empty that dead drop in Frankfurt, assuming it wasn't empty to start with. He had come up with a plausible story to tell his secretary about why he had needed to get to Frankfurt first. He had rehearsed it in his mind. Could he have forgotten to actually say it to her? Damn. Double damn. But yes, it seemed possible. He found keeping up with all this administrative crap frustrating beyond measure.

A first-class seat on TWA, the usual cosseting stewardesses, and some champagne soothed him. He decided he would just empty the poste restante box after meeting CITADEL. What the hell, no problem. He turned his mind to CITADEL. He probably should have prepared an agenda and been ready to task CITADEL, but the briefing in the Deputy Director's conference room had gone so badly, and so unexpectedly, that he had cut it off before things got out of hand. Why was the normally docile bigot list group cutting up stroppy, as the MI6 guys used to say? That old queen Withers could be expected to do the usual stonewalling about never divulging any information lest the source be compromised. That was why the Clandestine Service ended up running so damn few operations.

Was his normal cadre of well-placed snoops failing him? Like other senior officers, he knew the internal rumor mills and gossip sessions had hoovered up far more useful information than ever came in on the cable traffic. Had somebody set the dogs on him? Was he being second-guessed by one of those stupid tiger teams, or whatever they called them, who went sneaking around second-guessing every action a senior officer took? Those damn Monday morning quarterbacks had a lot more clout than they deserved. But the Deputy Director himself had expressed concern with INGRESS and CITADEL. He thought the INGRESS business was as dead and buried as the people involved, but CITADEL worried him.

He had only jumped the gun a little on surfacing the West German — what was his name? — oh, yes, Kirst, Hans Georg Kirst, because the boss wanted to test the material and was concerned about holding out on the Germans. Was this too much of a test? Was this what he wanted? Was it too much too soon? Was his action premature? He worried and gnawed on the question after they had darkened the cabin for the night. The champagne wasn't helping him think any better but it was damping down the fear that he had put a foot wrong. Well, when in doubt it was best to just bluff it out. Most of the people he dealt with at his level were more interested in holding onto their jobs than winning an argument.

Turning to CITADEL again, he did wish he'd had time, or taken the time, to think about what he wanted to talk to CITADEL about besides what had happened in Luxembourg. Oh well, something would come to him. In the end, he decided on a nice nap.

Bonn was cool and gray in the late November light of early morning. West Germany around Bonn and Luxembourg had a tendency to be that way from November to May. Van Claire took the airport shuttle into the city. The shuttle left him in the square in front of the railroad station and he went in. He bought a ticket and six British newspapers and the *Herald Trib* and went into the first-class restaurant for an omelet and coffee. He meant to do some operational planning while having breakfast. Instead he got caught up in a *Times* article and had to hurry to make his train. The jet lag had arrived in force, and he was feeling terribly weary.

Koblenz was pretty, even on a gloomy day. He was glad he hadn't brought the two men from S ecurity with him. They weren't needed since CITADEL was entirely harmless, and van Claire didn't like having them plodding around behind him. He walked down to the river and turned west along the broad sidewalk that ran alongside the Rhine. As usual, CITADEL materialized from somewhere and fell into step beside him. He started to talk but van Claire held up a hand.

"What was that business in Luxembourg about? The shootings that were in the paper? Was that you?"

CITADEL tried extra hard not to show his relief. They had gotten to the German in time! Instead he snorted with laughter. "Hardly. That drunken German was stumbling around Moscow making an ass of himself and hinting broadly that he was working for CIA and the West Germans: the BND no less. He was also looking for bribes and was trying to make contact with the local Mafiosi." CITADEL looked sad. "I regret that there are such people in the Soviet Union, and they are always sniffing around the Ministry of Trade. They try to make money off the socialist governments in Africa whom we support." He shook his head in disbelief at the venality of mankind. "I have no idea what happened in Luxembourg or what he was doing there, but from the newspapers it looked to us like his American case officer was trying to rescue him, from whom? The BND? The Russian mafia? The Africans?"

"Carpenter wasn't the case officer," van Claire said without thinking. Oh, God, how do I take that back? I just surfaced that kid to the KGB. But then, so what? The KGB knew about him, didn't they? Hell, they must have a list of damn near every case officer in the Agency.

CITADEL wished he hadn't heard that. He had pretty much talked Komsomol around to calling off the assassination squad for the American. The American was just some guy who happened to be there; why even bother to take the risk? But now this idiot had just confirmed that the shooter was CIA. Komsomol would insist on going forward now. Do I dare conceal this information from Komsomol? I most certainly do not.

"Why did you contact me? What do you have for me?"

"I have survived a close miss. But I think I see it ending in great opportunity." CITADEL gathered himself to launch into his prepared speech. He wasn't sure this latest idea of Komsomol's wasn't reaching too far, but orders were orders.

Walking beside him, van Claire was translating. "Close miss?" Oh, I bet he's scrambled "near miss" and "close call." OK, let's hear what he has to say.

"After I meet you last time I am called into Komsomol's office. He has two guys from Internal Security there and they berate me for slipping the tail I told you about." He looked at van Claire for confirmation. Van Claire nodded.

"I say no, no, I am not slipping tail. I am meeting openly with an American I met who finds me very *sympatisch*, no? This American, you of course, is senior American State Department official but maybe is really CIA. He is most upset about things they are doing in Vietnam and goes on and on about it. I am working to develop him. I give him your name; I told them you tell me about the German engineer in Dynamit Nobel and little Goshkorow. They get all excited and say this is good development. They congratulate me. Now I am in good smell with them."

"Good odor," van Claire said automatically.

"Yes. So Komsomol sends away two goons from Internal Security and says, 'I forget how good you are, Gregor. You are maybe man I need for big project.'"

"What's going to happen to the German and Goshkorow?" van Claire interrupted.

CITADEL tried not to look irritated. He made a dismissive flutter with his hand. "Nothing much, maybe they try to bribe German engineer into sharing with us what he is telling you. Good for the German: he makes double money. For Goshkorow, he gets punished. Maybe force him to retire on reduced pension. He's old man, not worth bothering with."

Van Claire was greatly relieved. He thought the KGB would be much harsher when they discovered a would-be defector.

"Anyway," CITADEL said, steering them back on the main topic. "Komsomol says, I am recommending you to Roman Gratchkenowsky. I almost faint with fear. You know who Roman Gratchkenowsky is?"

"Everybody does," van Claire said. "Head of KGB counterintelligence back almost to Beria's day."

"And a very scary man. Komsomol kills people because he loses his temper. Gratchkenowsky kills them by the thousand as part of a program. But he also runs high-level agents." CITADEL paused for effect. "Komsomol says Gratchkenowsky is personally running mole in CIA."

The mole! Van Claire stopped short in the middle of the promenade, then forced himself to move again. "And?"

"And he says he is recommending me to go to America and run this mole directly. Gratchkenowsky says it is getting too hard to run him through mail drops: the American is getting nervous that Angleton is close to catching him."

"Is he?" My God, van Claire thought. I'm asking a KGB agent what's going on in my own agency.

"Don't know. But Komsomol say it will take hand-holding, and I'm being considered to be the hand-holder."

"Did he say who the mole is?" Please, please tell me.

"No, just that he is very senior man in your CI Staff."

My God, it might even be Angleton himself.

"So you don't need a plane ticket anymore?"

"More than ever. But to California, not Washington. I need out. I am not stupid. I am not being called in because I am a good boy. They think this operation might be close to blowing up and if they can't handle it they need a Judas cow." He stopped. "No, a Judas *goat* to divert your FBI while they rescue the mole. The deal is, if I am sent to Washington I give you advance warning. We meet. I tell you who mole is. Within one week you help me escape. My price is up to $7 million, a new identity, resettlement in California or someplace equally warm. Deal?"

Van Claire sputtered, "Seven million is a hell of a lot of . . ." He stopped. "You have a deal, Mr. . . ."

"Arbarkian. Gregor Arbarkian."

CHAPTER SIXTEEN

At the same time that Arbarkian had slid out of his dark corner and joined van Claire on the promenade at Koblenz, Anne was picking Alicia up at the Luxembourg railroad station, three stops from Koblenz. It was only a short walk to their apartment, but Alicia didn't know the way and besides, their cover story was that Alicia was coming as her guest. Guests get picked up at the railroad station. When they got back Sam was sitting in the middle of the floor, building walls out of wooden blocks that the twins were taking great pleasure in knocking over.

Sam got up when they came in, gave Alicia a hug, pointed at the phone and shrugged. He had recently decided that he didn't know whether it was bugged or not, or by whom, but then he didn't know why they'd let him out of jail either, so why take chances? In training the TSD weirdoes had been of two minds. Half of the Technical Services Division staff was convinced that the Soviets lived in some science fiction world where their spy gear was always a generation ahead of the CIA's. It was marvelously imaginative. Wireless microphones the size of BBs could be rolled on the floor or under a carpet and pick up conversations 150 feet away. Or spike microphones could be trained on two men walking along on the other side of the Rhine and pick up what they were saying.

The other half of TSD believed that everything the KGB built was fabricated out of cast iron, weighed at least a quarter-ton, and made loud, suspicious noises when it was turned on. As for the CIA itself, the TSD guys said they could bug a phone all right. But if you wanted to bug a room, they asked case officers to be prepared for a mike-and-wire job. The listening post had to be at the other end of the wire, and the mike had to be buried in a wall or somewhere because the mike itself was as big as your thumb. So who knew?

They had to hurry. Alicia and Anne were supposed to spend the day having lunch with the Chief of Station at his house. There he would make official apologies for not having done anything for them, although they all knew that there hadn't been much the Bonn Station could have done. But just as Alicia was leaving Bonn a cable had come in from Headquarters — well, from Harvey, really — somebody was to drop everything and rush to Frankfurt and empty a dead drop: the poste restante box at the main post office. The Chief was still leery of involving his station officers in what looked like Harvey's suicide squad, so would Alicia mind doing this little errand? Secretaries were immune from Headquarters tong wars, since nobody ever noticed their existence. So Alicia was leaving as soon as Sam got through dictating his dispatch to her. Oh, and Anne said she was going with her.

When Sam bridled, Alicia gave him her best, most earnest smile. She was a secretary, not an operations officer, and a girl could use some help at a time like his. Besides, Anne had been stuck in the apartment for days, wringing her hands and worrying about Sam being in jail. She needed to see the bright lights and big city, you know? Sam didn't see Frankfurt as the bright lights and big city anybody had in mind, but nodded, resigned.

Alicia took her steno notebook out of her huge handbag. Then she reached in again and took out a parcel wrapped in brown paper and handed it to Sam. It was clearly heavy. "The boss said you might need this," she said. Curious, Sam unwrapped it. Good Lord: it was a .45 pistol and two extra clips of ammunition. They both sat there looking at it for a moment. Alicia said, enviously, "Cool."

Sam wasn't so sure. It was, to put it mildly, unusual for a CIA officer to be armed, in Europe anyway. For that matter, where in hell had the Chief gotten it? It wasn't like the Station had an armory. Oh, shit, I bet he took it off the Marine guards. They'll be pissed. He wouldn't go to the trouble of giving me a gun unless he thought I needed it. But why? He looked up and made eye contact with Alicia.

She knew what he was thinking. "The Chief said he didn't know if you'd need it or not, but he just had this feeling you might. I was wondering what he was talking about. I mean," she said, pointing at the pistol, "I didn't know what was in the package." She sat a moment, then flipped open her steno pad and looked at him expectantly.

Sam had spent the last two days preparing what he wanted to dictate. He started talking at an even 120 words a minute with Alicia keeping right up with him. In 17 minutes he was done. Anne was just coming out of the bedroom, looking more stunning than usual. She wore a very short black skirt and a white blouse, and was carrying a red raincoat.

"Wow," Sam said.

Anne was embarrassed. "The skirt's too short, but that's all they've been selling for the last two years. It's Mary Quant's fault. The British must be immune to cold weather. OK, Alicia, let's be off to Frankfurt. Have fun with the kiddies, dear. I'll be home late."

The express got them to Frankfurt in two hours and ten minutes. They were in the lead car in the first-class no-smoking section.

Alicia had pleaded with Anne to sit there. She had, she said, just quit smoking and didn't want to be tempted. Anne, sympathetic, agreed, although the thought of going without a cigarette for two hours was most unhappy-making.

"Is this the first time you've tried to quit?" Anne asked.

"Third time this month," Alicia had said. Oh, the sacrifices I make, Anne thought. Still, she and Alicia liked each other and they chatted amiably until they pulled in to Frankfurt, exactly on time as usual. Being in the first car, they were out of the train and heading for the post office across the square before most of the other passengers had even gotten off.

"This should only take a couple of minutes," Alicia said, then let out a little whimpering noise.

"What's wrong?" Anne asked. "Are you all right?"

"The fat guy behind us. I've seen him at Headquarters. It's van Claire. It's the guy this is all about. Shit. He must be heading for the post office too. C'mon."

They rushed across the street and into the post office. The formal German name for the German post office is Post and Telegraphic Service. In a German post office you could send a telegram, buy a money order, and pay your rent, your taxes, and your health insurance. You could also book a long-distance telephone call or make local calls. And, of course, you could mail packages and buy stamps. There were lots of people there doing lots of things. The lines were long, but fortunately only two people at the poste restante window.

Alicia turned towards the poste restante line. "Delay him," she said.

"How?"

Alicia looked her up and down. She smiled. ""You'll think of something."

Anne got the hint. There were any number of big wooden benches around, and she took one that faced the front door. It was also in sight of the poste restante window. She took off her coat, sat down and waited.

Clay van Claire showed up not a minute behind them. He walked in, looked around. You could almost see his lips moving as he spelled out "poste restante." Anne was startled. It was the man she and Sam had seen a couple of months ago, walking along the promenade at Koblenz. She forgot about that and focused on her timing. As he started moving towards the window Anne crossed her legs.

Women's hosiery makers hadn't caught up with the newly fashionable short skirts, so the hose and garter belt that worked fine for the longer 1950s fashions resulted in some fine displays of leg ten years later.

Clay van Claire started across the lobby and stopped dead when he saw a flash of bare thigh above the stocking top.

At the same time Anne looked up, flashed him her most alluring smile, popped off the bench and walked quickly towards him. It was not for nothing that she and her girlfriends had practiced their dumb bimbo routines in high school. Sometimes they threw in a Southern accent for effect. Anne decided to skip the Southern accent today.

"Oh, sir, you look like you speak English. Do you speak English? Oh, please say you speak English." She rushed up to him and placed a restraining hand on his chest. Mary Kay Campbell from Savannah, Georgia, had taught her the trick. "Keep your hand on 'em, and keep them talkin', darlin'. It'll keep their hands off you." Van Claire stood there, mesmerized.

Anne's cover story was that she was a little less than bright and was supposed to meet a friend here, she thought. But then she thought she remembered that it was supposed to be in front of American Express, and did he know where AmEx was? She chattered and twinkled at him, once glancing right and seeing Alicia had moved up a place in line. She saw him glance at her ring finger, which was bare, since she had slipped the wedding and engagement rings into her purse. There was a telltale ring of whiter skin left where they had been though.

Thinking quickly, she smiled at him. "Freddy and I are separated. He's such a prude. Are you a prude?" Then she twinkled again. Mary Kay had been Miss Calhoun County or something down in Georgia. She said beauty contestants learned by age 12 how to cock their heads, wrinkle their noses and twinkle. It seemed to have a salutary effect on the already besotted van Claire. Hurry up, Alicia, hurry up; I'm running out of things to say and do, she thought.

He was just clearing his throat preparatory to telling her that he was no prude and perhaps they might go somewhere where he could prove it when Anne saw that Alicia was just leaving the poste restante counter and heading for the door.

So she squealed. "Ooh, now I remember where AmEx is. Thank you." She stood on tiptoe and pecked him on the cheek and then turned and fled.

Van Claire, a little bewildered, looked after her. Damn! He half-turned to chase after her when he remembered what he'd come here for. Instead he strode over to the poste restante window. The next customer had left and the clerk was just walking away. "Hey you," van Claire said, rather more loudly than he needed to, and thrust the post office authorization at him.

The clerk looked at the box number and frowned: "But the lady in front of you just picked up the mail from that box," he said. Being German, he said it in German.

"What? What?" van Claire said, again too loudly. Why can't these damn people speak English?

The clerk, realizing the man with the loud voice was just another foreigner, pointed at the box number on the card and said, "No mail. Is *leer* — empty."

Van Claire felt himself relax. Thank God. It was empty. INGRESS never left a message. He was safe. Then he felt aggrieved that he had to come all the way up here from Koblenz just to find out that he needn't have. Damn, this operational stuff is a pain in the ass. Oh well, time to go home and tell the Deputy Director it was time to cut Counterintelligence out of any contact with the CITADEL operation. Or maybe anything else, for that matter. Let's see, should he change his ticket and fly out of Frankfurt? No, he'd let a concierge do that. What he needed was a hotel posh enough to have a concierge. He headed back to the tourist kiosk inside the main railroad station.

Anne and Alicia had fled in the other direction, across the street and into an attractive-looking cafe with windows looking out on the river. They were both a little out of breath.

"Ick," Anne gasped. "I hope I never have to do that again." Then she paused and said "Although come to think of it, it was kind of fun. That's got to be the oldest trick in the book."

"Yes," said Alicia. "But it works every time. At least for people who look like you."

Anne looked her over. "All you have to do is be female. I'll show you a couple of things you can do with makeup when we get a chance. But never mind that; was there anything in the drop?"

"Yes, this," Alicia said, taking a sealed envelope out of her huge purse. "Let's see what we have here." She opened it and read it.

"Oh, God. Poor man. And that's who Goshkorow is."

"Who?"

"A Soviet trade official who wants to defect. It's a note from Dieter Volkmann to Mr. Navarre. It's dated October 20 and it says, 'Mr. Navarre, I have just seen Mr. Goshkorow killed by Russians. They saw me and I am fleeing. Please help me, Dieter.'"

"Who's Mr. Navarre?" Anne asked.

"Clay van Claire."

"But didn't he tell the DDP he didn't know anything about Goshkorow? And I thought he didn't meet Dieter again. This says he did."

"Damn right. Fat boy has some explaining to do. I'll get this off to Harvey tonight."

"But who was Goshkorow — I mean, besides being a Soviet trade official?"

"Well, we know Dieter was at a trade congress right here in Frankfurt on the 12th. Those all take place at the convention center down the street." She pointed to her right.

They sat there for a while.

"I know what you're thinking," Anne said.

"And I know what you're thinking," Alicia said.

"But I'm just a dependent."

"And I'm just a secretary."

"But we don't have to shoot anybody, so we don't need Sam."

"And Harvey's not here to do it himself, so how do we do it?" Alicia thought for a minute, and then said, "I know." It was late afternoon, but the stores stayed open until seven. It seemed only fair since they closed for two hours at lunchtime. There are as many camera stores as watch shops in West Germany, which meant there was one on nearly every corner.

Alicia, with Anne following, walked into the first camera store she saw and bought a nice-looking Asahi Pentax. She paid for it with a bundle of cash. "Ops money," she whispered to Anne. "Harvey says always carry a lot when you're working. You might need to make a friend fast." They walked out the door and headed along the Bahnhofstrasse for the conference center.

"Here's where you stand around just out of sight while I see what I can dig up," Alicia said. She looked apologetic. "Sorry, Anne, but if it's a woman she's maybe going to resent a glamour puss like you and clam up. If it's a man I'll come get you and turn you loose."

The Germans are nothing if not dutiful, and they work long hours to prove it. The same nice lady was on duty at the reception desk at the conference center office. Alicia approached her looking timid and worried, or at least she hoped so.

"Oh, I wonder if you can help me. I'm from the Ghehri Camera Store. We just got the currency release" — whatever that is, Alicia thought, but it sounded official — "and can deliver Mr. Goshkorow's camera. But the only address we have is 'c/o the Conference Center.' Can that be right?"

The lady had started giving her full attention at the word "Goshkorow." Alicia looked earnest and sympathetic and the lady went into the whole story of poor Mr. Goshkorow and his heart attack.

"Oh, dear," Alicia said mournfully. "And he never got his nice new camera." She thought a moment. "He came to the store with a friend, a German gentleman . . ."

"Oh, you must mean Mr. Volkmann," and she told her all about Mr. Volkmann rushing out just before the news came of Mr. Goshkorow's heart attack. "But I read in the paper that he was killed just the next day in Luxembourg by some robbers. What an awful coincidence."

Alicia looked crestfallen. Then she glared at the camera as if it were all the camera's fault. "I don't know what we're going to do with the camera. I mean, it's paid for . . ."

"Oh," said the nice lady. "Maybe Mr. Arbarkian, Mr. Goshkorow's boss, would know. He was here that day, and he comes here all the time for trade conferences. Wait a minute, we have his address. He's the one who signed the contract for the rental of the meeting hall." She went off towards the filing cabinet behind her, looked through it with German efficiency, and came back with a sheet of paper. "Here, I'll copy the address down for you. At least he can get the camera to poor Mr. Goshkorow's family."

Two minutes later Anne and Alicia were walking back towards the station, heading for the consulate. Anne had been writing briefing papers for three years and Alicia knew the jargon: between the two of them they were determined to write a cable that would knock Headquarters' socks off. Anne could then take a train back to Luxembourg, while Alicia sent the cable from the commo center. Alicia was glowing with excitement. "Harvey's just going to love this. It ties INGRESS and CITADEL together and puts van Claire on the hot seat. Hot dog. The big mystery solved by the secretary and the housewife. Take that, James Bond."

CHAPTER SEVENTEEN

Late that night the gendarme at the *Hopital Civile* in Luxembourg was fighting to stay awake and guard the prisoner in the locked private room. The *Hopital* was small, but big enough for a small city whose populace avoided hospitals when they could. It had four floors, with an average of twenty rooms per floor on the top two floors. There was a reception hall and offices on the ground floor and there were two operating rooms on the European first floor.

Luxembourg was still in many ways an old farm city, and the tendency was to prefer to go to bed at dark and get up at dawn. Electric lights had interfered with that, of course, but old preferences die hard. The half-dozing guard started. He thought he heard a noise. He got out of his chair and looked around, then walked five steps to the connecting corridor and looked down the hall.

Fire! Jesus, there were flames coming out from under the door of a supply closet. He ran down the corridor, looking for a fire extinguisher. There it was, another fifty feet down the hall. He ran to it, pulled it off the wall, frantically read the directions, turned it upside down and ran back towards the fire. He must have yelled, although he didn't remember doing it, for the door four doors down opened and the floor nurse stuck her head out, looking to see what was going on.

He took off his coat, wrapped it around the doorknob, and opened the door. A rush of flames leapt out, and he turned the fire extinguisher on and stood, legs spread, in the middle of the hall spraying the flames. It took two minutes to empty the fire extinguisher. The flames were pretty much beaten down when the floor nurse came dragging a second extinguisher. In another two minutes the fire was out.

Remembering why he was there, the gendarme walked quickly back to his post while the nurse waited for the firemen. He checked the door; it was still locked. He was relieved. The *Wachtmeister* had told him not to leave his post under any circumstances. If he had to pee he was to call somebody up from the front desk to cover for him while he ran to the toilet two doors down. It would be best to check, though. He got the key out of his pocket and unlocked the door, noticing that the knob felt a little loose. He'd best report that.

Inside, the room was half-lit, which he always thought made it extra hard for the poor patient to get some sleep. Still, this Soviet, or Russian, was in a coma, so that shouldn't be a problem. His tubes and wire were attached but the monitor was buzzing angrily. He looked at the patient, then at the monitor. Oh God, he wasn't breathing. He hit the alarm, and the night nurse came running. The hospital was too small to have a doctor on duty at night, but the night nurse had emergency training. Not, however, for this kind of emergency. In the end a doctor couldn't have helped either.

An hour later the firemen were still there, the doctor had come, and the night-duty officer from the Surete was there with two policemen. Kurt had the duty that night, as he did every fifth night. Junior officers worked the midnight shift. The brass needed their sleep to keep a clear head so they could make important decisions during regular office hours.

He took extensive notes: the gendarme leaving his post to put a fire out, the smell of gasoline in what was left of the supply closet, the slightly loosened doorknob, and the dead man. We'll never know who he was now, Kurt thought. He examined the hospital bed and the dead patient closely. The pillow looked a little off. Like what? Like it had been taken out from under the patient's head, used to smother him and then put back? That was purely conjecture on his part. Still, if you string everything together you might suspect a not quite as discreet as hoped-for murder.

Evidence? Probably nothing. The gendarme would have covered any fingerprints on the doorknob with his own. They'd take fingerprints anyway, and get an expert opinion on whether the lock had been forced, although it obviously had been. Discreetly, but not discreetly enough. The nearest pathologist was either in Belguim or all the way to Frankfurt. The Luxembourg docs could deliver a baby or set a broken leg, but after that your guess was as good as theirs. But he'd try to get the pathologist. And he'd look up the professor from the Slavic Languages Department at the university whom the Surete had brought in to listen to the patient's mumblings. He taught Russian, but it was all very hush-hush as to what language the patient had been babbling in. Kurt snorted: as if a seven-year-old couldn't have figured it out by now. If she had actually heard anything useful he would have known by now anyway.

Assuming he was right, it had been well-planned. Divert the gendarme. Slip in and smother the prisoner; leave no traces. Except that they had. As usual in government operations, the planning had been smoother than the doing. But somebody had scouted this place out. The most obvious candidate was the man who had been here only two days ago, the one the gendarme had followed all over town. He had been to the university, he had been to the hospital, and he had scouted out Sam's apartment. The last thought made him shiver. But then the idiot who had followed the man, who said he was a journalist, had broken off when he had gone to the railroad station.

"Why?" Kurt had asked the cop and his boss. "Why the hell didn't you get on the train and follow him?"

They had been shocked and affronted. But inspector, the train was leaving the jurisdiction of Luxembourg. They had no police powers outside Luxembourg. Besides, they didn't have tickets.

Kurt could have kicked them. "You were supposed to follow him, not arrest him. You don't need police powers for that. And you don't need a ticket. Just flash your ID at the conductor." Every cop in Europe had been riding the trains for free since forever by waving an ID card and they damn well knew it. Damn mule-headed peasants with kepis on their thick heads. He'd yelled at them until he felt a little better. Then he felt bad about it.

Then he got mad again. Oh, they'd never prove it, but the KGB had made sure the second guy in the Gambrinus attack would never wake up and say something embarrassing. And the guy was a Russian goon. This meant that Sam had killed one and a half KGB men, which meant that the Soviets were going to come looking for him. It was an article of faith that the KGB took care of its own. They would go to great lengths to exchange or rescue or otherwise free agents who had been captured and avenge agents who had been killed. On the other hand, they'd kill their own without thinking twice about it, but outsiders weren't allowed to.

The reason Kurt had been so angry for so long was that his bosses had let Sam out on a short leash. They wanted him to wander around Luxembourg like a Judas goat until something happened. They hadn't even bothered to follow him. Maybe that was some idiot compromise between the ones who wanted to keep him in jail and the ones who thought he had a reasonable case of self-defense. Either way, how cavalier can you get? He looked at his watch. It was past dawn and he would be getting off shift soon. He determined that tomorrow he was going to go in and have it out with his bosses. Screw his career. Sam wasn't a close friend or anything, but he was a nice man and his next-door neighbor and he deserved better than to be left bouncing around town like a toy balloon that had gotten loose. He stomped down to the ground-floor office to find a phone and see if he could dig up a pathologist.

Sam woke up just after dawn. Anne had gotten home late last night, full of stories that were told with a mixture of great solemnity and giggles, depending on the topic. Clearly, the whole story was falling into place. Or was it? It was obvious that Dieter had been running from the people who killed Goshkorow; his note said so. But why had the KGB killed Goshkorow in the first place? Had Dieter bungled and somehow surfaced him to the Soviets, or, more obviously, had Van Claire done it?

This is all way above my pay grade, Sam decided, slipping out of bed, picking up his running shoes, and tiptoeing for the door. Maybe a run will clear my head. On the way out he stopped, hesitated, and then unlocked the drawer in the kitchen. He took out the .45 and stuffed it in his pants, where it pressed against the middle of his back. It felt kind of silly and overdramatic to be carrying a gun in peaceful Luxembourg, but God knows he'd needed one two weeks ago. Besides, the Chief of Station wasn't given to dramatics, and he'd stuck his neck out, wrangling the .45 from the Marine detachment at the embassy. He either knows or suspects something.

He eased out of the building and began trotting up the Rue du St Esprit, where it became the Rue Sigeroi, the road that led to the path along the cliff beside the River Alzette. In two hundred yards he was clear of the city and in open farm country of gently rolling hills. Those crisp, always freshly mown farm fields always looked like postcards. The cows in the fields gave him uninterested glances as he trotted by. He had started out doing the old T&T shuffle, a half-trot that loosened things up and gave his body time to adjust to the insult of having to exercise at dawn. Named for the Marine

Corps Training and Test Regiment, the T&T shuffle had been executed by thousands of officer candidates for tens of thousands of miles since God knows when.

He thought about the Marine lieutenant who was the Bonn embassy Marine detachment commander. He would not have been happy to have had his arm twisted by the Chief. Now he had a pistol adrift from the armory and a lot of explaining to do if the inspector general suddenly dropped by for an inventory or if, God forbid, those crazy spies used it on somebody. Sam ran on. He was running against the traffic, of which there was precisely none. He had seen and heard one tractor in a field off to his left, but that was it. He thought through what had been going on in these last days, trying to put things together.

Six minutes later he was still chugging along when he heard the first car of the morning coming up behind him. He had paid no particular attention. It was full light and he was running on the other side of the road. But then two things did attract his attention. First, the car was really hauling. This made little sense on a narrow road that went from one place where no one was in a hurry to an even smaller place that was hardly worth getting to. The other was that he heard tires on gravel. The car wasn't on the paved road! The car was on his side of the road! He threw himself at the ditch just as the car hit him.

Oh. Ouch. Shit. God, that hurt. He had zoned out for a few seconds. Now it all came back to him in a rush. He hurt all over. He opened his eyes. He was still alive, so the car must have almost missed him. Maybe it did and he was just hurting from jumping into the ditch at a full-tilt run. Fifty yards up the Rue du St Esprit, a dark-gray car had screeched to a stop and the doors flew open. Three men jumped out, spread out, and came towards him, crouching.

Crouching? Spread out? These weren't rescuers or worried motorists, rushing to his aid. This was a tactical formation. The men were dressed in black and they ran at him, their arms spread apart. They were attacking.

Sam rolled to his left, pulled the gun out, jacked a round into the chamber, flipped the safety off, and had one second to run through the Marine Corps five-paragraph order, the immortal USMC decision process. <u>Situation</u>: these guys just tried to kill me and now they are attacking. Then he had an alternate Situation: my brain is scrambled and these are just concerned civilians. <u>Mission</u>: survive. <u>Execution</u>: shoot. Alternate Execution: don't shoot. <u>Administration</u>: a round in the chamber, more in the magazine. <u>Command and Control</u>: It's just me out here. If I'm right, the police will find a hit-and-run sometime today and that's that. If I'm wrong, the *Luxemburger Wort* is going to headline: American Killer Kills Again!

He fired. The leading guy spun around and fell down. The other two rushed forward, pistols drawn now, and with their free hands pulled their colleague back toward the car. Still backing away, pointing the pistols but not firing, they got to the car, pushed their colleague in, and drove away, very fast.

What in hell was that all about? Sam tried to think. He could swear his brain hurt as much as his body did. C'mon brain, let's get with the program. I know you're having another bad morning, but I could use some help here. What was that all about? While his brain was mulling over his request, he checked his body. Everything hurt, but not broken-hurt. He couldn't see any blood. This was all good. Not wonderful, but good. He tried standing up. Ouch. Ouch ouch. There; he had done it. He tried walking. Stiff, but not bad.

At this point his brain decided it was time to help him out. It said: those guys were trying to kill you, Sam. Concerned motorists don't wave guns at people they've just bounced off their car's front fender. They were trying to kill you quietly; otherwise they would have started shooting themselves. And yes, your aim was shaky: you just nicked the guy. If you don't believe me, look around, there's a little blood on the road, but not much. Now go home before somebody comes along and starts asking questions. Sam pushed the gun back into his pants and limped off, trying for a very slow T&T shuffle. He kept looking over his shoulder to see if the three guys were coming back for another try.

It was just after 7:15 a.m. when Kurt walked into the tiny elevator lobby of his apartment building. He was startled to see Sam leaning against the wall, waiting for the elevator. Sam looked like hell. His clothes were torn and grass-stained, and Sam was holding himself very carefully, the way people do when they are in pain.

"Sam, what is happening to you?"

"Oh, hi, Kurt. Nothing much: I was out running and fell into a ditch and really creamed myself."

"Creamed?"

"A figure of speech. It means it was a big impact when I landed."

"Ahh." Kurt was immediately suspicious. Sam looked too roughed-up and upset to have just taken a minor fall. And this "fall" happened only a few hours after somebody had probably smothered that Russian Sam had kicked in the head.

Sam was uncomfortable. Here I am with a recently fired pistol in my pants standing six inches away from a *Surete* inspector in full uniform. And the inspector, who had been grumpy and distant for the last week — well, who wouldn't be with a suspected murderer for a next-door neighbor — is suddenly trying to be friendly in an awkward way.

The elevator arrived, making its customary *bong!* noise. Kurt opened the door and held it for Sam. The elevator was tiny. It held just two people crowded together. Well, it held four if you included the twins. The protocol was tricky. Do you stand one in front of the other, both facing the door? That would be weird in such a small space. Or do you stand face to face, chests touching. That could be fun if you are with Anne; less so if you're with another large guy. Guys standing chest to chest could lead to misunderstandings. They settled for stuffing themselves in at a slight slant and traveled slowly upwards in silence. Sam thought Abbott and Costello or the Marx brothers could do a lot with this situation.

When they got to the sixth floor — finally — Kurt got out first and held the door again for Sam. When Sam came out Kurt took him by the arm and pushed him gently — but it was still a push — against his apartment door and stood facing him, nose to nose.

"Not to bullshit me, please, Sam. What happened to you just now?"

Sam hesitated. He supposed that sometimes it was permissible for a spy to tell the truth. "Some guys in a car sideswiped me. I jumped out of the way in time. They took off. And no, I don't know who they are and I didn't get a license-plate number." Well, that was kind of close to telling the truth.

Kurt patted Sam on the chest. "You be very careful." He wanted to say, "That guy you kicked in the head is dead, just this morning, maybe on purpose," but he didn't. What good would it do? He turned to go into his own apartment. "You didn't shoot anybody today, did you?" He said it in a ha-ha, ho-ho kind of way.

"Just one," Sam ha-ha'd in return and opened his door.

At noon the Chief of Station locked the contents of his inbox in the safe and headed for the restaurant across the street from the Foreign Ministry. It was time to have a chat with one of the big boys in the German CIA, the BND. His opposite number, a burly German, was precisely on time. Sometimes, the Chief thought, I wish one of these guys would get the zipper on their fly stuck or something and show up late. What would they say?

The foreplay was minimal. The German and the American services had been cautiously friendly since not all that long after the end of WW II. There had been some terribly messed-up times getting the BND started: the odious General Gehlen (or was he a hero?), the ex-Nazis who kept popping up in key BND jobs and the later prominent defections of BND officers to the Soviets or East Germans. CIA couldn't say much about the Nazis since they'd hired a boatload themselves in the years right after the end of the war. But the defections to the Russians? Best to grit one's teeth and keep murmuring polite phrases..

Over an expensive lunch, since the German knew the American was buying, the Chief laid a few cards on the table. "It has come to our attention that you might not be aware that the German journalist who was killed in Luxembourg a couple of weeks ago had been of assistance to us in the past. We are now in possession of information that leads us to believe he was killed because he may have seen the murder of a Russian in Frankfurt the same day."

The German hesitated. Should he admit the he already knew this or feign surprise and great interest? He settled for, "Really?"

"Really. If all you're going to say is 'really,' I'll call for the check now."

The German decided he'd rather not play poker with this man. "You are telling me the German was a CIA agent because why?"

"Because you need to know why he got killed. Two guys don't show up in a one-horse town like Luxembourg and kill somebody, apparently with a very sophisticated poison, because he looked at some other guy's wife wrong. This was a KGB hit that got broken up by a friend of the German."

"One-horse town?" The silence again.

"It's a figure of speech from American Western movies. I regret using it." The Chief turned towards the waiter. "*Ober, Zahl bitte,*" he said, calling for the bill.

The German waved the waiter away. "We perhaps know part of this story. We didn't know why the American came to riding to the rescue." The Germans liked American Westerns too.

"Which part of the story did you know?"

"Is the American CIA?"

It was horse-trading time. Without realizing it, both men had wiggled themselves more comfortably into their chairs and got ready to deal. They sat there looking at each other, each waiting for the other to speak first. After a long pause the Chief raised his head and started looking around for the waiter again.

The German gave in. "We don't know if Goshkorow was murdered or not. The body was shipped out that night back to Russia. But we are told the German killed in Luxembourg was injected with some compound with a long name that causes the same characteristics as the results of a fatal heart attack. So both men die the same day of apparently the same cause. We don't believe in coincidences either. What you don't know is that second man the American attacked did not die right away. He is in the hospital in a coma, but sometimes he cries out. He cries out in Russian. The Luxembourg people" — and here he nodded approvingly — "had a Russian speaker listen to his ramblings. She heard nothing significant except that his mother lives out in some town three hundred miles from Volgograd and he was speaking in Russian. We heard he died last night. Was the American CIA?"

That was a quick change of topic. The Chief decided to play. "Yes, Carpenter is a trainee who was sent to Luxembourg to learn German. He has — and had — no, I repeat, no operational duties."

"So he was not the German's case officer?"

The Chief folded his hands and smiled earnestly at the German. Trading time again.

The German reached into his breast pocket and took out a three-by-five photograph. It was a very grainy head and shoulders shot of a man coming out of a building. It was obviously an enlargement of a photo taken from some distance away. "We would like to know who this man is. He was seen walking around Luxembourg last week. He said he was a journalist but we are not so sure."

"I'll try and find out for you as soon as possible who he is. And no, Carpenter was not the case officer. As I said, he had no,

I repeat, no operational duties in Luxembourg, West Germany, or anywhere else." Hmm, COS thought, this is the same guy Sam took a picture of last week, and fits the description of Goshkorow's boss that the German receptionist gave to Anne and Alicia. He looked at the German. "I think, though, that he's a Soviet named Arbarkian."

Amid assertions of mutual high regard and frequent references to America's and West Germany's long and warm liaison relationship, the two men parted, but not until after the American had paid the bill.

At four p.m. Kurt walked into the prefecture's office building and headed for the stairs. Most days he would, often almost unconsciously, reflect on the fact that the prefecture had maintained an office here for more than two hundred years. He sometimes wondered what kind of crimes the Luxembourgoise had got up to back then. Today, though, he was focused only on the fact that he was going to commit career suicide. He was going to ask — no, demand — that his bosses stop leaving Sam hanging out like a target on the rifle range and either get him some protection, put him back in jail, or kick him out of the country. Let the Americans worry about him, assuming that they were worried at all, which he doubted.

He had stopped to inspect himself in the mirror in the men's toilet, checking to make sure his jacket was correct, and that his kepi was on at the right angle. Everything adjusted, he headed for the Chief Inspector's office. As he walked into the outer office the Chief Inspector, who was talking to his secretary, looked over and smiled, if you could call that frosty grimace a smile. "Ah, good, just the man I want to see. Come in."

In his office he waved Kurt to a chair, held up a hand when Kurt started to speak, and looked directly at him. "The American you questioned in the Gambrinus murder cases is going to be unofficially deported. Tomorrow morning, as a matter of fact. I explained to them" — and at "them" he glanced upwards towards the prosecutor's office on the top floor — "that even a student has bills to pay and an apartment lease and whatnot, but they are adamant. The Germans tell us the CIA Chief in Bonn has been asking questions. Our masters don't want to know about what happened at the hospital this morning. They know the Russian's dead but have their fingers in their ears about the fire and the cop leaving the patient unattended. They have decided upstairs that maybe it is better for the Germans and the Americans not to know we screwed up." He leaned forward. "That is your doing. You planted the seeds that this was probably a KGB murder. They don't know what to do about murders by foreign intelligence services with no evidence and no witnesses. Now the BND tells us the CIA has admitted that this Carpenter is a CIA agent, a trainee they claim." He snorted. "They certainly trained him to shoot anyway."

The Chief Inspector went on. "Bonn wiggled their eyebrows at the front office when they learned the American had been walking around loose. The front office promptly decided this was too complicated for them to deal with. They want the whole problem to go away. Right now the whole problem is the American, so he is going to go away. There's a plane at ten a.m. tomorrow. Carpenter and his wife and children are to be on it. You will drive him over yourself and walk him right onto the airplane. After that he is CIA's problem. You will also have your people clean up the mess caused by his sudden departure. See if you can get him to come up with the money to pay his bills. If you have to, go see the comptroller and see what you can get out of the contingency fund. Icelandic Airlines has been spoken to and they will have the tickets ready."

Kurt nodded. Icelandic was the only airline offering flights to the United States from Luxembourg. For that matter, Luxembourg was the only airport in Europe Icelandic had landing rights for. Consequently, Icelandic was always eager to cooperate with the Luxembourg authorities.

"Here is his passport, "the Chief continued. " He won't need his Luxembourg driver's license and his residence permit anymore." The Chief Inspector opened a manila envelope, took a passport out, and handed it to Kurt. "Now, my secretary said you wanted to see me. What about?"

"It was a matter concerning this case, Herr Chief Inspector. But our conversation has answered all my concerns. Are we worried that the newspapers will make inquiry into what the outcome of the Gambrinus deaths will be?"

"I'm not, but upstairs is. The current thinking is that we are going to take any reporter who gets too nosy aside and murmur the magic words "national security," and trust that that will shut them up. If it doesn't, you" — and he pointed his finger at Kurt — "are in charge of coming up with something to tell them."

"I'm not too good at indirection, Herr Chief Inspector."

"Then you have an excellent opportunity here to learn. This is no longer a criminal investigation. This is a matter of national security, of politics in the front office, and of the Duchy of Luxembourg's relationship with the BND and CIA. These matters far transcend the importance of finding out who murdered that German and why." He said the last sentence with an air of angry irritation. "Now go make sure our skirts are clean," he said, and waved Kurt, and the Gambrinus killings, out of his presence.

Out on the street, Kurt sighed mightily. Well, he thought, I didn't have to make a noble gesture and sacrifice my career for Sam after all. On the other hand, I have an equally excellent chance of getting busted back down to patrolman again if I screw up this new assignment. How on earth am I going to clean up this mess? The brass doesn't know how so they tell me to do it. Well, orders are orders. Let's start by going home and surprising Sam. God, I hope Angelica doesn't think this was my idea.

CHAPTER EIGHTEEN

Four bedraggled people straggled into Dulles airport around noon the next day. The Icelandic flight had been on time into New York, but the United flight to Dulles had been delayed, and traveling with little children was not an unalloyed pleasure. The twins had been quite good, all things considered. But little kids don't react well to sudden change. Neither, Sam thought, do their parents. The five-hour time difference and the seven-hour flight mostly cancelled each other out on the clock, but nobody had told their bodies.

Kurt had knocked on their door at seven the night before and told them, looking at the floor as he did, that they were going to be more or less deported the next morning. Kurt looked splendidly official in full officer's kit, complete with Sam Browne belt and the little pistol. The papers duly presented, Kurt was pushed aside by his wife. Angelica had been hovering in the hallway, glaring at Kurt as if the whole thing were his idea. She took the twins next door to her apartment and set them to playing with her daughters, reminding them that the apartment doors were going to stay open and Mütti better not hear any squabbling. Then she came back and accelerated Kurt's explanations by translating his German.

For a rather stolid police inspector, Kurt had really been pretty ingenious about getting this show on the road. Rather than plodding along, he had gotten up on his toes and executed an impressive series of bureaucratic *jetes*. He had taken the local Icelandic Air guy aside and sworn him to secrecy and made him a co-conspirator in what was described as a counterintelligence operation. Delighted to be involved in something new and interesting and, well, very *secret*, the Icelandic Air guy had come up with a van to take them to the airport, waived the excess baggage fees, gotten them seats on the morning plane, and arranged for the ticket charges to disappear into a series of interdepartmental memoranda between various finance offices.

The Volkswagen dealer had been delighted to do the government a favor and swore on his mother's head that he would get a top price for Sam and Anne's VW bug. Sam didn't look forward to working out how to settle things with Finance and Accounting when he got home. It was the government's quasi-personal car, not his. The QP car had been a bone of contention anyway. Grant Natz had questioned what a staffer under student cover would be doing with a car; COS Bonn had countered by asking what an American with a wife and two children was going to do without one.

Kurt had taken his kepi off and was rubbing his forehead when the topic of what to do with the furniture came up. He finally said he'd think of something later. Then he told Sam and Anne an edited version of why the hurry. The Surete had decided not to charge Sam with anything, since their preliminary investigation showed that he had acted in self-defense. At the same time his actions were at the very least undesirable, since shooting people in crowded restaurants was frowned upon regardless of the circumstances, and that therefore his residence permit was being revoked.

Kurt didn't see how to explain the suddenness of it all, nor why he had been detailed to oversee the process. He started on a rambling story, but Sam held up a hand. "We get it, Kurt. Your bosses want a problem to go away. We're the problem, and we're going away. The rest gets swept under the rug. You're the junior guy in the office, so they handed you the broom."

Kurt didn't argue. Anne said, "Kurt, do you mind if I call my friend Alicia and tell her we're leaving?"

The call made Anne and Alicia proud of their new skills at not saying anything directly. Alicia had been home reading when Anne called. Alicia was very happy that Sam had been sprung, and wished them bon voyage. As it turned out she was going on home leave imminently, so maybe they would see each other. Wasn't that an interesting coincidence? Bye-bye, kiss, kiss.

The next morning nothing would do as far as the Duchy's brass was concerned but that Sam had to ride with Kurt in a police car with a driver, so they couldn't say much. It wouldn't do for the driver to suspect that the inspector was on friendly terms with what, as far as the street cops knew, was a killer, and possibly a double murderer.

In the Icelandic van behind them were Anne and the kids and Angelica and her kids, and a mountain of air freight containing all their clothing and the infrastructure that two three-year-olds required. Sam glanced over his shoulder at the little procession and decided it was as discreet as a Fourth of July parade. All it needed was a jeep with a ring-mounted .50-caliber machine gun to finish it off.

At the airport, and out of the driver's sight, Sam had shaken Kurt's hands with both of his, and thanked him for going way beyond anything he had a right to hope for. Particularly from a cop who had, after all, been conducting a murder investigation with him as the prime suspect. Kurt didn't say much and just stood there looking stoic. Anne and Angelica cried a little, and the kids, who had been frolicking around the departure hall, caught their parents' mood and became subdued.

On the flight home they sat together in the plane, which was half-empty as usual, and tried to figure out what to do next. The twins, wrongfully stuffed with chocolate again, were sleeping in sky cots two rows behind them.

"If life were fair," Anne said, "the Director himself would meet you in the foyer at Headquarters with a brass band and give you a medal for trying to save Dieter."

"And what do you estimate is the likelihood is of that happening?"

"Oh, zero I guess. Sam, are you sure you want to work for these people?"

"I don't even know if I have the choice. They aren't going to be delighted that I made the front page of the *International Herald Tribune*."

"You think they're going to fire you?"

"Europe Division certainly will if they have the chance. I wonder how long it would take me to work my way up from bagging groceries at Safeway to something big like being a cashier."

"Oh, you'd do fine."

"Hmm. I'm sure employers are hungry out there for a 27-year-old ex-student who can't speak German and is probably on the Interpol watch list."

"Silly." Still, it was something to think about. She could always go back to the Bureau of the Budget. But what would Sam do? He certainly didn't seem to be the Mr. Mom type.

They went through everything that had happened as the plane flew westward. The only new thing they discovered was that Anne had seen van Claire both in Frankfurt and walking along the Rhine river in Koblenz. Sam had tied the other man in Koblenz to the guy who had been prowling around Luxembourg, looking at their apartment. Was that guy the Mr. Arbarkian from the Soviet Trade Mission that the nice lady at the Frankfurt convention center had told Alicia about? Was Arbarkian CITADEL? The description Alicia had gotten certainly fit.

They finally decided they had shared everything. Well, almost everything. Anne had fussed over him when he had come home scratched and rumpled yesterday. Sam saw no reason to upset her more by telling her about the three guys who had tried to turn him into a wet spot on the Rue du St Esprit. Of course, Sam didn't know that Kurt had not told him about the probable murder of the second Russian the same day, and for the same reason.

Dulles was as majestic and empty as ever, except for the lines at the too-few pay phones. When they got their turn, Anne's mother's cries of delight practically echoed across the empty concourse; then a car rental and arranging for the air freight to be shipped to Anne's mother's house, and they were off for Bethesda, Maryland.

Bethesda was a small Maryland suburb a couple miles over the state line from the District of Columbia. CIA people liked Bethesda and nearby Carderock Springs and Kensington because it was relatively inexpensive, close to the new Beltway and the Cabin John Bridge. The bridge connected them to the George Washington Parkway and made for a 20-minute commute to Headquarters. Better-off CIA people lived in Georgetown in the District, or North Arlington, Virginia. It would have been even closer to live in McLean, Virginia, which was after all Headquarters' mailing address, but the area was mostly farmland and there weren't many houses to buy.

Anne's parents lived in a standard postwar white clapboard house with one and a half bathrooms and three bedrooms. The half-bathroom was something of a coup. Most D.C. houses had just the one bathroom upstairs, although there were a few new developments that actually featured two full bathrooms. Some people thought that was a little excessive. Besides, who wanted to have to clean *two* bathrooms?

Sam's taciturn father-in-law surprised everybody, possibly including himself, by treating Sam like a returning hero. He was an important person at Treasury, and Treasury Department people spent a lot of time keeping their mouths shut. Sam had been depressed at the prospect of returning home with his head under his arm, possibly unemployed, and certainly a most unsuccessful second lieutenant spy. So the unexpected praise cheered him greatly.

Anne's mother was overjoyed. Her beautiful daughter and her beautiful grandsons and her brave son-in-law were home and free. She had already called Sam's parents in Connecticut with the good news, and Sam headed off to do the same. His in-laws were kind enough not to dwell on Sam's former jailbird status, and talked of other things instead. Like most Washington government families, they did not ask Sam why he had shot up the Gambrinus, although, like most Washington government families, they were dying to.

The next morning Sam was on the phone to the German Desk on the unsecure black line. An unfamiliar voice answered the phone by, as usual, giving the extension number. Sam identified himself, explained that he was back in Washington, and asked for reporting instructions. The voice was guarded, even suspicious. No, Ross Callahan was not available. He took Sam's telephone number — well, his father-in-law's number — and said he would check. Then he hung up. That, Sam thought, wasn't exactly a triumphal return to Headquarters.

By mid afternoon he hadn't heard anything, so he tried the German Desk again. The same suspicious voice told him he would be contacted and that it was not necessary for him to check in again; i.e. don't call us, we'll call you.

At four thirty the phone rang and his mother-in-law got it. After saying something or other he couldn't hear, she said, "It's for you, Sam, dear."

Sam took the phone. "Sam Carpenter."

"Welcome home," Harvey Masters said.

"Thanks."

"Report to room 2C34 tomorrow. Call me at this extension when you get to the lobby. Don't talk to the German Desk or anybody in EUR."

"Shit. I didn't know; I called in this morning."

There was a sigh. "Oh well, they'd find out soon enough anyway. How are Anne and the boys? They survive this mess all right?"

"Yes, thank you."

"I have to go. See you in the morning." He hung up.

Sam put the phone down, relieved and pleased. He was relieved that somebody in the Agency admitted that he existed, and pleased that Harvey was concerned for his family. Hmmm, he thought, Harvey didn't ask me how I was. He decided that was a kind of compliment: Harvey just assumed I would be all right, like I was one of the grown-ups now. At this rate I might even make First Lieutenant. He went off to tell Anne his news.

Room 2C34 was as barren as ever when Sam arrived the next morning. It had taken a determined effort by an attractive woman who introduced herself to Sam as Maria DeAngelo to get him there. The people in the badge office by the front door had claimed Sam didn't exist. Maria went and fetched a slender, earnest young man who was appropriately named Ernest, short for Ernie Barringer. Ernie started talking to the badge clerks in a deferential, soft voice, using lots of acronyms, until the clerks started looking in various file cabinets. Then they reluctantly admitted that Sam existed, and that yes, here was a directive they had received about him, and eventually they came up with a Headquarters badge and chain with Sam's picture on it and an impressive number of letters around the edges indicating that Sam had access to practically everything in the building

Harvey gave Sam a big hello. Old GRUMPY WOLF actually smiled and reintroduced him to Maria and Ernest. "Maria and Ernest are the reasons this dump actually works. Maria knows where all the paper is, and Ernie's the Headquarters version of Ross Callahan."

"Now here's the deal. The Deputy Director is concerned about two operations: INGRESS and CITADEL. He put together a little operations group which he unfortunately insists on calling a tiger team. It consists of me, Ross Callahan, Maria, and as of last week, Ernest, and as of today, you and your pal Alicia. She's off checking in at the moment. The Deputy didn't say so, but we're in charge of finding out things he probably doesn't want to know. How many things we find out that he doesn't want to know will determine what happens to us when this is all over. Judging from what we've found so far, I'd say we're all going to end up counting paperclips in a warehouse in Pennsylvania. Knowing that, do you want to join our merry band?"

Sam smiled and shrugged. "Sure."

"Good. I'm glad you volunteered, although it's not like you had a lot of choices. Your old pal Grant Natz, before the Deputy personally shipped his ass to Vietnam, got the European Division convinced you're another Charlie Whitman." Harvey was talking about the University of Texas student who had gone up into the university bell tower two years before and killed 16 people with his rifle. Unfortunately, Charlie was also an ex-Marine. Of course, Charlie had been an Eagle Scout too, and that hadn't had the right effect on him either. "Anyway, don't plan on going back to the German Desk anytime soon." Harvey checked his notes, and then looked up at Sam. "You still carrying?"

"I've got a field-stripped .45 in my air freight. I got semi-deported in a hurry and couldn't think of anything else to do with it."

Harvey raised an eyebrow. "Where'd you get it?"

"From Alicia. Bonn sent it."

Both of Harvey's eyebrows went up. "Our bookish Chief of Station is sending you .45s by courier? Jesus, he must have been worried. You didn't use it, did you?"

"Er, yes."

Harvey sighed again. "Tell me why I asked?" he said, looking upwards at the ceiling.

Sam explained about the three guys on the Rue du St Esprit.

"OK, the KGB's after you. Ernie, let's get some sidearms and concealed-carry permits for all hands. I'll try and get past the palace guard and get the Deputy to try and get the Soviets to knock it off, but meanwhile we're on our own."

Maria brightened. "May I shoot van Claire in the balls? Assuming he has any?"

Harvey ignored her and turned to Sam. "Where are you living?"

"We just rented an apartment out in Falls Church, off Route 7 behind George Marshall High School."

"We'll need your extra bedroom for one of us to stay there in shifts. Sorry, but you can't stay awake twenty-four hours a day and the KGB may well be coming after you here in the U.S."

Harvey pointed to Maria and changed the topic. "Sam, the first order of business is for you to debrief yourself to Maria. I need to know everything you know by close of business today." As Sam and Maria headed for two empty desks, the door opened and Alicia walked in. Sam walked over, grabbed her in a bear hug, and swung her around the room like they were tango dancers. He put her down and said, "I'm glad you're OK."

She looked up at him with a glorious smile on her plain face and said, "Same for you." Then, suddenly all business, she whipped out her steno pad, nodded for permission from Maria, and said, "Start talking, Tex." In minutes they were in deep conversation, Maria asking, Sam answering, and Alicia taking shorthand. Harvey looked at his little team and mentally shook his head. They're awfully good, dammit. They're going to come up with way more than anybody wants to hear.

Ross came in two hours later, looking brisk and un-jet-lagged. He did not look happy, though, even when he grabbed Maria for another tango and was preparing to continue when Harvey came back in. He was carrying a sheaf of papers and offhandedly murmured, "No sex in the office, please. How was Germany?"

"For me, it was old home week," Ross said. "For the Agency, it was a real *Schweineri*. Harvey, we're in a first-class mess out there. Kirst was the Socialists' golden boy. Willy Brandt and the Socialist brass treated him like a son, and he made the Socialists look good to everybody, even the left-wingers who are real Marxists. He was pro-American, he thought we and the French and the Brits saved Germany from itself, and was most accommodating to the Soviets, although only up to a point. He has a wife and three kids and led a blameless life.

"I talked to every creep and gossip-monger in West Germany. They've all been trying to get something on him since he was in fourth grade and there's nothing, absolutely no dirt that they can come up with. He's so clean even the baseless rumors never got a foothold. Plus his main work has been seeking a rapprochement with East Europe. As a point of honor all the material he works with is in the public domain. The point is, he didn't have access to anything the Soviets couldn't get by walking into the *Ausserminsiterium's* public reading room. Bottom line: he wasn't a Soviet agent."

"Why suicide then?"

"Don't know exactly. Most people are saying it was a version of, 'I bust my ass to save the world and this is what I get for it?' Despair? Fear that the charges would stick and humiliate his family? The CDU — the center-right party — was delighted that the Socialists had mud on their ice cream suit. So they were the ones who jumped at the chance to get him arrested and make a big stink. But I don't think they really believed the story either. Certainly, they let him out on his own recognizance. Whoever heard of letting a spy walk around town on his own?"

"So who benefits?"

"The Soviets. The last thing they want is for the Germans to go running around doing penance in East Europe and curtseying to the Poles and Czechs. They want a West Germany they can portray as a bunch of truculent, unreconstructed Nazis just waiting for a chance to dust off the brown-and-black uniforms they have hanging in the back of the closet and get down to business again. And they want the Poles and Czechs to stay dead afraid of the Germans so they'll put up with the Russian occupation as the lesser evil."

"So you think we got set up?"

"Yes. In spades."

Harvey went over and sat with Sam and Maria and Alicia. When they had finished, Harvey gathered them in a semicircle around him and said, "OK, I think we have as much information as we're going to get at this point. It's time to bell the cat."

CHAPTER NINETEEN

In Moscow, a tired Arbarkian was just closing the door behind him as he tiptoed out of Komsomol's office. As usual, his emotions bounced back and forth between fear and anger. Damn it to hell: Komsomol was ruining a perfectly good operation. Arbarkian had van Claire well in hand and here was their big chance to strew havoc at the top of the CIA hierarchy. And that belligerent fool was planning to throw it away by getting it entangled with an unnecessary assassination.

He had had a team of many of the best analysts of the First Chief Directorate working for a week, debating who should be fingered as the KGB's mole within the CIA. Every piece of information that the KGB had about the men who ran the CIA, and particularly its Clandestine Service, now the more bland "Directorate for Plans," was examined, pored over, and argued about. What were their vulnerabilities? What makes them susceptible to coercion?

Who drank too much? Well, it seemed they all did, but only one was a confirmed alcoholic. The trouble was the alcoholic Division Chief was a jolly sort, and his stumbling in mid afternoon from a half-day at Billy Martin's, incoherent and with his fly open, was considered an amusing eccentricity. Anybody junior to a Division Chief who came back from lunch in that condition would have been fired on the spot. But the upper ranks had their own code of conduct.

Half of them were unfaithful to their wives, and well more than half of the wives had returned the compliment. So there was nothing vulnerable there either. How could you suggest that a man could be coerced into serving the Soviets on the threat of revealing conduct that his peers all engaged in too?

How about homosexuality? The Americans were absolutely hysterical about the horrors of sodomy. Half the questions on their polygraph test, the dreaded FLUTTER, concerned inquiries as to whether the subject was prone to playing hide-the-weenie in the wrong orifices. But they could find no Oscar Wilde within the CIA's ranks. Well, they were a bunch of old spies after all, and any heavy breathing with choirboys was likely to be done very discreetly.

Money! Who appeared to be bribable? Here they ran into a further problem. Washington was a government town. The well-paid lawyers and lobbyists notwithstanding, the bulk of the moneyed class in Washington was the GS-14s and GS-15s, of whom there were several tens of thousands. The scattering of supergrades, the GS-16s thorough GS-18s, helped, but they were few and more or less dust on the table. So the economy of Washington's upper-middle class revolved around an economic elite who in the rest of the country would be considered middle-class at most. As a result, houses were cheap in Washington and everybody drove Chevrolets and Fords. Stepping up to a Mercury or a Pontiac was considered, well, you know, a little tacky.

And then, there was the small group of Washingtonians generally referred to as "the cave dwellers." These were the descendants of people who had bought building lots from George Washington back in his real estate developer days. They had been there ever since. They had boxcars full of money that they had inherited and that they did not work to increase. Instead, they preferred to run the government. As a result, most government agencies, especially glamorous ones like State and the CIA, were run by fifth- and sixth-generation money. Or, even better, men who had rich wives. The Kremlin would have to auction off the entire contents of the Hermitage to raise the cash to bribe one of them.

Stuck with these unavoidable truths, the group of analysts dithered until Arbarkian screamed at them. Then they took a collective deep breath and came up with a name. The candidate's name caused some to react with a "good luck with that" smirk, while others thought it might just work. Arbarkian took the name to Komsomol, who couldn't care less and snapped at him to get off his ass and get on with it. Komsomol wanted one last milking of van Claire and then to end the operation before the Americans wised up and realized they were being duped.

If Komsomol now sent Arbarkian to the U.S. with the Roman Gratchkenowsky story and instructions to maybe exfiltrate the fictitious CIA mole, that would be one thing. Or they could just let van Claire denounce the supposed mole and stir up a shitstorm. The storm could last for months or even years, and that would be another great victory. But how to do this? Komsomol had a rat's intuition for the clandestine but not a rat's patience to gnaw at things until he got what he wanted. He sent for Arbarkian.

There were operational problems. Komsomol wasn't to be moved on killing the American. He ignored Arbarkian's protests that the American may well not have known he was dealing with Russians, never mind KGB employees, when he started shooting. And he was certainly justified in shooting when the supposedly highly trained Thirteenth Directorate assassination team had tried to run him down on the Rue du St Esprit, was he not? Most important, there was the unspoken protocol between the CIA and the KGB not to harm each other's officers, which had been in effect since shortly after the end of World War II. Were they going to abrogate that? Arbarkian left hanging the unspoken question: Did they have the permission of their superiors to do this? Did Andropov know and approve? He bet not. Arbarkian left Komsomol's office sadder and only slightly wiser. Well, off to Washington, and let's see what happens.

The next day van Claire got a handwritten letter postmarked Washington, D.C., whose return address was given as being from a fraternity brother from college he hadn't heard from in twenty years. Curious, he opened it.

"Dear Clay," it said. "I have a delightful new boss who is sending me to Washington for some liaison work with various government agencies. Could I perhaps drop by your house next Thursday at around 5:30 or 6 p.m.? We could have drinks and tell war stories. By the way, I finally remembered the name of that Smith girl you were so hot to boink all those years ago. Lest I forget, if it is permissible, could I have a copy of the State Department phone book? I want to look up some our classmates. I'll call you when I hit town and confirm." The signature was a scribble.

Van Claire sat back and started putting things together. It was from CITADEL, of course. Remembering the name of the Smith girl? He thought some more. Then, oh my God, he's telling me that he has the name of the mole. He has the name of the mole! Oh sweet Jesus, I am going to be a legend in CIA. I'm going to be the next Deputy Director. Maybe, someday, perhaps, even the Director of Central Intelligence? Oh my. That would be so very, very nice.

Now what's this about the State Department phone book? Well, my cover job is State, but . . . oh, of course: CITADEL wanted something juicy to impress his new boss. Let's see if I can come up with something that's not too damaging but looks pretty hot. And I'll have to get my wife out of here. That'll be no problem; she's always off doing something at night. Sometimes he wondered if she was seeing somebody. Nah, he decided, she's so boring in bed she couldn't excite a sailor on leave. He got dressed and went to the office.

His secretary, his third in a year — damn women were always sneaking off to other jobs — was stewing when he got to work. "Mr. van Claire, Travel is being awfully difficult about those first-class tickets for your last trip to West Germany. They said even the DCI travels tourist. What shall I do?"

"I don't know. Tell them I have a compression of the fifth vertebra and require first-class accommodations when I travel. Don't bother me with this administrative crap." He went into his office, closed the door, and started trying to think of what bonbons he could bring CITADEL.

CHAPTER TWENTY

"OK, folks, let's gather around. I just got through talking to Craig Withers. I had him go to the Deputy's people — the Deputy doesn't want to be seen with me for obvious reasons — and they all poo-pooed the idea that the KGB could be gunning for Sam. Ridiculous, they said — not in the United States. Sam's making the whole Rue du St Esprit business up to make himself look good. Jesus wept. So they're not going to get the Deputy to go to the KGB and tell them to knock it off and they're not providing Sam any security. My last and only option is to include Sam in the CITADEL briefing and appeal directly to the Deputy for some security for him. Here's the briefing. It's damn short — tiny steps for little feet — so give a listen, please."

Harvey was standing by his desk. The others pushed their chairs into a semicircle around him. Ross was next-most-senior, so he concentrated on looking officer-like and relaxed. Sam and Maria looked neutral. Alicia and Ernie, who had been working like puppies gnawing on a fresh bone, actually looked like they were having a good time.

Harvey began: "There are five things our group wishes to bring to your attention. Item one: at the outset CITADEL offered the name of Hans Georg Kirst as a Stasi agent. He did this, he said, to establish his bona fides. All of our subsequent investigations show that not only was Kirst most probably not a Stasi agent but that his loss has caused great harm to our interests in Germany.

"Second, the name of an asset of the German Station was sent up to the DDP's office a week before Mr. van Claire's first meeting with CITADEL. Two weeks after that meeting the German asset, an engineer at Dynamit Nobel, was approached by what appeared to be a Soviet agent who demanded he cooperate with them or his name would be given to his employer as a CIA agent. The German refused and was fired by Dynamit Nobel shortly thereafter.

"Third, in early November Mr. van Claire met with both INGRESS, the German journalist, and, later in the day, with CITADEL. At the first meeting Mr. van Claire was given the name of a Russian would-be defector, a man named Goshkorow. The next day Goshkorow and the German journalist died of apparent heart attacks. I say apparent because in the German's case the heart attack was proved to be brought on by a poison administered by two Russian-speaking men. The poisoning of the German might have gone unnoticed if it had not been broken up by the intervention of a CIA officer. I might note here that Mr. van Claire has denied to the Deputy Director that he met INGRESS that day. We have ample evidence that he did.

"Fourth, the material CITADEL had presented to us is, with the exception of one set of valuable information on GRU plans and intentions, is *Spielmaterial* of quite high quality but nevertheless the kind usually used in KGB deception operations. It is of no value to us and much of it is meant to mislead us and cause us to expend time and energy on wild goose chases.

"Fifth, CITADEL, who presented himself to Mr. van Claire as a high-ranking KGB official, is actually a mid-level case officer named Gregor Arbarkian. One of his known activities was to scout out the Luxembourg hospital where the Russian injured in the INGRESS poisoning attempt was a patient and the residence of the CIA officer who broke up the INGRESS assassination. Two days after this, the hospitalized Russian died under mysterious circumstances and an attempt was made to assassinate the CIA officer.

"Consequently, I recommend that back-channel representations be made at as a high a level as is deemed necessary to warn, threaten, insist or cajole the KGB into desisting from CITADEL's campaign to assassinate the CIA officer. Thank you."

Harvey looked up. "That's it."

"That ought to do it," Ross said. The others nodded. Sam said "thank you."

Harvey said, "I think it's time to make an appointment to see The Man."

Harvey dialed the Deputy's extension on the red line. Margaret, the tall, gray-haired woman whose husband was a college professor, answered. They had known each other since OSS days. It was the friendly nodding acquaintance of people who had known each other for a long time, but not very well. Harvey had been overseas for the last twenty-two years, after all.

"Harvey, how nice to hear your voice. I heard that the boss had you downstairs someplace doing something interesting for him."

"That's why I'm calling, Margaret. I have done what I was supposed to do and it's time to report my findings to him. Can you set me up to see him? I'm afraid it's rather urgent, so today if possible."

There was a long silence at the other end. Harvey, concerned, said, "Ah, Margaret, are you still there?"

"Yes, dear. I, er, well; the situation is that he said that when you checked in I was to tell you that Craig Withers was to handle the briefing."

Harvey sat back in his chair. Oh damn, the Muffled Fart Brigade was going take over and bury this somewhere out beyond West Parking. He sighed.

Margaret heard the sigh. "Let me call you back, Harvey. There's someone here." She probably meant the other secretary, Jennifer, who had won the crown as the world's biggest gossip two years running. Or it could be the boss himself. Margaret said goodbye and hung up.

Fifteen minutes later, Harvey's red line rang. He answered with a wary "Hello?"

"It's Margaret, Harvey. I can talk now. Jennifer is off showing her breasts to someone." Jennifer, besides being a champion gossip, was devoted to wearing the 1950s brassieres that made a women's *balcons* project straight out from their bodies like the nose cones of rockets. There had been a TV personality called Dagmar who had the largest such set, and men had taken to calling ladies' chests Dagmars, and were much given to discussing the engineering stresses involved in designing an undergarment that was holding everything up and out in such a noteworthy fashion. "The boss has a problem. Your friend van Claire has been running all over town beating his chest and letting everybody know he's about to destroy Angleton and the CI staff. The damn fool has no sense of operational security."

"What on earth is he saying?"

"That's just it: he's saying that a defector is about to give him the name of the mole that Angleton's been looking for and that it's actually someone in CI staff."

"I thought CITADEL was run on a bigot-list basis."

"Not when van Claire's in charge. The word is he's been out lunching with Allen Dulles and Bissell and that entire crowd, and you know how the old boys' network likes to drop juicy bits at Georgetown dinners and receptions."

"Dammit, they're all retired. And the president himself fired Dulles and Bissell. They're the last people who should be hearing about this."

"This is Washington, Harvey. They're the first people to hear about this. And getting fired by President Kennedy makes you a hero in some circles."

"That's all the more reason I need to talk to the DDP. Why is he putting Withers into the game now?"

"Harvey, the boss is under the gun. He's got every heavyweight in the old boys' club cheering for van Claire. I know what you're going to do: Dr. Harvey Masters is going to come marching into his office and make a masterly presentation during which he's going to nail Clay van Claire's withered balls to the wall, just under the portrait of Allen Dulles. And what's the boss supposed to do then? Slap you on the back and thank you? Be realistic, Harvey. Do you want to end up cleaning the toilets in the executive men's room? And do think the boss is going to let himself get in a position where he ends up as your assistant? Now call Withers and let him strike up the band. Goodbye, dear." Margaret hung up.

Harvey looked in his notes for Wither's extension number.

A half-hour later Withers slid into the team's office like he had oiled his hand-sewn moccasins. Well, they looked more like slippers than shoes. In some ways Craig Withers reminded Harvey of pictures he had seen in the National Gallery of eighteenth- and nineteenth-century courtiers and diplomats circling around the throne room, all skinny legs and frock coats and oily expressions, oozing their way forward to tell the boss something the boss might want to hear. Withers is our own Count Metternich, Harvey thought. Well, Metternich had a pretty good batting average.

"Well, Harvey. How nice to see you again."

Harvey rose and shook the proffered hand. "It's nice to see you again too, Craig," he lied. "I am given to understand that you have been selected to brief The Man on our task group's findings."

Withers raised his eyebrows slightly in feigned surprise. "Do tell. I can't say I am delighted to have been the one selected."

"I'd be happy to step in if you prefer."

Withers raised a hand. "No, no. You will be blunt, and I will not. But don't look so unhappy, Harvey. I hold Mr. van Claire in the same high level of admiration as you do. You may rely on me to do my best."

Oh, dear, Harvey thought. That means he's going to be the *banderillero*, and plant little pinpricks on the charging bull, but not be the matador with the sword. Damn.

"Perhaps you might tell me what you have prepared," Withers said.

Harvey took a deep breath and began the briefing; Withers listened intently and took an occasional note.

The next morning at eleven Craig Withers appeared in the Deputy Director's conference room to make his presentation. He did not know that a preliminary meeting on the matter had already been held in the men's room at nine a.m. Withers, who knew his way around a thousand briefings and a thousand conference rooms, assumed that most of the seven men before him had already made up their minds. He could have recited "The Charge of the Light Brigade" for all some of them cared. But the Deputy was the one to make the decision, and he would listen carefully. Withers knew he would really only be talking to him.

Introductions were made and were all necessarily perfunctory: they all knew each other. The Deputy had three of his deputies present, plus a GS-17 from Soviet Bloc and the Chief of Europe himself. The seventh man he knew was from the Director of Central Intelligence's office, although he only knew him to nod to in the halls and in meetings. Still, the fact that a representative from the Director's office would descend from the throne room to catch this meeting was both noteworthy and unsettling. Craig wished that Headquarters briefers had that electronic thing fighter pilots had. The Air Force called it IFF: Identification Friend or Foe. He could use one.

Craig guessed that the room was approximately evenly split for and against whatever it was he was going to say. Clay had been patrolling the halls and buttonholing people on the command floors of the Clandestine Service for a week now. God knows what he'd been up to in Washington dining and drawing rooms.

The Deputy had looked twice at the man from the Director's office. Clearly he was not happy to have him there keeping an eye on him, and not happy that the Director had found out about this at all. The three-martini lunches at Billy Martin's Carriage House had clearly superseded the bigot list.

At a nod from the Deputy, Withers gave them his friendliest, least oily smile and launched into the briefing. He was standing in front of the conference table, which had been turned sideways, with the seven men all seated in a row along the long side. It looked like a shortened version of *The Last Supper*, except everyone was wearing dark-gray suits and no one looked like Jesus. Standing at the civilian version of parade rest, Craig delivered Harvey's briefing more or less verbatim, although in a more neutral tone than Harvey might have used. When he finished he put his feet together, standing almost at attention, and made a tiny forward bending motion which could have been perceived as a bow.

"Is that all?" a GS-17 asked, obviously surprised.

"Yes sir."

"No conclusions and recommendations?"

"We defer to you gentlemen."

They didn't seem pleased. It left them little to argue about.

The Deputy cleared his throat. "I am most unhappy to learn about this assassination business. Who are you talking about?"

"A GS-11 named Sam Carpenter."

"Ah, the Luxembourg business. Could it be viewed as retaliation for that?"

"It should be explained to the KGB that Carpenter had no knowledge they were KGB, or even Russian, and that as they had drawn weapons it was clearly a matter of self-defense, sir."

"Thank you, Craig, and thank Harvey and the task force for me for doing such a thorough job. Ask them to continue and complete their work with all due haste, since Mr. van Claire has reported that CITADEL is coming to Washington within two days."

Craig Withers walked into room 2C34 and closed the door very carefully behind him. When he turned around again, six people were looking at him. He waved in the general direction of the desks and chairs and drew out a desk chair for himself. He sat down rather primly, pinching his pants at the crease at the knee and holding them to make sure the trousers didn't ride up and expose too much of his long black socks. He gave the six a wry smile.

"Well, they didn't have much to say." Then he gave them a recital of the response to his briefing. "They did say as I was leaving that you were to hurry because CITADEL is coming here."

"Kind of Delphic," Ross said.

"The brass never show their hands to the enlisted men," Harvey said. "It means they didn't want to hear what we told them so we're to keep going and either prove CITADEL is a dangle or admit it could be genuine. But at least it sounds like the DDP might be going to do something for Sam."

"Are you sure?" Maria asked.

"Pretty sure," Harvey said. "We better mount guard on Sam for a while until we hear something though. Meanwhile, we need to get back to work. Anybody have any idea what CITADEL is doing coming to Washington?"

Nobody did. Ross said, "At least we'll be playing on home ground."

Sam said, "Harvey, we can't. It's against the law for CIA to operate domestically."

"Will somebody pull Dudley Do-Right's hat down over his ears, please?" Ross said. "C'mon, Sam, van Claire and CITADEL are operating here, so so are we. Make believe you're in Luxembourg and get on with it."

"I can't," Sam, said. Then he stopped to think. "Yes I can. I'm a CIA agent and CIA agents aren't supposed to play by the rules. OK, I'm in."

Ross smiled. "Besides, you're not an agent, Sam. You're a case officer. Case officers don't have scruples. It's OK for agents to have them; nobody cares what they think," Ross said.

"Enough with the funnies, folks," Harvey said. "Let's try and get organized. I'll be the first to admit I'm at a loss on how to proceed. Our premise is that CITADEL is a dangle. Van Claire is being suckered into giving him more and more valuable information in return for CITADEL's promise to give us the name of the mole in CIA, who he says is a supergrade on the CI staff."

"Which narrows it down to six people, including Angleton."

"And also included Bill Hood, the guy who's flying cover for us."

"Or is he?"

"Do I smell paranoia?"

"The likelihood of it being either of them is zero. If they leaked to the KGB the whole CIA would be destroyed in twenty minutes."

"What if we're wrong?" Maria interrupted. "What if the mole is real? It *is* possible, after all."

"But not likely," Ross replied.

Harvey cleared his throat rather loudly. "Let's not talk like Headquarters people. We shall stick to our thesis that operation CITADEL is a dangle. Let's do this," Harvey said. "We mount a surveillance operation, try and keep an eye on van Claire, and, if we can, CITADEL when he shows up. And then we just watch. If something happens which will prove our assumption that this is a dangle, then we act on it. If nothing does, or if we lose them and don't know what happened, then we just accept defeat gracelessly and wait for them to come for us. Agreed?"

There were nods all around.

OK, let's get this show on the road," Harvey said. "Ernie, get rental cars for everybody, including yourself. Get a truck too. I don't want six beige Plymouth sedans. It would look like an AARP surveillance team. Wait a minute." He turned to Sam. "OK if Anne plays? She's good at surveillance. She doesn't have to, but it's your ass on the line so she may want to."

Sam smiled. "I'll ask, but I know the answer's yes. Harvey, I thought you said she was too good-looking for surveillance work."

"I can fix that," Alicia said. They all turned to look at Alicia. Alicia didn't look like her normal homely little self. She looked better. A lot better in fact. Alicia saw the scrutiny and smiled. "Anne's been showing me makeup tricks. She also showed me how she can ugly herself up. She did something with an eyebrow pencil and some stuff so that even van Claire wouldn't recognize her. Well, he would if got up close, but probably not at a distance." Then they noticed that Alicia and Ernie were sitting very close together. Well, isn't that sweet, Maria thought. They'll be sorry.

"Make it seven cars, then, Ernie," Harvey continued. "And while you're at it, get everybody a Minox camera and a regular camera too. Maybe we can have some pictures when it comes time for show and tell.

"Maria, find out everything you can about van Claire: where does he live, what's the most likely commuting pattern. As soon as you do, Sam and Ross: go scope the place out, see what the opportunities are for observation posts. Anybody know anything about bugging phones?"

No hands went up. Then Ernie said, "I can find somebody."

Harvey reflected. "No, too many people to get involved. My fault for bringing it up. Let's follow the military's KISS rule."

"KISS?"

"Keep It Simple, Stupid. Let's settle for an OP. Get going, report in here. Extension 3587 rolls over to two more lines and there's no cutoff, so let the phone keep ringing until I or whoever's here answers. Tell me every single thing that happens, even the boring stuff, and let's see if we can put everything together. Now get going."

By two thirty p.m. Sam and Ross were out cruising van Claire's neighborhood. He lived on Abercrombie Street in Chevy Chase, a block off Connecticut Avenue and a half-mile from the D.C. line. It was all residential on one side of Connecticut. On the other side there were two posh country clubs, the Chevy Chase and Columbia country clubs.

Van Clair's side of Connecticut Avenue was all big houses on small lots, stuffed close to each other on heavily treed, winding roads. Most of the roads trickled down to dead ends in a stream valley park. There were cars parked on the narrow streets and an endless number of plumbers' and electricians' trucks and unmarked white panel trucks for God knows what.

Ross and Sam were sitting in a white panel truck themselves. They were a block down from van Claire's house. "Lotta money here," Ross said to Sam, looking at all the trucks. "I think these people have little men come in to sharpen their pencils for them."

"Which means there'll be a lot of maids and stuff looking out windows while the homeowners are downtown generating money to pay for all this," Sam said. "So we can't be here long without attracting attention."

"If we sit in the front seat. Nobody will see us in the back."

"The back of the van has no windows."

"It's about to," Ross said, taking a box with a heavy drill and a number of bits out of the bag of stuff they had bought at hardware store in the district. "All we need is a few discreet holes. And don't go all Calvinist on me. We'll pay Hertz for fucking up their truck in due course." He slipped between the seats and went into the empty back of the van. Sam followed him.

Harvey had gotten on the phone and called his wife in Cleveland. "Charlotte," he said when she answered the phone, "you used to be a respectable suburban housewife before I dragged you off to Europe. What do respectable suburban housewives do during the day?"

"How nice to hear your voice, dear. And thank you for inquiring how I am and how the family is. Your daughter is pregnant again, by the way. Now that we've gotten all that out of the way, we can get back to covert operations. Respectable suburban housewives raise children, shop for food, do things related to keeping the house looking nice even though their husbands won't notice, and do volunteer work."

"Volunteer work like what?"

"The Red Cross, church groups, the League of Women Voters in the East, the Junior League out here. I do a lot of that stuff in West Germany, not that you've noticed."

As usual, the dry remarks went right over Harvey's head. "Thanks, sweetie. When are you coming back here?"

"You're up to something. Why don't you call me when it's safe? Bye-bye." She hung up.

At eight the next morning they had another group meeting in room 2C34. "Let's begin. Ernie has cameras for you and will show you how to use a Minox."

Ernie did. The tiny cameras were, as far as Sam knew, the only spy gear that actually worked. That and high-ASA film, which was brand-new and still classified. Three months before, the Agency had actually issued ASA 800 film for use in the field.

When Ernie was finished, Harvey continued. "Sam and Ross have scouted van Claire's home. I have made a little deal with Margaret, the Deputy's secretary, to keep an eye on van Claire here at the office. Maria?"

"That nice man I met in the Office of Security when we were checking the guys who went with van Claire to Koblenz?" Maria said. "Well, he told me CITADEL flew in to Dulles last night and was met by an embassy car and taken to the Sixteenth Street Hilton, the one by the Soviet Chancellery. We've got an OP/LP just up the street, and Alicia and Ernie will go there and keep an eye out."

"Good. Thanks to my wife's remarks, Anne and Maria will be going to the new library on Connecticut Avenue this morning, the one three blocks from van Claire's house. They're supposed to be setting up a conference for the League of Women Voters, so they have permission to use a room in the basement until the library closes at 8 p.m. tonight. That'll give the women and a husband or two someplace to hide during the day so we don't have to lurk around the neighborhood. There's a phone booth in the lobby of the library, so we have communications. I doubt anything will happen there, but it's best to cover the bases. Let's all get off to our places and sit and wait. This is the hard part. Anybody who's ever manned a listening post or an observation post will tell you that."

"Yeah," Ross said. "Remember that OP they had across the street from the Soviet Consulate in Salzburg?"

"They told us about it at the Farm when we in training," Sam said. "The OP operators were going nuts from boredom so they took a Nikon camera, screwed a Russian 500-millimeter lens on it and got a German automatic shutter advance. Then they tried something TSD had come up with called a sensor. Every time somebody walked up to the Soviet Consulate, the motion detector sensor would signal the camera to take a picture and then advance the film one frame."

"Did it work?"

"After a fashion. They came back in a week: they had a drum magazine of film on it, All 500 exposures were used. Noteworthy, since not many people visit the consulate."

"And?"

"And it was October and they had 500 pictures of falling leaves. The sensor was *very* sensitive."

"Well, let's stick to eyeballs. Everybody go off and concentrate on not being bored. Call in every time *anything* happens. Ross and Sam, you stay here and be ready to rush off to the scene of whatever it is that happens."

When the others had left, Harvey put his forehead on the table and groaned. "Look at me. I'm a fifty-four-year-old spy, an OSS Jedburgh, and I just set up a League of Women Voters undercover operation in the Chevy Chase library."

Ross and Sam, who had had trouble making a suitably inconspicuous hole in the panel truck, lit cigarettes and looked on sympathetically.

CHAPTER TWENTY-ONE

Clay van Claire's day started out rotten and then turned worse. He cut himself shaving and couldn't get the toilet paper bandages to stick on right. One fell off and got a drop of blood on the shirt he was planning to wear, so he had to throw it in the hamper and get another one. He came down to breakfast in a foul mood.

His wife looked at him uninterestedly. He had been telling her for years that he liked a breakfast of bacon and eggs over easy. She had told him where the frying pan was. So he settled for Special K as usual. He didn't like Special K. She was smoking, the newspaper and a cup of coffee in front of her.

"I have a business meeting here tonight, around six. It's confidential. Could you maybe visit a friend or something?"

"I'll be at the club, then. Probably be late," she said, not looking up from the paper. He looked at her. She was, he had to admit, still pretty good-looking in a Ladies Who Lunch sort of way. She was out a lot recently, come to think of it. Could she . . . ? Nah, besides, they hadn't even been in the sack for weeks. She seemed uninterested.

When he went to start his Mercedes, the car just sat there. Son of a bitch. The damn thing cost an arm and leg and spent half its time in the shop. Call AAA? He didn't have time to wait. He went back inside.

"My car won't start again. Can I take yours?"

"I need it. I have a lunch."

He called the Deputy's office. Margaret was there early as usual and answered.

"This is van Claire. Send a car for me. Mine's broken again." He hung up.

"And good morning to you, too," Margaret said to the dial tone. She called the motor pool. Van Claire acted like the pool cars were his own.

When van Claire got to the office he made his ritual visit to the executive men's room but today didn't join in the usual caustic chatter about what losers the Redskins were and the office gossip about who was going to get the German Station if the incumbent retired. He was thinking of his meeting tonight.

What was he going to do with CITADEL? CITADEL was going to give him the mole's name tonight, but he wanted something damn juicy to keep the *Rezident* off his back. Then he wanted solid assurances that his money was going to come through.

Yesterday, after a monumental shouting match in a crowded Deputy Director's conference room, it had been agreed to wire one million dollars to a Guernsey bank account as earnest money. The bank transfer had been made last night. For security reasons CI staff had not been invited to the meeting, but everyone else who could possibly manage a reason to be there had been there. The people at the meeting had not been admiring. After forty-five minutes of back-and-forth, the questions they really wanted to ask came out.

"Clay, why did you lie to the boss?"

"I've explained that to him to his satisfaction. Next question." Actually, he had given a long and groveling apology, which had not been accepted. The Deputy's bottom line was that Clay either came back tomorrow with the mole's name or he was fired.

"You gave two agents to the KGB and got a third one killed in the process. Why are you still employed here?"

"Did you Headquarters commandos ever hear of operational necessity? I traded a couple of minor agents for a chance to find the mole who's destroying us. I should be commended for having the balls to do that. You people don't have any, so you wouldn't understand. And may I remind you that the Deputy Director signed off on all this? Shall we go in and discuss this with him?" That finally shut them up, even though the Deputy hadn't signed off on anything.

Today he was in a quandary. What could he get for CITADEL that wouldn't leave his fingerprints all over it? A secondary consideration was what could he get that wouldn't be too damaging to the CIA. Certainly he didn't want to blow another agent. That Kirst business had had a lot of back blast. Why couldn't CITADEL have brought him someone more obviously a KGB agent? He paced around the office, trying to think. At the same time he was so excited he could hardly stand it. In a few hours he would have the name of the mole! A few hours after that, he assumed, he would be in the Deputy's office, or even the Director's, gravely accepting their congratulations and offering sage advice on how to advance the operation as they went forward together. But first things first. What will I have to give CITADEL?

He almost smacked himself on the forehead when it came to him. The DDP's reading files, you idiot. You take it, you announce you're going to read it, and march off to your office. Sometime thereafter you decide you're coming down with something and have them drive you home. You simply take the file off the clipboard, slip it in your briefcase, and take it home with you. There's nothing there except all those code names that CITADEL could never figure out anyway and a bunch of stories a day ahead, or more often, a day behind Reuters and AP. Give CITADEL a look and bring it back in the morning.

It was a lock. The guards were supposed to stop people leaving the building on a random basis and check their briefcases to see if they were carrying any classified material home to work on. That was, of course, forbidden. It fact, it was a security violation. The first security violation got you a formal written warning, which went into your personnel records. On a second violation you got suspended for two weeks without pay. For a third security violation you got fired. But there was no danger of that today. He'd be going down to the executive motor pool in the basement for a ride home and the guards there didn't do anything except look obsequious.

Tomorrow morning you come in early, open your safe, slip the file onto the clipboard, and turn it in. You tell Margaret or whoever that you threw it your safe last night without thinking to tell her and you're so sorry. You'd better act damn sorry, he reminded himself. Margaret's a bear on security and she'll be on her uppers, having spent half the evening running around trying to find the clipboard with the reading files on it. Serve her right. She was always kind of haughty with him.

Harvey spent the day sitting in 2C34 waiting for the phone to ring. It did, but not often. Downtown, Alicia and Ernie were sitting side by side peering through the slats of the Venetian blinds at the CIA LP/OP on Sixteenth Street by the Soviet Chancellery. Alicia was checking the chancellery; Ernie was looking at the front door of the Hilton a block away. They had photos of CITADEL, binoculars, cameras, snacks, coffee, and an agreement to cover each other when one had to go to the bathroom.

Being an observer in an observation post is tedious and stressful. On the one hand you are just sitting there, waiting. On the other hand if your mind wanders and you miss seeing the person you're hoping to see slip in or out of the building, you've screwed the whole thing up. So you have to pay close attention even if your mind screams at you that it's bored and wants to go to the movies. But Alicia and Ernie were perfectly happy. For one thing they had decided that they really, really liked each other. That made them perfectly happy to get paid to sit beside each other and chat all day long. For another this was, after all, a clandestine operation. They were finally CIA agents, not just a secretary and a clerk.

At nine thirty Ernie had a hit. Arbarkian, CITADEL rather, walked out of the Hilton and headed north. He nudged Alicia. "Here he comes."

"Now I've got him," she said. Not surprisingly, CITADEL walked up to the front door of the Soviet Chancellery and walked in. In the next few minutes three other men walked in at intervals. She reported this to Harvey.

In Chevy Chase, Anne and Maria called to report that they had been warmly welcomed at the library and were attracting no attention in their room in the basement. Anne had taken the twins from her mother for an hour and strollered them through van Claire's neighborhood. The first time she went by she saw nothing. The second time she saw a tow truck that said Metropolitan Motors on the side hauling away a Mercedes sedan, a big one. At lunchtime Maria went for a walk and noted that the other car in van Claire's driveway was gone. Presumably the house was now empty. She noted two houses close to his were being extensively remodeled, and that some of the craftsmen's trucks looked like they had been parked there overnight. That would come in handy for Ross and Sam if they needed to dump their van nearby.

Ross and Sam were in 2C34 with Harvey, awaiting orders. Ross, a veteran of the stakeout and OP world, sat quietly, drawing on some inner patience and just waiting. Sam settled down to read a copy of *P. S. Wilkinson*; he identified with the title character. Harvey was feeling the first little black tremors of despair. This isn't going to work, he thought.

At four fifteen van Claire announced he wasn't feeling well and told his secretary to call the garage and have a motor pool car ready to take him home. He closed and locked his safe, put on his coat and hat, picked up his briefcase and left.

Ten minutes later Margaret, the DDP's secretary, kept her agreement with Harvey and gave van Claire's secretary a ring. "Susan, is Clay still around? I think the boss might want to see him later."

"He just left, Margaret. Said he wasn't feeling well. Should I call the motor pool? They have radio telephones in the executive cars."

"No, no, not necessary at all. Oh, by the way, did he give you the reading file back? He made a big thing about taking it just now."

"He didn't give it to me. Should I open his safe and take a look for it?"

"Would you please? I'm not sure the boss is through with it. Call me back, OK?"

"Sure. Bye."

Five minutes later Susan called back. "It wasn't in his safe. I can't find it, Margaret."

"Oh, thanks, Susan. Never mind. One of the other officers must have it. I'll just have to ask around. Thank you."

Margaret hung up the phone and considered what might, or might not, have happened. The Deputy Director's reading file was a collection of cables and an occasional dispatch that were the highlights of the previous day's CIA activities worldwide. The chief reports officer put it together every day, put the assembled cables on a clipboard, and circulated it to the Deputy and his senior staff. Since nobody could be expected to remember a thousand cryptonyms, names and places and brief explanatory notes were penciled in to explain where necessary. It was a gross violation of security of course, but the only way to ensure perfect security was to have no operations at all.

Keeping track of the reading file was a major headache for the secretaries. Since it was a digest of everything going on in the clandestine world on a given day, it really was the family jewels. Yet it was handled almost as cavalierly as the morning's *New York Times*. At least no secretary had had to retrieve it from the executive men's room yet. Ordinarily, this would be just another minor irritation in the day's occupation, but Harvey had asked her to keep an eye on van Claire and call him if anything noteworthy happened. This was noteworthy. She reached for the phone.

When Harvey answered she said, "I think Fatso took the Deputy's reading file home with him," and hung up before Harvey could thank her.

Harvey turned to Ross and Sam. "Saddle up, boys. Van Claire's heading home. He's got the DDP's reading file with him. Don't get a hernia tailing him. You know where he's going. Go to the library, check in here, and let's hope something happens."

At 4:27 p.m. CITADEL walked out the front door of the Soviet Chancellery and headed south on Sixteenth Street. Alicia was on the phone instantly.

"He's moving, Harvey."

"Follow him, please. You on foot; Ernie takes a car."

She hung up and ran out of the office. Ernie was right behind her.

"Luck," she said and blew him a kiss as she ran for the front door. Ernie ran for the door that led to the basement garage.

Alicia was out the door and scanning the street. She saw CITADEL; she didn't see any countersurveillance. She concentrated on looking invisible and wandered after him. He turned right on K Street and, after a suitable interval, so did she. He walked up to Farragut Square at Connecticut and K and stopped at a bus stop. There were eight people already there. CITADEL made nine and she was the tenth. She slipped in between two tall people. Hell, everybody was taller than she was.

Rush hour had started, and the L bus line was a principal route to the Maryland suburbs. L6 and L8 express buses loaded up in the Federal Triangle down by the Mall, stopped once at Farragut

Square to pick up passengers, and then ran as an express to the Maryland line at Chevy Chase Circle, where it turned into a local and started dropping people off at every second street corner. A bus drew up, already almost full. Somehow CITADEL worked his way onto the bus. Alicia, less trained but equally gifted, was two people behind him. She managed to slip past him and end up squished in the aisle twenty feet farther back, where she disappeared in the crowd of standees.

Ernie, in a Hertz Ford, was doing all right for a guy who didn't know how to do this. He'd had the sense to follow Alicia, not CITADEL, and had managed to go slowly and miss lights so that he stayed comfortably behind her. He didn't check his tail: nobody had told him to. He was caught at the light while CITADEL and Alicia waited for the bus, and was behind them when they got on. He didn't see how they'd done it, but six of the people ahead of them in line were still standing there looking pissed when the absolutely full bus pulled away from the curb without them.

After that it was a piece of cake. The bus was an express now, so it inched along, not stopping unless everyone else did too. Traffic was very heavy, so Ernie and the bus were locked into position and stayed within a couple of cars of each other all the way up Connecticut Avenue. After Chevy Chase Circle they were in Maryland and the bus started dropping people off. At the fourth stop CITADEL got out, looked around, and headed down Abercrombie Street.

CITADEL glanced around. There was no one else on the street. Not, he thought, that he cared. If CIA wanted to follow him that was fine with him. He'd rather expected that, but van Claire was remarkably careless about tradecraft. CITADEL's own people would be around somewhere. He'd been appalled that that shit Komsomol had sent a hit team with him with orders to find and kill the American, preferably in a dramatic fashion. Mixing a delicate operation like van Claire with a killing was profoundly stupid. But then Komsomol was profoundly stupid.

CITADEL wondered how tonight's meeting would go off. If van Claire laughed or got angry when he told him the name of the CIA mole that the KGB analysts had selected, then the operation would be over. But if van Claire actually bought the name of the supposed mole and went haring off with it, he'd have to follow the operational plan and keep going.

Two blocks later Alicia got off the bus. Ernie slid to the curb and opened the door for her.

"Turn right and right and let's see if he went to van Claire's," she said. He did, and CITADEL had. It was well after dark, but there were streetlights. They saw him walking up the driveway as they went by the cross street. "Keep going," Alicia said. "Let's head for the library."

The room in the basement was on a corridor off the stairway one floor down from the library itself. It made a textbook-perfect place for a discreet rendezvous. Alicia slipped in, gave Anne a finger wave and got on the phone to Harvey. "CITADEL just went into van Claire's house."

Harvey sat back in his chair and sighed a very large sigh. My God, he had guessed right. Well, it was logical after all. Washington was crawling with spies from fifty different countries, counterspies, the FBI and the Secret Service running around protecting people and carefully examining passersby. Why not disappear into a posh residential neighborhood far from the madding crowd?

Now Anne had taken the phone. "Sam and Ross just came in. Ross took the panel truck and is parking it somewhere near van Claire's house. Sam is here. Instructions?"

"Tell Sam to join Ross and wait. See what they can see. Van Claire has the Deputy's reading file with him. At the moment I'm damned if I can think what to do about it. I'm open for ideas."

Sam left the library, got in a Hertz Chevy Malibu parked out back, and drove the five blocks to Abercrombie Street. Damn. It was well after dark and rich people didn't work late, apparently. The streets were full of cars. He saw the panel truck tucked in behind another truck at the remodeling site two doors down from van Claire's and then he saw a parking spot next to van Claire's driveway. The school solution would be to drive past it and find some other place to park. Screw it, Sam thought. We might need wheels close by. He pulled in, parked, and got out of the car. They had taped the solenoids in the car doors so that the interior lights didn't come on when the doors were opened. Sam pressed his door closed. He was wearing dark jeans and a black jacket. He had a black ski mask on.

Ross nodded as he got in the truck. "CITADEL went in five minutes ago. What did Harvey say?"

"See what we can see. He says van Claire has the Deputy's reading file."

"He's going to give that to CITADEL? Jesus." He looked out the windshield. "Can't see much from here. How are you at sneaking around backyards?"

"Not half as good as those boys from Texarkana in the Marines, but OK. You sure this is following orders?"

"More or less. Harvey would have been precise if he wanted us to just sit here."

They went out the back of the truck and circled around the block to come up on van Claire's house from the back. It was cold, and nobody was outside. The houses had tons of shrubbery, fences that weren't hard to get around or over, and surprisingly few dogs, though they did hear one bark from inside a house. Maria had confirmed that Chevy Chase had strict rules about dogs. If dogs went outside they were on a leash, and both the town and the neighbors were eager to enforce the rule.

Ross had a black balaclava and dark clothes too, so they were nearly invisible as they edged through the azaleas in van Claire's backyard. They moved to the back of the house. It was a truncated stockbroker Tudor, scrunched up to fit the small lot, but still very large. There was a big porch with jalousie windows, now shut tight in back. Ross nudged Sam and they went around the edge of the yard to the four stairs that led from the porch to the backyard. Ross reached up and tested the door. It was locked, of course. Ross took a credit card out of his wallet and slipped the lock. As he had hoped, the door opened; rich people never bothered with deadbolts.

The back of the house was in darkness, but light shone through from a front room. The kitchen door wasn't locked. They slipped into the kitchen and skulked down the hallway. Both men peeled off their ski masks. They could hear van Claire and CITADEL talking.

"Look, you confirmed that the million dollars was deposited into your Guernsey account, right? And yes, you have to be debriefed, and yes, it will take time. Several weeks, possibly."

There was a snort of laughter, presumably from CITADEL. "We debriefed Lonsdale and Burgess and McLean for three years each and they were our agents all along. How long?"

"Well, I don't know exactly. I'll find out for you."

"Thank you, I guess. What do you have for me?"

"Who is the mole?" Sam wasn't sure, but van Claire's voice sounded a little wavery.

There was a long, long silence.

Then, from CITADEL: "Is this room bugged?"

"No, of course not."

"In Russia the answer would be, 'yes, of course.' Here, I will whisper in your ear, so you will be the first to know."

There was a sound of movement, then van Claire's voice. "Well, I'll be a son of a bitch."

"You like that." CITADEL sounded disappointed. Why? He should be delighted, Sam thought. CITADEL clearly knew something he didn't.

"Now what do you have for me?"

The 2nd Lieutenant Spy

There was the sound of the clasps on a briefcase snapping open.

Sam and Ross looked at each other in the dim light. Harvey had said, "See what you can see." He hadn't said anything about horning in on the meeting. Still, if Harvey was right, van Claire was about to hand the KGB the family jewels. What had Staff Sergeant Mills said? "When in doubt, young gentlemen, get off the pot and DO SOMETHING." Sam nodded towards the room but Ross was already moving in that direction.

"Good evening, folks," Ross said in what he hoped was a cheery voice. "I'm from the library, and your book is overdue." Sam had stood to the side, covering the room. His hand was in his jacket, his fingers wrapped around the .45. Who knew how CITADEL would react? Christ, for that matter, who knew how van Claire would react?

The living room looked like the scene from a training film. CITADEL and van Claire were sitting in overstuffed leather chairs. The chairs were both deep burgundy brown and clearly expensive. On the Louis XVI coffee table between them sat a sheaf of papers. Even from ten feet away Ross could see that they were CIA cables. It was the Deputy's reading file. Thank you, Lord. If that had been anything else he and Sam — well, the whole crew of them — would be fired and probably prosecuted.

CITADEL had a Minox camera in his hand and was just setting the focus when they walked in. He froze, waiting for their next move.

Clay van Claire erupted in anger. He sprang to his feet, face red and arms waving. "Who are you? What are you two jackasses doing here? Get out! I'm calling the police." He stormed toward the phone.

"Oh, please do call the police, Mr. van Claire. We're from the Deputy Director's office; He wants his reading file back."

"You're ours? You're CIA?" van Claire screamed.

Sam and Ross reached in their pockets, produced their Headquarters passes and showed him.

"Get out. Get out now. You fucking idiots are ruining a sensitive operation."

Ross stepped over to the coffee table and picked up the briefing papers. "Certainly, sir; good night."

"No you don't. Goddamn it, I don't know who you are." Van Claire stormed over to the phone and dialed. It was 6:15, and nobody answered the Deputy's phone. Office hours were over. Van Claire stood for a second, steaming. He wanted the Clandestine Services watch officer. He wanted these two picked up and dragged off by the Office of Security. He didn't know the phone number. He didn't really know any CIA phone numbers except his own and the front office's. He supposed he could call the CIA number in the phone book and argue with the operator, who would probably refuse to even admit that there was a Clandestine Services watch officer. Goddamn it. Action this day! He would go out to Headquarters and find the watch officer and have these two idiots hauled off. Shit: his car was in the shop.

He spun around and pointed a finger at Sam. "You. Gimme your car keys."

Sam glanced at Ross, who to his surprise nodded slightly.

"Yes, sir. It's the Chevy Malibu at the foot of the driveway." Sam held out the keys to van Claire, who snatched them and stormed out, not even stopping to take a coat. Over his shoulder he said, looking at CITADEL, "Coming with me?"

Arbarkian was no Winston Churchill. No action this day. Think, plot, and plan. He sat with his knees primly together and shook his head slightly, wishing he could disappear into the big chair. Van Claire saw the head shake and kept going.

After the door slammed behind him, Ross sat down in the chair van Claire had just vacated and gave CITADEL a warm smile. "Mr. Arbarkian, let's have a nice chat. We have a lot to chat about."

Arbarkian sat there, returning the smile but saying nothing. Ross was about to speak again when the room was filled with a *WHOOMP* sound that was instantly familiar to all three of them. They froze. It was the sound of a car bomb going off.

Sam knew. The *whoomp* had sounded glorious at the abandoned Naval Air Station where the CIA trained people in demolitions. Then it was the sound of a surplus GSA sedan being blown up by Sam with a soap dish full of C-3, a magnet and a two-minute-and-thirty-second acid-fused blasting cap under the gas tank. Then it was fun.

Sam was out of the chair and out the door in one long motion, pistol in hand. He ran down the front steps and stopped dead in the middle of van Claire's front lawn. The Malibu had had a three-quarters-full tank of gas, and it had all blown. Sam's rental Chevrolet Malibu was engulfed in flames. He could see van Claire in the driver's seat, somehow still erect but blackened like something in a horror movie. It was then he realized that it was his rental and that the corpse was supposed to be him.

He had taken his jacket off and wrapped it around his hand, intending to try to open the door and rescue van Claire. He looked at the flaming wreck. Not possible, he decided. No way, no chance.

Inside, Ross had jumped to his feet as Sam ran out the door. He stepped around the coffee table and headed for Arbarkian.

Arbarkian raised his hands, palms out. "That wasn't me! I'm a street man like you." He sounded very frightened. He was: the look on Ross's face made his intentions clear.

"Bullshit. That was you in Luxembourg scouting the kid's apartment. That was you scouting the hospital where the Russian got suffocated. That was your people who tried to run the kid down on the rue de St Esprit." He pulled Arbarkian out of the chair and shook him like a rat."

"I was only following orders."

"That's what Eichmann said at his trial. Fat load of good it did him."

"Stop. Please stop. What do you want?"

Ross dropped him back in the expensive chair. "For starters, who ordered the kid to be killed?"

"Ivan Komsomol. My boss."

"Why?"

"An eye for an eye. The Luxembourg shooting."

"What name did you just whisper in van Claire's ear?"

Arbarkian hesitated. Ross moved towards him again, and again Arbarkian lifted his hands defensively.

"William Hood."

Ross burst out laughing. "Christ, you expect anybody to believe that? If Hood was your guy we would have been swept off the map all over the world. Now I suppose you'll tell me Michael Suslov is a CIA agent."

Arbarkian looked nervous. "It's not like that."

"What's it like, then? This whole operation is a dangle, isn't it? Answer me, damn you." Ross pulled his gun out of its shoulder holster, flipping the safety off as he did so.

Arbarkian looked him right in the eye. "Go ahead and shoot then. If I answer your question either way I am dead." He was thinking of really defecting. Maybe they wouldn't take it out on Anna and the two children. Oh, yes they would. He pressed his knees together, and then put his hands on them, and then waited for the man to do whatever it was he was going to do.

Ross took a deep breath, pulled himself together, put his gun away, and sat down in van Claire's chair. "Let's talk," he said

The police and the fire trucks got there with commendable speed. The fire station was only three blocks away, two doors up from the library actually, and the police were good about patrolling this quite wealthy area. The firemen glanced at Sam and the house and then went to work on the car. Sam, his brain working again, for which he thanked it profusely, had had time to put his pistol away and put his jacket back on to cover his shoulder holster. He was holding his Headquarters badge out at arm's length when the first cops rolled up.

"We have a national security problem here," he said to the first cop. "Could you patch a call through to the CIA Watch Office in Langley and tell them what's happened?"

The cop had no more idea of how to patch a call through to the CIA than he did to get J. Edgar Hoover on the phone. But this was Washington and this kind of thing happened here. He treated Sam carefully, but more or less as a colleague rather than a suspect, which was what Sam had had in mind. He passed this attitude on to the other cops who were arriving.

The first cops into the house found two men in the living room, one also flashing a CIA Headquarters badge and one claiming diplomatic immunity. The one claiming diplomatic immunity had picked up the phone and was dialing. The guy with the CIA badge waved irritably at the cops to let the man continue.

After that van Claire's house looked like the site of a law enforcement convention. Within a half-hour the Montgomery County arson squad was all over the remains of Sam's Chevrolet, and the medical examiner was supervising the removal of van Claire's body, or what was left of it. A few of the neighbors who were standing at the edge of the yellow crime tape on van Claire's front lawn heard some heavy-set men talking to the cops. From what the men said the neighbors decided the men were from CIA Security. At least that was what they thought they heard before they were shooed away.

Anne, Maria, Alicia, and Ernie had come barreling up in Ernie's rental just as the first fire trucks arrived. At that point Sam was still standing on the lawn, just zipping up his jacket. He saw them and waved them off. He couldn't remember the Marine Corps hand

and arm signals so he gave a thumbs-up and the twins' bye-bye wave. They got the message and headed for Langley to tell Harvey what little they knew. Sam turned to go inside. They all knew it was going to be a long night. The CIA would be stonewalling; the cops would not like that. In the middle of it all a Lincoln Town Car with diplomatic plates pulled up and a man who looked like a rug salesman walked out of the house, got in, and was driven away without anyone saying a word in protest. What was that all about? the shivering neighbors asked one another.

By four a.m. Ross was back in room 2C34, his weary head in his hands. Harvey, looking pretty bleary himself, sat opposite him. Sam had stretched out on the floor, and, accustomed to the Marines' ability to find uncomfortable places to bivouac, was sound asleep.

"Run through it one more time, Ross, and then I'll write it up and we can get some sleep," Harvey said.

"I could have killed him, Harvey. I should have killed him. I didn't. I let him go." Harvey nodded sympathetically. He had killed a number of people. A couple had been in cold blood after he saw Mauthausen. But he couldn't have aced Arbarkian in van Claire's living room either. The Cold War is a figure of speech, he thought, not a real war. There was still a veneer of civilization left in Cold War operations, Komsomol's practices excepted.

"I had a couple of minutes before the cops and the firemen and all showed up and I tried to hustle Arbarkian into defecting. I told him he was as good as dead anyway. Komsomol was going to blame everything on him and he knew it. But he wouldn't bite. He just sat there. I think he was trying to come up with a plan that didn't involve committing himself. Good luck with that."

"You didn't have much choice except to let him go. You're not a cop; you can't arrest him. And there's no evidence to give the Montgomery County cops that would give them probable cause to arrest him, and besides he's got diplomatic immunity."

"I still think he was a damn fool to go back. He'll either be dead or mining uranium with his bare hands out on the Arctic Circle somewhere within a week."

"In his situation, I'm not sure what I would have done. He's probably got a family."

"Yeah, he mentioned that. But everybody in a situation like that starts harping about Mama and the kids and maybe a babushka and all that crap." Ross paused. "He said his wife's name was Anna. I don't know if he's even married. Who the hell knows?"

"One more time," Harvey said. "Did any civilians make you and Sam? How about the others?"

"Sam and I were using work names, of course. They're registered aliases with limited backup. They're enough to rent the cars and whatnot, and the telephone number for the 649th Air Force Replacement Command. Central Cover staff actually answers it. But the *Washington Post* would see through it in a minute if they check."

"And the others?"

"Sam waved them off, just after the explosion, and before the cops and the firemen showed up. They're clean."

"Let's hope so." Anne and Maria and Alicia and Ernie had been sent off to their respective beds. Ernie was in charge of returning the remaining cars, but was told to wait until they could come up with a good story about why they were one car short. Anne had thought to go back and thank the library people and said the League of Women Voters had had enough excitement for the evening and were closing up shop. The librarians had agreed with her.

"We have to thank Feeny from the Office of Security. He got us out of there before the press showed up." Feeny, a red-faced retired D.C. cop, had shown surprising finesse. He had grabbed the Montgomery County watch commander, who had just arrived, and in three sentences got further inquiries adjourned to CIA

Headquarters, cops and all. How he had gotten the Montgomery cops to agree to conduct an inquiry out of their jurisdiction was one for the textbooks.

"Good, good. No sign of the bombers, of course?"

"Of course. Arbarkian fenced and danced around, but once he had fingered Komsomol as having ordered Sam's killing he shut up. At least I scared him into doing that," Ross said reflectively. "You know, Harvey, I came damn near killing him. I mean, right after the explosion, when we all realized they were after Sam, not van Claire. He said he didn't think Komsomol would be stupid enough, or angry enough, to mix hitting Sam in the middle of the van Claire operation. Then he just shrugged and smiled."

"And he wouldn't admit it was a dangle?"

"Nope. He stayed *stumm* on that."

"It would have been a damn sight easier if he had admitted it. Now half those idiots on the sixth floor will think it was a real operation." The hall door clicked and started to open.

Craig Withers slid into the room. Clearly his slithering shoes still worked at 4 a.m. He was wearing a three-piece charcoal-gray suit that he had not bought in a department store. His glance went to Sam on the floor. "Our young warrior is resting? Or is he dead or wounded?"

"Asleep."

"One hopes he doesn't awake fit, rested and ready to cause more turmoil."

"Now it's his fault somebody tried to kill him and got van Claire instead? That's rich."

"This is Headquarters, Harvey. Many little games have been interrupted. Mostly they're shit-scared: van Claire was one of them. Well, one of us, to be honest. I must include myself. I mean, it's bad enough to have the KGB's assassins running around trying to pick off young Lochinvar here, but blowing up a supergrade is quite beyond the pale."

The 2nd Lieutenant Spy

For all his snide comments, Craig did seem a little rattled. Talking in robust terms about intelligence operations in a Headquarters conference room did not match up well with actually blowing CIA executives up. The first was fun, like playing golf. The second was, well, not like playing golf. And to have one of their own, a member of the Clandestine Service's men's room club incinerated in his own driveway. And in Chevy Chase yet.

"I'll try and write something up for you right away, Craig," Harvey said in tired, strained voice.

"Get some sleep, dear boy. Come in after lunch. Right now they're busy with matters of protocol and damage control. Who do we rouse out of bed at four a.m., and what do we tell them and in which order should they be called? Should the White House be called? Should the Director do it? And who wakens the Director? The Clandestine Services watch officer is browning his trousers trying to guess right."

Withers went on. "Already both the *New York Times* and the *Washington Post* traced the rental car back to a Mr. Ernest somebody or other who works for the 649th Air Force Replacement Command, or so it might seem. They came asking our press office if this Ernest person was ours. We said go ask the Air Force. They said the Air Force was unconvincing and they suspect us, since van Claire was rather open about boasting to the neighbors about whom he worked for. Plus a neighbor ran to the window when the bomb went off and saw a young man come charging out of van Claire's house with a pistol in his hand. He gave a remarkably accurate description of Sleeping Beauty there," he said, pointing at the sleeping Sam.

Harvey stared at him. "Dear boy" my ass. Harvey was years older than Withers. Well, maybe Withers was just trying to be avuncular. He is, after all, going out of his way to tell the peasants what's going on up in the castle. But he was still a condescending so-and-so. Harvey prodded Sam with a toe. "Up and at 'em, Tex."

As if roused by a USMC drill instructor, Sam was instantly awake and on his feet, smiling politely. "Sorry, dozed off."

"Sack rat. You've been lying there like a corpse for two hours," Ross said, a trifle enviously.

Sam looked embarrassed. "Sorry. I did that after they tried to run me down on the Rue du St Esprit too. Came home and slept for hours. Anne said at the time it made her worried that I was acting so weirdly. Anyway, I'm OK now. What's up?"

Harvey turned to Withers. "An excellent question. What now?" He was looking at Withers with his eyebrows raised.

Withers made a graceful, somewhat enigmatic gesture with his right hand. "The Deputy just called in; he'll be here shortly. He asked if you and your people were involved in all this. When told that the answer was 'of course,' he is reported to have laughed and said, 'Tell Harvey and his people to stand by. I'll be in touch.'"

CHAPTER TWENTY-TWO

The Minister, meeting the Body, and going before it, either into the Church or towards the Grave, shall say or sing: "I am the resurrection and the life, saith the Lord: he that believeth in me, though he were dead, yet shall he live: and whosoever liveth and believeth in me, shall never die."

The Order for the Burial of the Dead was being followed in the Episcopal manner. And there was nothing more Episcopal than Washington's National Cathedral. Sitting on top of St. Alban's Hill, where Massachusetts and Wisconsin Avenues meet. Its spire can be seen all over the city. St. Alban's Hill is the tallest point in D.C. (Capitol Hill, after all, could more accurately be described as Jenkins Hillock). Construction had begun in 1921 and was expected to take at least a hundred years, as cathedrals are wont to do. Everyone was surprised at how quickly it went up, and now it had been the gathering place of Washington's great and good for ceremonial occasions for forty years.

Sam and Anne were ten rows back. He looked around at the packed cathedral and was struck by the pious fraud of it all. The cathedral was full, such was the draw of having the opportunity to look sorrowful in front of all the CIA brass and hundreds of others from the Washington Establishment. The murmurs running up and down the pews were that a Supreme Court Justice was there, and two Cabinet members, one from a major department — Commerce, they thought.

There had been a stir just after Sam and Anne had arrived when a motorcade swept up to the cathedral steps, complete with black Secret Service Chevrolet Suburbans and motorcycle outriders. Breaths had been held. Was it? Was it? In the end, the answer was no. It was only the Vice President. But upon consideration, he would do. Those in attendance plotted how they might end up close enough to him after the ceremony to have an opportunity to mention their names and say something obsequious.

Anne was looking around too, biting her lip a little. She had memories of an Episcopal church in Connecticut, the one she went to when she was a little girl. The ceremony had always started with, "Dearly beloved," and the words of the Book of Common Prayer had lent a wondrous luster to weddings and baptisms. Whatever your station in life, the Book started you out and packed you off with language fit for a king.

What is going to happen to us now, she wondered? Sam had said that their little task force had been hurriedly disbanded. Harvey and Alicia and Ross had all been sent back to Germany. "Deported," actually, Sam had said, and put out of reach of inquiring minds at Headquarters. Ernie was buried back in Records and Maria had been plopped down at a desk in the German Branch and given a few name traces to do. Sam had been told to stay away from Headquarters and to stay home and await further instructions.

Hear my prayer, O Lord . . . for I am a stranger with Thee, and a sojourner, as all my fathers were.

The priest had the look of a middle-aged executive himself, she thought. He had a strong voice and a practiced manner and was clearly used to addressing large crowds of important people.

She wondered what had or hadn't happened to the amiable Sam. He had been getting angrier and angrier as it appeared clear to him, and to her too, that he had been set adrift by the Agency and more or less forgotten about. Sam was worried for her and the boys. Here they were in a little apartment in Falls Church. Was the KGB going to come after them again? When Sam had gone out for groceries that first night he had first dropped down into the push-up position behind their ratty old car and checked the bottom of the gas tank for explosives. Then he had opened the hood and rummaged around checking for extra wiring by the ignition coil. Then, for she was peeking out the window and saw all this, he took a deep breath, opened the car door, hopped in and started it. When the car started normally and headed for the Safeway, she realized she had been holding her breath too.

What a way to live. Sam had asked her in an embarrassed tone if she might consider going back to the Bureau of the Budget so he could resign and go job hunting. She could, she supposed. Certainly her boss and the Associate Administrator had made it clear that they would be delighted to have her back. But there was still the KGB to worry about.

But that worry lasted only from the day van Claire had been killed through the next day. Yesterday morning a plain gray Ford sedan with the little round hubcaps that screamed "unmarked police car" arrived in their parking lot. A large man got out, knocked on their door, and when Sam had cautiously opened it, displayed Office of Security credentials. The large man nodded approvingly at the .45 Sam was holding in his right hand, pointed at the floor.

"You won't need that anymore unless the Russians have been taking stupid pills," he said. He would be there for the next eight hours with his partner, a large black man with linebacker's shoulders. They would introduce the next shift when the time came.

Please don't go outside without taking one of them along. And maybe the kids could stay inside today?

Then Craig Withers had called. "Good morning," he chirped, as if nothing untoward had occurred. "Just thought I'd let you know that Maria and Ernie are back with me to do a little, um, tidying up. Oh, and the reason I called is that a car will pick you up at 9:45 sharp and take you to van Claire's funeral tomorrow. Have a nice day." He hung up before Sam could open his mouth. Clearly, there had been a policy shift on the sixth floor. But the funeral? Why?

That explained the dark-green Mercury, one of the executive cars from the motor pool in the Headquarters basement, that had arrived this morning. The first person out of it was a rather miffed-looking woman with very large breasts who said she'd been assigned to babysit the twins. The car took them to the National Cathedral, where they found they had seats in the tenth row. Someone was making a point by seating them up front, where they could be seen.

We brought nothing into this world, and it is certain we can carry nothing out.

Sam suddenly sat up straighter. Of course! He was an idiot not to have seen it sooner. Of course this was a fraud! This whole thing was a large, loud message to Andropov and the KGB that the Washington establishment, not just the CIA, was thoroughly pissed about van Claire. His and Anne's tenth-row presence at the funeral was to send the message that they were now a protected species.

Man, that is born of a woman, hath but a short time to live, and is full of misery.

Well, that sounds about right, Sam thought.

The priest looked out at the crowd he was addressing. The Vice President was looking right at him. He had an earnest look on his face and was giving him his full attention. The Vice President certainly knew how to go to a funeral. The wiseguys said that was a Vice President's principal duty after all, so he should be good at it.

Many of the rest of the crowd were quietly glancing around, seeing who was there and who might be spoken to after this was over. The priest glanced at the front row. The widow was checking her watch again. It would appear that Mrs. van Claire was not going to have to be restrained from throwing herself into her husband's grave. He wondered how many of them, or even if any of them, believed in God anymore. He raised his hands and said:

O spare me a little, that I may recover my strength, before I go hence, and be no more seen.

Think about that, you Pharisees and hypocrites, he mused, and then chastised himself for that most un-Christian thought.

CHAPTER TWENTY-THREE

Christmas passed, and then January, slowly as January always does. The two Office of Security men had disappeared two days after the funeral. Sam and Anne hoped that meant the Deputy Director had made an informal deal with the KGB, but no one had bothered to tell them, of course. So Sam and Anne sat around and watched as the twins slowly and sweetly destroyed the little apartment. The twins didn't mean to, of course, but things spilled, and toys banged the cheap drywall.

Around the world CIA operations plodded on. Vietnam stayed the same, but in Laos some Agency people were spending more time doing drug deals with and for Major General Vang Pao than fighting the Pathet Lao and North Vietnamese regulars. In Africa and South America the KGB and CIA continued their proxy war. But in the rest of the world, and particularly in Europe, the twenty-year effort to penetrate the KGB and GRU had ground to a halt. The van Claire mess was a good part of it.

Every morning the discussion amidst the clouds of cigar and cigarette smoke in the executive men's room on the sixth floor of

Headquarters began with an acerbic critique of the previous day's efforts to square the circle. There were three topics of conversation. First, had Andropov called off the KGB assassination squad? Those who had read the reports knew that van Claire's death was an outgrowth of the attempt to kill a lowly career trainee in revenge for his inadvertent role in killing two KGB security men. But many, and unfortunately many of the more senior folk, had missed that part and now assumed that van Claire's death was a deliberate assassination of a senior CIA officer. Were they now at personal risk? This possibility wonderfully attracted their attention.

Second, had CITADEL been a real operation or a dangle? If it was real, that raised the third topic: could Bill Hood of all people possibly be the CIA's Kim Philby? That was about as likely as Dick Helms or Cord Meyer or Allen Dulles or Desmond Fitzgerald or any of the old World War II and OSS crowd. The speculation went on and on.

One morning, around the fourth or fifth day of February, Sam looked at Anne and said, "You know, this is exactly the same situation Ross was in after he broke up that operation the Stasi was running against van Claire in Frankfurt. They left him sitting by the phone for four months while they yelled and screamed at each other about who they could blame for it."

"Well, he got rehabilitated. They made him deputy chief of the German Desk."

"That wasn't a promotion. They put him there so Grant Natz could keep an eye on him and look for a chance to can him. And speaking of promotion, look at this." He handed her a single piece of paper. It said "Office of Personnel" at the top, but did not specify for which agency. The note was short:

"This is to advise you that the GS-12 promotion board met on January 14th 1969. You were not selected for promotion to GS-12."

Anne was instantly sympathetic. "Oh, my poor sweetie. That's so unfair."

Sam shrugged. "That'll teach me to open the mail."

"Well, I still say that's not fair. It's not your fault you ended up out in the boonies. Besides, I bet you are the best shot in your trainee class."

Her attempt to humor him didn't humor him. He patted her hand. "Nice try, babe. I still have my Headquarters pass. They didn't specifically forbid me to enter the building. They just said, 'Stay home and await instructions.' I can stretch that to go in and see Central Cover staff and see what they'll let me say about my, you'll pardon the expression, 'CIA career' in public."

"Once you do that you'll be breaking cover, and then you can't change your mind. You'll have to leave."

"That's precisely what I have in mind. It's all over. Can't you hear the Fat Lady singing?"

"Sweetie, patience isn't exactly your long suit. Why don't you go to the library and find a book or two to read? Wait a little longer. Tell you what, give it a week. If nothing happens you can go negotiate with Personnel, and then Central Cover. You know, do it by the book for a change."

He stroked her long black hair and said, "I'm sorry. I'm just feeling sorry for myself. I'm going over to the high school and run around their track for an hour. Maybe the KGB will be out and I'll get a chance to practice sprinting." He saw her flinch. "That's a joke, baby. The KGB really has been called off. Headquarters is just covering their bet by using me as the wind dummy."

"Wind dummy?"

"A buddy in jump school told me: the Eighty-Second Airborne uses a wind dummy. It's a couple of sacks that weigh about as much as a paratrooper strapped to a chute. They throw it out the plane door on the first pass over the drop zone. They want to see which way the wind is blowing at whatever height they're going to jump from. The joke is, if the colonel is pissed at you he uses you as the wind dummy, see if you drift too close to the power lines or whatever's down there."

"That's not much of a joke."

"Well, the Eighty-Second thinks it's funny."

"Be careful, please. I'm still not sure they're not out there waiting for you."

"They're not. They would've got me by now if they were."

"Thank you, dear. Now I feel much better."

At Headquarters, room 2C34 had been activated again. Craig Withers had been charged with the task of "tidying up." He had plucked Maria and Ernie from their exiles and set them to work pulling at the various Irish pennants dangling from parts of their previous investigations. Withers had never heard the term, but Ernie had explained that Sam had told him about it. An "Irish pennant" was a loose thread on a uniform or webbed gear or marching pack that a Marine drill instructor could pull on and then berate the owner about. Neither Sam nor Ernie knew where the expression came from.

Withers, who hated loose ends, looked it up. Apparently it was a slur against the Irish evolving from Royal Navy complaints about loose rigging in the nineteenth century. Whatever it was, there were plenty of them around. The intelligence analysts had pieced together the hundreds of pages in two sets of microfilmed documents CITADEL had given van Claire. They were generally of the opinion that the bulk it was all of a work: an extremely clever mass of disinformation. If it had been followed up on, it would have had half the Clandestine Service chasing down rabbit holes for a decade.

But not all of the information was meant to mislead. The third set of documents, the two hundred and thirty-eight pages on the GRU, the KGB's military counterpart and sometimes competitor, was, many thought, right on the mark and extremely valuable. In the end, there were twenty-seven disseminations that came from it. Since even one dissemination — an intelligence report deemed solid enough and important enough to be sent out to State and the White House and the Pentagon — was deemed an important success, twenty-seven was a bonanza.

What left the analysts mystified was why these golden pieces of information were included in the mess of otherwise misleading or entirely false material. Withers was wringing his hands. The Deputy wanted a definitive analysis of the CITADEL operation. Most important, he wanted to know whether van Claire had been a sucker or a saint.

Then there were the scribbled notes that were found sitting in an unmarked file folder in the back of van Claire's safe. The idiot had actually not destroyed his and Dieter Volkmann's notes. Instead, he had put them in the back of his safe for what? For safekeeping? Jesus, how dumb can you get? With infinite patience, and the help of a handwriting expert borrowed from the Support Directorate, Ernie and Maria pieced together van Claire's hastily taken notes from his meeting with INGRESS. With them were Dieter's notes in his tiny handwriting. It turned out that poor Dieter was a natural. He had gotten the outlines of two Soviet gambits in Guinea-Bissau and Ghana that were themselves worthy of three more disseminations. The fact that the information was three months old was immaterial. Things moved so slowly through the tortuous channels of the African governments involved that the deals were still pending. Thus, Dieter's stories were still fresh and new.

And, just to muddle the story further, someone had withdrawn the million dollars from CITADEL's Guernsey bank account. But where was CITADEL? To nobody's surprise the FBI had reported that CITADEL was seen at Dulles airport getting on a TWA flight to New York. There he had boarded an Aeroflot flight for Kiev. Why Kiev rather than Moscow? Who knew? Ernie and Maria were all set to try to find out who had taken the money, and where those persons had taken it. The Office of Finance would be sure to ask some pointed questions, and soon.

Altogether it was a real dog's breakfast, as those who hung around the MI6 liaison officers would say. Clay van Claire had clearly surfaced the German engineer and poor old Goshkorow to the KGB. He had clearly been suckered on the maybe-Czech defector in Frankfurt. But he had also been the source of thirty intelligence disseminations, which was on average two months' product for the Clandestine Services in these lean times. Was he a bungling hero or something else? The DDP was not grateful for Withers' mixed report. Withers was told to go back and try harder. The "or else" was barely implied, but Craig got the message.

In the middle of all this, Maria had slipped out to Falls Church and made an entirely unauthorized visit to Sam and Anne. She passed a message from Harvey that it looked like they were in the top of the fifth inning in what might turn out to be a doubleheader. Harvey said Sam should stand down, take his pack off, and stay home and do push-ups until the mess got sorted out. Sam, who had planned to go to Headquarters at the end of the week and resign, sat, squirmed, and finally agreed. After all, what could be more fun that spending February in Falls Church, sitting and looking out the window at the dreary winter?

CHAPTER TWENTY-FOUR

On the night of February 15, 1969, the Marine guard at the visitors' entrance to the American Embassy in Montevideo, Uruguay, called up to the embassy's night duty officer. Lance Corporal Kyle Johansson was a prime example of a Marine who had been selected for embassy duty. He had a GCT (IQ to civilians) of 110, which made him eligible for Officer Candidate's School and was in all other ways the A. J. Squared Away Marine right off a recruiting poster. True, he got a little wild on liberty, but Marines were supposed to do that.

"Sir, Mr. Walker is here to see you." It was three o'clock in the morning, but Lance Corporal Johansson sounded like this was an entirely routine event. Around the world and for the last twenty years, "Mr. Walker is here to see you" was the open code for telling a CIA station that a prospective defector had arrived at their door.

The night duty officer was Terry McGowan, two CT classes ahead of Sam. He was instantly alert, making a quick phone call and then hurrying to the elevator to go downstairs and see what he had on his hands. Once the elevator door opened he slowed to what he hoped was a relaxed walk and headed, smiling pleasantly, to the guard station.

The man awaiting him looked like the Viking warriors he had seen in the pictures in the books he had read in the sixth grade. Tall, blond, square-shouldered and with a lantern jaw, the man looked not at all like a defector. Terry held out a welcoming hand and ushered the man into the little conference room just behind the guard station, which was set up for meetings like this. He flicked the two switches for the lights and the third to start the hidden tape recorder.

Terry sat the man down, took a chair on the other side of the metal desk, and said, "Good evening, sir. My name is Leslie Harris. May I offer you a cup of coffee? And may I ask how much time you can spare me this evening?"

Leslie Harris was one of Terry's registered aliases, "good evening" was a stretch for three a.m., and the first question CIA officers ask prospective defectors is how much time they have before everybody has to worry about someone noticing that the defector is not where he is supposed to be,

"I will save you a lot of trouble, Mr. Harris, or whatever your name is. I am Pytor Rostenkowsky. I am a KGB officer with the first Chief Directorate, a second secretary at the Soviet Embassy here, and the KGB *Rezident*. I have been involved in an, um, incident and am surely about to be recalled and suffer severe penalties. Consequently I wish to immigrate to the United States immediately."

"May I ask what this incident was, Mr. Rostenkowsky?" Terry said as he accepted the Soviet's proffered passport and pressed a buzzer under the kneehole of the desk.

"It is a matter of great embarrassment." The Russian's English was BBC correct but not perfect. "It involves a prostitute and an, um, incident."

"We shall return to that topic later then," Terry said smoothly. "Let us assume for the moment that you are who you say you are.

What would you like us to do for you, and what do you propose to do for us in return?" Terry McGowan forced himself to speak slowly and look calm. He was, of course, terribly excited. This encounter was right out of the training sessions at the Farm. Now he had to remember the intricate steps as they started the dance. Was this a real defector or a dangle? Was he even a Russian? He sure looked like a Swede, but then a lot of Russians, Poles and Ukrainians looked like Swedes, courtesy of Charles XII's failed invasion of Russia in 1708. Charles may have lost the war, but his soldiers sure left a lot of blue-eyed kiddies behind in their wake.

There was a discreet tap at the door. Terry stood up and said, "I need to give a colleague your passport for a moment, if I may?" He opened the door, a hand reached in, and he put the passport in the hand, which withdrew and closed the door behind it.

Terry returned to his chair, sat, and smiled brightly again. "You were just telling me what you might do to help us."

"Actually, you were going to tell me what you can do for me." For the first time Terry noticed that the Russian had been drinking, possibly a lot. Montevideo was so full of smells of perfumed flowers and other exotic things that the odor of vodka was rather faint. "I want a new name, some money, and a job. I want to live in the Canal Zone. It is warm and far from Russia and America."

"None of that is impossible," Terry said. "But perhaps you might tell me a few things which would facilitate our interest in helping you?" In short, Terry thought, gimme something that is both valuable and might establish your bona fides.

Terry looked straight at him. "Do you have any knowledge of a KGB penetration of CIA?"

"No."

"Any rumors?"

"No."

Terry thought about the next question for a moment. "Your people recently blew up a CIA officer in a car bombing in the Washington, D.C., area. Tell me about that."

The Russian smiled a kind of smirk. "Ah, you want gossip. That is easy. The KGB gossips like old babushkas hanging over the back fence. What I hear is that this was a great up-fuck." Terry didn't dream of interrupting him to correct his use of the vernacular.

The Russian continued: "Is big stink in Moscow. Andropov is not happy with car bombing on front page of every newspaper in the world, particularly when he finds out the Thirteenth Department people blew up the wrong man. Naturally we deny the whole thing as capitalist lies. But I hear the guy who ordered the killing — his name is Komsomol, I think — was transferred to the Ninth Chief Directorate to run counterintelligence operations in Chechnya.

"That is a promotion or a demotion, depending on how you look at it. It is more prestigious to be in First Directorate. Ninth is just guard duty and security sweeps. But for a man like Komsomol, being reassigned to a job where he's *supposed* to shoot people might make him very happy."

"How about a man named Arbarkian?"

"I know him, trained with him. Good man, very sly. Gossip says he was recalled because of car bombing mess."

"What happened to him?"

"Nothing good, I imagine. Up-fucks must be blamed on someone: he was the case officer. He was, how do you use the idiom, the low man on the totem pole? What is a totem pole?"

"I'll explain later. What was Arbarkian's rank?"

The man shrugged. "Senior case officer. About a lieutenant colonel perhaps."

"What were his duties?"

"Agent handling, of course."

"Anything else? Inspecting *Rezidenturas*, perhaps?"

A chuckle. "He's not the inspector type. He sits at his oar and rows."

"Did you hear any rumors that Arbarkian was going to defect?"

The Russian snorted. "Never happen. Arbarkian is company man. Also married, children. They would be punished."

"Ever hear of a man named Goshkorow?"
"No."
"Dieter Volkmann?"
"No."
"Bill Hood?"
"I hear his name a few times. He is a big wheel. That is all I hear."
"Clay van Claire?"
The Russian smiled. "Oh, yes."
"The Czech in Frankfurt?"
The Russian laughed, a very harsh sound. "That was dangle we ran with the Stasi in West Germany that got screwed up. But it proved the basic point, that you people are gullible. Particularly van Claire, which is why I smile. They use it as a case study in training."
"How about Roman Gratchkenowsky?"
"You did not hear?"
"Hear what?"
"Gratchkenowsky is old and has gotten funny in the head, so he has big office but nobody goes in anymore except old Bolsheviks to drink and tell stories, if they can remember the endings."
"Who is in charge of counterintelligence then?"
"Dmitri Popov, since six months now. You did not know this? You do not seem to know much about KGB." Rostenkowsky looked worried. Could these people handle a defection without getting him killed?

Terry McGowan was debating how or whether to respond to this when there was another discreet tap on the door. As Terry went to answer it the door opened and a hand held out Rostenkowsky's passport. When Terry took it the hand gave a thumbs up and closed the door behind it again.

Terry sat down and leaned forward. "We might have a deal here. Let's talk about what you have been doing here in Montevideo," he said.

CHAPTER TWENTY-FIVE

Four days after Pytor Rostenkowsky defected, somebody passed The Word down the chain of command. The gist of The Word was "Enough, already." As usual, it wasn't clear who had said it. But whatever the source, The Word was heard loud and clear throughout the Clandestine Service. Pencils were downed, heads came up, and there was attentive waiting by all hands for further instructions.

Rostenkowsky was not the sole reason for The Word. True, his request for defection had been accepted, at least tentatively, and he and Terry McGowan had been ferried out to the Montevideo airport in an embassy van and flown in an Air America cargo plane to Washington. They had proceeded in steps via Fort Sherman, Panama and Homestead Air Force Base outside Miami for refueling. Terry had been promoted to GS-13, an action that surprised and pleased him. He had, after all, just followed the cookbook instructions on how to handle a defector. But everybody from the DCI on down was happy that for once somebody had finally done what they were supposed to do and not screwed things up.

The Rostenkowsky revelations tipped the scales, but just barely. True, the business about Gratchkenowsky running Bill Hood was now shown to be a load of crap. And now it was doubly proven that Arbarkian was no high-level commissar as he had presented himself to van Claire. Rostenkowsky hadn't heard anything about a mole within the CIA.

But the defector hadn't absolutely, positively proved CITADEL was a hoax. While it made it highly likely, there were still some things he said that gave hope and comfort to the Headquarters naysayers. Plus, he was, by his own admission, a really rotten human being, which didn't help in establishing his bona fides. His credentials were not improved when word came back from the Montevideo police that the, um, incident, involved the death of a twelve-year-old boy. No wonder he had wanted to defect.

Still, what he had revealed was enough to cause the DDP to schedule a colloquy with most of the Chiefs of Station in Europe to do some gentle head-banging. The gentleness was required because many of the people who would disagree with what the Deputy Director was about to do still had a lot of clout in and out of the CIA and it would not do to goad them. Allen Dulles had just died, "finally," some said, but his followers lingered on.

Most of the CIA's operations were untouched by what happened next. The war in Vietnam ground on, as did the newly created China Operations Division, grimly determined to find out the name of their adversary. And, of course, Jim Angleton and the CI staff paid no attention to any of them and continued their hunt for the elusive, but, in the minds of many, fictitious mole.

The Europe and Soviet Bloc divisions at Headquarters needed some shaking up. They had overreacted to Angleton's incursions and had settled down to doing almost nothing. The Chiefs of Station pleadings for Headquarters to pretty please get off their asses and let them do *something* had been ignored. Instead, Headquarters had settled down to a life of meetings, coordinating meaningless cables, and personal and personnel feuds.

So the Deputy Director started at the top. The Chief of Europe was eased out and given a prestigious-sounding assignment in the Director's office that involved liaising and coordinating intelligence findings with other government agencies. It was a job the Chief of Europe, a notorious bully, would be no good at. It was expected that people in other agencies would stop returning his calls within days and that he would be left to wither, raging and storming around his plush but isolated office. Another move resulted in E. Howard Hunt and the California professor with no intelligence background disappearing from Europe's front office to lesser jobs somewhere.

The Chief of Support for Europe, the one who had let Sam sit and stew after the Frankfurt slot had been cancelled, had already moved on to a tour in Vietnam, where he had been caught doing a very bad job of embezzling operational funds and unceremoniously fired by Tom Polgar, Chief of Station, Saigon. His successor, a hanky-in-the-sleeve type, was so ineffectual that he too was quietly ousted. The demotion received bad reviews at the Metropolitan Club downtown and there had been bleatings of protest on the Georgetown cocktail circuit.

Grant Natz, Sam's former branch Chief, had been dispatched to Vietnam months before, by order of the Deputy himself. Natz had originally been appalled at the thought of being posted to somewhere in the jungle. But upon reflection, the assignment as liaison officer to a South Vietnamese combat police battalion had its appeal. Operation Phoenix would allow him to be very, very hard on his enemies. Hell, he could have them interrogated, tortured, and even executed.

But it had apparently taken some coaxing to get Natz off the airplane in Saigon, The Saigon Station people said it had dawned on Natz on the flight over that the Viet Cong and the North Vietnamese also had guns and might actually be minded to shoot him. Fortunately, his Saigon office was surrounded by the U.S. Army and his few forays into the field were taken in an M113 armored personnel carrier with lots of South Vietnamese MPs riding shotgun. Unfortunately for Natz his personality did not wear well in a war zone, where tempers are frayed to start with. Somebody fragged him within two weeks of his arrival. It was all hushed up, of course, and attributed to the Viet Cong. At the Albanian Shithole the talk of who fragged Natz was closely divided. The choices were the South Vietnamese or his own colleagues.

Van Claire was awarded the Intelligence Star posthumously. Management declared its intention of posting his name in the lobby as soon as the mural to the CIA's fallen was completed. Privately, Rostenkowsky's revelation that van Claire had been selected for the CITADEL affair because he had proven to be a sucker in the Czech business in Frankfurt pretty much shut up van Claire's supporters. They settled for the medal, and went on to grumble and snipe about something else.

The big news was reserved for the Deputy's conference with the European Chiefs of station. Like all high-level personnel shifts, those affected had been sounded out in advance, so many of the attendees would have to pretend to be shocked, pleased or surprised when the announcements came from the podium.

Harvey and Chief of Station West Germany adjourned to a corner of the Albanian Shithole for a quiet talk. It was mid afternoon and the regulars were back at work, so they had the place to themselves.

"What's going to happen at show and tell this afternoon?" Harvey asked.

"Oh, a lot and a little. It's mostly rearranging the deck chairs, but it might help. At least I hope it will. But, well, I don't know . . . "

"Care to give some examples?"

"Not to go any further until it's announced, but they talked me into taking over as Chief of Europe."

"Well, hot damn! That's good news. *Mozel tov*."

"Hmm. I don't know. Some of the driftwood in the front office is gone, but I'll still be stuck with the others. And the courtiers in the Deputy's and the Director's office aren't going to be happy with an outsider in the captain's chair, so there'll be resistance to anything I want to do. And Angleton's still got the cork in the operations bottle. The Deputy and the Director just won't tell him to sit down and shut up."

"I thought the Bill Hood business put paid to that? I mean, it has to be obvious to even the village idiot that the whole CITADEL business was a KGB dangle," Harvey said.

"Well, yes and no. Bill Hood is taking over as Chief of Station Germany. Making Bill Hood Chief is supposed to make it clear that he is not the mole. But now the courtiers are sniping and saying that moving him to Germany is just Angleton's way of getting him out of Counterintelligence so Angleton can continue the search for the real mole. Who, of course, they still think is Bill Hood, Germany or no Germany."

"Jesus."

"So that may not work. By the way, I talked to Bill and we agree: Ross Callahan may be the best street man in Europe, but indoors he can barely figure out how to take the cover off a typewriter. So we're going to send his pal Maria out there along with Ernie, the kid from Records who's so good at getting things done up. Ross will be Mr. Outside and they'll be Mr. and Miss Insiders. I wish I had them." He brightened. "Maybe I can make a deal with Bill."

The Chief paused. "But there's still the Irish pennant about all that really good GRU stuff on Soviet military intelligence ops that was buried in the crap CITADEL handed us. What was that about? Do you know?"

"Has it occurred to anybody that the KGB is just as screwed up as we are and somebody put it in by accident?" Harvey said.

"Hmm. Alternatively, the KGB is just as sneaky as we are and they put it in to confuse us, which is exactly what's happening. Or just to stick a shiv in the GRU? They are the KGB's competitor after all."

"Yes. My head hurts more and more lately. I think it's time to retire."

"Harvey, please don't. I can't make you a Chief of Station because you're only a GS-14. But I can offer you the GS-15 Deputy slot in Germany. Bill Hood is all for it. There's a hell of a lot to be done there. Between the embassies in Bonn and the banks in Frankfurt we could have a field day."

Harvey was quiet. "Thank you. I hadn't been expecting that at all. Let me think a minute. No, to hell with thinking about it. Charlotte and I really like West Germany. Plus I'd have a chance to actually run some operations for a change. I might be able to set a few things right too. Maybe get Alicia into the CT program and some money for Dieter Volkmann's parents. Central Cover can come up with an insurance policy or something. We owe them. Thank you, I accept."

"You could start with Charlie Berringer, the ITT guy Sam spotted in Luxembourg. He's given us a bunch of good stuff on what the Russians are up to in Africa. By the way, how did that task force you were running for the Deputy end up?"

"We found lots of things he didn't want to hear about and inadvertently created a situation where van Claire got turned into a crispy critter. That ended up on the front page of every newspaper in the world. Other than that was a smashing success."

"I suspect you're skipping the part about doing enough good things so that you survived and ended up back in Frankfurt. And I personally thank the God I don't believe in for having van Claire start that car instead of young Sam. Harvey, are we sure the Soviets have calmed down and are going to leave Sam alone?"

"I think so," Harvey said. "But I don't know so. You can never tell. My reading is that they consider themselves even: van Claire for the two KGB security goons in Luxembourg. And according to Rostenkowsky, the guy who ordered Sam to be capped is off killing peasants in Chechnya."

"Where is Sam these days?"

"In exile in an apartment out in the boondocks somewhere in Falls Church. I can use him in Frankfurt."

"Mmm. I had a go-around with the Deputy about him."

"What's the boss's problem?"

"That front-page picture of him in the *Herald Trib* taking target practice on the KGB goons. The boss says that's not very clandestine."

"So we put him in Frankfurt under official cover and let him be a magnet for everybody in the business. Hell, he'd have a ball."

"That's what I told the DDP. He waffled around and then said, 'Oh hell, go ahead.'"

"So we go ahead?"

"That depends on whether we can talk Sam into it. If I were he I'd quit and sell encyclopedias door-to-door before I'd come back to this place. You want to take a shot at it?"

"What's his phone number?"

Sam was rereading Hugh Thomas's book on the Spanish Civil War. It had caused a sensation when it came out in 1961. At least it had in his college. Finally there was a history of that sad war that wasn't written in the whining keen of the communist dialectic or the lip-smacking delight of the right. Here was the thrilling language of a Cambridge don, ostensibly neutral, who concealed his socialist leanings quite admirably. Sam was caught up in it all over again and jumped when the phone by his elbow rang. Startled, he said a word. The twins heard it and ran happily to Anne. "Mommy, Daddy said 'shit.'"

Sam answered.

"Sam, it's Harvey. How are you?"

"I'm fine, Harvey, but what's going on?" Sam stood up and walked around as far as the telephone cord would let him. " I didn't hear any overseas operator. Are you here in the U.S.? Don't tell me you went and retired?" Damn, Sam thought, I can't visualize GRUMPY WOLF playing golf in Florida. In the mood he was in the last time I saw him, if anybody handed him a No. 3 wood he'd likely hit somebody with it.

"No, no. The Chief and I are in town for a meeting. We, ah, have a job for you, that is if you're still interested."

Sam just stood there. From the kitchen, Anne looked at him inquiringly. "Who is it, dear?" she said.

CPSIA information can be obtained
at www.ICGtesting.com
Printed in the USA
BVHW04s0302230318
511387BV00019B/216/P